Von Arnim's Classics: Elizabeth and I
Enchanted April

Elizabeth and Her German Garden

May 7th.—I love my garden. I am writing in it now in the late afternoon loveliness, much interrupted by the mosquitoes and the temptation to look at all the glories of the new green leaves washed half an hour ago in a cold shower. Two owls are perched near me, and are carrying on a long conversation that I enjoy as much as any warbling of nightingales. The gentleman owl says [[musical notes occur here in the printed text]], and she answers from her tree a little way off, [[musical notes]], beautifully assenting to and completing her lord's remark, as becomes a properly constructed German she-owl. They say the same thing over and over again so emphatically that I think it must be something nasty about me; but I shall not let myself be frightened away by the sarcasm of owls.

This is less a garden than a wilderness. No one has lived in the house, much less in the garden, for twenty-five years, and it is such a pretty old place that the people who might have lived here and did not, deliberately preferring the horrors of a flat in a town, must have belonged to that vast number of eyeless and earless persons of whom the world seems chiefly composed. Noseless too, though it does not sound pretty; but the greater part of my spring happiness is due to the scent of the wet earth and young leaves.

I am always happy (out of doors be it understood, for indoors there are servants and furniture) but in quite different ways, and my spring happiness bears no resemblance to my summer or autumn happiness, though it is not more intense, and there were days last winter when I danced for sheer joy out in my frost-bound garden, in spite of my years and children. But I did it behind a bush, having a due regard for the decencies.

There are so many bird-cherries round me, great trees with branches sweeping the grass, and they are so wreathed just now with white blossoms and tenderest green that the garden looks like a wedding. I never saw such masses of them; they seemed to fill the place. Even across a little stream that bounds the garden on the east, and right in the middle of the cornfield beyond, there is an immense one, a picture of grace and glory against the cold blue of the spring sky.

My garden is surrounded by cornfields and meadows, and beyond are great stretches of sandy heath and pine forests, and where the forests leave off the bare heath begins again; but the forests are beautiful in their lofty, pink-stemmed vastness, far overhead the crowns of softest gray-green, and underfoot a bright green wortleberry carpet, and everywhere the breathless silence; and the bare heaths are beautiful too, for one can see across them into eternity almost, and to go out on to them with one's face towards the setting sun is like going into the very presence of God.

In the middle of this plain is the oasis of birdcherries and greenery where I spend my happy days, and in the middle of the oasis is the gray stone house with many gables where I pass my reluctant nights. The house is very old, and has been added to at various times. It was a convent before the Thirty Years' War, and the vaulted chapel, with its brick floor worn by pious peasant knees, is now used as a hall. Gustavus Adolphus and his Swedes passed through more than once, as is duly recorded in archives still preserved, for we are on what was then the high-road between Sweden and Brandenburg the unfortunate. The Lion of the North was no doubt an estimable person and acted wholly up to his convictions, but he must have sadly upset the peaceful nuns, who were not without convictions of their own, sending them out on to the wide, empty plain to piteously seek some life to replace the life of silence here.

From nearly all the windows of the house I can look out across the plain, with no obstacle in the shape of a hill, right away to a blue line of distant forest, and on the west side uninterruptedly to the setting sun—nothing but a green, rolling plain, with a sharp edge against the sunset. I love those west windows better than any others, and have chosen my bedroom on that side of the house so that even times of hair-brushing may not be entirely lost, and the young woman who attends to such matters has been taught to fulfil her duties about a mistress recumbent in an easychair before an open window, and not to profane with chatter that sweet and solemn time. This girl is grieved at my habit of living almost in the garden, and all her ideas as to the sort of life a respectable German lady should lead have got into a sad muddle since she came to me. The people round about are persuaded that I am, to put it as kindly as possible, exceedingly eccentric, for the news has travelled that I spend the day out of doors with a book, and that no mortal eye has ever yet seen me sew or cook. But why cook when you can get some one to cook for you? And as for sewing, the maids will hem the sheets better and quicker than I could, and all forms of needlework of the fancy order are inventions of the evil one for keeping the foolish from applying their heart to wisdom.

We had been married five years before it struck us that we might as well make use of this place by coming down and living in it. Those five years were spent in a flat in a town, and during their whole interminable length I was perfectly miserable and perfectly healthy, which disposes of the ugly notion that has at times disturbed me that my happiness here is less due to the garden than to a good digestion. And while we were wasting our lives there, here was this dear place with dandelions up to the very door, all the paths grass-grown and completely effaced, in winter so lonely, with nobody but the north wind taking the least notice of it, and in May—in all those five lovely Mays—no one to look at the wonderful bird-cherries and still more wonderful masses of lilacs, everything glowing and blowing, the virginia creeper madder every year, until at last, in October, the very roof was wreathed with blood-red tresses, the owls and the squirrels and all the blessed little birds reigning supreme, and not a living creature ever entering the empty house except the snakes, which got into the habit during those silent years of wriggling up the south wall into the rooms on that side whenever the old housekeeper opened the windows. All that was here,— peace, and happiness, and a reasonable life,—and yet it never struck me to come and live in it. Looking back I am astonished, and can in no way account for the tardiness of my discovery that here, in this far-away corner, was my kingdom of heaven. Indeed, so little did it enter my head to even use the place in summer, that I submitted to weeks of seaside life with all its horrors every year; until at last, in the early spring of last year, having come down for the opening of the village school, and wandering out afterwards into the bare and desolate garden, I don't know what smell of wet earth or rotting leaves brought back my childhood with a rush and all the happy days I had spent in a garden. Shall I ever forget that day? It was the beginning of my real life, my coming of age as it were, and entering into my kingdom. Early March, gray, quiet skies, and brown, quiet earth; leafless and sad and lonely enough out there in the damp and silence, yet there I stood feeling the same rapture of pure delight in the first breath of spring that I used to as a child, and the five wasted years fell from me like a cloak, and the world was full of hope, and I vowed myself then and there to nature, and have been happy ever since.

My other half being indulgent, and with some faint thought perhaps that it might be as well to look after the place, consented to live in it at any rate for a time; whereupon followed six specially blissful weeks from the end of April into June, during which I was here alone, supposed to be superintending the painting and papering, but as a matter of fact only going into the house when the workmen had gone out of it.

How happy I was! I don't remember any time quite so perfect since the days when I was too little to do lessons and was turned out with sugar on my eleven o'clock bread and butter on to a lawn closely strewn with dandelions and daisies. The sugar on the bread and butter has lost its charm, but I love the dandelions and daisies even more passionately now than then, and never would endure to see them all mown away if I were not certain that in a day or two they would be pushing up their little faces again as jauntily as ever. During those six weeks I lived in a world of dandelions and delights. The dandelions carpeted the three lawns,—they used to be lawns, but have long since blossomed out into meadows filled with every sort of pretty weed,—and under and among the groups of leafless oaks and beeches were blue hepaticas, white anemones, violets, and celandines in sheets. The celandines in particular delighted me with their clean, happy brightness, so beautifully trim and newly varnished, as though they too had had the painters at work on them. Then, when the anemones went, came a few stray periwinkles and Solomon's Seal, and all the birdcherries blossomed in a burst. And then, before I had a little got used to the joy of their flowers against the sky, came the lilacs—masses and masses of them, in clumps on the grass, with other shrubs and trees by the side of walks, and one great continuous bank of them half a mile long right past the west front of the house, away down as far as one could see, shining glorious against a background of firs. When that time came, and when, before it was over, the acacias all blossomed too, and four great clumps of pale, silvery-pink peonies flowered under the south windows, I felt so absolutely happy, and blest, and thankful, and grateful, that I really cannot describe it. My days seemed to melt away in a dream of pink and purple peace.

There were only the old housekeeper and her handmaiden in the house, so that on the plea of not giving too much trouble I could indulge what my other half calls my fantaisie dereglee as regards meals—that is to say, meals so simple that they could be brought out to the lilacs on a tray; and I lived, I remember, on salad and bread and tea the whole time, sometimes a very tiny pigeon appearing at lunch to save me, as the old lady thought, from starvation. Who but a woman could have stood salad for six weeks, even salad sanctified by the presence and scent of the most gorgeous lilac masses? I did, and grew in grace every day, though I have never liked it since. How often now, oppressed by the necessity of assisting at three dining-room meals daily, two of which are conducted by the functionaries held indispensable to a proper maintenance of the family dignity, and all of which are pervaded by joints of meat, how often do I think of my salad days, forty in number, and of the blessedness of being alone as I was then alone!

And then the evenings, when the workmen had all gone and the house was left to emptiness and echoes, and the old housekeeper had gathered up her rheumatic limbs into her bed, and my little room in quite another part of the house had been set ready, how reluctantly I used to leave the friendly frogs and owls, and with my heart somewhere down in my shoes lock the door to the garden behind me, and pass through the long series of echoing south rooms full of shadows and ladders and ghostly pails of painters' mess, and humming a tune to make myself believe I liked it, go rather slowly across the brick-floored hall, up the creaking stairs, down the long whitewashed passage, and with a final rush of panic whisk into my room and double lock and bolt the door!

There were no bells in the house, and I used to take a great dinner-bell to bed with me so that at least I might be able to make a noise if frightened in the night, though what good it would have been I don't know, as there was no one to hear. The housemaid slept in another little cell opening out of mine, and we two were the only living creatures in the great empty west wing. She evidently did not believe in ghosts, for I could hear how she fell asleep immediately after getting into bed; nor do I believe in them, "mais je les redoute," as a French lady said, who from her books appears to have been strongminded.

The dinner-bell was a great solace; it was never rung, but it comforted me to see it on the chair beside my bed, as my nights were anything but placid, it was all so strange, and there were such queer creakings and other noises. I used to lie awake for hours, startled out of a light sleep by the cracking of some board, and listen to the indifferent snores of the girl in the next room. In the morning, of course, I was as brave as a lion and much amused at the cold perspirations of the night before; but even the nights seem to me now to have been delightful, and myself like those historic boys who heard a voice in every wind and snatched a fearful joy. I would gladly shiver through them all over again for the sake of the beautiful purity of the house, empty of servants and upholstery.

How pretty the bedrooms looked with nothing in them but their cheerful new papers! Sometimes I would go into those that were finished and build all sorts of castles in the air about their future and their past. Would the nuns who had lived in them know their little white-washed cells again, all gay with delicate flower papers and clean white paint? And how astonished they would be to see cell No. 14 turned into a bathroom, with a bath big enough to insure a cleanliness of body equal to their purity of soul! They would look upon it as a snare of the tempter; and I know that in my own case I only began to be shocked at the blackness of my nails the day that I began to lose the first whiteness of my soul by falling in love at fifteen with the parish organist, or rather with the glimpse of surplice and Roman nose and fiery moustache which was all I ever saw of him, and which I loved to distraction for at least six months; at the end of which time, going out with my governess one day, I passed him in the street, and discovered that his unofficial garb was a frock-coat combined with a turn-down collar and a "bowler" hat, and never loved him any more.

The first part of that time of blessedness was the most perfect, for I had not a thought of anything but the peace and beauty all round me. Then he appeared suddenly who has a right to appear when and how he will and rebuked me for never having written, and when I told him that I had been literally too happy to think of writing, he seemed to take it as a reflection on himself that I could be happy alone. I took him round the garden along the new paths I had had made, and showed him the acacia and lilac glories, and he said that it was the purest selfishness to enjoy myself when neither he nor the offspring were with me, and that the lilacs wanted thoroughly pruning. I tried to appease him by offering him the whole of my salad and toast supper which stood ready at the foot of the little verandah steps when we came back, but nothing appeased that Man of Wrath, and he said he would go straight back to the neglected family. So he went; and the remainder of the precious time was disturbed by twinges of conscience (to which I am much subject) whenever I found myself wanting to jump for joy. I went to look at the painters every time my feet were for taking me to look at the garden; I trotted diligently up and down the passages; I criticised and suggested and commanded more in one day than I had done in all the rest of the time; I wrote regularly and sent my love; but I could not manage to fret and yearn. What are you to do if your conscience is clear and your liver in order and the sun is shining?

May 10th.—I knew nothing whatever last year about gardening and this year know very little more, but I have dawnings of what may be done, and have at least made one great stride—from ipomaea to tea-roses.

The garden was an absolute wilderness. It is all round the house, but the principal part is on the south side and has evidently always been so. The south front is one-storied, a long series of rooms opening one into the other, and the walls are covered with virginia creeper. There is a little verandah in the middle, leading by a flight of rickety wooden steps down into what seems to have been the only spot in the whole place that was ever cared for. This is a semicircle cut into the lawn and edged with privet, and in this semicircle are eleven beds of different sizes bordered with box and arranged round a sun-dial, and the sun-dial is very venerable and moss-grown, and greatly beloved by me. These beds were the only sign of any attempt at gardening to be seen (except a solitary crocus that came up all by itself each spring in the grass, not because it wanted to, but because it could not help it), and these I had sown with ipomaea, the whole eleven, having found a German gardening book, according to which ipomaea in vast quantities was the one thing needful to turn the most hideous desert into a paradise. Nothing else in that book was recommended with anything like the same warmth, and being entirely ignorant of the quantity of seed necessary, I bought ten pounds of it and had it sown not only in the eleven beds but round nearly every tree, and then waited in great agitation for the promised paradise to appear. It did not, and I learned my first lesson. Luckily I had sown two great patches of sweetpeas which made me very happy all the summer, and then there were some sunflowers and a few hollyhocks under the south windows, with Madonna lilies in between. But the lilies, after being transplanted, disappeared to my great dismay, for how was I to know it was the way of lilies? And the hollyhocks turned out to be rather ugly colours, so that my first summer was decorated and beautified solely by sweet-peas. At present we are only just beginning to breathe after the bustle of getting new beds and borders and paths made in time for this summer. The eleven beds round the sun-dial are filled with roses, but I see already that I have made mistakes with some. As I have not a living soul with whom to hold communion on this or indeed on any matter, my only way of learning is by making mistakes. All eleven were to have been carpeted with purple pansies, but finding that I had not enough and that nobody had any to sell me, only six have got their pansies, the others being sown with dwarf mignonette. Two of the eleven are filled with Marie van Houtte roses, two with Viscountess Folkestone, two with Laurette Messimy, one with Souvenir de la Malmaison, one with Adam and Devoniensis, two with Persian Yellow and Bicolor, and one big bed behind the sun-dial with three sorts of red roses (seventy-two in all), Duke of Teck, Cheshunt Scarlet, and Prefet de Limburg. This bed is, I am sure, a mistake, and several of the others are, I think, but of course I must wait and see, being such an ignorant person. Then I have had two long beds made in the grass on either side of the semicircle, each sown with mignonette, and one filled with Marie van Houtte, and the other with Jules Finger and the Bride; and in a warm corner under the drawing-room windows is a bed of Madame Lambard, Madame de Watteville, and Comtesse Riza du Parc; while farther down the garden, sheltered on the north and west by a group of beeches and lilacs, is another large bed, containing Rubens, Madame Joseph Schwartz, and the Hon. Edith Gifford. All these roses are dwarf; I have only two standards in the whole garden, two Madame George Bruants, and they look like broomsticks. How I long for the day when the tea-roses open their buds! Never did I look forward so intensely to anything; and every day I go the rounds, admiring what the dear little things have achieved in the twenty-four hours in the way of new leaf or increase of lovely red shoot.

The hollyhocks and lilies (now flourishing) are still under the south windows in a narrow border on the top of a grass slope, at the foot of which I have sown two long borders of sweetpeas facing the rose beds, so that my roses may have something almost as sweet as themselves to look at until the autumn, when everything is to make place for more tea-roses. The path leading away from this semicircle down the garden is bordered with China roses, white and pink, with here and there a Persian Yellow. I wish now I had put tea-roses there, and I have misgivings as to the effect of the Persian Yellows among the Chinas, for the Chinas are such wee little baby things, and the Persian Yellows look as though they intended to be big bushes.

There is not a creature in all this part of the world who could in the least understand with what heart-beatings I am looking forward to the flowering of these roses, and not a German gardening book that does not relegate all tea-roses to hot-houses, imprisoning them for life, and depriving them for ever of the breath of God. It was no doubt because I was so ignorant that I rushed in where Teutonic angels fear to tread and made my tea-roses face a northern winter; but they did face it under fir branches and leaves, and not one has suffered, and they are looking to-day as happy and as determined to enjoy themselves as any roses, I am sure, in Europe.

May 14th.—To-day I am writing on the verandah with the three babies, more persistent than mosquitoes, raging round me, and already several of the thirty fingers have been in the ink-pot and the owners consoled when duty pointed to rebukes. But who can rebuke such penitent and drooping sunbonnets? I can see nothing but sunbonnets and pinafores and nimble black legs.

These three, their patient nurse, myself, the gardener, and the gardener's assistant, are the only people who ever go into my garden, but then neither are we ever out of it. The gardener has been here a year and has given me notice regularly on the first of every month, but up to now has been induced to stay on. On the first of this month he came as usual, and with determination written on every feature told me he intended to go in June, and that nothing should alter his decision. I don't think he knows much about gardening, but he can at least dig and water, and some of the things he sows come up, and some of the plants he plants grow, besides which he is the most unflaggingly industrious person I ever saw, and has the great merit of never appearing to take the faintest interest in what we do in the garden. So I have tried to keep him on, not knowing what the next one may be like, and when I asked him what he had to complain of and he replied "Nothing," I could only conclude that he has a personal objection to me because of my eccentric preference for plants in groups rather than plants in lines. Perhaps, too, he does not like the extracts from gardening books I read to him sometimes when he is planting or sowing something new. Being so helpless myself, I thought it simpler, instead of explaining, to take the book itself out to him and let him have wisdom at its very source, administering it in doses while he worked. I quite recognise that this must be annoying, and only my anxiety not to lose a whole year through some stupid mistake has given me the courage to do it. I laugh sometimes behind the book at his disgusted face, and wish we could be photographed, so that I may be reminded in twenty years' time, when the garden is a bower of loveliness and I learned in all its ways, of my first happy struggles and failures.

All through April he was putting the perennials we had sown in the autumn into their permanent places, and all through April he went about with a long piece of string making parallel lines down the borders of beautiful exactitude and arranging the poor plants like soldiers at a review. Two long borders were done during my absence one day, and when I explained that I should like the third to have plants in groups and not in lines, and that what I wanted was a natural effect with no bare spaces of earth to be seen, he looked even more gloomily hopeless than usual; and on my going out later on to see the result, I found he had planted two long borders down the sides of a straight walk with little lines of five plants in a row—first five pinks, and next to them five rockets, and behind the rockets five pinks, and behind the pinks five rockets, and so on with different plants of every sort and size down to the end. When I protested, he said he had only carried out my orders and had known it would not look well; so I gave in, and the remaining borders were done after the pattern of the first two, and I will have patience and see how they look this summer, before digging them up again; for it becomes beginners to be humble.

If I could only dig and plant myself! How much easier, besides being so fascinating, to make your own holes exactly where you want them and put in your plants exactly as you choose instead of giving orders that can only be half understood from the moment you depart from the lines laid down by that long piece of string! In the first ecstasy of having a garden all my own, and in my burning impatience to make the waste places blossom like a rose, I did one warm Sunday in last year's April during the servants' dinner hour, doubly secure from the gardener by the day and the dinner, slink out with a spade and a rake and feverishly dig a little piece of ground and break it up and sow surreptitious ipomaea, and run back very hot and guilty into the house, and get into a chair and behind a book and look languid just in time to save my reputation. And why not? It is not graceful, and it makes one hot; but it is a blessed sort of work, and if Eve had had a spade in Paradise and known what to do with it, we should not have had all that sad business of the apple.

What a happy woman I am living in a garden, with books, babies, birds, and flowers, and plenty of leisure to enjoy them! Yet my town acquaintances look upon it as imprisonment, and burying, and I don't know what besides, and would rend the air with their shrieks if condemned to such a life. Sometimes I feel as if I were blest above all my fellows in being able to find my happiness so easily. I believe I should always be good if the sun always shone, and could enjoy myself very well in Siberia on a fine day. And what can life in town offer in the way of pleasure to equal the delight of any one of the calm evenings I have had this month sitting alone at the foot of the verandah steps, with the perfume of young larches all about, and the May moon hanging low over the beeches, and the beautiful silence made only more profound in its peace by the croaking of distant frogs and hooting of owls? A cockchafer darting by close to my ear with a loud hum sends a shiver through me, partly of pleasure at the reminder of past summers, and partly of fear lest he should get caught in my hair. The Man of Wrath says they are pernicious creatures and should be killed. I would rather get the killing done at the end of the summer and not crush them out of such a pretty world at the very beginning of all the fun.

This has been quite an eventful afternoon. My eldest baby, born in April, is five years old, and the youngest, born in June, is three; so that the discerning will at once be able to guess the age of the remaining middle or

May baby. While I was stooping over a group of hollyhocks planted on the top of the only thing in the shape of a hill the garden possesses, the April baby, who had been sitting pensive on a tree stump close by, got up suddenly and began to run aimlessly about, shrieking and wringing her hands with every symptom of terror. I stared, wondering what had come to her; and then I saw that a whole army of young cows, pasturing in a field next to the garden, had got through the hedge and were grazing perilously near my tea-roses and most precious belongings. The nurse and I managed to chase them away, but not before they had trampled down a border of pinks and lilies in the cruellest way, and made great holes in a bed of China roses, and even begun to nibble at a Jackmanni clematis that I am trying to persuade to climb up a tree trunk. The gloomy gardener happened to be ill in bed, and the assistant was at vespers—as Lutheran Germany calls afternoon tea or its equivalent—so the nurse filled up the holes as well as she could with mould, burying the crushed and mangled roses, cheated for ever of their hopes of summer glory, and I stood by looking on dejectedly. The June baby, who is two feet square and valiant beyond her size and years, seized a stick much bigger than herself and went after the cows, the cowherd being nowhere to be seen. She planted herself in front of them brandishing her stick, and they stood in a row and stared at her in great astonishment; and she kept them off until one of the men from the farm arrived with a whip, and having found the cowherd sleeping peacefully in the shade, gave him a sound beating. The cowherd is a great hulking young man, much bigger than the man who beat him, but he took his punishment as part of the day's work and made no remark of any sort. It could not have hurt him much through his leather breeches, and I think he deserved it; but it must be demoralising work for a strong young man with no brains looking after cows. Nobody with less imagination than a poet ought to take it up as a profession.

After the June baby and I had been welcomed back by the other two with as many hugs as though we had been restored to them from great perils, and while we were peacefully drinking tea under a beech tree, I happened to look up into its mazy green, and there, on a branch quite close to my head, sat a little baby owl. I got on the seat and caught it easily, for it could not fly, and how it had reached the branch at all is a mystery. It is a little round ball of gray fluff, with the quaintest, wisest, solemn face. Poor thing! I ought to have let it go, but the temptation to keep it until the Man of Wrath, at present on a journey, has seen it was not to be resisted, as he has often said how much he would like to have a young owl and try and tame it. So I put it into a roomy cage and slung it up on a branch near where it had been sitting, and which cannot be far from its nest and its mother. We had hardly subsided again to our tea when I saw two more balls of fluff on the ground in the long grass and scarcely distinguishable at a little distance from small mole-hills. These were promptly united to their relation in the cage, and now when the Man of Wrath comes home, not only shall he be welcomed by a wife decked with the orthodox smiles, but by the three little longed-for owls. Only it seems wicked to take them from their mother, and I know that I shall let them go again some day—perhaps the very next time the Man of Wrath goes on a journey. I put a small pot of water in the cage, though they never could have tasted water yet unless they drink the raindrops off the beech leaves. I suppose they get all the liquid they need from the bodies of the mice and other dainties provided for them by their fond parents. But the raindrop idea is prettier.

May 15th.—How cruel it was of me to put those poor little owls into a cage even for one night! I cannot forgive myself, and shall never pander to the Man of Wrath's wishes again. This morning I got up early to see how they were getting on, and I found the door of the cage wide open and no owls to be seen. I thought of course that somebody had stolen them—some boy from the village, or perhaps the chastised cowherd. But looking about I saw one perched high up in the branches of the beech tree, and then to my dismay one lying dead on the ground. The third was nowhere to be seen, and is probably safe in its nest. The parents must have torn at the bars of the cage until by chance they got the door open, and then dragged the little ones out and up into the tree. The one that is dead must have been blown off the branch, as it was a windy night and its neck is broken. There is one happy life less in the garden to-day through my fault, and it is such a lovely, warm day—just the sort of weather for young soft things to enjoy and grow in. The babies are greatly distressed, and are digging a grave, and preparing funeral wreaths of dandelions.

Just as I had written that I heard sounds of arrival, and running out I breathlessly told the Man of Wrath how nearly I had been able to give him the owls he has so often said he would like to have, and how sorry I was they were gone, and how grievous the death of one, and so on after the voluble manner of women.

He listened till I paused to breathe, and then he said, "I am surprised at such cruelty. How could you make the mother owl suffer so? She had never done you any harm."

Which sent me out of the house and into the garden more convinced than ever that he sang true who sang—

Two paradises 'twere in one to live in Paradise alone.

May 16th.—The garden is the place I go to for refuge and shelter, not the house. In the house are duties and annoyances, servants to exhort and admonish, furniture, and meals; but out there blessings crowd round me at every step—it is there that I am sorry for the unkindness in me, for those selfish thoughts that are so much worse than they feel; it is there that all my sins and silliness are forgiven, there that I feel protected and at home, and every flower and weed is a friend and every tree a lover. When I have been vexed I run out to them for comfort, and when I have been angry without just cause, it is there that I find absolution. Did ever a woman have so many friends? And always the same, always ready to welcome me and fill me with cheerful thoughts. Happy children of a common Father, why should I, their own sister, be less content and joyous than they? Even in a thunder storm, when other people are running into the house, I run out of it. I do not like thunder storms—they frighten me for hours before they come, because I always feel them on the way; but it is odd that I should go for shelter to the garden. I feel better there, more taken care of, more petted. When it thunders, the April baby says, "There's lieber Gott scolding those angels again." And once, when there was a storm in the night, she complained loudly, and wanted to know why lieber Gott didn't do the scolding in the daytime, as she had been so tight asleep. They all three speak a wonderful mixture of German and English, adulterating the purity of their native tongue by putting in English words in the middle of a German sentence. It always reminds me of Justice tempered by Mercy. We have been cowslipping to-day in a little wood dignified by the name of the Hirschwald, because it is the happy hunting-ground of innumerable deer who fight there in the autumn evenings, calling each other out to combat with bayings that ring through the silence and send agreeable shivers through the lonely listener. I often walk there in September, late in the evening, and sitting on a fallen tree listen fascinated to their angry cries. We made cowslip balls sitting on the grass. The babies had never seen such things nor had imagined anything half so sweet. The Hirschwald is a little open wood of silver birches and springy turf starred with flowers, and there is a tiny stream meandering amiably about it and decking itself in June with yellow flags. I have dreams of having a little cottage built there, with the daisies up to the door, and no path of any sort—just big enough to hold myself and one baby inside and a purple clematis outside. Two rooms—a bedroom and a kitchen. How scared we would be at night, and how completely happy by day! I know the exact spot where it should stand, facing south-east, so that we should get all the cheerfulness of the morning, and close to the stream, so that we might wash our plates among the flags. Sometimes, when in the mood for society, we would invite the remaining babies to tea and entertain them with wild strawberries on plates of horse-chestnut leaves; but no one less innocent and easily pleased than a baby would be permitted to darken the effulgence of our sunny cottage—indeed, I don't suppose that anybody wiser would care to come. Wise people want so many things before they can even begin to enjoy themselves, and I feel perpetually apologetic when with them, for only being able to offer them that which I love best myself—apologetic, and ashamed of being so easily contented.

The other day at a dinner party in the nearest town (it took us the whole afternoon to get there) the women after dinner were curious to know how I had endured the winter, cut off from everybody and snowed up sometimes for weeks.

"Ah, these husbands!" sighed an ample lady, lugubriously shaking her head; "they shut up their wives because it suits them, and don't care what their sufferings are."

Then the others sighed and shook their heads too, for the ample lady was a great local potentate, and one began to tell how another dreadful husband had brought his young wife into the country and had kept her there, concealing her beauty and accomplishments from the public in a most cruel manner, and how, after spending a certain number of years in alternately weeping and producing progeny, she had quite lately run away with somebody unspeakable—I think it was the footman, or the baker, or some one of that sort.

"But I am quite happy," I began, as soon as I could put in a word.

"Ah, a good little wife, making the best of it," and the female potentate patted my hand, but continued gloomily to shake her head.

"You cannot possibly be happy in the winter entirely alone," asserted another lady, the wife of a high military authority and not accustomed to be contradicted.

"But I am."

"But how can you possibly be at your age? No, it is not possible."

"But I am."

"Your husband ought to bring you to town in the winter."

"But I don't want to be brought to town."

"And not let you waste your best years buried." "But I like being buried."

"Such solitude is not right."

"But I'm not solitary."

"And can come to no good." She was getting quite angry.

There was a chorus of No Indeeds at her last remark, and renewed shaking of heads.

"I enjoyed the winter immensely," I persisted when they were a little quieter; "I sleighed and skated, and then there were the children, and shelves and shelves full of—" I was going to say books, but stopped. Reading is an occupation for men; for women it is reprehensible waste of time. And how could I talk to them of the happiness I felt when the sun shone on the snow, or of the deep delight of hear-frost days?

"It is entirely my doing that we have come down here," I proceeded, "and my husband only did it to please me."

"Such a good little wife," repeated the patronising potentate, again patting my hand with an air of understanding all about it, "really an excellent little wife. But you must not let your husband have his own way too much, my dear, and take my advice and insist on his bringing you to town next winter." And then they fell to talking about their cooks, having settled to their entire satisfaction that my fate was probably lying in wait for me too, lurking perhaps at that very moment behind the apparently harmless brass buttons of the man in the hall with my cloak.

I laughed on the way home, and I laughed again for sheer satisfaction when we reached the garden and drove between the quiet trees to the pretty old house; and when I went into the library, with its four windows open to the moonlight and the scent, and looked round at the familiar bookshelves, and could hear no sounds but sounds of peace, and knew that here I might read or dream or idle exactly as I chose with never a creature to disturb me, how grateful I felt to the kindly Fate that has brought me here and given me a heart to understand my own blessedness, and rescued me from a life like that I had just seen—a life spent with the odours of other people's dinners in one's nostrils, and the noise of their wrangling servants in one's ears, and parties and tattle for all amusement.

But I must confess to having felt sometimes quite crushed when some grand person, examining the details of my home through her eyeglass, and coolly dissecting all that I so much prize from the convenient distance of the open window, has finished up by expressing sympathy with my loneliness, and on my protesting that I like it, has murmured, "sebr anspruchslos." Then indeed I have felt ashamed of the fewness of my wants; but only for a moment, and only under the withering influence of the eyeglass; for, after all, the owner's spirit is the same spirit as that which dwells in my servants—girls whose one idea of happiness is to live in a town where there are others of their sort with whom to drink beer and dance on Sunday afternoons. The passion for being for ever with one's fellows, and the fear of being left for a few hours alone, is to me wholly incomprehensible. I can entertain myself quite well for weeks together, hardly aware, except for the pervading peace, that I have been alone at all. Not but what I like to have people staying with me for a few days, or even for a few weeks, should they be as anspruchslos as I am myself, and content with simple joys; only, any one who comes here and would be happy must have something in him; if he be a mere blank creature, empty of head and heart, he will very probably find it dull. I should like my house to be often full if I could find people capable of enjoying themselves. They should be welcomed and sped with equal heartiness; for truth compels me to confess that, though it pleases me to see them come, it pleases me just as much to see them go.

On some very specially divine days, like today, I have actually longed for some one else to be here to enjoy the beauty with me. There has been rain in the night, and the whole garden seems to be singing—not the untiring birds only, but the vigorous plants, the happy grass and trees, the lilac bushes—oh, those lilac bushes! They are all out to-day, and the garden is drenched with the scent. I have brought in armfuls, the picking is such a delight, and every pot and bowl and tub in the house is filled with purple glory, and the servants think there is going to be a party and are extra nimble, and I go from room to room gazing at the sweetness, and the windows are all flung open so as to join the scent within to the scent without; and the servants gradually discover that there is no party, and wonder why the house should be filled with flowers for one woman by herself, and I long more and more for a kindred spirit—it seems so greedy to have so much loveliness to oneself—but kindred spirits are so very, very rare; I might almost as well cry for the moon. It is true that my garden is full of friends, only they are—dumb.

June 3rd.—This is such an out-of-the-way corner of the world that it requires quite unusual energy to get here at all, and I am thus delivered from casual callers; while, on the other hand, people I love, or people who love me, which is much the same thing, are not likely to be deterred from coming by the roundabout train journey and the long drive at the end. Not the least of my many blessings is that we have only one neighbour. If you have to have neighbours at all, it is at least a mercy that there should be only one; for with people dropping in at all hours and wanting to talk to you, how are you to get on with your life, I should like to know, and read your books, and dream your dreams to your satisfaction? Besides, there is always the certainty that either you or the dropper-in will say something that would have been better left unsaid, and I have a holy horror of gossip and mischief-making. A woman's tongue is a deadly weapon and the most difficult thing in the world to keep in order, and things slip off it with a facility nothing short of appalling at the very moment when it ought to be most quiet. In such cases the only safe course is to talk steadily about cooks and children, and to pray that the visit may not be too prolonged, for if it is you are lost. Cooks I have found to be the best of all subjects—the most phlegmatic flush into life at the mere word, and the joys and sufferings connected with them are experiences common to us all. Luckily, our neighbour and his wife are both busy and charming, with a whole troop of flaxenhaired little children to keep them occupied, besides the business of their large estate. Our intercourse is arranged on lines of the most beautiful simplicity. I call on her once a year, and she returns the call a fortnight later; they ask us to dinner in the summer, and we ask them to dinner in the winter. By strictly keeping to this, we avoid all danger of that closer friendship which is only another name for frequent quarrels. She is a pattern of what a German country lady should be, and is not only a pretty woman but an energetic and practical one, and the combination is, to say the least, effective. She is up at daylight superintending the feeding of the stock, the butter-making, the sending off of the milk for sale; a thousand things get done while most people are fast asleep, and before lazy folk are well at breakfast she is off in her pony-carriage to the other farms on the place, to rate the "mamsells," as the head women are called, to poke into every corner, lift the lids off the saucepans, count the new-laid eggs, and box, if necessary, any careless dairymaid's ears. We are allowed by law to administer "slight corporal punishment" to our servants, it being left entirely to individual taste to decide what "slight" shall be, and my neighbour really seems to enjoy using this privilege, judging from the way she talks about it. I would give much to be able to peep through a keyhole and see the dauntless little lady, terrible in her wrath and dignity, standing on tiptoe to box the ears of some great strapping girl big enough to eat her. The making of cheese and butter and sausages excellently well is a work which requires brains, and is, to my thinking, a very admirable form of activity, and entirely worthy of the attention of the intelligent. That my neighbour is intelligent is at once made evident by the bright alertness of her eyes—eyes that nothing escapes, and that only gain in prettiness by being used to some good purpose. She is a recognised authority for miles around on the mysteries of sausage-making, the care of calves, and the slaughtering of swine; and with all her manifold duties and daily prolonged absences from home, her children are patterns of health and neatness, and of what dear little German children, with white pigtails and fearless eyes and thick legs, should be. Who shall say that such a life is sordid and dull and unworthy of a high order of intelligence? I protest that to me it is a beautiful life, full of wholesome outdoor work, and with no room for those listless moments of depression and boredom, and of wondering what you will do next, that leave wrinkles round a pretty woman's eyes, and are not unknown even to the most brilliant. But while admiring my neighbour, I don't think I shall ever try to follow in her steps, my talents not being of the energetic and organising variety, but rather of that order which makes their owner almost lamentably prone to take up a volume of poetry and wander out to where the kingcups grow, and, sitting on a willow trunk beside a little stream, forget the very existence of everything but green pastures and still waters, and the glad blowing of the wind across the joyous fields. And it would make me perfectly wretched to be confronted by ears so refractory as to require boxing.

Sometimes callers from a distance invade my solitude, and it is on these occasions that I realise how absolutely alone each individual is, and how far away from his neighbour; and while they talk (generally about babies, past, present, and to come), I fall to wondering at the vast and impassable distance that separates one's own soul from the soul of the person sitting in the next chair. I am speaking of comparative strangers, people who are forced to stay a certain time by the eccentricities of trains, and in whose presence you grope about after common interests and shrink back into your shell on finding that you have none. Then a frost slowly settles down on me and I grow each minute more benumbed and speechless, and the babies feel the frost in the air and look vacant, and the callers go through the usual form of wondering who they most take after, generally settling the question by saying that the May baby, who is the beauty, is like her father, and that the two more or less plain ones are the image of me, and this decision, though I know it of old and am sure it is coming, never fails to depress me as much as though I heard it for the first time. The babies are very little and inoffensive and good, and it is hard that they should be used as a means of filling up gaps in conversation, and their features pulled to pieces one by one, and all their weak points noted and criticised, while they stand smiling shyly in the operator's face, their very smile drawing forth comments on the shape of their mouths; but, after all, it does not occur very often, and they are one of those few interests one has in common with other people, as everybody seems to have babies. A garden, I have discovered, is by no means a fruitful topic, and it is amazing how few persons really love theirs—they all pretend they do, but you can hear by the very tone of their voice what a lukewarm affection it is. About June their interest is at its warmest, nourished by agreeable supplies of strawberries and roses; but on reflection I don't know a single person within twenty miles who really cares for his garden, or has discovered the treasures of happiness that are buried in it, and are to be found if sought for diligently, and if needs be with tears. It is after these rare calls that I experience the only moments of depression from which I ever suffer, and then I am angry at myself, a well-nourished person, for allowing even a single precious hour of life to be spoil: by anything so indifferent. That is the worst of being fed enough, and clothed enough, and warmed enough, and of having everything you can reasonably desire—on the least provocation you are made uncomfortable and unhappy by such abstract discomforts as being shut out from a nearer approach to your neighbour's soul; which is on the face of it foolish, the probability being that he hasn't got one.

The rockets are all out. The gardener, in a fit of inspiration, put them right along the very front of two borders, and I don't know what his feelings can be now that they are all flowering and the plants behind are completely hidden; but I have learned another lesson, and no future gardener shall be allowed to run riot among my rockets in quite so reckless a fashion. They are charming things, as delicate in colour as in scent, and a bowl of them on my writing-table fills the room with fragrance. Single rows, however, are a mistake; I had masses of them planted in the grass, and these show how lovely they can be. A border full of rockets, mauve and white, and nothing else, must be beautiful; but I don't know how long they last nor what they look like when they have done flowering. This I shall find out in a week or two, I suppose. Was ever a would-be gardener left so entirely to his own blundering? No doubt it would be a gain of years to the garden if I were not forced to learn solely by my failures, and if I had some kind creature to tell me when to do things. At present the only flowers in the garden are the rockets, the pansies in the rose beds, and two groups of azaleas—mollis and pontica. The azaleas have been and still are gorgeous; I only planted them this spring and they almost at once began to flower, and the sheltered corner they are in looks as though it were filled with imprisoned and perpetual sunsets. Orange, lemon, pink in every delicate shade—what they will be next year and in succeeding years when the bushes are bigger, I can imagine from the way they have begun life. On gray, dull days the effect is absolutely startling. Next autumn I shall make a great bank of them in front of a belt of fir trees in rather a gloomy nook. My tea-roses are covered with buds which will not open for at least another week, so I conclude this is not the sort of climate where they will flower from the very beginning of June to November, as they are said to do.

July 11th.—There has been no rain since the day before Whitsunday, five weeks ago, which partly, but not entirely, accounts for the disappointment my beds have been. The dejected gardener went mad soon after Whitsuntide, and had to be sent to an asylum. He took to going about with a spade in one hand and a revolver in the other, explaining that he felt safer that way, and we bore it quite patiently, as becomes civilised beings who respect each other's prejudices, until one day, when I mildly asked him to tie up a fallen creeper—and after he bought the revolver my tones in addressing him were of the mildest, and I quite left off reading to him aloud—he turned round, looked me straight in the face for the first time since he has been here, and said, "Do I look like Graf X—— ——(a great local celebrity), or like a monkey?" After which there was nothing for it but to get him into an asylum as expeditiously as possible. There was no gardener to be had in his place, and I have only just succeeded in getting one; so that what with the drought, and the neglect, and the gardener's madness, and my blunders, the garden is in a sad condition; but even in a sad condition it is the dearest place in the world, and all my mistakes only make me more determined to persevere.

The long borders, where the rockets were, are looking dreadful. The rockets have done flowering, and, after the manner of rockets: in other walks of life, have degenerated into sticks; and nothing else in those borders intends to bloom this summer. The giant poppies I had planted out in them in April have either died off or remained quite small, and so have the columbines; here and there a delphinium droops unwillingly, and that is all. I suppose poppies cannot stand being moved, or perhaps they were not watered enough at the time of transplanting; anyhow, those borders are going to be sown to-morrow with more poppies for next year; for poppies I will have, whether they like it or not, and they shall not be touched, only thinned out.

Well, it is no use being grieved, and after all, directly I come out and sit under the trees, and look at the dappled sky, and see the sunshine on the cornfields away on the plain, all the disappointment smooths itself out, and it seems impossible to be sad and discontented when everything about me is so radiant and kind.

To-day is Sunday, and the garden is so quiet, that, sitting here in this shady corner watching the lazy shadows stretching themselves across the grass, and listening to the rooks quarrelling in the treetops, I almost expect to hear English church bells ringing for the afternoon service. But the church is three miles off, has no bells, and no afternoon service. Once a fortnight we go to morning prayer at eleven and sit up in a sort of private box with a room behind, whither we can retire unobserved when the sermon is too long or our flesh too weak, and hear ourselves being prayed for by the blackrobed parson. In winter the church is bitterly cold; it is not heated, and we sit muffled up in more furs than ever we wear out of doors; but it would of course be very wicked for the parson to wear furs, however cold he may be, so he puts on a great many extra coats under his gown, and, as the winter progresses, swells to a prodigious size. We know when spring is coming by the reduction in his figure. The congregation sit at ease while the parson does the praying for them, and while they are droning the long-drawn-out chorales, he retires into a little wooden box just big enough to hold him. He does not come out until he thinks we have sung enough, nor do we stop until his appearance gives us the signal. I have often thought how dreadful it would be if he fell ill in his box and left us to go on singing. I am sure we should never dare to stop, unauthorised by the Church. I asked him once what he did in there; he looked very shocked at such a profane question, and made an evasive reply.

If it were not for the garden, a German Sunday would be a terrible day; but in the garden on that day there is a sigh of relief and more profound peace, nobody raking or sweeping or fidgeting; only the little flowers themselves and the whispering trees.

I have been much afflicted again lately by visitors—not stray callers to be got rid of after a due administration of tea and things you are sorry afterwards that you said, but people staying in the house and not to be got rid of at all. All June was lost to me in this way, and it was from first to last a radiant month of heat and beauty; but a garden where you meet the people you saw at breakfast, and will see again at lunch and dinner, is not a place to be happy in. Besides, they had a knack of finding out my favourite seats and lounging in them just when I longed to lounge myself; and they took books out of the library with them, and left them face downwards on the seats all night to get well drenched with dew, though they might have known that what is meat for roses is poison for books; and they gave me to understand that if they had had the arranging of the garden it would have been finished long ago—whereas I don't believe a garden ever is finished. They have all gone now, thank heaven, except one, so that I have a little breathing space before others begin to arrive. It seems that the place interests people, and that there is a sort of novelty in staying in such a deserted corner of the world, for they were in a perpetual state of mild amusement at being here at all. Irais is the only one left. She is a young woman with a beautiful, refined face, and her eyes and straight, fine eyebrows are particularly lovable. At meals she dips her bread into the salt-cellar, bites a bit off, and repeats the process, although providence (taking my shape) has caused salt-spoons to be placed at convenient intervals down the table. She lunched to-day on beer, Schweine-koteletten, and cabbage-salad with caraway seeds in it, and now I hear her through the open window, extemporising touching melodies in her charming, cooing voice. She is thin, frail, intelligent, and lovable, all on the above diet. What better proof can be needed to establish the superiority of the Teuton than the fact that after such meals he can produce such music? Cabbage salad is a horrid invention, but I don't doubt its utility as a means of encouraging thoughtfulness; nor will I quarrel with it, since it results so poetically, any more than I quarrel with the manure that results in roses, and I give it to Irais every day to make her sing. She is the sweetest singer I have ever heard, and has a charming trick of making up songs as she goes along. When she begins, I go and lean out of the window and look at my little friends out there in the borders while listening to her music, and feel full of pleasant sadness and regret. It is so sweet to be sad when one has nothing to be sad about.

The April baby came panting up just as I had written that, the others hurrying along behind, and with flaming cheeks displayed for my admiration three brand-new kittens, lean and blind, that she was carrying in her pinafore, and that had just been found motherless in the woodshed.

"Look," she cried breathlessly, "such a much!"

I was glad it was only kittens this time, for she had been once before this afternoon on purpose, as she informed me, sitting herself down on the grass at my feet, to ask about the lieber Gott, it being Sunday and her pious little nurse's conversation having run, as it seems, on heaven and angels. Her questions about the lieber Gott are better left unrecorded, and I was relieved when she began about the angels.

"What do they wear for clothes?" she asked in her German-English.

"Why, you've seen them in pictures," I answered, "in beautiful, long dresses, and with big, white wings." "Feathers?" she asked.

"I suppose so,—and long dresses, all white and beautiful."

"Are they girlies?"

"Girls? Ye—es."

"Don't boys go into the Himmel?"

"Yes, of course, if they're good."

"And then what do they wear?" "Why, the same as all the other angels, I suppose."

"Dwesses?"

She began to laugh, looking at me sideways as though she suspected me of making jokes. "What a funny Mummy!" she said, evidently much amused. She has a fat little laugh that is very infectious.

"I think," said I, gravely, "you had better go and play with the other babies."

She did not answer, and sat still a moment watching the clouds. I began writing again.

"Mummy," she said presently.

"Well?"

"Where do the angels get their dwesses?"

I hesitated. "From lieber Gott," I said.

"Are there shops in the Himmel?"

"Shops? No."

"But, then, where does lieber Gott buy their dwesses?"

"Now run away like a good baby; I'm busy."

"But you said yesterday, when I asked about lieber Gott, that you would tell about Him on Sunday, and it is Sunday. Tell me a story about Him." There was nothing for it but resignation, so I put down my pencil with a sigh. "Call the others, then."

She ran away, and presently they all three emerged from the bushes one after the other, and tried all together to scramble on to my knee. The April baby got the knee as she always seems to get everything, and the other two had to sit on the grass.

I began about Adam and Eve, with an eye to future parsonic probings. The April baby's eyes opened wider and wider, and her face grew redder and redder. I was surprised at the breathless interest she took in the story—the other two were tearing up tufts of grass and hardly listening. I had scarcely got to the angels with the flaming swords and announced that that was all, when she burst out, "Now I'll tell about it. Once upon a time there was Adam and Eva, and they had plenty of clothes, and there was no snake, and lieber Gott wasn't angry with them, and they could eat as many apples as they liked, and was happy for ever and ever—there now!"

She began to jump up and down defiantly on my knee.

"But that's not the story," I said rather helplessly. "Yes, yes! It's a much nicelier one! Now another."

"But these stories are true," I said severely; "and it's no use my telling them if you make them up your own way afterwards."

"Another! another!" she shrieked, jumping up and down with redoubled energy, all her silvery curls flying.

I began about Noah and the flood.

"Did it rain so badly?" she asked with a face of the deepest concern and interest.

"Yes, all day long and all night long for weeks and weeks——"

"And was everybody so wet?"

"Yes—"

"But why didn't they open their umbwellas?"

Just then I saw the nurse coming out with the tea-tray.

"I'll tell you the rest another time," I said, putting her off my knee, greatly relieved; "you must all go to Anna now and have tea."

"I don't like Anna," remarked the June baby, not having hitherto opened her lips; "she is a stupid girl."

The other two stood transfixed with horror at this statement, for, besides being naturally extremely polite, and at all times anxious not to hurt any one's feelings, they had been brought up to love and respect their kind little nurse.

The April baby recovered her speech first, and lifting her finger, pointed it at the criminal in just indignation. "Such a child will never go into the Himmel," she said with great emphasis, and the air of one who delivers judgment.

September 15th.—This is the month of quiet days, crimson creepers, and blackberries; of mellow afternoons in the ripening garden; of tea under the acacias instead of the too shady beeches; of wood-fires in the library in the chilly evenings. The babies go out in the afternoon and blackberry in the hedges; the three kittens, grown big and fat, sit cleaning themselves on the sunny verandah steps; the Man of Wrath shoots partridges across the distant stubble; and the summer seems as though it would dream on for ever. It is hard to believe that in three months we shall probably be snowed up and certainly be cold. There is a feeling about this month that reminds me of March and the early days of April, when spring is still hesitating on the threshold and the garden holds its breath in expectation. There is the same mildness in the air, and the sky and grass have the same look as then; but the leaves tell a different tale, and the reddening creeper on the house is rapidly approaching its last and loveliest glory.

My roses have behaved as well on the whole as was to be expected, and the Viscountess Folkestones and Laurette Messimys have been most beautiful, the latter being quite the loveliest things in the garden, each flower an exquisite loose cluster of coral-pink petals, paling at the base to a yellow-white. I have ordered a hundred standard tea-roses for planting next month, half of which are Viscountess Folkestones, because the tea-roses have such a way of hanging their little heads that one has to kneel down to be able to see them well in the dwarf forms—not but what I entirely approve of kneeling before such perfect beauty, only it dirties one's clothes. So I am going to put standards down each side of the walk under the south windows, and shall have the flowers on a convenient level for worship. My only fear is, that they will stand the winter less well than the dwarf sorts, being so difficult to pack up snugly. The Persian Yellows and Bicolors have been, as I predicted, a mistake among the tea-roses; they only flower twice in the season and all the rest of the time look dull and moping; and then the Persian Yellows have such an odd smell and so many insects inside them eating them up. I have ordered Safrano tea-roses to put in their place, as they all come out next month and are to be grouped in the grass; and the semicircle being immediately under the windows, besides having the best position in the place, must be reserved solely for my choicest treasures. I have had a great many disappointments, but feel as though I were really beginning to learn. Humility, and the most patient perseverance, seem almost as necessary in gardening as rain and sunshine, and every failure must be used as a stepping-stone to something better. I had a visitor last week who knows a great deal about gardening and has had much practical experience. When I heard he was coming, I felt I wanted to put my arms right round my garden and hide it from him; but what was my surprise and delight when he said, after having gone all over it, "Well, I think you have done wonders." Dear me, how pleased I was! It was so entirely unexpected, and such a complete novelty after the remarks I have been listening to all the summer. I could have hugged that discerning and indulgent critic, able to look beyond the result to the intention, and appreciating the difficulties of every kind that had been in the way. After that I opened my heart to him, and listened reverently to all he had to say, and treasured up his kind and encouraging advice, and wished he could stay here a whole year and help me through the seasons. But he went, as people one likes always do go, and he was the only guest I have had whose departure made me sorry.

The people I love are always somewhere else and not able to come to me, while I can at any time fill the house with visitors about whom I know little and care less. Perhaps, if I saw more of those absent ones, I would not love them so well—at least, that is what I think on wet days when the wind is howling round the house and all nature is overcome with grief; and it has actually happened once or twice when great friends have been staying with me that I have wished, when they left, I might not see them again for at least ten years. I suppose the fact is, that no friendship can stand the breakfast test, and here, in the country, we invariably think it our duty to appear at breakfast. Civilisation has done away with curl-papers, yet at that hour the soul of the Hausfrau is as tightly screwed up in them as was ever her grandmother's hair; and though my body comes down mechanically, having been trained that way by punctual parents, my soul never thinks of beginning to wake up for other people till lunch-time, and never does so completely till it has been taken out of doors and aired in the sunshine. Who can begin conventional amiability the first thing in the morning? It is the hour of savage instincts and natural tendencies; it is the triumph of the Disagreeable and the Cross. I am convinced that the Muses and the Graces never thought of having breakfast anywhere but in bed.

November 11th.—When the gray November weather came, and hung its soft dark clouds low and unbroken over the brown of the ploughed fields and the vivid emerald of the stretches of winter corn, the heavy stillness weighed my heart down to a forlorn yearning after the pleasant things of childhood, the petting, the comforting, the warming faith in the unfailing wisdom of elders. A great need of something to lean on, and a great weariness of independence and responsibility took possession of my soul; and looking round for support and comfort in that transitory mood, the emptiness of the present and the blankness of the future sent me back to the past with all its ghosts. Why should I not go and see the place where I was born, and where I lived so long; the place where I was so magnificently happy, so exquisitely wretched, so close to heaven, so near to hell, always either up on a cloud of glory, or down in the depths with the waters of despair closing over my head? Cousins live in it now, distant cousins, loved with the exact measure of love usually bestowed on cousins who reign in one's stead; cousins of practical views, who have dug up the flower-beds and planted cabbages where roses grew; and though through all the years since my father's death I have held my head so high that it hurt, and loftily refused to listen to their repeated suggestions that I should revisit my old home, something in the sad listlessness of the November days sent my spirit back to old times with a persistency that would not be set aside, and I woke from my musings surprised to find myself sick with longing. It is foolish but natural to quarrel with one's cousins, and especially foolish and natural when they have done nothing, and are mere victims of chance. Is it their fault that my not being a boy placed the shoes I should otherwise have stepped into at their disposal? I know it is not; but their blamelessness does not make me love them more. "Noch ein dummes Frauenzimmer!" cried my father, on my arrival into the world—he had three of them already, and I was his last hope,—and a dummes Frauenzimmer I have remained ever since; and that is why for years I would have no dealings with the cousins in possession, and that is why, the other day, overcome by the tender influence of the weather, the purely sentimental longing to join hands again with my childhood was enough to send all my pride to the winds, and to start me off without warning and without invitation on my pilgrimage.

I have always had a liking for pilgrimages, and if I had lived in the Middle Ages would have spent most of my time on the way to Rome. The pilgrims, leaving all their cares at home, the anxieties of their riches or their debts, the wife that worried and the children that disturbed, took only their sins with them, and turning their backs on their obligations, set out with that sole burden, and perhaps a cheerful heart. How cheerful my heart would have been, starting on a fine morning, with the smell of the spring in my nostrils, fortified by the approval of those left behind, accompanied by the pious blessings of my family, with every step getting farther from the suffocation of daily duties, out into the wide fresh world, out into the glorious free world, so poor, so penitent, and so happy! My dream, even now, is to walk for weeks with some friend that I love, leisurely wandering from place to place, with no route arranged and no object in view, with liberty to go on all day or to linger all day, as we choose; but the question of luggage, unknown to the simple pilgrim, is one of the rocks on which my plans have been shipwrecked, and the other is the certain censure of relatives, who, not fond of walking themselves, and having no taste for noonday naps under hedges, would be sure to paralyse my plans before they had grown to maturity by the honest horror of their cry, "How very unpleasant if you were to meet any one you know!" The relative of five hundred years back would simply have said, "How holy!"

My father had the same liking for pilgrimages—indeed, it is evident that I have it from him—and he encouraged it in me when I was little, taking me with him on his pious journeys to places he had lived in as a boy. Often have we been together to the school he was at in Brandenburg, and spent pleasant days wandering about the old town on the edge of one of those lakes that lie in a chain in that wide green plain; and often have we been in Potsdam, where he quartered as a lieutenant, the Potsdam pilgrimage including hours in the woods around and in the gardens of Sans Souci, with the second volume of Carlyle's Frederick under my father's arm; and often did we spend long summer days at the house in the Mark, at the head of the same blue chain of lakes, where his mother spent her young years, and where, though it belonged to cousins, like everything else that was worth having, we could wander about as we chose, for it was empty, and sit in the deep windows of rooms where there was no furniture, and the painted Venuses and cupids on the ceiling still smiled irrelevantly and stretched their futile wreaths above the emptiness beneath. And while we sat and rested, my father told me, as my grandmother had a hundred times told him, all that had happened in those rooms in the far-off days when people danced and sang and laughed through life, and nobody seemed ever to be old or sorry.

There was, and still is, an inn within a stone's throw of the great iron gates, with two very old lime trees in front of it, where we used to lunch on our arrival at a little table spread with a red and blue check cloth, the lime blossoms dropping into our soup, and the bees humming in the scented shadows overhead. I have a picture of the house by my side as I write, done from the lake in old times, with a boat full of ladies in hoops and powder in the foreground, and a youth playing a guitar. The pilgrimages to this place were those I loved the best.

But the stories my father told me, sometimes odd enough stories to tell a little girl, as we wandered about the echoing rooms, or hung over the stone balustrade and fed the fishes in the lake, or picked the pale dog-roses in the hedges, or lay in the boat in a shady reed-grown bay while he smoked to keep the mosquitoes off, were after all only traditions, imparted to me in small doses from time to time, when his earnest desire not to raise his remarks above the level of dulness supposed to be wholesome for Backfische was neutralised by an impulse to share his thoughts with somebody who would laugh; whereas the place I was bound for on my latest pilgrimage was filled with living, first-hand memories of all the enchanted years that lie between two and eighteen. How enchanted those years are is made more and more clear to me the older I grow. There has been nothing in the least like them since; and though I have forgotten most of what happened six months ago, every incident, almost every day of those wonderful long years is perfectly distinct in my memory.

But I had been stiffnecked, proud, unpleasant, altogether cousinly in my behaviour towards the people in possession. The invitations to revisit the old home had ceased. The cousins had grown tired of refusals, and had left me alone. I did not even know who lived in it now, it was so long since I had had any news. For two days I fought against the strong desire to go there that had suddenly seized me, and assured myself that I would not go, that it would be absurd to go, undignified, sentimental, and silly, that I did not know them and would be in an awkward position, and that I was old enough to know better. But who can foretell from one hour to the next what a woman will do? And when does she ever know better? On the third morning I set out as hopefully as though it were the most natural thing in the world to fall unexpectedly upon hitherto consistently neglected cousins, and expect to be received with open arms.

It was a complicated journey, and lasted several hours. During the first part, when it was still dark, I glowed with enthusiasm, with the spirit of adventure, with delight at the prospect of so soon seeing the loved place again; and thought with wonder of the long years I had allowed to pass since last I was there. Of what I should say to the cousins, and of how I should introduce myself into their midst, I did not think at all: the pilgrim spirit was upon me, the unpractical spirit that takes no thought for anything, but simply wanders along enjoying its own emotions. It was a quiet, sad morning, and there was a thick mist. By the time I was in the little train on the light railway that passed through the village nearest my old home, I had got over my first enthusiasm, and had entered the stage of critically examining the changes that had been made in the last ten years. It was so misty that I could see nothing of the familiar country from the carriage windows, only the ghosts of pines in the front row of the forests; but the railway itself was a new departure, unknown in our day, when we used to drive over ten miles of deep, sandy forest roads to and from the station, and although most people would have called it an evident and great improvement, it was an innovation due, no doubt, to the zeal and energy of the reigning cousin; and who was he, thought I, that he should require more conveniences than my father had found needful? It was no use my telling myself that in my father's time the era of light railways had not dawned, and that if it had, we should have done our utmost to secure one; the thought of my cousin, stepping into my shoes, and then altering them, was odious to me. By the time I was walking up the hill from the station I had got over this feeling too, and had entered a third stage of wondering uneasily what in the world I should do next. Where was the intrepid courage with which I had started? At the top of the first hill I sat down to consider this question in detail, for I was very near the house now, and felt I wanted time. Where, indeed, was the courage and joy of the morning? It had vanished so completely that I could only suppose that it must be lunch time, the observations of years having led to the discovery that the higher sentiments and virtues fly affrighted on the approach of lunch, and none fly quicker than courage. So I ate the lunch I had brought with me, hoping that it was what I wanted; but it was chilly, made up of sandwiches and pears, and it had to be eaten under a tree at the edge of a field; and it was November, and the mist was thicker than ever and very wet—the grass was wet with it, the gaunt tree was wet with it, I was wet with it, and the sandwiches were wet with it. Nobody's spirits can keep up under such conditions; and as I ate the soaked sandwiches, I deplored the headlong courage more with each mouthful that had torn me from a warm, dry home where I was appreciated, and had brought me first to the damp tree in the damp field, and when I had finished my lunch and dessert of cold pears, was going to drag me into the midst of a circle of unprepared and astonished cousins. Vast sheep loomed through the mist a few yards off. The sheep dog kept up a perpetual, irritating yap. In the fog I could hardly tell where I was, though I knew I must have played there a hundred times as a child. After the fashion of woman directly she is not perfectly warm and perfectly comfortable, I began to consider the uncertainty of human life, and to shake my head in gloomy approval as lugubrious lines of pessimistic poetry suggested themselves to my mind.

Now it is clearly a desirable plan, if you want to do anything, to do it in the way consecrated by custom, more especially if you are a woman. The rattle of a carriage along the road just behind me, and the fact that I started and turned suddenly hot, drove this truth home to my soul. The mist hid me, and the carriage, no doubt full of cousins, drove on in the direction of the house; but what an absurd position I was in! Suppose the kindly mist had lifted, and revealed me lunching in the wet on their property, the cousin of the short and lofty letters, the unangenehme Elisabeth! "Die war doch immer verdreht," I could imagine them hastily muttering to each other, before advancing wreathed in welcoming smiles. It gave me a great shock, this narrow escape, and I got on to my feet quickly, and burying the remains of my lunch under the gigantic molehill on which I had been sitting, asked myself nervously what I proposed to do next. Should I walk back to the village, go to the Gasthof, write a letter craving permission to call on my cousins, and wait there till an answer came? It would be a discreet and sober course to pursue; the next best thing to having written before leaving home. But the Gasthof of a north German village is a dreadful place, and the remembrance of one in which I had taken refuge once from a thunderstorm was still so vivid that nature itself cried out against this plan. The mist, if anything, was growing denser. I knew every path and gate in the place. What if I gave up all hope of seeing the house, and went through the little door in the wall at the bottom of the garden, and confined myself for this once to that? In such weather I would be able to wander round as I pleased, without the least risk of being seen by or meeting any cousins, and it was after all the garden that lay nearest my heart. What a delight it would be to creep into it unobserved, and revisit all the corners I so well remembered, and slip out again and get away safely without any need of explanations, assurances, protestations, displays of affection, without any need, in a word, of that exhausting form of conversation, so dear to relations, known as Redensarten! The mist tempted me. I think if it had been a fine day I would have gone soberly to the Gasthof and written the conciliatory letter; but the temptation was too great, it was altogether irresistible, and in ten minutes I had found the gate, opened it with some difficulty, and was standing with a beating heart in the garden of my childhood.

Now I wonder whether I shall ever again feel thrills of the same potency as those that ran through me at that moment. First of all I was trespassing, which is in itself thrilling; but how much more thrilling when you are trespassing on what might just as well have been your own ground, on what actually was for years your own ground, and when you are in deadly peril of seeing the rightful owners, whom you have never met, but with whom you have quarrelled, appear round the corner, and of hearing them remark with an inquiring and awful politeness "I do not think I have the pleasure—?" Then the place was unchanged. I was standing in the same mysterious tangle of damp little paths that had always been just there; they curled away on either side among the shrubs, with the brown tracks of recent footsteps in the centre of their green stains, just as they did in my day. The overgrown lilac bushes still met above my head. The moisture dripped from the same ledge in the wall on to the sodden leaves beneath, as it had done all through the afternoons of all those past Novembers. This was the place, this damp and gloomy tangle, that had specially belonged to me. Nobody ever came to it, for in winter it was too dreary, and in summer so full of mosquitoes that only a Backfisch indifferent to spots could have borne it. But it was a place where I could play unobserved, and where I could walk up and down uninterrupted for hours, building castles in the air. There was an unwholesome little arbour in one dark corner, much frequented by the larger black slug, where I used to pass glorious afternoons making plans. I was for ever making plans, and if nothing came of them, what did it matter? The mere making had been a joy. To me this out-of-the-way corner was always a wonderful and a mysterious place, where my castles in the air stood close together in radiant rows, and where the strangest and most splendid adventures befell me; for the hours I passed in it and the people I met in it were all enchanted.

Standing there and looking round with happy eyes, I forgot the existence of the cousins. I could have cried for joy at being there again. It was the home of my fathers, the home that would have been mine if I had been a boy, the home that was mine now by a thousand tender and happy and miserable associations, of which the people in possession could not dream. They were tenants, but it was my home. I threw my arms round the trunk of a very wet fir tree, every branch of which I remembered, for had I not climbed it, and fallen from it, and torn and bruised myself on it uncountable numbers of times? and I gave it such a hearty kiss that my nose and chin were smudged into one green stain, and still I did not care. Far from caring, it filled me with a reckless, Backfisch pleasure in being dirty, a delicious feeling that I had not had for years. Alice in Wonderland, after she had drunk the contents of the magic bottle, could not have grown smaller more suddenly than I grew younger the moment I passed through that magic door. Bad habits cling to us, however, with such persistency that I did mechanically pull out my handkerchief and begin to rub off the welcoming smudge, a thing I never would have dreamed of doing in the glorious old days; but an artful scent of violets clinging to the handkerchief brought me to my senses, and with a sudden impulse of scorn, the fine scorn for scent of every honest Backfisch, I rolled it up into a ball and flung it away into the bushes, where I daresay it is at this moment. "Away with you," I cried, "away with you, symbol of conventionality, of slavery, of pandering to a desire to please—away with you, miserable little lace-edged rag!" And so young had I grown within the last few minutes that I did not even feel silly.

As a Backfisch I had never used handkerchiefs—the child of nature scorns to blow its nose—though for decency's sake my governess insisted on giving me a clean one of vast size and stubborn texture on Sundays. It was stowed away unfolded in the remotest corner of my pocket, where it was gradually pressed into a beautiful compactness by the other contents, which were knives. After a while, I remember, the handkerchief being brought to light on Sundays to make room for a successor, and being manifestly perfectly clean, we came to an agreement that it should only be changed on the first and third Sundays in the month, on condition that I promised to turn it on the other Sundays. My governess said that the outer folds became soiled from the mere contact with the other things in my pocket, and that visitors might catch sight of the soiled side if it was never turned when I wished to blow my nose in their presence, and that one had no right to give one's visitors shocks. "But I never do wish———" I began with great earnestness. "Unsinn," said my governess, cutting me short.

After the first thrills of joy at being there again had gone, the profound stillness of the dripping little shrubbery frightened me. It was so still that I was afraid to move; so still, that I could count each drop of moisture falling from the oozing wall; so still, that when I held my breath to listen, I was deafened by my own heart-beats. I made a step forward in the direction where the arbour ought to be, and the rustling and jingling of my clothes terrified me into immobility. The house was only two hundred yards off; and if any one had been about, the noise I had already made opening the creaking door and so foolishly apostrophising my handkerchief must have been noticed. Suppose an inquiring gardener, or a restless cousin, should presently loom through the fog, bearing down upon me? Suppose Fraulein Wundermacher should pounce upon me suddenly from behind, coming up noiselessly in her galoshes, and shatter my castles with her customary triumphant "Fetzt halte ich dich aber fest!" Why, what was I thinking of? Fraulein Wundermacher, so big and masterful, such an enemy of day-dreams, such a friend of das Praktische, such a lover of creature comforts, had died long ago, had been succeeded long ago by others, German sometimes, and sometimes English, and sometimes at intervals French, and they too had all in their turn vanished, and I was here a solitary ghost. "Come, Elizabeth," said I to myself impatiently, "are you actually growing sentimental over your governesses? If you think you are a ghost, be glad at least that you are a solitary one. Would you like the ghosts of all those poor women you tormented to rise up now in this gloomy place against you? And do you intend to stand here till you are caught?" And thus exhorting myself to action, and recognising how great was the risk I ran in lingering, I started down the little path leading to the arbour and the principal part of the garden, going, it is true, on tiptoe, and very much frightened by the rustling of my petticoats, but determined to see what I had come to see and not to be scared away by phantoms.

How regretfully did I think at that moment of the petticoats of my youth, so short, so silent, and so woollen! And how convenient the canvas shoes were with the india rubber soles, for creeping about without making a sound! Thanks to them I could always run swiftly and unheard into my hiding-places, and stay there listening to the garden resounding with cries of "Elizabeth! Elizabeth! Come in at once to your lessons!" Or, at a different period, "Ou etes-vous donc, petite sotte?" Or at yet another period, "Warte nur, wenn ich dich erst habe!" As the voices came round one corner, I whisked in my noiseless clothes round the next, and it was only Fraulein Wundermacher, a person of resource, who discovered that all she needed for my successful circumvention was galoshes. She purchased a pair, wasted no breath calling me, and would come up silently, as I stood lapped in a false security lost in the contemplation of a squirrel or a robin, and seize me by the shoulders from behind, to the grievous unhinging of my nerves. Stealing along in the fog, I looked back uneasily once or twice, so vivid was this disquieting memory, and could hardly be reassured by putting up my hand to the elaborate twists and curls that compose what my maid calls my Frisur, and that mark the gulf lying between the present and the past; for it had happened once or twice, awful to relate and to remember, that Fraulein Wundermacher, sooner than let me slip through her fingers, had actually caught me by the long plait of hair to whose other end I was attached and whose English name I had been told was pigtail, just at the instant when I was springing away from her into the bushes; and so had led me home triumphant, holding on tight to the rope of hair, and muttering with a broad smile of special satisfaction, "Diesmal wirst du mir aber nicht entschlupfen!" Fraulein Wundermacher, now I came to think of it, must have been a humourist. She was certainly a clever and a capable woman. But I wished at that moment that she would not haunt me so persistently, and that I could get rid of the feeling that she was just behind in her galoshes, with her hand stretched out to seize me. Passing the arbour, and peering into its damp recesses, I started back with my heart in my mouth. I thought I saw my grandfather's stern eyes shining in the darkness. It was evident that my anxiety lest the cousins should catch me had quite upset my nerves, for I am not by nature inclined to see eyes where eyes are not. "Don't be foolish, Elizabeth," murmured my soul in rather a faint voice, "go in, and make sure." "But I don't like going in and making sure," I replied. I did go in, however, with a sufficient show of courage, and fortunately the eyes vanished. What I should have done if they had not I am altogether unable to imagine. Ghosts are things that I laugh at in the daytime and fear at night, but I think if I were to meet one I should die. The arbour had fallen into great decay, and was in the last stage of mouldiness. My grandfather had had it made, and, like other buildings, it enjoyed a period of prosperity before being left to the ravages of slugs and children, when he came down every afternoon in summer and drank his coffee there and read his Kreuzzeitung and dozed, while the rest of us went about on tiptoe, and only the birds dared sing. Even the mosquitoes that infested the place were too much in awe of him to sting him; they certainly never did sting him, and I naturally concluded it must be because he had forbidden such familiarities. Although I had played there for so many years since his death, my memory skipped them all, and went back to the days when it was exclusively his. Standing on the spot where his armchair used to be, I felt how well I knew him now from the impressions he made then on my child's mind, though I was not conscious of them for more than twenty years. Nobody told me about him, and he died when I was six, and yet within the last year or two, that strange Indian summer of remembrance that comes to us in the leisured times when the children have been born and we have time to think, has made me know him perfectly well. It is rather an uncomfortable thought for the grown-up, and especially for the parent, but of a salutary and restraining nature, that though children may not understand what is said and done before them, and have no interest in it at the time, and though they may forget it at once and for years, yet these things that they have seen and heard and not noticed have after all impressed themselves for ever on their minds, and when they are men and women come crowding back with surprising and often painful distinctness, and away frisk all the cherished little illusions in flocks.

I had an awful reverence for my grandfather. He never petted, and he often frowned, and such people are generally reverenced. Besides, he was a just man, everybody said; a just man who might have been a great man if he had chosen, and risen to almost any pinnacle of worldly glory. That he had not so chosen was held to be a convincing proof of his greatness; for he was plainly too great to be great in the vulgar sense, and shrouded himself in the dignity of privacy and potentialities. This, at least, as time passed and he still did nothing, was the belief of the simple people around. People must believe in somebody, and having pinned their faith on my grandfather in the promising years that lie round thirty, it was more convenient to let it remain there. He pervaded our family life till my sixth year, and saw to it that we all behaved ourselves, and then he died, and we were glad that he should be in heaven. He was a good German (and when Germans are good they are very good) who kept the commandments, voted for the Government, grew prize potatoes and bred innumerable sheep, drove to Berlin once a year with the wool in a procession of waggons behind him and sold it at the annual Wollmarkt, rioted soberly for a few days there, and then carried most of the proceeds home, hunted as often as possible, helped his friends, punished his children, read his Bible, said his prayers, and was genuinely astonished when his wife had the affectation to die of a broken heart. I cannot pretend to explain this conduct. She ought, of course, to have been happy in the possession of so good a man; but good men are sometimes oppressive, and to have one in the house with you and to live in the daily glare of his goodness must be a tremendous business. After bearing him seven sons and three daughters, therefore, my grandmother died in the way described, and afforded, said my grandfather, another and a very curious proof of the impossibility of ever being sure of your ground with women. The incident faded more quickly from his mind than it might otherwise have done for its having occurred simultaneously with the production of a new kind of potato, of which he was justly proud. He called it Trost in Trauer, and quoted the text of Scripture Auge um Auge, Zabn um Zahn, after which he did not again allude to his wife's decease. In his last years, when my father managed the estate, and he only lived with us and criticised, he came to have the reputation of an oracle. The neighbours sent him their sons at the beginning of any important phase in their lives, and he received them in this very arbour, administering eloquent and minute advice in the deep voice that rolled round the shrubbery and filled me with a vague sense of guilt as I played. Sitting among the bushes playing muffled games for fear of disturbing him, I supposed he must be reading aloud, so unbroken was the monotony of that majestic roll. The young men used to come out again bathed in perspiration, much stung by mosquitoes, and looking bewildered; and when they had got over the impression made by my grandfather's speech and presence, no doubt forgot all he had said with wholesome quickness, and set themselves to the interesting and necessary work of gaining their own experience. Once, indeed, a dreadful thing happened, whose immediate consequence was the abrupt end to the long and close friendship between us and our nearest neighbour. His son was brought to the arbour and left there in the usual way, and either he must have happened on the critical half hour after the coffee and before the Kreuzzeitung, when my grandfather was accustomed to sleep, or he was more courageous than the others and tried to talk, for very shortly, playing as usual near at hand, I heard my grandfather's voice, raised to an extent that made me stop in my game and quake, saying with deliberate anger, "Hebe dich weg von mir, Sohn des Satans!" Which was all the advice this particular young man got, and which he hastened to take, for out he came through the bushes, and though his face was very pale, there was an odd twist about the corners of his mouth that reassured me. This must have happened quite at the end of my grandfather's life, for almost immediately afterwards, as it now seems to me, he died before he need have done because he would eat crab, a dish that never agreed with him, in the face of his doctor's warning that if he did he would surely die. "What! am I to be conquered by crabs?" he demanded indignantly of the doctor; for apart from loving them with all his heart he had never yet been conquered by anything. "Nay, sir, the combat is too unequal—do not, I pray you, try it again," replied the doctor. But my grandfather ordered crabs that very night for supper, and went in to table with the shining eyes of one who is determined to conquer or die, and the crabs conquered, and he died. "He was a just man," said the neighbours, except that nearest neighbour, formerly his best friend, "and might have been a great one had he so chosen." And they buried him with profound respect, and the sunshine came into our home life with a burst, and the birds were not the only creatures that sang, and the arbour, from having been a temple of Delphic utterances, sank into a home for slugs.

Musing on the strangeness of life, and on the invariable ultimate triumph of the insignificant and small over the important and vast, illustrated in this instance by the easy substitution in the arbour of slugs for grandfathers, I went slowly round the next bend of the path, and came to the broad walk along the south side of the high wall dividing the flower garden from the kitchen garden, in which sheltered position my father had had his choicest flowers. Here the cousins had been at work, and all the climbing roses that clothed the wall with beauty were gone, and some very neat fruit trees, tidily nailed up at proper intervals, reigned in their stead. Evidently the cousins knew the value of this warm aspect, for in the border beneath, filled in my father's time in this month of November with the wallflowers that were to perfume the walk in spring, there was a thick crop of—I stooped down close to make sure—yes, a thick crop of radishes. My eyes filled with tears at the sight of those radishes, and it is probably the only occasion on record on which radishes have made anybody cry. My dear father, whom I so passionately loved, had in his turn passionately loved this particular border, and spent the spare moments of a busy life enjoying the flowers that grew in it. He had no time himself for a more near acquaintance with the delights of gardening than directing what plants were to be used, but found rest from his daily work strolling up and down here, or sitting smoking as close to the flowers as possible. "It is the Purest of Humane pleasures, it is the Greatest Refreshment to the Spirits of Man," he would quote (for he read other things besides the Kreuzzeitung), looking round with satisfaction on reaching this fragrant haven after a hot day in the fields. Well, the cousins did not think so. Less fanciful, and more sensible as they probably would have said, their position plainly was that you cannot eat flowers. Their spirits required no refreshment, but their bodies needed much, and therefore radishes were more precious than wallflowers. Nor was my youth wholly destitute of radishes, but they were grown in the decent obscurity of odd kitchen garden corners and old cucumber frames, and would never have been allowed to come among the flowers. And only because I was not a boy here they were profaning the ground that used to be so beautiful. Oh, it was a terrible misfortune not to have been a boy! And how sad and lonely it was, after all, in this ghostly garden. The radish bed and what it symbolised had turned my first joy into grief. This walk and border me too much of my father reminded, and of all he had been to me. What I knew of good he had taught me, and what I had of happiness was through him. Only once during all the years we lived together had we been of different opinions and fallen out, and it was the one time I ever saw him severe. I was four years old, and demanded one Sunday to be taken to church. My father said no, for I had never been to church, and the German service is long and exhausting. I implored. He again said no. I implored again, and showed such a pious disposition, and so earnest a determination to behave well, that he gave in, and we went off very happily hand in hand. "Now mind, Elizabeth," he said, turning to me at the church door, "there is no coming out again in the middle. Having insisted on being brought, thou shalt now sit patiently till the end." "Oh, yes, oh, yes," I promised eagerly, and went in filled with holy fire. The shortness of my legs, hanging helplessly for two hours midway between the seat and the floor, was the weapon chosen by Satan for my destruction. In German churches you do not kneel, and seldom stand, but sit nearly the whole time, praying and singing in great comfort. If you are four years old, however, this unchanged position soon becomes one of torture. Unknown and dreadful things go on in your legs, strange prickings and tinglings and dartings up and down, a sudden terrifying numbness, when you think they must have dropped off but are afraid to look, then renewed and fiercer prickings, shootings, and burnings. I thought I must be very ill, for I had never known my legs like that before. My father sitting beside me was engrossed in the singing of a chorale that evidently had no end, each verse finished with a long-drawn-out hallelujah, after which the organ played by itself for a hundred years—by the organist's watch, which was wrong, two minutes exactly—and then another verse began. My father, being the patron of the living, was careful to sing and pray and listen to the sermon with exemplary attention, aware that every eye in the little church was on our pew, and at first I tried to imitate him; but the behaviour of my legs became so alarming that after vainly casting imploring glances at him and seeing that he continued his singing unmoved, I put out my hand and pulled his sleeve.

"Hal-le-lu-jah," sang my father with deliberation; continuing in a low voice without changing the expression of his face, his lips hardly moving, and his eyes fixed abstractedly on the ceiling till the organist, who was also the postman, should have finished his solo, "Did I not tell thee to sit still, Elizabeth?" "Yes, but——" "Then do it." "But I want to go home." "Unsinn." And the next verse beginning, my father sang louder than ever. What could I do? Should I cry? I began to be afraid I was going to die on that chair, so extraordinary were the sensations in my legs. What could my father do to me if I did cry? With the quick instinct of small children I felt that he could not put me in the corner in church, nor would he whip me in public, and that with the whole village looking on, he was helpless, and would have to give in. Therefore I tugged his sleeve again and more peremptorily, and prepared to demand my immediate removal in a loud voice. But my father was ready for me. Without interrupting his singing, or altering his devout expression, he put his hand slowly down and gave me a hard pinch—not a playful pinch, but a good hard unmistakeable pinch, such as I had never imagined possible, and then went on serenely to the next hallelujah. For a moment I was petrified with astonishment. Was this my indulgent father, my playmate, adorer, and friend? Smarting with pain, for I was a round baby, with a nicely stretched, tight skin, and dreadfully hurt in my feelings, I opened my mouth to shriek in earnest, when my father's clear whisper fell on my ear, each word distinct and not to be misunderstood, his eyes as before gazing meditatively into space, and his lips hardly moving, "Elizabeth, wenn du schreist, kneife ich dich bis du platzt." And he finished the verse with unruffled decorum—

"Will Satan mich verschlingen,
So lass die Engel singen
    Hallelujah!"

We never had another difference. Up to then he had been my willing slave, and after that I was his.

With a smile and a shiver I turned from the border and its memories to the door in the wall leading to the kitchen garden, in a corner of which my own little garden used to be. The door was open, and I stood still a moment before going through, to hold my breath and listen. The silence was as profound as before. The place seemed deserted; and I should have thought the house empty and shut up but for the carefully tended radishes and the recent footmarks on the green of the path. They were the footmarks of a child. I was stooping down to examine a specially clear one, when the loud caw of a very bored looking crow sitting on the wall just above my head made me jump as I have seldom in my life jumped, and reminded me that I was trespassing. Clearly my nerves were all to pieces, for I gathered up my skirts and fled through the door as though a whole army of ghosts and cousins were at my heels, nor did I stop till I had reached the remote corner where my garden was. "Are you enjoying yourself, Elizabeth?" asked the mocking sprite that calls itself my soul: but I was too much out of breath to answer.

This was really a very safe corner. It was separated from the main garden and the house by the wall, and shut in on the north side by an orchard, and it was to the last degree unlikely that any one would come there on such an afternoon. This plot of ground, turned now as I saw into a rockery, had been the scene of my most untiring labours. Into the cold earth of this north border on which the sun never shone I had dug my brightest hopes. All my pocket money had been spent on it, and as bulbs were dear and my weekly allowance small, in a fatal hour I had borrowed from Fraulein Wundermacher, selling her my independence, passing utterly into her power, forced as a result till my next birthday should come round to an unnatural suavity of speech and manner in her company, against which my very soul revolted. And after all, nothing came up. The labour of digging and watering, the anxious zeal with which I pounced on weeds, the poring over gardening books, the plans made as I sat on the little seat in the middle gazing admiringly and with the eye of faith on the trim surface so soon to be gemmed with a thousand flowers, the reckless expenditure of pfennings, the humiliation of my position in regard to Fraulein Wundermacher,—all, all had been in vain. No sun shone there, and nothing grew. The gardener who reigned supreme in those days had given me this big piece for that sole reason, because he could do nothing with it himself. He was no doubt of opinion that it was quite good enough for a child to experiment upon, and went his way, when I had thanked him with a profuseness of gratitude I still remember, with an unmoved countenance. For more than a year I worked and waited, and watched the career of the flourishing orchard opposite with puzzled feelings. The orchard was only a few yards away, and yet, although my garden was full of manure, and water, and attentions that were never bestowed on the orchard, all it could show and ever did show were a few unhappy beginnings of growth that either remained stationary and did not achieve flowers, or dwindled down again and vanished. Once I timidly asked the gardener if he could explain these signs and wonders, but he was a busy man with no time for answering questions, and told me shortly that gardening was not learned in a day. How well I remember that afternoon, and the very shape of the lazy clouds, and the smell of spring things, and myself going away abashed and sitting on the shaky bench in my domain and wondering for the hundredth time what it was that made the difference between my bit and the bit of orchard in front of me. The fruit trees, far enough away from the wall to be beyond the reach of its cold shade, were tossing their flower-laden heads in the sunshine in a carelessly well-satisfied fashion that filled my heart with envy. There was a rise in the field behind them, and at the foot of its protecting slope they luxuriated in the insolent glory of their white and pink perfection. It was May, and my heart bled at the thought of the tulips I had put in in November, and that I had never seen since. The whole of the rest of the garden was on fire with tulips; behind me, on the other side of the wall, were rows and rows of them,—cups of translucent loveliness, a jewelled ring flung right round the lawn. But what was there not on the other side of that wall? Things came up there and grew and flowered exactly as my gardening books said they should do; and in front of me, in the gay orchard, things that nobody ever troubled about or cultivated or noticed throve joyously beneath the trees,—daffodils thrusting their spears through the grass, crocuses peeping out inquiringly, snowdrops uncovering their small cold faces when the first shivering spring days came. Only my piece that I so loved was perpetually ugly and empty. And I sat in it thinking of these things on that radiant day, and wept aloud.

Then an apprentice came by, a youth who had often seen me busily digging, and noticing the unusual tears, and struck perhaps by the difference between my garden and the profusion of splendour all around, paused with his barrow on the path in front of me, and remarked that nobody could expect to get blood out of a stone. The apparent irrelevance of this statement made me weep still louder, the bitter tears of insulted sorrow; but he stuck to his point, and harangued me from the path, explaining the connection between north walls and tulips and blood and stones till my tears all dried up again and I listened attentively, for the conclusion to be drawn from his remarks was plainly that I had been shamefully taken in by the head gardener, who was an unprincipled person thenceforward to be for ever mistrusted and shunned. Standing on the path from which the kindly apprentice had expounded his proverb, this scene rose before me as clearly as though it had taken place that very day; but how different everything looked, and how it had shrunk! Was this the wide orchard that had seemed to stretch away, it and the sloping field beyond, up to the gates of heaven? I believe nearly every child who is much alone goes through a certain time of hourly expecting the Day of Judgment, and I had made up my mind that on that Day the heavenly host would enter the world by that very field, coming down the slope in shining ranks, treading the daffodils under foot, filling the orchard with their songs of exultation, joyously seeking out the sheep from among the goats. Of course I was a sheep, and my governess and the head gardener goats, so that the results could not fail to be in every way satisfactory. But looking up at the slope and remembering my visions, I laughed at the smallness of the field I had supposed would hold all heaven.

Here again the cousins had been at work. The site of my garden was occupied by a rockery, and the orchard grass with all its treasures had been dug up, and the spaces between the trees planted with currant bushes and celery in admirable rows; so that no future little cousins will be able to dream of celestial hosts coming towards them across the fields of daffodils, and will perhaps be the better for being free from visions of the kind, for as I grew older, uncomfortable doubts laid hold of my heart with cold fingers, dim uncertainties as to the exact ultimate position of the gardener and the governess, anxious questionings as to how it would be if it were they who turned out after all to be sheep, and I who—? For that we all three might be gathered into the same fold at the last never, in those days, struck me as possible, and if it had I should not have liked it.

"Now what sort of person can that be," I asked myself, shaking my head, as

I contemplated the changes before me, "who could put a rockery among vegetables and currant bushes? A rockery, of all things in the gardening world, needs consummate tact in its treatment. It is easier to make mistakes in forming a rockery than in any other garden scheme. Either it is a great success, or it is great failure; either it is very charming, or it is very absurd. There is no state between the sublime and the ridiculous possible in a rockery." I stood shaking my head disapprovingly at the rockery before me, lost in these reflections, when a sudden quick pattering of feet coming along in a great hurry made me turn round with a start, just in time to receive the shock of a body tumbling out of the mist and knocking violently against me.

It was a little girl of about twelve years old.

"Hullo!" said the little girl in excellent English; and then we stared at each other in astonishment.

"I thought you were Miss Robinson," said the little girl, offering no apology for having nearly knocked me down. "Who are you?"

"Miss Robinson? Miss Robinson?" I repeated, my eyes fixed on the little girl's face, and a host of memories stirring within me. "Why, didn't she marry a missionary, and go out to some place where they ate him?"

The little girl stared harder. "Ate him? Marry? What, has she been married all this time to somebody who's been eaten and never let on? Oh, I say, what a game!" And she threw back her head and laughed till the garden rang again.

"O hush, you dreadful little girl!" I implored, catching her by the arm, and terrified beyond measure by the loudness of her mirth. "Don't make that horrid noise—we are certain to be caught if you don't stop——"

The little girl broke off a shriek of laughter in the middle and shut her mouth with a snap. Her eyes, round and black and shiny like boot buttons, came still further out of her head. "Caught?" she said eagerly. "What, are you afraid of being caught too? Well, this is a game!" And with her hands plunged deep in the pockets of her coat she capered in front of me in the excess of her enjoyment, reminding me of a very fat black lamb frisking round the dazed and passive sheep its mother.

It was clear that the time had come for me to get down to the gate at the end of the garden as quickly as possible, and I began to move away in that direction. The little girl at once stopped capering and planted herself squarely in front of me. "Who are you?" she said, examining me from my hat to my boots with the keenest interest.

I considered this ungarnished manner of asking questions impertinent, and, trying to look lofty, made an attempt to pass at the side.

The little girl, with a quick, cork-like movement, was there before me. "Who are you?" she repeated, her expression friendly but firm. "Oh, I—I'm a pilgrim," I said in desperation.

"A pilgrim!" echoed the little girl. She seemed struck, and while she was struck I slipped past her and began to walk quickly towards the door in the wall. "A pilgrim!" said the little girl, again, keeping close beside me, and looking me up and down attentively. "I don't like pilgrims. Aren't they people who are always walking about, and have things the matter with their feet? Have you got anything the matter with your feet?"

"Certainly not," I replied indignantly, walking still faster. "And they never wash, Miss Robinson says. You don't either, do you?"

"Not wash? Oh, I'm afraid you are a very badly brought-up little girl—oh, leave me alone—I must run—"

"So must I," said the little girl, cheerfully, "for Miss Robinson must be close behind us. She nearly had me just before I found you." And she started running by my side.

The thought of Miss Robinson close behind us gave wings to my feet, and, casting my dignity, of which, indeed, there was but little left, to the winds, I fairly flew down the path. The little girl was not to be outrun, and though she panted and turned weird colours, kept by my side and even talked. Oh, I was tired, tired in body and mind, tired by the different shocks I had received, tired by the journey, tired by the want of food; and here I was being forced to run because this very naughty little girl chose to hide instead of going in to her lessons.

"I say—this is jolly—" she jerked out.

"But why need we run to the same place?" I breathlessly asked, in the vain hope of getting rid of her. "Oh, yes—that's just—the fun. We'd get on—together—you and I—"

"No, no," said I, decided on this point, bewildered though I was.

"I can't stand washing—either—it's awful—in winter—and makes one have—chaps."

"But I don't mind it in the least," I protested faintly, not having any energy left.

"Oh, I say!" said the little girl, looking at my face, and making the sound known as a guffaw. The familiarity of this little girl was wholly revolting. We had got safely through the door, round the corner past the radishes, and were in the shrubbery. I knew from experience how easy it was to hide in the tangle of little paths, and stopped a moment to look round and listen. The little girl opened her mouth to speak. With great presence of mind I instantly put my muff in front of it and held it there tight, while I listened. Dead silence, except for the laboured breathing and struggles of the little girl.

"I don't hear a sound," I whispered, letting her go again. "Now what did you want to say?" I added, eyeing her severely.

"I wanted to say," she panted, "that it's no good pretending you wash with a nose like that."

"A nose like that! A nose like what?" I exclaimed, greatly offended; and though I put up my hand and very tenderly and carefully felt it, I could find no difference in it. "I am afraid poor Miss Robinson must have a wretched life," I said, in tones of deep disgust.

The little girl smiled fatuously, as though I were paying her compliments. "It's all green and brown," she said, pointing. "Is it always like that?"

Then I remembered the wet fir tree near the gate, and the enraptured kiss it had received, and blushed.

"Won't it come off?" persisted the little girl.

"Of course it will come off," I answered, frowning.

"Why don't you rub it off?"

Then I remembered the throwing away of the handkerchief, and blushed again.

"Please lend me your handkerchief," I said humbly, "I—I have lost mine." There was a great fumbling in six different pockets, and then a handkerchief that made me young again merely to look at it was produced. I took it thankfully and rubbed with energy, the little girl, intensely interested, watching the operation and giving me advice. "There—it's all right now—a little more on the right—there—now it's all off."

"Are you sure? No green left?" I anxiously asked.

"No, it's red all over now," she replied cheerfully. "Let me get home," thought I, very much upset by this information, "let me get home to my dear, uncritical, admiring babies, who accept my nose as an example of what a nose should be, and whatever its colour think it beautiful." And thrusting the handkerchief back into the little girl's hands, I hurried away down the path. She packed it away hastily, but it took some seconds for it was of the size of a small sheet, and then came running after me. "Where are you going?" she asked surprised, as I turned down the path leading to the gate.

"Through this gate," I replied with decision.

"But you mustn't—we're not allowed to go through there——"

So strong was the force of old habits in that place that at the words not allowed my hand dropped of itself from the latch; and at that instant a voice calling quite close to us through the mist struck me rigid.

"Elizabeth! Elizabeth!" called the voice, "Come in at once to your lessons—Elizabeth! Elizabeth!"

"It's Miss Robinson," whispered the little girl, twinkling with excitement; then, catching sight of my face, she said once more with eager insistence, "Who are you?"

"Oh, I'm a ghost!" I cried with conviction, pressing my hands to my forehead and looking round fearfully.

"Pooh," said the little girl.

It was the last remark I heard her make, for there was a creaking of approaching boots in the bushes, and seized by a frightful panic I pulled the gate open with one desperate pull, flung it to behind me, and fled out and away down the wide, misty fields.

The Gotha Almanach says that the reigning cousin married the daughter of a Mr. Johnstone, an Englishman, in 1885, and that in 1886 their only child was born, Elizabeth.

November 20th.—Last night we had ten degrees of frost (Fahrenheit), and I went out the first thing this morning to see what had become of the tea-roses, and behold, they were wide awake and quite cheerful—covered with rime it is true, but anything but black and shrivelled. Even those in boxes on each side of the verandah steps were perfectly alive and full of buds, and one in particular, a Bouquet d'Or, is a mass of buds, and would flower if it could get the least encouragement. I am beginning to think that the tenderness of tea-roses is much exaggerated, and am certainly very glad I had the courage to try them in this northern garden. But I must not fly too boldly in the face of Providence, and have ordered those in the boxes to be taken into the greenhouse for the winter, and hope the Bouquet d'Or, in a sunny place near the glass, may be induced to open some of those buds. The greenhouse is only used as a refuge, and kept at a temperature just above freezing, and is reserved entirely for such plants as cannot stand the very coldest part of the winter out of doors. I don't use it for growing anything, because I don't love things that will only bear the garden for three or four months in the year and require coaxing and petting for the rest of it. Give me a garden full of strong, healthy creatures, able to stand roughness and cold without dismally giving in and dying. I never could see that delicacy of constitution is pretty, either in plants or women. No doubt there are many lovely flowers to be had by heat and constant coaxing, but then for each of these there are fifty others still lovelier that will gratefully grow in God's wholesome air and are blessed in return with a far greater intensity of scent and colour.

We have been very busy till now getting the permanent beds into order and planting the new tea-roses, and I am looking forward to next summer with more hope than ever in spite of my many failures. I wish the years would pass quickly that will bring my garden to perfection! The Persian Yellows have gone into their new quarters, and their place is occupied by the tearose Safrano; all the rose beds are carpeted with pansies sown in July and transplanted in October, each bed having a separate colour. The purple ones are the most charming and go well with every rose, but I have white ones with Laurette Messimy, and yellow ones with Safrano, and a new red sort in the big centre bed of red roses. Round the semicircle on the south side of the little privet hedge two rows of annual larkspurs in all their delicate shades have been sown, and just beyond the larkspurs, on the grass, is a semicircle of standard tea and pillar roses.

In front of the house the long borders have been stocked with larkspurs, annual and perennial, columbines, giant poppies, pinks, Madonna lilies, wallflowers, hollyhocks, perennial phloxes, peonies, lavender, starworts, cornflowers, Lychnis chalcedonica, and bulbs packed in wherever bulbs could go. These are the borders that were so hardly used by the other gardener. The spring boxes for the verandah steps have been filled with pink and white and yellow tulips. I love tulips better than any other spring flower; they are the embodiment of alert cheerfulness and tidy grace, and next to a hyacinth look like a wholesome, freshly tubbed young girl beside a stout lady whose every movement weighs down the air with patchouli. Their faint, delicate scent is refinement itself; and is there anything in the world more charming than the sprightly way they hold up their little faces to the sun. I have heard them called bold and flaunting, but to me they seem modest grace itself, only always on the alert to enjoy life as much as they can and not afraid of looking the sun or anything else above them in the face. On the grass there are two beds of them carpeted with forget-me-nots; and in the grass, in scattered groups, are daffodils and narcissus. Down the wilder shrubbery walks foxgloves and mulleins will (I hope) shine majestic; and one cool corner, backed by a group of firs, is graced by Madonna lilies, white foxgloves, and columbines.

In a distant glade I have made a spring garden round an oak tree that stands alone in the sun—groups of crocuses, daffodils, narcissus, hyacinths, and tulips, among such flowering shrubs and trees as Pirus Malus spectabilis, floribunda, and coronaria; Prunus Juliana, Mahaleb, serotina, triloba, and Pissardi; Cydonias and Weigelias in every colour, and several kinds of Crataegus and other May lovelinesses. If the weather behaves itself nicely, and we get gentle rains in due season, I think this little corner will be beautiful—but what a big "if" it is! Drought is our great enemy, and the two last summers each contained five weeks of blazing, cloudless heat when all the ditches dried up and the soil was like hot pastry. At such times the watering is naturally quite beyond the strength of two men; but as a garden is a place to be happy in, and not one where you want to meet a dozen curious eyes at every turn, I should not like to have more than these two, or rather one and a half—the assistant having stork-like proclivities and going home in the autumn to his native Russia, returning in the spring with the first warm winds. I want to keep him over the winter, as there is much to be done even then, and I sounded him on the point the other day. He is the most abject-looking of human beings—lame, and afflicted with a hideous eye-disease; but he is a good worker and plods along unwearyingly from sunrise to dusk.

"Pray, my good stork," said I, or German words to that effect, "why don't you stay here altogether, instead of going home and rioting away all you have earned?"

"I would stay," he answered, "but I have my wife there in Russia."

"Your wife!" I exclaimed, stupidly surprised that the poor deformed creature should have found a mate—as though there were not a superfluity of mates in the world—"I didn't know you were married?"

"Yes, and I have two little children, and I don't know what they would do if I were not to come home. But it is a very expensive journey to Russia, and costs me every time seven marks."

"Seven marks!"

"Yes, it is a great sum."

I wondered whether I should be able to get to Russia for seven marks, supposing I were to be seized with an unnatural craving to go there.

All the labourers who work here from March to December are Russians and Poles, or a mixture of both. We send a man over who can speak their language, to fetch as many as he can early in the year, and they arrive with their bundles, men and women and babies, and as soon as they have got here and had their fares paid, they disappear in the night if they get the chance, sometimes fifty of them at a time, to go and work singly or in couples for the peasants, who pay them a pfenning or two more a day than we do, and let them eat with the family. From us they get a mark and a half to two marks a day, and as many potatoes as they can eat. The women get less, not because they work less, but because they are women and must not be encouraged. The overseer lives with them, and has a loaded revolver in his pocket and a savage dog at his heels. For the first week or two after their arrival, the foresters and other permanent officials keep guard at night over the houses they are put into. I suppose they find it sleepy work; for certain it is that spring after spring the same thing happens, fifty of them getting away in spite of all our precautions, and we are left with our mouths open and much out of pocket. This spring, by some mistake, they arrived without their bundles, which had gone astray on the road, and, as they travel in their best clothes, they refused utterly to work until their luggage came. Nearly a week was lost waiting, to the despair of all in authority.

Nor will any persuasions induce them to do anything on Saints' days, and there surely never was a church so full of them as the Russian Church. In the spring, when every hour is of vital importance, the work is constantly being interrupted by them, and the workers lie sleeping in the sun the whole day, agreeably conscious that they are pleasing themselves and the Church at one and the same time—a state of perfection as rare as it is desirable. Reason unaided by Faith is of course exasperated at this waste of precious time, and I confess that during the first mild days after the long winter frost when it is possible to begin to work the ground, I have sympathised with the gloom of the Man of Wrath, confronted in one week by two or three empty days on which no man will labour, and have listened in silence to his remarks about distant Russian saints.

I suppose it was my own superfluous amount of civilisation that made me pity these people when first I came to live among them. They herd together like animals and do the work of animals; but in spite of the armed overseer, the dirt and the rags, the meals of potatoes washed down by weak vinegar and water, I am beginning to believe that they would strongly object to soap, I am sure they would not wear new clothes, and I hear them coming home from their work at dusk singing. They are like little children or animals in their utter inability to grasp the idea of a future; and after all, if you work all day in God's sunshine, when evening comes you are pleasantly tired and ready for rest and not much inclined to find fault with your lot. I have not yet persuaded myself, however, that the women are happy. They have to work as hard as the men and get less for it; they have to produce offspring, quite regardless of times and seasons and the general fitness of things; they have to do this as expeditiously as possible, so that they may not unduly interrupt the work in hand; nobody helps them, notices them, or cares about them, least of all the husband. It is quite a usual thing to see them working in the fields in the morning, and working again in the afternoon, having in the interval produced a baby. The baby is left to an old woman whose duty it is to look after babies collectively. When I expressed my horror at the poor creatures working immediately afterwards as though nothing had happened, the Man of Wrath informed me that they did not suffer because they had never worn corsets, nor had their mothers and grandmothers. We were riding together at the time, and had just passed a batch of workers, and my husband was speaking to the overseer, when a woman arrived alone, and taking up a spade, began to dig. She grinned cheerfully at us as she made a curtesy, and the overseer remarked that she had just been back to the house and had a baby.

"Poor, poor woman!" I cried, as we rode on, feeling for some occult reason very angry with the Man of Wrath. "And her wretched husband doesn't care a rap, and will probably beat her to-night if his supper isn't right. What nonsense it is to talk about the equality of the sexes when the women have the babies!"

"Quite so, my dear," replied the Man of Wrath, smiling condescendingly. "You have got to the very root of the matter. Nature, while imposing this agreeable duty on the woman, weakens her and disables her for any serious competition with man. How can a person who is constantly losing a year of the best part of her life compete with a young man who never loses any time at all? He has the brute force, and his last word on any subject could always be his fist."

I said nothing. It was a dull, gray afternoon in the beginning of November, and the leaves dropped slowly and silently at our horses' feet as we rode towards the Hirschwald.

"It is a universal custom," proceeded the Man of Wrath, "amongst these Russians, and I believe amongst the lower classes everywhere, and certainly commendable on the score of simplicity, to silence a woman's objections and aspirations by knocking her down. I have heard it said that this apparently brutal action has anything but the maddening effect tenderly nurtured persons might suppose, and that the patient is soothed and satisfied with a rapidity and completeness unattainable by other and more polite methods. Do you suppose," he went on, flicking a twig off a tree with his whip as we passed, "that the intellectual husband, wrestling intellectually with the chaotic yearnings of his intellectual wife, ever achieves the result aimed at? He may and does go on wrestling till he is tired, but never does he in the very least convince her of her folly; while his brother in the ragged coat has got through the whole business in less time than it takes me to speak about it. There is no doubt that these poor women fulfil their vocation far more thoroughly than the women in our class, and, as the truest: happiness consists in finding one's vocation quickly and continuing in it all one's days, I consider they are to be envied rather than not, since they are early taught, by the impossibility of argument with marital muscle, the impotence of female endeavour and the blessings of content."

"Pray go on," I said politely.

"These women accept their beatings with a simplicity worthy of all praise, and far from considering themselves insulted, admire the strength and energy of the man who can administer such eloquent rebukes. In Russia, not only may a man beat his wife, but it is laid down in the catechism and taught all boys at the time of confirmation as necessary at least once a week, whether she has done anything or not, for the sake of her general health and happiness."

I thought I observed a tendency in the Man of Wrath rather to gloat over these castigations.

"Pray, my dear man," I said, pointing with my whip, "look at that baby moon so innocently peeping at us over the edge of the mist just behind that silver birch; and don't talk so much about women and things you don't understand. What is the use of your bothering about fists and whips and muscles and all the dreadful things invented for the confusion of obstreperous wives? You know you are a civilised husband, and a civilised husband is a creature who has ceased to be a man.

"And a civilised wife?" he asked, bringing his horse close up beside me and putting his arm round my waist, "has she ceased to be a woman?"

"I should think so indeed,—she is a goddess, and can never be worshipped and adored enough."

"It seems to me," he said, "that the conversation is growing personal."

I started off at a canter across the short, springy turf. The Hirschwald is an enchanted place on such an evening, when the mists lie low on the turf, and overhead the delicate, bare branches of the silver birches stand out clear against the soft sky, while the little moon looks down kindly on the damp November world. Where the trees thicken into a wood, the fragrance of the wet earth and rotting leaves kicked up by the horses' hoofs fills my soul with delight. I particularly love that smell,—it brings before me the entire benevolence of Nature, for ever working death and decay, so piteous in themselves, into the means of fresh life and glory, and sending up sweet odours as she works.

December 7th.—I have been to England. I went for at least a month and stayed a week in a fog and was blown home again in a gale. Twice I fled before the fogs into the country to see friends with gardens, but it was raining, and except the beautiful lawns (not to be had in the Fatherland) and the infinite possibilities, there was nothing to interest the intelligent and garden-loving foreigner, for the good reason that you cannot be interested in gardens under an umbrella. So I went back to the fogs, and after groping about for a few days more began to long inordinately for Germany. A terrific gale sprang up after I had started, and the journey both by sea and land was full of horrors, the trains in Germany being heated to such an extent that it is next to impossible to sit still, great gusts of hot air coming up under the cushions, the cushions themselves being very hot, and the wretched traveller still hotter.

But when I reached my home and got out of the train into the purest, brightest snow-atmosphere, the air so still that the whole world seemed to be listening, the sky cloudless, the crisp snow sparkling underfoot and on the trees, and a happy row of three beaming babies awaiting me, I was consoled for all my torments, only remembering them enough to wonder why I had gone away at all.

The babies each had a kitten in one hand and an elegant bouquet of pine needles and grass in the other, and what with the due presentation of the bouquets and the struggles of the kittens, the hugging and kissing was much interfered with. Kittens, bouquets, and babies were all somehow squeezed into the sleigh, and off we went with jingling bells and shrieks of delight. "Directly you comes home the fun begins," said the May baby, sitting very close to me. "How the snow purrs!" cried the April baby, as the horses scrunched it up with their feet. The June baby sat loudly singing "The King of Love my Shepherd is," and swinging her kitten round by its tail to emphasise the rhythm.

The house, half-buried in the snow, looked the very abode of peace, and I ran through all the rooms, eager to take possession of them again, and feeling as though I had been away for ever. When I got to the library I came to a standstill,—ah, the dear room, what happy times I have spent in it rummaging amongst the books, making plans for my garden, building castles in the air, writing, dreaming, doing nothing! There was a big peat fire blazing half up the chimney, and the old housekeeper had put pots of flowers about, and on the writing-table was a great bunch of violets scenting the room. "Oh, how good it is to be home again!" I sighed in my satisfaction. The babies clung about my knees, looking up at me with eyes full of love. Outside the dazzling snow and sunshine, inside the bright room and happy faces—I thought of those yellow fogs and shivered. The library is not used by the Man of Wrath; it is neutral ground where we meet in the evenings for an hour before he disappears into his own rooms—a series of very smoky dens in the southeast corner of the house. It looks, I am afraid, rather too gay for an ideal library; and its colouring, white and yellow, is so cheerful as to be almost frivolous. There are white bookcases all round the walls, and there is a great fireplace, and four windows, facing full south, opening on to my most cherished bit of garden, the bit round the sun-dial; so that with so much colour and such a big fire and such floods of sunshine it has anything but a sober air, in spite of the venerable volumes filling the shelves. Indeed, I should never be surprised if they skipped down from their places, and, picking up their leaves, began to dance. With this room to live in, I can look forward with perfect equanimity to being snowed up for any time Providence thinks proper; and to go into the garden in its snowed-up state is like going into a bath of purity. The first breath on opening the door is so ineffably pure that it makes me gasp, and I feel a black and sinful object in the midst of all the spotlessness. Yesterday I sat out of doors near the sun-dial the whole afternoon, with the thermometer so many degrees below freezing that it will be weeks finding its way up again; but there was no wind, and beautiful sunshine, and I was well wrapped up in furs. I even had tea brought out there, to the astonishment of the menials, and sat till long after the sun had set, enjoying the frosty air. I had to drink the tea very quickly, for it showed a strong inclination to begin to freeze. After the sun had gone down the rooks came home to their nests in the garden with a great fuss and fluttering, and many hesitations and squabbles before they settled on their respective trees. They flew over my head in hundreds with a mighty swish of wings, and when they had arranged themselves comfortably, an intense hush fell upon the garden, and the house began to look like a Christmas card, with its white roof against the clear, pale green of the western sky, and lamplight shining in the windows.

I had been reading a Life of Luther, lent me by our parson, in the intervals between looking round me and being happy. He came one day with the book and begged me to read it, having discovered that my interest in Luther was not as living as it ought to be; so I took it out with me into the garden, because the dullest book takes on a certain saving grace if read out of doors, just as bread and butter, devoid of charm in the drawing-room, is ambrosia eaten under a tree. I read Luther all the afternoon with pauses for refreshing glances at the garden and the sky, and much thankfulness in my heart. His struggles with devils amazed me; and I wondered whether such a day as that, full of grace and the forgiveness of sins, never struck him as something to make him relent even towards devils. He apparently never allowed himself just to be happy. He was a wonderful man, but I am glad I was not his wife.

Our parson is an interesting person, and untiring in his efforts to improve himself. Both he and his wife study whenever they have a spare moment, and there is a tradition that she stirs her puddings with one hand and holds a Latin grammar in the other, the grammar, of course, getting the greater share of her attention. To most German Hausfraus the dinners and the puddings are of paramount importance, and they pride themselves on keeping those parts of their houses that are seen in a state of perpetual and spotless perfection, and this is exceedingly praiseworthy; but, I would humbly inquire, are there not other things even more important? And is not plain living and high thinking better than the other way about? And all too careful making of dinners and dusting of furniture takes a terrible amount of precious time, and—and with shame I confess that my sympathies are all with the pudding and the grammar. It cannot be right to be the slave of one's household gods, and I protest that if my furniture ever annoyed me by wanting to be dusted when I wanted to be doing something else, and there was no one to do the dusting for me, I would cast it all into the nearest bonfire and sit and warm my toes at the flames with great contentment, triumphantly selling my dusters to the very next pedlar who was weak enough to buy them. Parsons' wives have to do the housework and cooking themselves, and are thus not only cooks and housemaids, but if they have children—and they always do have children—they are head and under nurse as well; and besides these trifling duties have a good deal to do with their fruit and vegetable garden, and everything to do with their poultry. This being so, is it not pathetic to find a young woman bravely struggling to learn languages and keep up with her husband? If I were that husband, those puddings would taste sweetest to me that were served with Latin sauce. They are both severely pious, and are for ever engaged in desperate efforts to practise what they preach; than which, as we all know, nothing is more difficult. He works in his parish with the most noble self-devotion, and never loses courage, although his efforts have been several times rewarded by disgusting libels pasted up on the street-corners, thrown under doors, and even fastened to his own garden wall. The peasant hereabouts is past belief low and animal, and a sensitive, intellectual parson among them is really a pearl before swine. For years he has gone on unflinchingly, filled with the most living faith and hope and charity, and I sometimes wonder whether they are any better now in his parish than they were under his predecessor, a man who smoked and drank beer from Monday morning to Saturday night, never did a stroke of work, and often kept the scanty congregation waiting on Sunday afternoons while he finished his postprandial nap. It is discouraging enough to make most men give in, and leave the parish to get to heaven or not as it pleases; but he never seems discouraged, and goes on sacrificing the best part of his life to these people when all his tastes are literary, and all his inclinations towards the life of the student. His convictions drag him out of his little home at all hours to minister to the sick and exhort the wicked; they give him no rest, and never let him feel he has done enough; and when he comes home weary, after a day's wrestling with his parishioners' souls, he is confronted on his doorstep by filthy abuse pasted up on his own front door. He never speaks of these things, but how shall they be hid? Everybody here knows everything that happens before the day is over, and what we have for dinner is of far greater general interest than the most astounding political earthquake. They have a pretty, roomy cottage, and a good bit of ground adjoining the churchyard. His predecessor used to hang out his washing on the tombstones to dry, but then he was a person entirely lost to all sense of decency, and had finally to be removed, preaching a farewell sermon of a most vituperative description, and hurling invective at the Man of Wrath, who sat up in his box drinking in every word and enjoying himself thoroughly. The Man of Wrath likes novelty, and such a sermon had never been heard before. It is spoken of in the village to this day with bated breath and awful joy.

December 22nd.—Up to now we have had a beautiful winter. Clear skies, frost, little wind, and, except for a sharp touch now and then, very few really cold days. My windows are gay with hyacinths and lilies of the valley; and though, as I have said, I don't admire the smell of hyacinths in the spring when it seems wanting in youth and chastity next to that of other flowers, I am glad enough now to bury my nose in their heavy sweetness. In December one cannot afford to be fastidious; besides, one is actually less fastidious about everything in the winter. The keen air braces soul as well as body into robustness, and the food and the perfume disliked in the summer are perfectly welcome then.

I am very busy preparing for Christmas, but have often locked myself up in a room alone, shutting out my unfinished duties, to study the flower catalogues and make my lists of seeds and shrubs and trees for the spring. It is a fascinating occupation, and acquires an additional charm when you know you ought to be doing something else, that Christmas is at the door, that children and servants and farm hands depend on you for their pleasure, and that, if you don't see to the decoration of the trees and house, and the buying of the presents, nobody else will. The hours fly by shut up with those catalogues and with Duty snarling on the other side of the door. I don't like Duty—everything in the least disagreeable is always sure to be one's duty. Why cannot it be my duty to make lists and plans for the dear garden? "And so it is," I insisted to the Man of Wrath, when he protested against what he called wasting my time upstairs. "No," he replied sagely; "your garden is not your duty, because it is your Pleasure."

What a comfort it is to have such wells of wisdom constantly at my disposal! Anybody can have a husband, but to few is it given to have a sage, and the combination of both is as rare as it is useful. Indeed, in its practical utility the only thing I ever saw to equal it is a sofa my neighbour has bought as a Christmas surprise for her husband, and which she showed me the last time I called there—a beautiful invention, as she explained, combining a bedstead, a sofa, and a chest of drawers, and into which you put your clothes, and on top of which you put yourself, and if anybody calls in the middle of the night and you happen to be using the drawing-room as a bedroom, you just pop the bedclothes inside, and there you are discovered sitting on your sofa and looking for all the world as though you had been expecting visitors for hours.

"Pray, does he wear pyjamas?" I inquired.

But she had never heard of pyjamas.

It takes a long time to make my spring lists. I want to have a border all yellow, every shade of yellow from fieriest orange to nearly white, and the amount of work and studying of gardening books it costs me will only be appreciated by beginners like myself. I have been weeks planning it, and it is not nearly finished. I want it to be a succession of glories from May till the frosts, and the chief feature is to be the number of "ardent marigolds"— flowers that I very tenderly love—and nasturtiums. The nasturtiums are to be of every sort and shade, and are to climb and creep and grow in bushes, and show their lovely flowers and leaves to the best advantage. Then there are to be eschscholtzias, dahlias, sunflowers, zinnias, scabiosa, portulaca, yellow violas, yellow stocks, yellow sweet-peas, yellow lupins— everything that is yellow or that has a yellow variety. The place I have chosen for it is a long, wide border in the sun, at the foot of a grassy slope crowned with lilacs and pines, and facing southeast. You go through a little pine wood, and, turning a corner, are to come suddenly upon this bit of captured morning glory. I want it to be blinding in its brightness after the dark, cool path through the wood.

That is the idea. Depression seizes me when I reflect upon the probable difference between the idea and its realisation. I am ignorant, and the gardener is, I do believe, still more so; for he was forcing some tulips, and they have all shrivelled up and died, and he says he cannot imagine why. Besides, he is in love with the cook, and is going to marry her after Christmas, and refuses to enter into any of my plans with the enthusiasm they deserve, but sits with vacant eye dreamily chopping wood from morning till night to keep the beloved one's kitchen fire well supplied. I cannot understand any one preferring cooks to marigolds; those future marigolds, shadowy as they are, and whose seeds are still sleeping at the seedsman's, have shone through my winter days like golden lamps.

I wish with all my heart I were a man, for of course the first thing I should do would be to buy a spade and go and garden, and then I should have the delight of doing everything for my flowers with my own hands and need not waste time explaining what I want done to somebody else. It is dull work giving orders and trying to describe the bright visions of one's brain to a person who has no visions and no brain, and who thinks a yellow bed should be calceolarias edged with blue.

I have taken care in choosing my yellow plants to put down only those humble ones that are easily pleased and grateful for little, for my soil is by no means all that it might be, and to most plants the climate is rather trying. I feel really grateful to any flower that is sturdy and willing enough to flourish here. Pansies seem to like the place and so do sweet-peas; pinks don't, and after much coaxing gave hardly any flowers last summer. Nearly all the roses were a success, in spite of the sandy soil, except the tea-rose Adam, which was covered with buds ready to open, when they suddenly turned brown and died, and three standard Dr. Grills which stood in a row and simply sulked. I had been very excited about Dr. Grill, his description in the catalogues being specially fascinating, and no doubt I deserved the snubbing I got. "Never be excited, my dears, about anything," shall be the advice I will give the three babies when the time comes to take them out to parties, "or, if you are, don't show it. If by nature you are volcanoes, at least be only smouldering ones. Don't look pleased, don't look interested, don't, above all things, look eager. Calm indifference should be written on every feature of your faces. Never show that you like any one person, or any one thing. Be cool, languid, and reserved. If you don't do as your mother tells you and are just gushing, frisky, young idiots, snubs will be your portion. If you do as she tells you, you'll marry princes and live happily ever after."

Dr. Grill must be a German rose. In this part of the world the more you are pleased to see a person the less is he pleased to see you; whereas, if you are disagreeable, he will grow pleasant visibly, his countenance expanding into wider amiability the more your own is stiff and sour. But I was not Prepared for that sort of thing in a rose, and was disgusted with Dr. Grill. He had the best place in the garden—warm, sunny, and sheltered; his holes were prepared with the tenderest care; he was given the most dainty mixture of compost, clay, and manure; he was watered assiduously all through the drought when more willing flowers got nothing; and he refused to do anything but look black and shrivel. He did not die, but neither did he live—he just existed; and at the end of the summer not one of him had a scrap more shoot or leaf than when he was first put in in April. It would have been better if he had died straight away, for then I should have known what to do; as it is, there he is still occupying the best place, wrapped up carefully for the winter, excluding kinder roses, and probably intending to repeat the same conduct next year. Well, trials are the portion of mankind, and gardeners have their share, and in any case it is better to be tried by plants than persons, seeing that with plants you know that it is you who are in the wrong, and with persons it is always the other way about—and who is there among us who has not felt the pangs of injured innocence, and known them to be grievous?

I have two visitors staying with me, though I have done nothing to provoke such an infliction, and had been looking forward to a happy little Christmas alone with the Man of Wrath and the babies. Fate decreed otherwise. Quite regularly, if I look forward to anything, Fate steps in and decrees otherwise; I don't know why it should, but it does. I had not even invited these good ladies—like greatness on the modest, they were thrust upon me. One is Irais, the sweet singer of the summer, whom I love as she deserves, but of whom I certainly thought I had seen the last for at least a year, when she wrote and asked if I would have her over Christmas, as her husband was out of sorts, and she didn't like him in that state. Neither do I like sick husbands, so, full of sympathy, I begged her to come, and here she is. And the other is Minora.

Why I have to have Minora I don't know, for I was not even aware of her existence a fortnight ago. Then coming down cheerfully one morning to breakfast—it was the very day after my return from England—I found a letter from an English friend, who up till then had been perfectly innocuous, asking me to befriend Minora. I read the letter aloud for the benefit of the Man of Wrath, who was eating Spickgans, a delicacy much sought after in these parts. "Do, my dear Elizabeth," wrote my friend, "take some notice of the poor thing. She is studying art in Dresden, and has nowhere literally to go for Christmas. She is very ambitious and hardworking—"

"Then," interrupted the Man of Wrath, "she is not pretty. Only ugly girls work hard."

"—and she is really very clever—"

"I do not like clever girls, they are so stupid," again interrupted the Man of Wrath.

"—and unless some kind creature like yourself takes pity on her she will be very lonely."

"Then let her be lonely."

"Her mother is my oldest friend, and would be greatly distressed to think that her daughter should be alone in a foreign town at such a season."

"I do not mind the distress of the mother."

"Oh, dear me," I exclaimed impatiently, "I shall have to ask her to come!"
"If you should be inclined," the letter went on, "to play the good Samaritan, dear Elizabeth, I am positive you would find Minora a bright, intelligent companion—"

"Minora?" questioned the Man of Wrath.

The April baby, who has had a nursery governess of an altogether alarmingly zealous type attached to her person for the last six weeks, looked up from her bread and milk.

"It sounds like islands," she remarked pensively.

The governess coughed.

"Majora, Minora, Alderney, and Sark," explained her pupil.

I looked at her severely.

"If you are not careful, April," I said, "you'll be a genius when you grow up and disgrace your parents."

Miss Jones looked as though she did not like Germans. I am afraid she despises us because she thinks we are foreigners—an attitude of mind quite British and wholly to her credit; but we, on the other hand, regard her as a foreigner, which, of course, makes things complicated.

"Shall I really have to have this strange girl?" I asked, addressing nobody in particular and not expecting a reply.

"You need not have her," said the Man of Wrath composedly, "but you will. You will write to-day and cordially invite her, and when she has been here twenty-four hours you will quarrel with her. I know you, my dear."

"Quarrel! I? With a little art-student?" Miss Jones cast down her eyes. She is perpetually scenting a scene, and is always ready to bring whole batteries of discretion and tact and good taste to bear on us, and seems to know we are disputing in an unseemly manner when we would never dream it ourselves but for the warning of her downcast eyes. I would take my courage in both hands and ask her to go, for besides this superfluity of discreet behaviour she is, although only nursery, much too zealous, and inclined to be always teaching and never playing; but, unfortunately, the April baby adores her and is sure there never was any one so beautiful before. She comes every day with fresh accounts of the splendours of her wardrobe, and feeling descriptions of her umbrellas and hats; and Miss Jones looks offended and purses up her lips. In common with most governesses, she has a little dark down on her upper lip, and the April baby appeared one day at dinner with her own decorated in faithful imitation, having achieved it after much struggling, with the aid of a lead pencil and unbounded love. Miss Jones put her in the corner for impertinence. I wonder why governesses are so unpleasant. The Man of Wrath says it is because they are not married. Without venturing to differ entirely from the opinion of experience, I would add that the strain of continually having to set an example must surely be very great. It is much easier, and often more pleasant, to be a warning than an example, and governesses are but women, and women are sometimes foolish, and when you want to be foolish it must be annoying to have to be wise.

Minora and Irais arrived yesterday together; or rather, when the carriage drove up, Irais got out of it alone, and informed me that there was a strange girl on a bicycle a little way behind. I sent back the carriage to pick her up, for it was dusk and the roads are terrible.

"But why do you have strange girls here at all?" asked Irais rather peevishly, taking off her hat in the library before the fire, and otherwise making herself very much at home; "I don't like them. I'm not sure that they're not worse than husbands who are out of order. Who is she? She would bicycle from the station, and is, I am sure, the first woman who has done it. The little boys threw stones at her."

"Oh, my dear, that only shows the ignorance of the little boys. Never mind her. Let us have tea in peace before she comes." "But we should be much happier without her," she grumbled. "Weren't we happy enough in the summer, Elizabeth—just you and I?"

"Yes, indeed we were," I answered heartily, putting my arms round her. The flame of my affection for Irais burns very brightly on the day of her arrival; besides, this time I have prudently provided against her sinning with the salt-cellars by ordering them to be handed round like vegetable dishes. We had finished tea and she had gone up to her room to dress before Minora and her bicycle were got here. I hurried out to meet her, feeling sorry for her, plunged into a circle of strangers at such a very personal season as Christmas. But she was not very shy; indeed, she was less shy than I was, and lingered in the hall, giving the servants directions to wipe the snow off the tyres of her machine before she lent an attentive ear to my welcoming remarks.

"I couldn't make your man understand me at the station," she said at last, when her mind was at rest about her bicycle; "I asked him how far it was, and what the roads were like, and he only smiled. Is he German? But of course he is—how odd that he didn't understand. You speak English very well,—very well indeed, do you know." By this time we were in the library, and she stood on the hearth-rug warming her back while I poured her out some tea.

"What a quaint room," she remarked, looking round, "and the hall is so curious too. Very old, isn't it? There's a lot of copy here."

The Man of Wrath, who had been in the hall on her arrival and had come in with us, began to look about on the carpet. "Copy" he inquired, "Where's copy?"

"Oh—material, you know, for a book. I'm just jotting down what strikes me in your country, and when I have time shall throw it into book form." She spoke very loud, as English people always do to foreigners.

"My dear," I said breathlessly to Irais, when I had got into her room and shut the door and Minora was safely in hers, "what do you think—she writes books!"

"What—the bicycling girl?"

"Yes—Minora—imagine it!"

We stood and looked at each other with awestruck faces.

"How dreadful!" murmured Irais. "I never met a young girl who did that before."

"She says this place is full of copy." "Full of what?"

"That's what you make books with."

"Oh, my dear, this is worse than I expected! A strange girl is always a bore among good friends, but one can generally manage her. But a girl who writes books—why, it isn't respectable! And you can't snub that sort of people; they're unsnubbable."

"Oh, but we'll try!" I cried, with such heartiness that we both laughed.

The hall and the library struck Minora most; indeed, she lingered so long after dinner in the hall, which is cold, that the Man of Wrath put on his fur coat by way of a gentle hint. His hints are always gentle.

She wanted to hear the whole story about the chapel and the nuns and Gustavus Adolphus, and pulling out a fat note-book began to take down what I said. I at once relapsed into silence.

"Well?" she said.

"That's all."

"Oh, but you've only just begun."

"It doesn't go any further. Won't you come into the library?"

In the library she again took up her stand before the fire and warmed herself, and we sat in a row and were cold. She has a wonderfully good profile, which is irritating. The wind, however, is tempered to the shorn lamb by her eyes being set too closely together.

Irais lit a cigarette, and leaning back in her chair, contemplated her critically beneath her long eyelashes. "You are writing a book?" she asked presently.

"Well—yes, I suppose I may say that I am. Just my impressions, you know, of your country. Anything that strikes me as curious or amusing—I jot it down, and when I have time shall work it up into something, I daresay."

"Are you not studying painting?"

"Yes, but I can't study that for ever. We have an English proverb: 'Life is short and Art is long'—too long, I sometimes think—and writing is a great relaxation when I am tired."

"What shall you call it?"

"Oh, I thought of calling it Journeyings in Germany. It sounds well, and would be correct. Or Jottings from German Journeyings,—I haven't quite decided yet which."

"By the author of Prowls in Pomerania, you might add," suggested Irais.

"And Drivel from Dresden," said I.

"And Bosh from Berlin," added Irais.

Minora stared. "I don't think those two last ones would do," she said, "because it is not to be a facetious book. But your first one is rather a good title," she added, looking at Irais and drawing out her note-book. "I think I'll just jot that down."

"If you jot down all we say and then publish it, will it still be your book?" asked Irais.

But Minora was so busy scribbling that she did not hear.

"And have you no suggestions to make, Sage?" asked Irais, turning to the Man of Wrath, who was blowing out clouds of smoke in silence.

"Oh, do you call him Sage?" cried Minora; "and always in English?"

Irais and I looked at each other. We knew what we did call him, and were afraid Minora would in time ferret it out and enter it in her note-book. The Man of Wrath looked none too well pleased to be alluded to under his very nose by our new guest as "him."

"Husbands are always sages," said I gravely.

"Though sages are not always husbands," said Irais with equal gravity.

"Sages and husbands—sage and husbands—" she went on musingly, "what does that remind you of, Miss Minora?"

"Oh, I know,—how stupid of me!" cried Minora eagerly, her pencil in mid-air and her brain clutching at the elusive recollection, "sage and,—why,—yes,—no,—yes, of course—oh," disappointedly, "but that's vulgar—I can't put it in."

"What is vulgar?" I asked.

"She thinks sage and onions is vulgar," said Irais languidly; "but it isn't, it is very good." She got up and walked to the piano, and, sitting down, began, after a little wandering over the keys, to sing.

"Do you play?" I asked Minora.

"Yes, but I am afraid I am rather out of practice."

I said no more. I know what that sort of playing is.

When we were lighting our bedroom candles Minora began suddenly to speak in an unknown tongue. We stared. "What is the matter with her?" murmured Irais.

"I thought, perhaps," said Minora in English, "you might prefer to talk German, and as it is all the same to me what I talk—" "Oh, pray don't trouble," said Irais. "We like airing our English—don't we, Elizabeth?"

"I don't want my German to get rusty though," said Minora; "I shouldn't like to forget it."

"Oh, but isn't there an English song," said Irais, twisting round her neck as she preceded us upstairs, "'Tis folly to remember, 'tis wisdom to forget'?"

"You are not nervous sleeping alone, I hope," I said hastily.

"What room is she in?" asked Irais.

"No. 12."

"Oh!—do you believe in ghosts?"

Minora turned pale.

"What nonsense," said I; "we have no ghosts here. Good-night. If you want anything, mind you ring."

"And if you see anything curious in that room," called Irais from her bedroom door, "mind you jot it down."

December 27th—It is the fashion, I believe, to regard Christmas as a bore of rather a gross description, and as a time when you are invited to over-eat yourself, and pretend to be merry without just cause. As a matter of fact, it is one of the prettiest and most poetic institutions possible, if observed in the proper manner, and after having been more or less unpleasant to everybody for a whole year, it is a blessing to be forced on that one day to be amiable, and it is certainly delightful to be able to give presents without being haunted by the conviction that you are spoiling the recipient, and will suffer for it afterward. Servants are only big children, and are made just as happy as children by little presents and nice things to eat, and, for days beforehand, every time the three babies go into the garden they expect to meet the Christ Child with His arms full of gifts. They firmly believe that it is thus their presents are brought, and it is such a charming idea that Christmas would be worth celebrating for its sake alone.

As great secrecy is observed, the preparations devolve entirely on me, and it is not very easy work, with so many people in our own house and on each of the farms, and all the children, big and little, expecting their share of happiness. The library is uninhabitable for several days before and after, as it is there that we have the trees and presents. All down one side are the trees, and the other three sides are lined with tables, a separate one for each person in the house. When the trees are lighted, and stand in their radiance shining down on the happy faces, I forget all the trouble it has been, and the number of times I have had to run up and down stairs, and the various aches in head and feet, and enjoy myself as much as anybody. First the June baby is ushered in, then the others and ourselves according to age, then the servants, then come the head inspector and his family, the other inspectors from the different farms, the mamsells, the bookkeepers and secretaries, and then all the children, troops and troops of them—the big ones leading the little ones by the hand and carrying the babies in their arms, and the mothers peeping round the door. As many as can get in stand in front of the trees, and sing two or three carols; then they are given their presents, and go off triumphantly, making room for the next batch. My three babies sang lustily too, whether they happened to know what was being sung or not. They had on white dresses in honour of the occasion, and the June baby was even arrayed in a low-necked and short-sleeved garment, after the manner of Teutonic infants, whatever the state of the thermometer. Her arms are like miniature prize-fighter's arms—I never saw such things; they are the pride and joy of her little nurse, who had tied them up with blue ribbons, and kept on kissing them. I shall certainly not be able to take her to balls when she grows up, if she goes on having arms like that.

When they came to say good-night, they were all very pale and subdued. The April baby had an exhausted-looking Japanese doll with her, which she said she was taking to bed, not because she liked him, but because she was so sorry for him, he seemed so very tired. They kissed me absently, and went away, only the April baby glancing at the trees as she passed and making them a curtesy.

"Good-bye, trees," I heard her say; and then she made the Japanese doll bow to them, which he did, in a very languid and blase fashion. "You'll never see such trees again," she told him, giving him a vindictive shake, "for you'll be brokened long before next time."

She went out, but came back as though she had forgotten something. "Thank the Christkind so much, Mummy, won't you, for all the lovely things He brought us. I suppose you're writing to Him now, isn't you?"

I cannot see that there was anything gross about our Christmas, and we were perfectly merry without any need to pretend, and for at least two days it brought us a little nearer together, and made us kind. Happiness is so wholesome; it invigorates and warms me into piety far more effectually than any amount of trials and griefs, and an unexpected pleasure is the surest means of bringing me to my knees. In spite of the protestations of some peculiarly constructed persons that they are the better for trials, I don't believe it. Such things must sour us, just as happiness must sweeten us, and make us kinder, and more gentle. And will anybody affirm that it behoves us to be more thankful for trials than for blessings? We were meant to be happy, and to accept all the happiness offered with thankfulness—indeed, we are none of us ever thankful enough, and yet we each get so much, so very much, more than we deserve. I know a woman— she stayed with me last summer—who rejoices grimly when those she loves suffer. She believes that it is our lot, and that it braces us and does us good, and she would shield no one from even unnecessary pain; she weeps with the sufferer, but is convinced it is all for the best. Well, let her continue in her dreary beliefs; she has no garden to teach her the beauty and the happiness of holiness, nor does she in the least desire to possess one; her convictions have the sad gray colouring of the dingy streets and houses she lives amongst—the sad colour of humanity in masses. Submission to what people call their "lot" is simply ignoble. If your lot makes you cry and be wretched, get rid of it and take another; strike out for yourself; don't listen to the shrieks of your relations, to their gibes or their entreaties; don't let your own microscopic set prescribe your goings-out and comings-in; don't be afraid of public opinion in the shape of the neighbour in the next house, when all the world is before you new and shining, and everything is possible, if you will only be energetic and independent and seize opportunity by the scruff of the neck.

"To hear you talk," said Irais, "no one would ever imagine that you dream away your days in a garden with a book, and that you never in your life seized anything by the scruff of its neck. And what is scruff? I hope I have not got any on me." And she craned her neck before the glass.

She and Minora were going to help me decorate the trees, but very soon Irais wandered off to the piano, and Minora was tired and took up a book; so I called in Miss Jones and the babies—it was Miss Jones's last public appearance, as I shall relate—and after working for the best part of two days they were finished, and looked like lovely ladies in widespreading, sparkling petticoats, holding up their skirts with glittering fingers. Minora wrote a long description of them for a chapter of her book which is headed Noel,—I saw that much, because she left it open on the table while she went to talk to Miss Jones. They were fast friends from the very first, and though it is said to be natural to take to one's own countrymen, I am unable altogether to sympathise with such a reason for sudden affection.

"I wonder what they talk about?" I said to Irais yesterday, when there was no getting Minora to come to tea, so deeply was she engaged in conversation with Miss Jones.

"Oh, my dear, how can I tell? Lovers, I suppose, or else they think they are clever, and then they talk rubbish."

"Well, of course, Minora thinks she is clever."

"I suppose she does. What does it matter what she thinks? Why does your governess look so gloomy? When I see her at luncheon I always imagine she must have just heard that somebody is dead. But she can't hear that every day. What is the matter with her?"

"I don't think she feels quite as proper as she looks," I said doubtfully; I was for ever trying to account for Miss Jones's expression.

"But that must be rather nice," said Irais. "It would be awful for her if she felt exactly the same as she looks."

At that moment the door leading into the schoolroom opened softly, and the April baby, tired of playing, came in and sat down at my feet, leaving the door open; and this is what we heard Miss Jones saying—

"Parents are seldom wise, and the strain the conscientious place upon themselves to appear so before their children and governess must be terrible. Nor are clergymen more pious than other men, yet they have continually to pose before their flock as such. As for governesses, Miss Minora, I know what I am saying when I affirm that there is nothing more intolerable than to have to be polite, and even humble, to persons whose weaknesses and follies are glaringly apparent in every word they utter, and to be forced by the presence of children and employers to a dignity of manner in no way corresponding to one's feelings. The grave father of a family, who was probably one of the least respectable of bachelors, is an interesting study at his own table, where he is constrained to assume airs of infallibility merely because his children are looking at him. The fact of his being a parent does not endow him with any supreme and sudden virtue; and I can assure you that among the eyes fixed upon him, not the least critical and amused are those of the humble person who fills the post of governess."

"Oh, Miss Jones, how lovely!" we heard Minora say in accents of rapture, while we sat transfixed with horror at these sentiments. "Do you mind if I put that down in my book? You say it all so beautifully."

"Without a few hours of relaxation," continued Miss Jones, "of private indemnification for the toilsome virtues displayed in public, who could wade through days of correct behaviour? There would be no reaction, no room for better impulses, no place for repentance. Parents, priests, and governesses would be in the situation of a stout lady who never has a quiet moment in which she can take off her corsets."

"My dear, what a firebrand!" whispered Irais. I got up and went in. They were sitting on the sofa, Minora with clasped hands, gazing admiringly into Miss Jones's face, which wore a very different expression from the one of sour and unwilling propriety I have been used to seeing.

"May I ask you to come to tea?" I said to Minora. "And I should like to have the children a little while."

She got up very reluctantly, but I waited with the door open until she had gone in and the two babies had followed. They had been playing at stuffing each other's ears with pieces of newspaper while Miss Jones provided Minora with noble thoughts for her work, and had to be tortured afterward with tweezers. I said nothing to Minora, but kept her with us till dinner-time, and this morning we went for a long sleigh-drive. When we came in to lunch there was no Miss Jones.

"Is Miss Jones ill?" asked Minora.

"She is gone," I said.

"Gone?"

"Did you never hear of such things as sick mothers?" asked Irais blandly; and we talked resolutely of something else.

All the afternoon Minora has moped. She had found a kindred spirit, and it has been ruthlessly torn from her arms as kindred spirits so often are. It is enough to make her mope, and it is not her fault, poor thing, that she should have preferred the society of a Miss Jones to that of Irais and myself.

At dinner Irais surveyed her with her head on one side. "You look so pale," she said; "are you not well?"

Minora raised her eyes heavily, with the patient air of one who likes to be thought a sufferer. "I have a slight headache," she replied gently.

"I hope you are not going to be ill," said Irais with great concern, "because there is only a cow-doctor to be had here, and though he means well, I believe he is rather rough." Minora was plainly startled. "But what do you do if you are ill?" she asked.

"Oh, we are never ill," said I; "the very knowledge that there would be no one to cure us seems to keep us healthy."

"And if any one takes to her bed," said Irais, "Elizabeth always calls in the cow-doctor."

Minora was silent. She feels, I am sure, that she has got into a part of the world peopled solely by barbarians, and that the only civilised creature besides herself has departed and left her at our mercy. Whatever her reflections may be her symptoms are visibly abating.

January 1st.—The service on New Year's Eve is the only one in the whole year that in the least impresses me in our little church, and then the very bareness and ugliness of the place and the ceremonial produce an effect that a snug service in a well-lit church never would. Last night we took Irais and Minora, and drove the three lonely miles in a sleigh. It was pitch-dark, and blowing great guns. We sat wrapped up to our eyes in furs, and as mute as a funeral procession.

"We are going to the burial of our last year's sins," said Irais, as we started; and there certainly was a funereal sort of feeling in the air. Up in our gallery pew we tried to decipher our chorales by the light of the spluttering tallow candles stuck in holes in the woodwork, the flames wildly blown about by the draughts. The wind banged against the windows in great gusts, screaming louder than the organ, and threatening to blow out the agitated lights together. The parson in his gloomy pulpit, surrounded by a framework of dusty carved angels, took on an awful appearance of menacing Authority as he raised his voice to make himself heard above the clatter. Sitting there in the dark, I felt very small, and solitary, and defenceless, alone in a great, big, black world. The church was as cold as a tomb; some of the candles guttered and went out; the parson in his black robe spoke of death and judgment; I thought I heard a child's voice screaming, and could hardly believe it was only the wind, and felt uneasy and full of forebodings; all my faith and philosophy deserted me, and I had a horrid feeling that I should probably be well punished, though for what I had no precise idea. If it had not been so dark, and if the wind had not howled so despairingly, I should have paid little attention to the threats issuing from the pulpit; but, as it was, I fell to making good resolutions. This is always a bad sign,—only those who break them make them; and if you simply do as a matter of course that which is right as it comes, any preparatory resolving to do so becomes completely superfluous. I have for some years past left off making them on New Year's Eve, and only the gale happening as it did reduced me to doing so last night; for I have long since discovered that, though the year and the resolutions may be new, I myself am not, and it is worse than useless putting new wine into old bottles.

"But I am not an old bottle," said Irais indignantly, when I held forth to her to the above effect a few hours later in the library, restored to all my philosophy by the warmth and light, "and I find my resolutions carry me very nicely into the spring. I revise them at the end of each month, and strike out the unnecessary ones. By the end of April they have been so severely revised that there are none left."

"There, you see I am right; if you were not an old bottle your new contents would gradually arrange themselves amiably as a part of you, and the practice of your resolutions would lose its bitterness by becoming a habit."

She shook her head. "Such things never lose their bitterness," she said, "and that is why I don't let them cling to me right into the summer. When May comes, I give myself up to jollity with all the rest of the world, and am too busy being happy to bother about anything I may have resolved when the days were cold and dark."

"And that is just why I love you," I thought. She often says what I feel.

"I wonder," she went on after a pause, "whether men ever make resolutions?"

"I don't think they do. Only women indulge in such luxuries. It is a nice sort of feeling, when you have nothing else to do, giving way to endless grief and penitence, and steeping yourself to the eyes in contrition; but it is silly. Why cry over things that are done? Why do naughty things at all, if you are going to repent afterward? Nobody is naughty unless they like being naughty; and nobody ever really repents unless they are afraid they are going to be found out."

"By 'nobody' of course you mean women, said Irais.

"Naturally; the terms are synonymous. Besides, men generally have the courage of their opinions."

"I hope you are listening, Miss Minora," said Irais in the amiably polite tone she assumes whenever she speaks to that young person.

It was getting on towards midnight, and we were sitting round the fire, waiting for the New Year, and sipping Glubwein, prepared at a small table by the Man of Wrath. It was hot, and sweet, and rather nasty, but it is proper to drink it on this one night, so of course we did.

Minora does not like either Irais or myself. We very soon discovered that, and laugh about it when we are alone together. I can understand her disliking Irais, but she must be a perverse creature not to like me. Irais has poked fun at her, and I have been, I hope, very kind; yet we are bracketed together in her black books. It is also apparent that she looks upon the Man of Wrath as an interesting example of an ill-used and misunderstood husband, and she is disposed to take him under her wing, and defend him on all occasions against us. He never speaks to her; he is at all times a man of few words, but, as far as Minora is concerned, he might have no tongue at all, and sits sphinx-like and impenetrable while she takes us to task about some remark of a profane nature that we may have addressed to him. One night, some days after her arrival, she developed a skittishness of manner which has since disappeared, and tried to be playful with him; but you might as well try to be playful with a graven image. The wife of one of the servants had just produced a boy, the first after a series of five daughters, and at dinner we drank the health of all parties concerned, the Man of Wrath making the happy father drink a glass off at one gulp, his heels well together in military fashion. Minora thought the incident typical of German manners, and not only made notes about it, but joined heartily in the health-drinking, and afterward grew skittish.

She proposed, first of all, to teach us a dance called, I think, the Washington Post, and which was, she said, much danced in England; and, to induce us to learn, she played the tune to us on the piano. We remained untouched by its beauties, each buried in an easy-chair toasting our toes at the fire. Amongst those toes were those of the Man of Wrath, who sat peaceably reading a book and smoking. Minora volunteered to show us the steps, and as we still did not move, danced solitary behind our chairs. Irais did not even turn her head to look, and I was the only one amiable or polite enough to do so. Do I deserve to be placed in Minora's list of disagreeable people side by side with Irais? Certainly not. Yet I most surely am.

"It wants the music, of course," observed Minora breathlessly, darting in and out between the chairs, apparently addressing me, but glancing at the Man of Wrath.

No answer from anybody.

"It is such a pretty dance," she panted again, after a few more gyrations.

No answer.

"And is all the rage at home."

No answer.

"Do let me teach you. Won't you try, Herr Sage?"

She went up to him and dropped him a little curtesy. It is thus she always addresses him, entirely oblivious to the fact, so patent to every one else, that he resents it.

"Oh come, put away that tiresome old book," she went on gaily, as he did not move; "I am certain it is only some dry agricultural work that you just nod over. Dancing is much better for you." Irais and I looked at one another quite frightened. I am sure we both turned pale when the unhappy girl actually laid hold forcibly of his book, and, with a playful little shriek, ran away with it into the next room, hugging it to her bosom and looking back roguishly over her shoulder at him as she ran. There was an awful pause. We hardly dared raise our eyes. Then the Mall of Wrath got up slowly, knocked the ashes off the end of his cigar, looked at his watch, and went out at the opposite door into his own rooms, where he stayed for the rest of the evening. She has never, I must say, been skittish since.

"I hope you are listening, Miss Minora," said Irais, "because this sort of conversation is likely to do you good."

"I always listen when people talk sensibly," replied Minora, stirring her grog.

Irais glanced at her with slightly doubtful eyebrows. "Do you agree with our hostess's description of women?" she asked after a pause.

"As nobodies? No, of course I do not."

"Yet she is right. In the eye of the law we are literally nobodies in our country. Did you know that women are forbidden to go to political meetings here?" "Really?" Out came the note-book.

"The law expressly forbids the attendance at such meetings of women, children, and idiots."

"Children and idiots—I understand that," said Minora; "but women—and classed with children and idiots?"

"Classed with children and idiots," repeated Irais, gravely nodding her head. "Did you know that the law forbids females of any age to ride on the top of omnibuses or tramcars?"

"Not really?"

"Do you know why?"

"I can't imagine."

"Because in going up and down the stairs those inside might perhaps catch a glimpse of the stocking covering their ankles."

"But what—"

"Did you know that the morals of the German public are in such a shaky condition that a glimpse of that sort would be fatal to them?"

"But I don't see how a stocking—"

"With stripes round it," said Irais.

"And darns in it," I added, "—could possibly be pernicious?"

"'The Pernicious Stocking; or, Thoughts on the Ethics of Petticoats,'" said Irais. "Put that down as the name of your next book on Germany."

"I never know," complained Minora, letting her note-book fall, "whether you are in earnest or not."

"Don't you?" said Irais sweetly.

"Is it true," appealed Minora to the Man of Wrath, busy with his lemons in the background, "that your law classes women with children and idiots?"

"Certainly," he answered promptly, "and a very proper classification, too." We all looked blank. "That's rude," said I at last.

"Truth is always rude, my dear," he replied complacently. Then he added,

"If I were commissioned to draw up a new legal code, and had previously enjoyed the privilege, as I have been doing lately, of listening to the conversation of you three young ladies, I should make precisely the same classification."

Even Minora was incensed at this.

"You are telling us in the most unvarnished manner that we are idiots," said Irais.

"Idiots? No, no, by no means. But children,—nice little agreeable children. I very much like to hear you talk together. It is all so young and fresh what you think and what you believe, and not of the least consequence to any one.

"Not of the least consequence?" cried Minora. "What we believe is of very great consequence indeed to us."

"Are you jeering at our beliefs?" inquired Irais sternly.

"Not for worlds. I would not on any account disturb or change your pretty little beliefs. It is your chief charm that you always believe every-thing. How desperate would our case be if young ladies only believed facts, and never accepted another person's assurance, but preferred the evidence of their own eyes! They would have no illusions, and a woman without illusions is the dreariest and most difficult thing to manage possible."

"Thing?" protested Irais.

The Man of Wrath, usually so silent, makes up for it from time to time by holding forth at unnecessary length. He took up his stand now with his back to the fire, and a glass of Glubwein in his hand. Minora had hardly heard his voice before, so quiet had he been since she came, and sat with her pencil raised, ready to fix for ever the wisdom that should flow from his lips.

"What would become of poetry if women became so sensible that they turned a deaf ear to the poetic platitudes of love? That love does indulge in platitudes I suppose you will admit." He looked at Irais.

"Yes, they all say exactly the same thing," she acknowledged.

"Who could murmur pretty speeches on the beauty of a common sacrifice, if the listener's want of imagination was such as to enable her only to distinguish one victim in the picture, and that one herself?"

Minora took that down word for word,—much good may it do her.

"Who would be brave enough to affirm that if refused he will die, if his assurances merely elicit a recommendation to diet himself, and take plenty of outdoor exercise? Women are responsible for such lies, because they believe them. Their amazing vanity makes them swallow flattery so gross that it is an insult, and men will always be ready to tell the precise number of lies that a woman is ready to listen to. Who indulges more recklessly in glowing exaggerations than the lover who hopes, and has not yet obtained? He will, like the nightingale, sing with unceasing modulations, display all his talent, untiringly repeat his sweetest notes, until he has what he wants, when his song, like the nightingale's, immediately ceases, never again to be heard."

"Take that down," murmured Irais aside to Minora—unnecessary advice, for her pencil was scribbling as fast as it could.

"A woman's vanity is so immeasurable that, after having had ninety-nine object-lessons in the difference between promise and performance and the emptiness of pretty speeches, the beginning of the hundredth will find her lending the same willing and enchanted ear to the eloquence of flattery as she did on the occasion of the first. What can the exhortations of the strong-minded sister, who has never had these experiences, do for such a woman? It is useless to tell her she is man's victim, that she is his plaything, that she is cheated, down-trodden, kept under, laughed at, shabbily treated in every way—that is not a true statement of the case. She is simply the victim of her own vanity, and against that, against the belief in her own fascinations, against the very part of herself that gives all the colour to her life, who shall expect a woman to take up arms?"

"Are you so vain, Elizabeth?" inquired Irais with a shocked face, "and had you lent a willing ear to the blandishments of ninety-nine before you reached your final destiny?"

"I am one of the sensible ones, I suppose," I replied, "for nobody ever wanted me to listen to blandishments."

Minora sighed.

"I like to hear you talk together about the position of women," he went on, "and wonder when you will realise that they hold exactly the position they are fitted for. As soon as they are fit to occupy a better, no power on earth will be able to keep them out of it. Meanwhile, let me warn you that, as things now are, only strong-minded women wish to see you the equals of men, and the strong-minded are invariably plain. The pretty ones would rather see men their slaves than their equals."

"You know," said Irais, frowning, "that I consider myself strong-minded."

"And never rise till lunch-time?"

Irais blushed. Although I don't approve of such conduct, it is very convenient in more ways than one; I get through my housekeeping undisturbed, and whenever she is disposed to lecture me, I begin about this habit of hers. Her conscience must be terribly stricken on the point, for she is by no means as a rule given to meekness.

"A woman without vanity would be unattackable," resumed the Man of Wrath. "When a girl enters that downward path that leads to ruin, she is led solely by her own vanity; for in these days of policemen no young woman can be forced against her will from the path of virtue, and the cries of the injured are never heard until the destroyer begins to express his penitence for having destroyed. If his passion could remain at white-heat and he could continue to feed her ear with the protestations she loves, no principles of piety or virtue would disturb the happiness of his companion; for a mournful experience teaches that piety begins only where passion ends, and that principles are strongest where temptations are most rare."

"But what has all this to do with us?" I inquired severely.

"You were displeased at our law classing you as it does, and I merely wish to justify it," he answered. "Creatures who habitually say yes to everything a man proposes, when no one can oblige them to say it, and when it is so often fatal, are plainly not responsible beings."

"I shall never say it to you again, my dear man," I said.

"And not only that fatal weakness," he continued, "but what is there, candidly, to distinguish you from children? You are older, but not wiser,— really not so wise, for with years you lose the common sense you had as children. Have you ever heard a group of women talking reasonably together?"

"Yes—we do!" Irais and I cried in a breath.

"It has interested me," went on the Man of Wrath, "in my idle moments, to listen to their talk. It amused me to hear the malicious little stories they told of their best friends who were absent, to note the spiteful little digs they gave their best friends who were present, to watch the utter incredulity with which they listened to the tale of some other woman's conquests, the radiant good faith they displayed in connection with their own, the instant collapse into boredom, if some topic of so-called general interest, by some extraordinary chance, were introduced." "You must have belonged to a particularly nice set," remarked Irais.

"And as for politics," he said, "I have never heard them mentioned among women."

"Children and idiots are not interested in such things," I said.

"And we are much too frightened of being put in prison," said Irais.

"In prison?" echoed Minora.

"Don't you know," said Irais, turning to her "that if you talk about such things here you run a great risk of being imprisoned?"

"But why?"

"But why? Because, though you yourself may have meant nothing but what was innocent, your words may have suggested something less innocent to the evil minds of your hearers; and then the law steps in, and calls it dolus eventualis, and everybody says how dreadful, and off you go to prison and are punished as you deserve to be."

Minora looked mystified.

"That is not, however, your real reason for not discussing them," said the Man of Wrath; "they simply do not interest you. Or it may be, that you do not consider your female friends' opinions worth listening to, for you certainly display an astonishing thirst for information when male politicians are present. I have seen a pretty young woman, hardly in her twenties, sitting a whole evening drinking in the doubtful wisdom of an elderly political star, with every appearance of eager interest. He was a bimetallic star, and was giving her whole pamphletsful of information."

"She wanted to make up to him for some reason," said Irais, "and got him to explain his hobby to her, and he was silly enough to be taken in. Now which was the sillier in that case?"

She threw herself back in her chair and looked up defiantly, beating her foot impatiently on the carpet.

"She wanted to be thought clever," said the Man of Wrath. "What puzzled me," he went on musingly, "was that she went away apparently as serene and happy as when she came. The explanation of the principles of bimetallism produce, as a rule, a contrary effect."

"Why, she hadn't been listening," cried Irais, "and your simple star had been making a fine goose of himself the whole evening.

      "Prattle, prattle, simple star,
       Bimetallic, wunderbar.
      Though you're given to describe
      Woman as a dummes Weib.
      You yourself are sillier far,
      Prattling, bimetallic star!"

"No doubt she had understood very little," said the Man of Wrath, taking no notice of this effusion.

"And no doubt the gentleman hadn't understood much either." Irais was plainly irritated.

"Your opinion of woman," said Minora in a very small voice, "is not a high one. But, in the sick chamber, I suppose you agree that no one could take her place?"

"If you are thinking of hospital-nurses," I said, "I must tell you that I believe he married chiefly that he might have a wife instead of a strange woman to nurse him when he is sick."

"But," said Minora, bewildered at the way her illusions were being knocked about, "the sick-room is surely the very place of all others in which a woman's gentleness and tact are most valuable."

"Gentleness and tact?" repeated the Man of Wrath. "I have never met those qualities in the professional nurse. According to my experience, she is a disagreeable person who finds in private nursing exquisite opportunities for asserting her superiority over ordinary and prostrate mankind. I know of no more humiliating position for a man than to be in bed having his feverish brow soothed by a sprucely-dressed strange woman, bristling with starch and spotlessness. He would give half his income for his clothes, and probably the other half if she would leave him alone, and go away altogether. He feels her superiority through every pore; he never before realised how absolutely inferior he is; he is abjectly polite, and contemptibly conciliatory; if a friend comes to see him, he eagerly praises her in case she should be listening behind the screen; he cannot call his soul his own, and, what is far more intolerable, neither is he sure that his body really belongs to him; he has read of ministering angels and the light touch of a woman's hand, but the day on which he can ring for his servant and put on his socks in private fills him with the same sort of wildness of joy that he felt as a homesick schoolboy at the end of his first term." Minora was silent. Irais's foot was livelier than ever. The Man of Wrath stood smiling blandly down upon us. You can't argue with a person so utterly convinced of his infallibility that he won't even get angry with you; so we sat round and said nothing.

"If," he went on, addressing Irais, who looked rebellious, "you doubt the truth of my remarks, and still cling to the old poetic notion of noble, self-sacrificing women tenderly helping the patient over the rough places on the road to death or recovery, let me beg you to try for yourself, next time any one in your house is ill, whether the actual fact in any way corresponds to the picturesque belief. The angel who is to alleviate our sufferings comes in such a questionable shape, that to the unimaginative she appears merely as an extremely self-confident young woman, wisely concerned first of all in securing her personal comfort, much given to complaints about her food and to helplessness where she should be helpful, possessing an extraordinary capacity for fancying herself slighted, or not regarded as the superior being she knows herself to be, morbidly anxious lest the servants should, by some mistake, treat her with offensive cordiality, pettish if the patient gives more trouble than she had expected, intensely injured and disagreeable if he is made so courageous by his wretchedness as to wake her during the night—an act of desperation of which I was guilty once, and once only. Oh, these good women! What sane man wants to have to do with angels? And especially do we object to having them about us when we are sick and sorry, when we feel in every fibre what poor things we are, and when all our fortitude is needed to enable us to bear our temporary inferiority patiently, without being forced besides to assume an attitude of eager and grovelling politeness towards the angel in the house." There was a pause.

"I didn't know you could talk so much, Sage," said Irais at length.

"What would you have women do, then?" asked Minora meekly. Irais began to beat her foot up and down again,—what did it matter what Men of Wrath would have us do? "There are not," continued Minora, blushing, "husbands enough for every one, and the rest must do something."

"Certainly," replied the oracle. "Study the art of pleasing by dress and manner as long as you are of an age to interest us, and above all, let all women, pretty and plain, married and single, study the art of cookery. If you are an artist in the kitchen you will always be esteemed."

I sat very still. Every German woman, even the wayward Irais, has learned to cook; I seem to have been the only one who was naughty and wouldn't. "Only be careful," he went on, "in studying both arts, never to forget the great truth that dinner precedes blandishments and not blandishments dinner. A man must be made comfortable before he will make love to you; and though it is true that if you offered him a choice between Spickgans and kisses, he would say he would take both, yet he would invariably begin with the Spickgans, and allow the kisses to wait."

At this I got up, and Irais followed my example. "Your cynicism is disgusting," I said icily.

"You two are always exceptions to anything I may say," he said, smiling amiably.

He stooped and kissed Irais's hand. She is inordinately vain of her hands, and says her husband married her for their sake, which I can quite believe. I am glad they are on her and not on Minora, for if Minora had had them I should have been annoyed. Minora's are bony, with chilly-looking knuckles, ignored nails, and too much wrist. I feel very well disposed towards her when my eye falls on them. She put one forward now, evidently thinking it would be kissed too.

"Did you know," said Irais, seeing the movement, "that it is the custom here to kiss women's hands?"

"But only married women's," I added, not desiring her to feel out of it, "never young girls'."

She drew it in again. "It is a pretty custom," she said with a sigh; and pensively inscribed it in her book.

January 15th.—The bills for my roses and bulbs and other last year's horticultural indulgences were all on the table when I came down to breakfast this morning. They rather frightened me. Gardening is expensive, I find, when it has to be paid for out of one's own private pin-money. The Man of Wrath does not in the least want roses, or flowering shrubs, or plantations, or new paths, and therefore, he asks, why should he pay for them? So he does not and I do, and I have to make up for it by not indulging all too riotously in new clothes, which is no doubt very chastening. I certainly prefer buying new rose-trees to new dresses, if I cannot comfortably have both; and I see a time coming when the passion for my garden will have taken such a hold on me that I shall not only entirely cease buying more clothes, but begin to sell those that I already have. The garden is so big that everything has to be bought wholesale; and I fear I shall not be able to go on much longer with only one man and a stork, because the more I plant the more there will be to water in the inevitable drought, and the watering is a serious consideration when it means going backwards and forwards all day long to a pump near the house, with a little water-cart. People living in England, in almost perpetual mildness and moisture, don't really know what a drought is. If they have some weeks of cloudless weather, it is generally preceded and followed by good rains; but we have perhaps an hour's shower every week, and then comes a month or six weeks' drought. The soil is very light, and dries so quickly that, after the heaviest thunder-shower, I can walk over any of my paths in my thin shoes; and to keep the garden even moderately damp it should pour with rain regularly every day for three hours. My only means of getting water is to go to the pump near the house, or to the little stream that forms my eastern boundary, and the little stream dries up too unless there has been rain, and is at the best of times difficult to get at, having steep banks covered with forget-me-nots. I possess one moist, peaty bit of ground, and that is to be planted with silver birches in imitation of the Hirschwald, and is to be carpeted between the birches with flaming azaleas. All the rest of my soil is sandy—the soil for pines and acacias, but not the soil for roses; yet see what love will do—there are more roses in my garden than any other flower! Next spring the bare places are to be filled with trees that I have ordered: pines behind the delicate acacias, and startling mountain-ashes, oaks, copper-beeches, maples, larches, juniper-trees—was it not Elijah who sat down to rest under a juniper-tree? I have often wondered how he managed to get under it. It is a compact little tree, not more than two to three yards high here, and all closely squeezed up together. Perhaps they grew more aggressively where he was. By the time the babies have grown old and disagreeable it will be very pretty here, and then possibly they won't like it; and, if they have inherited the Man of Wrath's indifference to gardens, they will let it run wild and leave it to return to the state in which I found it. Or perhaps their three husbands will refuse to live in it, or to come to such a lonely place at all, and then of course its fate is sealed. My only comfort is that husbands don't flourish in the desert, and that the three will have to wait a long time before enough are found to go round. Mothers tell me that it is a dreadful business finding one husband; how much more painful then to have to look for three at once!—the babies are so nearly the same age that they only just escaped being twins. But I won't look. I can imagine nothing more uncomfortable than a son-in-law, and besides, I don't think a husband is at all a good thing for a girl to have. I shall do my best in the years at my disposal to train them so to love the garden, and out-door life, and even farming, that, if they have a spark of their mother in them, they will want and ask for nothing better. My hope of success is however exceedingly small, and there is probably a fearful period in store for me when I shall be taken every day during the winter to the distant towns to balls—a poor old mother shivering in broad daylight in her party gown, and being made to start after an early lunch and not getting home till breakfast-time next morning. Indeed, they have already developed an alarming desire to go to "partings" as they call them, the April baby announcing her intention of beginning to do so when she is twelve. "Are you twelve, Mummy?" she asked.

The gardener is leaving on the first of April, and I am trying to find another. It is grievous changing so often—in two years I shall have had three—because at each change a great part of my plants and plans necessarily suffers. Seeds get lost, seedlings are not pricked out in time, places already sown are planted with something else, and there is confusion out of doors and despair in my heart. But he was to have married the cook, and the cook saw a ghost and immediately left, and he is going after her as soon as he can, and meanwhile is wasting visibly away. What she saw was doors that are locked opening with a great clatter all by themselves on the hingeside, and then somebody invisible cursed at her. These phenomena now go by the name of "the ghost." She asked to be allowed to leave at once, as she had never been in a place where there was a ghost before. I suggested that she should try and get used to it; but she thought it would be wasting time, and she looked so ill that I let her go, and the garden has to suffer. I don't know why it should be given to cooks to see such interesting things and withheld from me, but I have had two others since she left, and they both have seen the ghost. Minora grows very silent as bed-time approaches, and relents towards Irais and myself; and, after having shown us all day how little she approves us, when the bedroom candles are brought she quite begins to cling. She has once or twice anxiously inquired whether Irais is sure she does not object to sleeping alone.

"If you are at all nervous, I will come and keep you company," she said; "I don't mind at all, I assure you."

But Irais is not to be taken in by such simple wiles, and has told me she would rather sleep with fifty ghosts than with one Minora.

Since Miss Jones was so unexpectedly called away to her parent's bedside I have seen a good deal of the babies; and it is so nice without a governess that I would put off engaging another for a year or two, if it were not that I should in so doing come within the reach of the arm of the law, which is what every German spends his life in trying to avoid. The April baby will be six next month, and, after her sixth birthday is passed, we are liable at any moment to receive a visit from a school inspector, who will inquire curiously into the state of her education, and, if it is not up to the required standard, all sorts of fearful things might happen to the guilty parents, probably beginning with fines, and going on crescendo to dungeons if, owing to gaps between governesses and difficulties in finding the right one, we persisted in our evil courses. Shades of the prison-house begin to close here upon the growing boy, and prisons compass the Teuton about on every side all through life to such an extent that he has to walk very delicately indeed if he would stay outside them and pay for their maintenance. Cultured individuals do not, as a rule, neglect to teach their offspring to read, and write, and say their prayers, and are apt to resent the intrusion of an examining inspector into their homes; but it does not much matter after all, and I daresay it is very good for us to be worried; indeed, a philosopher of my acquaintance declares that people who are not regularly and properly worried are never any good for anything. In the eye of the law we are all sinners, and every man is held to be guilty until he has proved that he is innocent.

Minora has seen so much of the babies that, after vainly trying to get out of their way for several days, she thought it better to resign herself, and make the best of it by regarding them as copy, and using them to fill a chapter in her book. So she took to dogging their footsteps wherever they went, attended their uprisings and their lyings down, engaged them, if she could, in intelligent conversation, went with them into the garden to study their ways when they were sleighing, drawn by a big dog, and generally made their lives a burden to them. This went on for three days, and then she settled down to write the result with the Man of Wrath's typewriter, borrowed whenever her notes for any chapter have reached the state of ripeness necessary for the process she describes as "throwing into form." She writes everything with a typewriter, even her private letters.

"Don't forget to put in something about a mother's knee," said Irais; "you can't write effectively about children without that." "Oh, of course I shall mention that," replied Minora.

"And pink toes," I added. "There are always toes, and they are never anything but pink."

"I have that somewhere," said Minora, turning over her notes.

"But, after all, babies are not a German speciality," said Irais, "and I don't quite see why you should bring them into a book of German travels. Elizabeth's babies have each got the fashionable number of arms and legs, and are exactly the same as English ones."

"Oh, but they can't be just the same, you know," said Minora, looking worried. "It must make a difference living here in this place, and eating such odd things, and never having a doctor, and never being ill. Children who have never had measles and those things can't be quite the same as other children; it must all be in their systems and can't get out for some reason or other. And a child brought up on chicken and rice-pudding must be different to a child that eats Spickgans and liver sausages. And they are different; I can't tell in what way, but they certainly are; and I think if I steadily describe them from the materials I have collected the last three days, I may perhaps hit on the points of difference."

"Why bother about points of difference?" asked Irais. "I should write some little thing, bringing in the usual parts of the picture, such as knees and toes, and make it mildly pathetic."

"But it is by no means an easy thing for me to do," said Minora plaintively; "I have so little experience of children."

"Then why write it at all?" asked that sensible person Elizabeth.

"I have as little experience as you," said Irais, "because I have no children; but if you don't yearn after startling originality, nothing is easier than to write bits about them. I believe I could do a dozen in an hour."

She sat down at the writing-table, took up an old letter, and scribbled for about five minutes. "There," she said, throwing it to Minora, "you may have it—pink toes and all complete."

Minora put on her eye-glasses and read aloud:

"When my baby shuts her eyes and sings her hymns at bed-time my stale and battered soul is filled with awe. All sorts of vague memories crowd into my mind—memories of my own mother and myself—how many years ago!—of the sweet helplessness of being gathered up half asleep in her arms, and undressed, and put in my cot, without being wakened; of the angels I believed in; of little children coming straight from heaven, and still being surrounded, so long as they were good, by the shadow of white wings,—all the dear poetic nonsense learned, just as my baby is learning it, at her mother's knee. She has not an idea of the beauty of the charming things she is told, and stares wide-eyed, with heavenly eyes, while her mother talks of the heaven she has so lately come from, and is relieved and comforted by the interrupting bread and milk. At two years old she does not understand angels, and does understand bread and milk; at five she has vague notions about them, and prefers bread and milk; at ten both bread and milk and angels have been left behind in the nursery, and she has already found out that they are luxuries not necessary to her everyday life. In later years she may be disinclined to accept truths second-hand, insist on thinking for herself, be earnest in her desire to shake off exploded traditions, be untiring in her efforts to live according to a high moral standard and to be strong, and pure, and good—"

"Like tea," explained Irais.

"—yet will she never, with all her virtues, possess one-thousandth part of the charm that clung about her when she sang, with quiet eyelids, her first reluctant hymns, kneeling on her mother's knees. I love to come in at bed-time and sit in the window in the setting sunshine watching the mysteries of her going to bed. Her mother tubs her, for she is far too precious to be touched by any nurse, and then she is rolled up in a big bath towel, and only her little pink toes peep out; and when she is powdered, and combed, and tied up in her night-dress, and all her curls are on end, and her ears glowing, she is knelt down on her mother's lap, a little bundle of fragrant flesh, and her face reflects the quiet of her mother's face as she goes through her evening prayer for pity and for peace."

"How very curious!" said Minora, when she had finished. "That is exactly what I was going to say."

"Oh, then I have saved you the trouble of putting it together; you can copy that if you like." "But have you a stale soul, Miss Minora?" I asked.

"Well, do you know, I rather think that is a good touch," she replied; "it will make people really think a man wrote the book. You know I am going to take a man's name."

"That is precisely what I imagined," said Irais. "You will call yourself John Jones, or George Potts, or some such sternly commonplace name, to emphasise your uncompromising attitude towards all feminine weaknesses, and no one will be taken in."

"I really think, Elizabeth," said Irais to me later, when the click of Minora's typewriter was heard hesitating in the next room, "that you and I are writing her book for her. She takes down everything we say. Why does she copy all that about the baby? I wonder why mothers' knees are supposed to be touching? I never learned anything at them, did you? But then in my case they were only stepmother's, and nobody ever sings their praises."

"My mother was always at parties," I said; "and the nurse made me say my prayers in French."

"And as for tubs and powder," went on Irais, "when I was a baby such things were not the fashion. There were never any bathrooms, and no tubs; our faces and hands were washed, and there was a foot-bath in the room, and in the summer we had a bath and were put to bed afterwards for fear we might catch cold. My stepmother didn't worry much; she used to wear pink dresses all over lace, and the older she got the prettier the dresses got. When is she going?"

"Who? Minora? I haven't asked her that."

"Then I will. It is really bad for her art to be neglected like this. She has been here an unconscionable time,—it must be nearly three weeks."

"Yes, she came the same day you did," I said pleasantly.

Irais was silent. I hope she was reflecting that it is not worse to neglect one's art than one's husband, and her husband is lying all this time stretched on a bed of sickness, while she is spending her days so agreeably with me. She has a way of forgetting that she has a home, or any other business in the world than just to stay on chatting with me, and reading, and singing, and laughing at any one there is to laugh at, and kissing the babies, and tilting with the Man of Wrath. Naturally I love her—she is so pretty that anybody with eyes in his head must love her—but too much of anything is bad, and next month the passages and offices are to be whitewashed, and people who have ever whitewashed their houses inside know what nice places they are to live in while it is being done; and there will be no dinner for Irais, and none of those succulent salads full of caraway seeds that she so devotedly loves. I shall begin to lead her thoughts gently back to her duties by inquiring every day anxiously after her husband's health. She is not very fond of him, because he does not run and hold the door open for her every time she gets up to leave the room; and though she has asked him to do so, and told him how much she wishes he would, he still won't. She stayed once in a house where there was an Englishman, and his nimbleness in regard to doors and chairs so impressed her that her husband has had no peace since, and each time she has to go out of a room she is reminded of her disregarded wishes, so that a shut door is to her symbolic of the failure of her married life, and the very sight of one makes her wonder why she was born; at least, that is what she told me once, in a burst of confidence. He is quite a nice, harmless little man, pleasant to talk to, good-tempered, and full of fun; but he thinks he is too old to begin to learn new and uncomfortable ways, and he has that horror of being made better by his wife that distinguishes so many righteous men, and is shared by the Man of Wrath, who persists in holding his glass in his left hand at meals, because if he did not (and I don't believe he particularly likes doing it) his relations might say that marriage has improved him, and thus drive the iron into his soul. This habit occasions an almost daily argument between one or other of the babies and myself.

"April, hold your glass in your right hand."

"But papa doesn't."

"When you are as old as papa you can do as you like."

Which was embellished only yesterday by Minora adding impressively, "And only think how strange it would look if everybody held their glasses so."

April was greatly struck by the force of this proposition.

January 28th.—It is very cold,—fifteen degrees of frost Reaumur, but perfectly delicious, still, bright weather, and one feels jolly and energetic and amiably disposed towards everybody. The two young ladies are still here, but the air is so buoyant that even they don't weigh on me any longer, and besides, they have both announced their approaching departure, so that after all I shall get my whitewashing done in peace, and the house will have on its clean pinafore in time to welcome the spring.

Minora has painted my portrait, and is going to present it as a parting gift to the Man of Wrath; and the fact that I let her do it, and sat meekly times innumerable, proves conclusively, I hope, that I am not vain. When Irais first saw it she laughed till she cried, and at once commissioned her to paint hers, so that she may take it away with her and give it to her husband on his birthday, which happens to be early in February. Indeed, if it were not for this birthday, I really think she would have forgotten to go at all; but birthdays are great and solemn festivals with us, never allowed to slip by unnoticed, and always celebrated in the presence of a sympathetic crowd of relations (gathered from far and near to tell you how well you are wearing, and that nobody would ever dream, and that really it is wonderful), who stand round a sort of sacrificial altar, on which your years are offered up as a burnt-offering to the gods in the shape of lighted pink and white candles, stuck in a very large, flat, jammy cake. The cake with its candles is the chief feature, and on the table round it lie the gifts each person present is more or less bound to give. As my birthday falls in the winter I get mittens as well as blotting-books and photograph-frames, and if it were in the summer I should get photograph-frames and blotting-books and no mittens; but whatever the present may be, and by whomsoever given, it has to be welcomed with the noisiest gratitude, and loudest exclamations of joy, and such words as entzuckend, reizend, herrlich, wundervoll, and suss repeated over and over again, until the unfortunate Geburtstagskind feels indeed that another year has gone, and that she has grown older, and wiser, and more tired of folly and of vain repetitions. A flag is hoisted, and all the morning the rites are celebrated, the cake eaten, healths drunk, speeches made, and hands nearly shaken off. The neighbouring parsons drive up, and when nobody is looking their wives count the candles in the cake; the active lady in the next Schlass spares time to send a pot of flowers, and to look up my age in the Gotha Almanach; a deputation comes from the farms headed by the chief inspector in white kid gloves who invokes Heaven's blessings on the gracious lady's head; and the babies are enchanted, and sit in a corner trying on all the mittens. In the evening there is a dinner for the relations and the chief local authorities, with more health-drinking and speechifying, and the next morning, when I come downstairs thankful to have done with it, I am confronted by the altar still in its place, cake crumbs and candle-grease and all, because any hasty removal of it would imply a most lamentable want of sentiment, deplorable in anybody, but scandalous and disgusting in a tender female. All birthdays are observed in this fashion, and not a few wise persons go for a short trip just about the time theirs is due, and I think I shall imitate them next year; only trips to the country or seaside in December are not usually pleasant, and if I go to a town there are sure to be relations in it, and then the cake will spring up mushroom-like from the teeming soil of their affection.

I hope it has been made evident in these pages how superior Irais and myself are to the ordinary weaknesses of mankind; if any further proof were needed, it is furnished by the fact that we both, in defiance of tradition, scorn this celebration of birthday rites. Years ago, when first I knew her, and long before we were either of us married, I sent her a little brass candlestick on her birthday; and when mine followed a few months later, she sent me a note-book. No notes were written in it, and on her next birthday I presented it to her; she thanked me profusely in the customary manner, and when my turn came I received the brass candlestick. Since then we alternately enjoy the possession of each of these articles, and the present question is comfortably settled once and for all, at a minimum of trouble and expense. We never mention this little arrangement except at the proper time, when we send a letter of fervid thanks.

This radiant weather, when mere living is a joy, and sitting still over the fire out of the question, has been going on for more than a week. Sleighing and skating have been our chief occupation, especially skating, which is more than usually fascinating here, because the place is intersected by small canals communicating with a lake and the river belonging to the lake, and as everything is frozen black and hard, we can skate for miles straight ahead without being obliged to turn round and come back again,—at all times an annoying, and even mortifying, proceeding. Irais skates beautifully: modesty is the only obstacle to my saying the same of myself; but I may remark that all Germans skate well, for the simple reason that every year of their lives, for three or four months, they may do it as much as they like. Minora was astonished and disconcerted by finding herself left behind, and arriving at the place where tea meets us half an hour after we had finished. In some places the banks of the canals are so high that only our heads appear level with the fields, and it is, as Minora noted in her book, a curious sight to see three female heads skimming along apparently by themselves, and enjoying it tremendously. When the banks are low, we appear to be gliding deliciously over the roughest ploughed fields, with or without legs according to circumstances. Before we start, I fix on the place where tea and a sleigh are to meet us, and we drive home again; because skating against the wind is as detestable as skating with it is delightful, and an unkind Nature arranges its blowing without the smallest regard for our convenience. Yesterday, by way of a change, we went for a picnic to the shores of the Baltic, ice-bound at this season, and utterly desolate at our nearest point. I have a weakness for picnics, especially in winter, when the mosquitoes cease from troubling and the ant-hills are at rest; and of all my many favourite picnic spots this one on the Baltic is the loveliest and best. As it is a three-hours' drive, the Man of Wrath is loud in his lamentations when the special sort of weather comes which means, as experience has taught him, this particular excursion. There must be deep snow, hard frost, no wind, and a cloudless sky; and when, on waking up, I see these conditions fulfilled, then it would need some very potent reason to keep me from having out a sleigh and going off. It is, I admit, a hard day for the horses; but why have horses if they are not to take you where you want to go to, and at the time you want to go? And why should not horses have hard days as well as everybody else? The Man of Wrath loathes picnics, and has no eye for nature and frozen seas, and is simply bored by a long drive through a forest that does not belong to him; a single turnip on his own place is more admirable in his eyes than the tallest, pinkest, straightest pine that ever reared its snow-crowned head against the setting sunlight. Now observe the superiority of woman, who sees that both are good, and after having gazed at the pine and been made happy by its beauty, goes home and placidly eats the turnip. He went once and only once to this particular place, and made us feel so small by his blast behaviour that I never invite him now. It is a beautiful spot, endless forest stretching along the shore as far as the eye can reach; and after driving through it for miles you come suddenly, at the end of an avenue of arching trees, upon the glistening, oily sea, with the orange-coloured sails of distant fishing-smacks shilling in the sunlight. Whenever I have been there it has been windless weather, and the silence so profound that I could hear my pulses beating. The humming of insects and the sudden scream of a jay are the only sounds in summer, and in winter the stillness is the stillness of death. Every paradise has its serpent, however, and this one is so infested by mosquitoes during the season when picnics seem most natural, that those of my visitors who have been taken there for a treat have invariably lost their tempers, and made the quiet shores ring with their wailing and lamentations. These despicable but irritating insects don't seem to have anything to do but to sit in multitudes on the sand, waiting for any prey Providence may send them; and as soon as the carriage appears they rise up in a cloud, and rush to meet us, almost dragging us out bodily, and never leave us until we drive away again. The sudden view of the sea from the messy, pine-covered height directly above it where we picnic; the wonderful stretch of lonely shore with the forest to the water's edge; the coloured sails in the blue distance; the freshness, the brightness, the vastness—all is lost upon the picnickers, and made worse than indifferent to them, by the perpetual necessity they are under of fighting these horrid creatures. It is nice being the only person who ever goes there or shows it to anybody, but if more people went, perhaps the mosquitoes would be less lean, and hungry, and pleased to see us. It has, however, the advantage of being a suitable place to which to take refractory visitors when they have stayed too long, or left my books out in the garden all night, or otherwise made their presence a burden too grievous to be borne; then one fine hot morning when they are all looking limp, I suddenly propose a picnic on the Baltic. I have never known this proposal fail to be greeted with exclamations of surprise and delight.

"The Baltic! You never told us you were within driving distance? How heavenly to get a breath of sea air on a day like this! The very thought puts new life into one! And how delightful to see the Baltic! Oh, please take us!" And then I take them.

But on a brilliant winter's day my conscience is as clear as the frosty air itself, and yesterday morning we started off in the gayest of spirits, even Minora being disposed to laugh immoderately on the least provocation.

Only our eyes were allowed to peep out from the fur and woollen wrappings necessary to our heads if we would come back with our ears and noses in the same places they were in when we started, and for the first two miles the mirth created by each other's strange appearance was uproarious,—a fact I mention merely to show what an effect dry, bright, intense cold produces on healthy bodies, and how much better it is to go out in it and enjoy it than to stay indoors and sulk. As we passed through the neighbouring village with cracking of whip and jingling of bells, heads popped up at the windows to stare, and the only living thing in the silent, sunny street was a melancholy fowl with ruffled feathers, which looked at us reproachfully, as we dashed with so much energy over the crackling snow.

"Oh, foolish bird!" Irais called out as we passed; "you'll be indeed a cold fowl if you stand there motionless, and every one prefers them hot in weather like this!"

And then we all laughed exceedingly, as though the most splendid joke had been made, and before we had done we were out of the village and in the open country beyond, and could see my house and garden far away behind, glittering in the sunshine; and in front of us lay the forest, with its vistas of pines stretching away into infinity, and a drive through it of fourteen miles before we reached the sea. It was a hoar-frost day, and the forest was an enchanted forest leading into fairyland, and though Irais and I have been there often before, and always thought it beautiful, yet yesterday we stood under the final arch of frosted trees, struck silent by the sheer loveliness of the place. For a long way out the sea was frozen, and then there was a deep blue line, and a cluster of motionless orange sails; at our feet a narrow strip of pale yellow sand; right and left the line of sparkling forest; and we ourselves standing in a world of white and diamond traceries. The stillness of an eternal Sunday lay on the place like a benediction.

Minora broke the silence by remarking that Dresden was pretty, but she thought this beat it almost.

"I don't quite see," said Irais in a hushed voice, as though she were in a holy place, "how the two can be compared."

"Yes, Dresden is more convenient, of course," replied Minora; after which we turned away and thought we would keep her quiet by feeding her, so we went back to the sleigh and had the horses taken out and their cloths put on, and they were walked up and down a distant glade while we sat in the sleigh and picnicked. It is a hard day for the horses,—nearly thirty miles there and back and no stable in the middle; but they are so fat and spoiled that it cannot do them much harm sometimes to taste the bitterness of life. I warmed soup in a little apparatus I have for such occasions, which helped to take the chilliness off the sandwiches,—this is the only unpleasant part of a winter picnic, the clammy quality of the provisions just when you most long for something very hot. Minora let her nose very carefully out of its wrappings, took a mouthful, and covered it up quickly again. She was nervous lest it should be frost-nipped, and truth compels me to add that her nose is not a bad nose, and might even be pretty on anybody else; but she does not know how to carry it, and there is an art in the angle at which one's nose is held just as in everything else, and really noses were intended for something besides mere blowing.

It is the most difficult thing in the world to eat sandwiches with immense fur and woollen gloves on, and I think we ate almost as much fur as anything, and choked exceedingly during the process. Minora was angry at this, and at last pulled off her glove, but quickly put it on again.

"How very unpleasant," she remarked after swallowing a large piece of fur.

"It will wrap round your pipes, and keep them warm," said Irais.

"Pipes!" echoed Minora, greatly disgusted by such vulgarity.

"I'm afraid I can't help you," I said, as she continued to choke and splutter; "we are all in the same case, and I don't know how to alter it." "There are such things as forks, I suppose," snapped Minora.

"That's true," said I, crushed by the obviousness of the remedy; but of what use are forks if they are fifteen miles off? So Minora had to continue to eat her gloves.

By the time we had finished, the sun was already low behind the trees and the clouds beginning to flush a faint pink. The old coachman was given sandwiches and soup, and while he led the horses up and down with one hand and held his lunch in the other, we packed up—or, to be correct, I packed, and the others looked on and gave me valuable advice.

This coachman, Peter by name, is seventy years old, and was born on the place, and has driven its occupants for fifty years, and I am nearly as fond of him as I am of the sun-dial; indeed, I don't know what I should do without him, so entirely does he appear to understand and approve of my tastes and wishes. No drive is too long or difficult for the horses if I want to take it, no place impossible to reach if I want to go to it, no weather or roads too bad to prevent my going out if I wish to: to all my suggestions he responds with the readiest cheerfulness, and smoothes away all objections raised by the Man of Wrath, who rewards his alacrity in doing my pleasure by speaking of him as an alter Esel. In the summer, on fine evenings, I love to drive late and alone in the scented forests, and when I have reached a dark part stop, and sit quite still, listening to the nightingales repeating their little tune over and over again after interludes of gurgling, or if there are no nightingales, listening to the marvellous silence, and letting its blessedness descend into my very soul. The nightingales in the forests about here all sing the same tune, and in the same key of (E flat). I don't know whether all nightingales do this, or if it is peculiar to this particular spot. When they have sung it once, they clear their throats a little, and hesitate, and then do it again, and it is the prettiest little song in the world. How could I indulge my passion for these drives with their pauses without Peter? He is so used to them that he stops now at the right moment without having to be told, and he is ready to drive me all night if I wish it, with no sign of anything but cheerful willingness on his nice old face. The Man of Wrath deplores these eccentric tastes, as he calls them, of mine; but has given up trying to prevent my indulging them because, while he is deploring in one part of the house, I have slipped out at a door in the other, and am gone before he can catch me, and have reached and am lost in the shadows of the forest by the time he has discovered that I am nowhere to be found.

The brightness of Peter's perfections are sullied however by one spot, and that is, that as age creeps upon him, he not only cannot hold the horses in if they don't want to be held in, but he goes to sleep sometimes on his box if I have him out too soon after lunch, and has upset me twice within the last year—once last winter out of a sleigh, and once this summer, when the horses shied at a bicycle, and bolted into the ditch on one side of the chaussee (German for high road), and the bicycle was so terrified at the horses shying that it shied too into the ditch on the other side, and the carriage was smashed, and the bicycle was smashed, and we were all very unhappy, except Peter, who never lost his pleasant smile, and looked so placid that my tongue clave to the roof of my mouth when I tried to make it scold him.

"But I should think he ought to have been thoroughly scolded on an occasion like that," said Minora, to whom I had been telling this story as we wandered on the yellow sands while the horses were being put in the sleigh; and she glanced nervously up at Peter, whose mild head was visible between the bushes above us. "Shall we get home before dark?" she asked. The sun had altogether disappeared behind the pines and only the very highest of the little clouds were still pink; out at sea the mists were creeping up, and the sails of the fishing-smacks had turned a dull brown; a flight of wild geese passed across the disc of the moon with loud cacklings. "Before dark?" echoed Irais, "I should think not. It is dark now nearly in the forest, and we shall have the loveliest moonlight drive back."

"But it is surely very dangerous to let a man who goes to sleep drive you," said Minora apprehensively.

"But he's such an old dear," I said.

"Yes, yes, no doubt," she replied tastily; "but there are wakeful old dears to be had, and on a box they are preferable."

Irais laughed. "You are growing quite amusing, Miss Minora," she said.

"He isn't on a box to-day," said I; "and I never knew him to go to sleep standing up behind us on a sleigh." But Minora was not to be appeased, and muttered something about seeing no fun in foolhardiness, which shows how alarmed she was, for it was rude.

Peter, however, behaved beautifully on the way home, and Irais and I at least were as happy as possible driving back, with all the glories of the western sky flashing at us every now and then at the end of a long avenue as we swiftly passed, and later on, when they had faded, myriads of stars in the narrow black strip of sky over our heads. It was bitterly cold, and Minora was silent, and not in the least inclined to laugh with us as she had been six hours before.

"Have you enjoyed yourself, Miss Minora?' inquired Irais, as we got out of the forest on to the chaussee, and the lights of the village before ours twinkled in the distance.

"How many degrees do you suppose there are now?" was Minora's reply to this question.

"Degrees?—Of frost? Oh, dear me, are you cold," cried Irais solicitously.

"Well, it isn't exactly warm, is it?" said Minora sulkily; and Irais pinched me. "Well, but think how much colder you would have been without all that fur you ate for lunch inside you," she said. "And what a nice chapter you will be able to write about the Baltic," said I. "Why, it is practically certain that you are the first English person who has ever been to just this part of it."

"Isn't there some English poem," said Irais, "about being the first who ever burst—"

"'Into that silent sea,'" finished Minora hastily. "You can't quote that without its context, you know."

"But I wasn't going to," said Irais meekly; "I only paused to breathe. I must breathe, or perhaps I might die."

The lights from my energetic friend's Schloss shone brightly down upon us as we passed round the base of the hill on which it stands; she is very proud of this hill, as well she may be, seeing that it is the only one in the whole district.

"Do you never go there?" asked Minora, jerking her head in the direction of the house.

"Sometimes. She is a very busy woman, and I should feel I was in the way if I went often."

"It would be interesting to see another North German interior," said Minora; "and I should be obliged if you would take me.

"But I can't fall upon her suddenly with a strange girl," I protested; "and we are not at all on such intimate terms as to justify my taking all my visitors to see her."

"What do you want to see another interior for?" asked Irais. "I can tell you what it is like; and if you went nobody would speak to you, and if you were to ask questions, and began to take notes, the good lady would stare at you in the frankest amazement, and think Elizabeth had brought a young lunatic out for an airing. Everybody is not as patient as Elizabeth," added Irais, anxious to pay off old scores.

"I would do a great deal for you, Miss Minora," I said, "but I can't do that."

"If we went," said Irais, "Elizabeth and I would be placed with great ceremony on a sofa behind a large, polished oval table with a crochetmat in the centre—it has got a crochet-mat in the centre, hasn't it?" I nodded. "And you would sit on one of the four little podgy, buttony, tasselly red chairs that are ranged on the other side of the table facing the sofa. They are red, Elizabeth?" Again I nodded. "The floor is painted yellow, and there is no carpet except a rug in front of the sofa. The paper is dark chocolate colour, almost black; that is in order that after years of use the dirt may not show, and the room need not be done up. Dirt is like wickedness, you see, Miss Minora—its being there never matters; it is only when it shows so much as to be apparent to everybody that we are ashamed of it. At intervals round the high walls are chairs, and cabinets with lamps on them, and in one corner is a great white cold stove—or is it majolica?" she asked, turning to me.

"No, it is white."

"There are a great many lovely big windows, all ready to let in the air and the sun, but they are as carefully covered with brown lace curtains under heavy stuff ones as though a whole row of houses were just opposite, with peering eyes at every window trying to look in, instead of there only being fields, and trees, and birds. No fire, no sunlight, no books, no flowers; but a consoling smell of red cabbage coming up under the door, mixed, in due season, with soapsuds."

"When did you go there?" asked Minora.

"Ah, when did I go there indeed? When did I not go there? I have been calling there all my life."

Minora's eyes rolled doubtfully first at me then at Irais from the depths of her head-wrappings; they are large eyes with long dark eyelashes, and far be it from me to deny that each eye taken by itself is fine, but they are put in all wrong.

"The only thing you would learn there," went on Irais, "would be the significance of sofa corners in Germany. If we three went there together, I should be ushered into the right-hand corner of the sofa, because it is the place of honour, and I am the greatest stranger; Elizabeth would be invited to seat herself in the left-hand corner, as next in importance; the hostess would sit near us in an arm-chair; and you, as a person of no importance whatever, would either be left to sit where you could, or would be put on a chair facing us, and with the entire breadth of the table between us to mark the immense social gulf that separates the married woman from the mere virgin. These sofa corners make the drawing of nice distinctions possible in a way that nothing else could. The world might come to an end, and create less sensation in doing it, than you would, Miss Minora, if by any chance you got into the right-hand corner of one. That you are put on a chair on the other side of the table places you at once in the scale of precedence, and exactly defines your social position, or rather your complete want of a social position." And Irais tilted her nose ever so little heavenwards.

"Note it," she added, "as the heading of your next chapter."

"Note what?" asked Minora impatiently.

"Why,'The Subtle Significance of Sofas', of course," replied Irais. "If," she continued, as Minora made no reply appreciative of this suggestion, "you were to call unexpectedly, the bad luck which pursues the innocent would most likely make you hit on a washing-day, and the distracted mistress of the house would keep you waiting in the cold room so long while she changed her dress, that you would begin to fear you were to be left to perish from want and hunger; and when she did appear, would show by the bitterness of her welcoming smile the rage that was boiling in her heart."

"But what has the mistress of the house to do with washing?"

"What has she to do with washing? Oh, you sweet innocent—pardon my familiarity, but such ignorance of country-life customs is very touching in one who is writing a book about them."

"Oh, I have no doubt I am very ignorant," said Minora loftily.

"Seasons of washing," explained Irais, "are seasons set apart by the Hausfrau to be kept holy. They only occur every two or three months, and while they are going on the whole house is in an uproar, every other consideration sacrificed, husband and children sunk into insignificance, and no one approaching, or interfering with the mistress of the house during these days of purification, but at their peril."

"You Don't Really Mean," Said Minora, "that You Only Wash Your Clothes Four Times A Year?

"Yes, I do mean it," replied Irais.

"Well, I think that is very disgusting," said Minora emphatically.

Irais raised those pretty, delicate eyebrows of hers. "Then you must take care and not marry a German," she said.

"But what is the object of it?" went on Minora.

"Why, to clean the linen, I suppose."

"Yes, yes, but why only at such long intervals?"

"It is an outward and visible sign of vast possessions in the shape of linen. If you were to want to have your clothes washed every week, as you do in England, you would be put down as a person who only has just enough to last that length of time, and would be an object of general contempt."

"But I should be a clean object," cried Minora, "and my house would not be full of accumulated dirt."

We said nothing—there was nothing to be said.

"It must be a happy land, that England of yours," Irais remarked after a while with a sigh—a beatific vision no doubt presenting itself to her mind of a land full of washerwomen and agile gentlemen darting at door-handles.

"It is a clean land, at any rate," replied Minora.

"I don't want to go and live in it," I said—for we were driving up to the house, and a memory of fogs and umbrellas came into my mind as I looked up fondly at its dear old west front, and I felt that what I want is to live and die just here, and that there never was such a happy woman as Elizabeth.

April 18th.—I have been so busy ever since Irais and Minora left that I can hardly believe the spring is here, and the garden hurrying on its green and flowered petticoat—only its petticoat as yet, for though the underwood is a fairyland of tender little leaves, the trees above are still quite bare.

February was gone before I well knew that it had come, so deeply was I engaged in making hot-beds, and having them sown with petunias, verbenas, and nicotina affinis; while no less than thirty are dedicated solely to vegetables, it having been borne in upon me lately that vegetables must be interesting things to grow, besides possessing solid virtues not given to flowers, and that I might as well take the orchard and kitchen garden under my wing. So I have rushed in with all the zeal of utter inexperience, and my February evenings were spent poring over gardening books, and my days in applying the freshly absorbed wisdom. Who says that February is a dull, sad, slow month in the country? It was of the cheerfullest, swiftest description here, and its mild days enabled me to get on beautifully with the digging and manuring, and filled my rooms with snowdrops. The longer I live the greater is my respect and affection for manure in all its forms, and already, though the year is so young, a considerable portion of its pin-money has been spent on artificial manure. The Man of Wrath says he never met a young woman who spent her money that way before; I remarked that it must be nice to have an original wife; and he retorted that the word original hardly described me, and that the word eccentric was the one required. Very well, I suppose I am eccentric, since even my husband says so; but if my eccentricities are of such a practical nature as to result later in the biggest cauliflowers and tenderest lettuce in Prussia, why then he ought to be the first to rise up and call me blessed.

I sent to England for vegetable-marrow seeds, as they are not grown here, and people try and make boiled cucumbers take their place; but boiled cucumbers are nasty things, and I don't see why marrows should not do here perfectly well. These, and primrose-roots, are the English contributions to my garden. I brought over the roots in a tin box last time I came from England, and am anxious to see whether they will consent to live here. Certain it is that they don't exist in the Fatherland, so I can only conclude the winter kills them, for surely, if such lovely things would grow, they never would have been overlooked. Irais is deeply interested in the experiment; she reads so many English books, and has heard so much about primroses, and they have got so mixed up in her mind with leagues, and dames, and Disraelis, that she longs to see this mysterious political flower, and has made me promise to telegraph when it appears, and she will come over. Bur they are not going to do anything this year, and I only hope those cold days did not send them off to the Paradise of flowers. I am afraid their first impression of Germany was a chilly one.

Irais writes about once a week, and inquires after the garden and the babies, and announces her intention of coming back as soon as the numerous relations staying with her have left,—"which they won't do," she wrote the other day, "until the first frosts nip them off, when they will disappear like belated dahlias—double ones of course, for single dahlias are too charming to be compared to relations. I have every sort of cousin and uncle and aunt here, and here they have been ever since my husband's birthday—not the same ones exactly, but I get so confused that I never know where one ends and the other begins. My husband goes off after breakfast to look at his crops, he says, and I am left at their mercy. I wish I had crops to go and look at—I should be grateful even for one, and would look at it from morning till night, and quite stare it out of countenance, sooner than stay at home and have the truth told me by enigmatic aunts. Do you know my Aunt Bertha? she, in particular, spends her time propounding obscure questions for my solution. I get so tired and worried trying to guess the answers, which are always truths supposed to be good for me to hear. 'Why do you wear your hair on your forehead?' she asks,—and that sets me off wondering why I do wear it on my forehead, and what she wants to know for, or whether she does know and only wants to know if I will answer truthfully. 'I am sure I don't know, aunt,' I say meekly, after puzzling over it for ever so long; 'perhaps my maid knows. Shall I ring and ask her?' And then she informs me that I wear it so to hide an ugly line she says I have down the middle of my forehead, and that betokens a listless and discontented disposition. Well, if she knew, what did she ask me for? Whenever I am with them they ask me riddles like that, and I simply lead a dog's life. Oh, my dear, relations are like drugs,—useful sometimes, and even pleasant, if taken in small quantities and seldom, but dreadfully pernicious on the whole, and the truly wise avoid them."

From Minora I have only had one communication since her departure, in which she thanked me for her pleasant visit, and said she was sending me a bottle of English embrocation to rub on my bruises after skating; that it was wonderful stuff, and she was sure I would like it; and that it cost two marks, and would I send stamps. I pondered long over this. Was it a parting hit, intended as revenge for our having laughed at her? Was she personally interested in the sale of embrocation? Or was it merely Minora's idea of a graceful return for my hospitality? As for bruises, nobody who skates decently regards it as a bruise-producing exercise, and whenever there were any they were all on Minora; but she did happen to turn round once, I remember, just as I was in the act of tumbling down for the first and only time, and her delight was but thinly veiled by her excessive solicitude and sympathy. I sent her the stamps, received the bottle, and resolved to let her drop out of my life; I had been a good Samaritan to her at the request of my friend, but the best of Samaritans resents the offer of healing oil for his own use. But why waste a thought on Minora at Easter, the real beginning of the year in defiance of calendars. She belongs to the winter that is past, to the darkness that is over, and has no part or lot in the life I shall lead for the next six months. Oh, I could dance and sing for joy that the spring is here! What a resurrection of beauty there is in my garden, and of brightest hope in my heart! The whole of this radiant Easter day I have spent out of doors, sitting at first among the windflowers and celandines, and then, later, walking with the babies to the Hirschwald, to see what the spring had been doing there; and the afternoon was so hot that we lay a long time on the turf, blinking up through the leafless branches of the silver birches at the soft, fat little white clouds floating motionless in the blue. We had tea on the grass in the sun, and when it began to grow late, and the babies were in bed, and all the little wind-flowers folded up for the night, I still wandered in the green paths, my heart full of happiest gratitude. It makes one very humble to see oneself surrounded by such a wealth of beauty and perfection anonymously lavished, and to think of the infinite meanness of our own grudging charities, and how displeased we are if they are not promptly and properly appreciated. I do sincerely trust that the benediction that is always awaiting me in my garden may by degrees be more deserved, and that I may grow in grace, and patience, and cheerfulness, just like the happy flowers I so much love.

The Enchanted April

Chapter 1

It began in a Woman's Club in London on a February afternoon—an uncomfortable club, and a miserable afternoon—when Mrs. Wilkins, who had come down from Hampstead to shop and had lunched at her club, took up The Times from the table in the smoking-room, and running her listless eye down the Agony Column saw this:

To Those Who Appreciate Wistaria and Sunshine. Small mediaeval Italian Castle on the shores of the Mediterranean to be Let furnished for the month of April. Necessary servants remain. Z, Box 1000, The Times.

That was its conception; yet, as in the case of many another, the conceiver was unaware of it at the moment.

So entirely unaware was Mrs. Wilkins that her April for that year had then and there been settled for her that she dropped the newspaper with a gesture that was both irritated and resigned, and went over to the window and stared drearily out at the dripping street.

Not for her were mediaeval castles, even those that are specially described as small. Not for her the shores in April of the Mediterranean, and the wisteria and sunshine. Such delights were only for the rich. Yet the advertisement had been addressed to persons who appreciate these things, so that it had been, anyhow addressed too to her, for she certainly appreciated them; more than anybody knew; more than she had ever told. But she was poor. In the whole world she possessed of her very own only ninety pounds, saved from year to year, put by carefully pound by pound, out of her dress allowance. She had scraped this sum together at the suggestion of her husband as a shield and refuge against a rainy day. Her dress allowance, given her by her father, was £100 a year, so that Mrs. Wilkins's clothes were what her husband, urging her to save, called modest and becoming, and her acquaintance to each other, when they spoke of her at all, which was seldom for she was very negligible, called a perfect sight.

Mr. Wilkins, a solicitor, encouraged thrift, except that branch of it which got into his food. He did not call that thrift, he called it bad housekeeping. But for the thrift which, like moth, penetrated into Mrs. Wilkins's clothes and spoilt them, he had much praise. "You never know," he said, "when there will be a rainy day, and you may be very glad to find you have a nest-egg. Indeed we both may."

Looking out of the club window into Shaftesbury Avenue—hers was an economical club, but convenient for Hampstead, where she lived, and for Shoolbred's, where she shopped—Mrs. Wilkins, having stood there some time very drearily, her mind's eye on the Mediterranean in April, and the wisteria, and the enviable opportunities of the rich, while her bodily eye watched the really extremely horrible sooty rain falling steadily on the hurrying umbrellas and splashing omnibuses, suddenly wondered whether perhaps this was not the rainy day Mellersh—Mellersh was Mr. Wilkins— had so often encouraged her to prepare for, and whether to get out of such a climate and into the small mediaeval castle wasn't perhaps what Providence had all along intended her to do with her savings. Part of her savings, of course; perhaps quite a small part. The castle, being mediaeval, might also be dilapidated, and dilapidations were surely cheap. She wouldn't in the least mind a few of them, because you didn't pay for dilapidations which were already there, on the contrary—by reducing the price you had to pay they really paid you. But what nonsense to think of it . . .

She turned away from the window with the same gesture of mingled irritation and resignation with which she had laid down The Times, and crossed the room towards the door with the intention of getting her mackintosh and umbrella and fighting her way into one of the overcrowded omnibuses and going to Shoolbred's on her way home and buying some soles for Mellersh's dinner—Mellersh was difficult with fish and liked only soles, except salmon—when she beheld Mrs. Arbuthnot, a woman she knew by sight as also living in Hampstead and belonging to the club, sitting at the table in the middle of the room on which the newspapers and magazines were kept, absorbed, in her turn, in the first page of The Times.

Mrs. Wilkins had never yet spoken to Mrs. Arbuthnot, who belonged to one of the various church sets, and who analysed, classified, divided and registered the poor; whereas she and Mellersh, when they did go out, went to the parties of impressionist painters, of whom in Hampstead there were many. Mellersh had a sister who had married one of them and lived up on the Heath, and because of this alliance Mrs. Wilkins was drawn into a circle which was highly unnatural to her, and she had learned to dread pictures. She had to say things about them, and she didn't know what to say. She used to murmur, "marvelous," and feel that it was not enough. But nobody minded. Nobody listened. Nobody took any notice of Mrs. Wilkins. She was the kind of person who is not noticed at parties. Her clothes, infested by thrift, made her practically invisible; her face was non-arresting; her conversation was reluctant; she was shy. And if one's clothes and face and conversation are all negligible, thought Mrs. Wilkins, who recognized her disabilities, what, at parties, is there left of one?

Also she was always with Wilkins, that clean-shaven, fine-looking man, who gave a party, merely by coming to it, a great air. Wilkins was very respectable. He was known to be highly thought of by his senior partners. His sister's circle admired him. He pronounced adequately intelligent judgments on art and artists. He was pithy; he was prudent; he never said a word too much, nor, on the other had, did he ever say a word too little. He produced the impression of keeping copies of everything he said; and he was so obviously reliable that it often happened that people who met him at these parties became discontented with their own solicitors, and after a period of restlessness extricated themselves and went to Wilkins.

Naturally Mrs. Wilkins was blotted out. "She," said his sister, with something herself of the judicial, the digested, and the final in her manner, "should stay at home." But Wilkins could not leave his wife at home. He was a family solicitor, and all such have wives and show them. With his in the week he went to parties, and with his on Sundays he went to church. Being still fairly young—he was thirty-nine—and ambitious of old ladies, of whom he had not yet acquired in his practice a sufficient number, he could not afford to miss church, and it was there that Mrs. Wilkins became familiar, though never through words, with Mrs. Arbuthnot.

She saw her marshalling the children of the poor into pews. She would come in at the head of the procession from the Sunday School exactly five minutes before the choir, and get her boys and girls neatly fitted into their allotted seats, and down on their little knees in their preliminary prayer, and up again on their feet just as, to the swelling organ, the vestry door opened, and the choir and clergy, big with the litanies and commandments they were presently to roll out, emerged. She had a sad face, yet she was evidently efficient. The combination used to make Mrs. Wilkins wonder, for she had been told by Mellersh, on days when she had only been able to get plaice, that if one were efficient one wouldn't be depressed, and that if one does one's job well one becomes automatically bright and brisk.

About Mrs. Arbuthnot there was nothing bright and brisk, though much in her way with the Sunday School children that was automatic; but when Mrs. Wilkins, turning from the window, caught sight of her in the club she was not being automatic at all, but was looking fixedly at one portion of the first page of The Times, holding the paper quite still, her eyes not moving. She was just staring; and her face, as usual, was the face of a patient and disappointed Madonna.

Mrs. Wilkins watched her a minute, trying to screw up courage to speak to her. She wanted to ask her if she had seen the advertisement. She did not know why she wanted to ask her this, but she wanted to. How stupid not to be able to speak to her. She looked so kind. She looked so unhappy. Why couldn't two unhappy people refresh each other on their way through this dusty business of life by a little talk—real, natural talk, about what they felt, what they would have liked, what they still tried to hope? And she could not help thinking that Mrs. Arbuthnot, too, was reading that very same advertisement. Her eyes were on the very part of the paper. Was she, too, picturing what it would be like—the colour, the fragrance, the light, the soft lapping of the sea among little hot rocks? Colour, fragrance, light, sea; instead of Shaftesbury Avenue, and the wet omnibuses, and the fish department at Shoolbred's, and the Tube to Hampstead, and dinner, and to-morrow the same and the day after the same and always the same . . .

Suddenly Mrs. Wilkins found herself leaning across the table. "Are you reading about the mediaeval castle and the wisteria?" she heard herself asking.

Naturally Mrs. Arbuthnot was surprised; but she was not half so much surprised as Mrs. Wilkins was at herself for asking.

Mrs. Arbuthnot had not yet to her knowledge set eyes on the shabby, lank, loosely-put-together figure sitting opposite her, with its small freckled face and big grey eyes almost disappearing under a smashed-down wet-weather hat, and she gazed at her a moment without answering. She was reading about the mediaeval castle and the wisteria, or rather had read about it ten minutes before, and since then had been lost in dreams—of light, of colour, of fragrance, of the soft lapping of the sea among little hot rocks . . .

"Why do you ask me that?" she said in her grave voice, for her training of and by the poor had made her grave and patient.

Mrs. Wilkins flushed and looked excessively shy and frightened. "Oh, only because I saw it too, and I thought perhaps—I thought somehow—" she stammered.

Whereupon Mrs. Arbuthnot, her mind being used to getting people into lists and divisions, from habit considered, as she gazed thoughtfully at Mrs. Wilkins, under what heading, supposing she had to classify her, she could most properly be put.

"And I know you by sight," went on Mrs. Wilkins, who, like all the shy, once she was started; lunged on, frightening herself to more and more speech by the sheer sound of what she had said last in her ears. "Every Sunday—I see you every Sunday in church—"

"In church?" echoed Mrs. Arbuthnot.

"And this seems such a wonderful thing—this advertisement about the wisteria—and—"

Mrs. Wilkins, who must have been at least thirty, broke off and wriggled in her chair with the movement of an awkward and embarrassed schoolgirl.

"It seems so wonderful," she went on in a kind of burst, "and—it is such a miserable day . . ."

And then she sat looking at Mrs. Arbuthnot with the eyes of an imprisoned dog.

"This poor thing," thought Mrs. Arbuthnot, whose life was spent in helping and alleviating, "needs advice."

She accordingly prepared herself patiently to give it.

"If you see me in church," she said, kindly and attentively, "I suppose you live in Hampstead too?"

"Oh yes," said Mrs. Wilkins. And she repeated, her head on its long thin neck drooping a little as if the recollection of Hampstead bowed her, "Oh yes."

"Where?" asked Mrs. Arbuthnot, who, when advice was needed, naturally first proceeded to collect the facts.

But Mrs. Wilkins, laying her hand softly and caressingly on the part of The Times where the advertisement was, as though the mere printed words of it were precious, only said, "Perhaps that is why this seems so wonderful."

"No—I think that's wonderful anyhow," said Mrs. Arbuthnot, forgetting facts and faintly sighing.

"Then you were reading it?"

"Yes," said Mrs. Arbuthnot, her eyes going dreamy again.

"Wouldn't it be wonderful?" murmured Mrs. Wilkins.

"Wonderful," said Mrs. Arbuthnot. Her face, which had lit up, faded into patience again. "Very wonderful," she said. "But it's no use wasting one's time thinking of such things."

"Oh, but it is," was Mrs. Wilkins's quick, surprising reply; surprising because it was so much unlike the rest of her—the characterless coat and skirt, the crumpled hat, the undecided wisp of hair straggling out, "And just the considering of them is worth while in itself—such a change from Hampstead—and sometimes I believe—I really do believe—if one considers hard enough one gets things."

Mrs. Arbuthnot observed her patiently. In what category would she, supposing she had to, put her?

"Perhaps," she said, leaning forward a little, "you will tell me your name. If we are to be friends"—she smiled her grave smile—"as I hope we are, we had better begin at the beginning."

"Oh yes—how kind of you. I'm Mrs. Wilkins," said Mrs. Wilkins. "I don't expect," she added, flushing, as Mrs. Arbuthnot said nothing, "that it conveys anything to you. Sometimes it—it doesn't seem to convey anything to me either. But"—she looked round with a movement of seeking help—"I am Mrs. Wilkins."

She did not like her name. It was a mean, small name, with a kind of facetious twist, she thought, about its end like the upward curve of a pugdog's tail. There it was, however. There was no doing anything with it. Wilkins she was and Wilkins she would remain; and though her husband encouraged her to give it on all occasions as Mrs. Mellersh-Wilkins she only did that when he was within earshot, for she thought Mellersh made Wilkins worse, emphasizing it in the way Chatsworth on the gate-posts of a villa emphasizes the villa.

When first he suggested she should add Mellersh she had objected for the above reason, and after a pause—Mellersh was much too prudent to speak except after a pause, during which presumably he was taking a careful mental copy of his coming observation—he said, much displeased, "But I am not a villa," and looked at her as he looks who hopes, for perhaps the hundredth time, that he may not have married a fool.

Of course he was not a villa, Mrs. Wilkins assured him; she had never supposed he was; she had not dreamed of meaning . . . she was only just thinking . . .

The more she explained the more earnest became Mellersh's hope, familiar to him by this time, for he had then been a husband for two years, that he might not by any chance have married a fool; and they had a prolonged quarrel, if that can be called a quarrel which is conducted with dignified silence on one side and earnest apology on the other, as to whether or no Mrs. Wilkins had intended to suggest that Mr. Wilkins was a villa.

"I believe," she had thought when it was at last over—it took a long while—"that anybody would quarrel about anything when they've not left off being together for a single day for two whole years. What we both need is a holiday."

"My husband," went on Mrs. Wilkins to Mrs. Arbuthnot, trying to throw some light on herself, "is a solicitor. He—" She cast about for something she could say elucidatory of Mellersh, and found: "He's very handsome."

"Well," said Mrs. Arbuthnot kindly, "that must be a great pleasure to you."

"Why?" asked Mrs. Wilkins.

"Because," said Mrs. Arbuthnot, a little taken aback, for constant intercourse with the poor had accustomed her to have her pronouncements accepted without question, "because beauty—handsomeness— is a gift like any other, and if it is properly used—"

She trailed off into silence. Mrs. Wilkins's great grey eyes were fixed on her, and it seemed suddenly to Mrs. Arbuthnot that perhaps she was becoming crystallized into a habit of exposition, and of exposition after the manner of nursemaids, through having an audience that couldn't but agree, that would be afraid, if it wished, to interrupt, that didn't know, that was, in fact, at her mercy.

But Mrs. Wilkins was not listening; for just then, absurd as it seemed, a picture had flashed across her brain, and there were two figures in it sitting together under a great trailing wisteria that stretched across the branches of a tree she didn't know, and it was herself and Mrs. Arbuthnot—she saw them—she saw them. And behind them, bright in sunshine, were old grey walls—the mediaeval castle —she saw it—they were there . . .

She therefore stared at Mrs. Arbuthnot and did not hear a word she said.

And Mrs. Arbuthnot stared too at Mrs. Wilkins, arrested by the expression on her face, which was swept by the excitement of what she saw, and was as luminous and tremulous under it as water in sunlight when it is ruffled by a gust of wind. At this moment, if she had been at a party, Mrs. Wilkins would have been looked at with interest.

They stared at each other; Mrs. Arbuthnot surprised, inquiringly, Mrs. Wilkins with the eyes of some one who has had a revelation. Of course. That was how it could be done. She herself, she by herself, couldn't afford it, and wouldn't be able, even if she could afford it, to go there all alone; but she and Mrs. Arbuthnot together . . .

She leaned across the table, "Why don't we try and get it?" she whispered.

Mrs. Arbuthnot became even more wide-eyed. "Get it?" she repeated.

"Yes," said Mrs. Wilkins, still as though she were afraid of being overheard. "Not just sit here and say How wonderful, and then go home to Hampstead without having put out a finger—go home just as usual and see about the dinner and the fish just as we've been doing for years and years and will go on doing for years and years. In fact," said Mrs. Wilkins, flushing to the roots of her hair, for the sound of what she was saying, of what was coming pouring out, frightened her, and yet she couldn't stop, "I see no end to it. There is no end to it. So that there ought to be a break, there ought to be intervals—in everybody's interests. Why, it would really be being unselfish to go away and be happy for a little, because we would come back so much nicer. You see, after a bit everybody needs a holiday."

"But—how do you mean, get it?" asked Mrs. Arbuthnot.

"Take it," said Mrs. Wilkins.

"Take it?"

"Rent it. Hire it. Have it."

"But—do you mean you and I?"

"Yes. Between us. Share. Then it would only cost half, and you look so—you look exactly as if you wanted it just as much as I do—as if you ought to have a rest—have something happy happen to you."

"Why, but we don't know each other."

"But just think how well we would if we went away together for a month! And I've saved for a rainy day—look at it—"

"She is unbalanced," thought Mrs. Arbuthnot; yet she felt strangely stirred.

"Think of getting away for a whole month—from everything—to heaven—"

"She shouldn't say things like that," thought Mrs. Arbuthnot. "The vicar—" Yet she felt strangely stirred. It would indeed be wonderful to have a rest, a cessation.

Habit, however, steadied her again; and years of intercourse with the poor made her say, with the slight though sympathetic superiority of the explainer, "But then, you see, heaven isn't somewhere else. It is here and now. We are told so."

She became very earnest, just as she did when trying patiently to help and enlighten the poor. "Heaven is within us," she said in her gentle low voice. "We are told that on the very highest authority. And you know the lines about the kindred points, don't you—"

"Oh yes, I know them," interrupted Mrs. Wilkins impatiently.

"The kindred points of heaven and home," continued Mrs. Arbuthnot, who was used to finishing her sentences. "Heaven is in our home."

"It isn't," said Mrs. Wilkins, again surprisingly.

Mrs. Arbuthnot was taken aback. Then she said gently, "Oh, but it is. It is there if we choose, if we make it."

"I do choose, and I do make it, and it isn't," said Mrs. Wilkins.

Then Mrs. Arbuthnot was silent, for she too sometimes had doubts about homes. She sat and looked uneasily at Mrs. Wilkins, feeling more and more the urgent need to getting her classified. If she could only classify Mrs. Wilkins, get her safely under her proper heading, she felt that she herself would regain her balance, which did seem very strangely to be slipping all to one side. For neither had she had a holiday for years, and the advertisement when she saw it had set her dreaming, and Mrs. Wilkins's excitement about it was infectious, and she had the sensation, as she listened to her impetuous, odd talk and watched her lit-up face, that she was being stirred out of sleep.

Clearly Mrs. Wilkins was unbalanced, but Mrs. Arbuthnot had met the unbalanced before—indeed she was always meeting them—and they had no effect on her own stability at all; whereas this one was making her feel quite wobbly, quite as though to be off and away, away from her compass points of God, Husband, Home and Duty—she didn't feel as if Mrs. Wilkins intended Mr. Wilkins to come too—and just for once be happy, would be both good and desirable. Which of course it wasn't; which certainly of course it wasn't. She, also, had a nest-egg, invested gradually in the Post Office Savings Bank, but to suppose that she would ever forget her duty to the extent of drawing it out and spending it on herself was surely absurd. Surely she couldn't, she wouldn't ever do such a thing? Surely she wouldn't, she couldn't ever forget her poor, forget misery and sickness as completely as that? No doubt a trip to Italy would be extraordinarily delightful, but there were many delightful things one would like to do, and what was strength given to one for except to help one not to do them?

Steadfast as the points of the compass to Mrs. Arbuthnot were the great four facts of life: God, Husband, Home, Duty. She had gone to sleep on these facts years ago, after a period of much misery, her head resting on them as on a pillow; and she had a great dread of being awakened out of so simple and untroublesome a condition. Therefore it was that she searched with earnestness for a heading under which to put Mrs. Wilkins, and in this way illumine and steady her own mind; and sitting there looking at her uneasily after her last remark, and feeling herself becoming more and more unbalanced and infected, she decided pro tem, as the vicar said at meetings, to put her under the heading Nerves. It was just possible that she ought to go straight into the category Hysteria, which was often only the antechamber to Lunacy, but Mrs. Arbuthnot had learned not to hurry people into their final categories, having on more than one occasion discovered with dismay that she had made a mistake; and how difficult it had been to get them out again, and how crushed she had been with the most terrible remorse.

Yes. Nerves. Probably she had no regular work for others, thought Mrs. Arbuthnot; no work that would take her outside herself. Evidently she was rudderless—blown about by gusts, by impulses. Nerves was almost certainly her category, or would be quite soon if no one helped her. Poor little thing, thought Mrs. Arbuthnot, her own balance returning hand in hand with her compassion, and unable, because of the table, to see the length of Mrs. Wilkins's legs. All she saw was her small, eager, shy face, and her thin shoulders, and the look of childish longing in her eyes for something that she was sure was going to make her happy. No; such things didn't make people happy, such fleeting things. Mrs. Arbuthnot had learned in her long life with Frederick—he was her husband, and she had married him at twenty and was not thirty-three—where alone true joys are to be found. They are to be found, she now knew, only in daily, in hourly, living for others; they are to be found only—hadn't she over and over again taken her disappointments and discouragements there, and come away comforted?—at the feet of God.

Frederick had been the kind of husband whose wife betakes herself early to the feet of God. From him to them had been a short though painful step. It seemed short to her in retrospect, but it had really taken the whole of the first year of their marriage, and every inch of the way had been a struggle, and every inch of it was stained, she felt at the time, with her heart's blood. All that was over now. She had long since found peace. And Frederick, from her passionately loved bridegroom, from her worshipped young husband, had become second only to God on her list of duties and forbearances. There he hung, the second in importance, a bloodless thing bled white by her prayers. For years she had been able to be happy only by forgetting happiness. She wanted to stay like that. She wanted to shut out everything that would remind her of beautiful things, that might set her off again long, desiring . . .

"I'd like so much to be friends," she said earnestly. "Won't you come and see me, or let me come to you sometimes? Whenever you feel as if you wanted to talk. I'll give you my address"—she searched in her handbag—"and then you won't forget." And she found a card and held it out.

Mrs. Wilkins ignored the card.

"It's so funny," said Mrs. Wilkins, just as if she had not heard her, "But I see us both—you and me—this April in the mediaeval castle."

Mrs. Arbuthnot relapsed into uneasiness. "Do you?" she said, making an effort to stay balanced under the visionary gaze of the shining grey eyes. "Do you?"

"Don't you ever see things in a kind of flash before they happen?" asked Mrs. Wilkins.

"Never," said Mrs. Arbuthnot.

She tried to smile; she tried to smile the sympathetic yet wise and tolerant smile with which she was accustomed to listen to the necessarily biased and incomplete view of the poor. She didn't succeed. The smile trembled out.

"Of course," she said in a low voice, almost as if she were afraid the vicar and the Savings Bank were listening, "it would be most beautiful—most beautiful—"

"Even if it were wrong," said Mrs. Wilkins, "it would only be for a month."

"That—" began Mrs. Arbuthnot, quite clear as to the reprehensibleness of such a point of view; but Mrs. Wilkins stopped her before she could finish.

"Anyhow," said Mrs. Wilkins, stopping her, "I'm sure it's wrong to go on being good for too long, till one gets miserable. And I can see you've been good for years and years, because you look so unhappy"— Mrs. Arbuthnot opened her mouth to protest—"and I—I've done nothing but duties, things for other people, ever since I was a girl, and I don't believe anybody loves me a bit—a bit—the b-better—and I long— oh, I long—for something else—something else—"

Was she going to cry? Mrs. Arbuthnot became acutely uncomfortable and sympathetic. She hoped she wasn't going to cry. Not there. Not in that unfriendly room, with strangers coming and going.

But Mrs. Wilkins, after tugging agitatedly at a handkerchief that wouldn't come out of her pocket, did succeed at last in merely apparently blowing her nose with it, and then, blinking her eyes very quickly once or twice, looked at Mrs. Arbuthnot with a quivering air of half humble, half frightened apology, and smiled.

"Will you believe," she whispered, trying to steady her mouth, evidently dreadfully ashamed of herself, "that I've never spoken to any one before in my life like this? I can't think, I simply don't know, what has come over me."

"It's the advertisement," said Mrs. Arbuthnot, nodding gravely.

"Yes," said Mrs. Wilkins, dabbing furtively at her eyes, "and us both being so—"—she blew her nose again a little—"miserable."

Chapter 2

Of course Mrs. Arbuthnot was not miserable—how could she be, she asked herself, when God was taking care of her?—but she let that pass for the moment unrepudiated, because of her conviction that here was another fellow-creature in urgent need of her help; and not just boots and blankets and better sanitary arrangements this time, but the more delicate help of comprehension, of finding the exact right words.

The exact right words, she presently discovered, after trying various ones about living for others, and prayer, and the peace to be found in placing oneself unreservedly in God's hands—to meet all these words Mrs. Wilkins had other words, incoherent and yet, for the moment at least, till one had had more time, difficult to answer—the exact right words were a suggestion that it would do no harm to answer the advertisement. Non-committal. Mere inquiry. And what disturbed Mrs. Arbuthnot about this suggestion was that she did not make it solely to comfort Mrs. Wilkins; she made it because of her own strange longing for the mediaeval castle.

This was very disturbing. There she was, accustomed to direct, to lead, to advise, to support—except Frederick; she long since had learned to leave Frederick to God—being led herself, being influenced and thrown off her feet, by just an advertisement, by just an incoherent stranger. It was indeed disturbing. She failed to understand her sudden longing for what was, after all, self-indulgence, when for years no such desire had entered her heart.

"There's no harm in simply asking," she said in a low voice, as if the vicar and the Savings Bank and all her waiting and dependent poor were listening and condemning.

"It isn't as if it committed us to anything," said Mrs. Wilkins, also in a low voice, but her voice shook.

They got up simultaneously—Mrs. Arbuthnot had a sensation of surprise that Mrs. Wilkins should be so tall—and went to a writing-table, and Mrs. Arbuthnot wrote to Z, Box 1000, The Times, for particulars. She asked for all particulars, but the only one they really wanted was the one about the rent. They both felt that it was Mrs. Arbuthnot who ought to write the letter and do the business part. Not only was she used to organizing and being practical, but she also was older, and certainly calmer; and she herself had no doubt too that she was wiser. Neither had Mrs. Wilkins any doubt of this; the very way Mrs. Arbuthnot parted her hair suggested a great calm that could only proceed from wisdom.

But if she was wiser, older and calmer, Mrs. Arbuthnot's new friend nevertheless seemed to her to be the one who impelled. Incoherent, she yet impelled. She appeared to have, apart from her need of help, an upsetting kind of character. She had a curious infectiousness. She led one on. And the way her unsteady mind leaped at conclusions—wrong ones, of course; witness the one that she, Mrs. Arbuthnot, was miserable—the way she leaped at conclusions was disconcerting.

Whatever she was, however, and whatever her unsteadiness, Mrs. Arbuthnot found herself sharing her excitement and her longing; and when the letter had been posted in the letter-box in the hall and actually was beyond getting back again, both she and Mrs. Wilkins felt the same sense of guilt.

"It only shows," said Mrs. Wilkins in a whisper, as they turned away from the letter-box, "how immaculately good we've been all our lives. The very first time we do anything our husbands don't know about we feel guilty."

"I'm afraid I can't say I've been immaculately good," gently protested Mrs. Arbuthnot, a little uncomfortable at this fresh example of successful leaping at conclusions, for she had not said a word about her feeling of guilt.

"Oh, but I'm sure you have—I see you being good—and that's why you're not happy."

"She shouldn't say things like that," thought Mrs. Arbuthnot. "I must try and help her not to."

Aloud she said gravely, "I don't know why you insist that I'm not happy. When you know me better I think you'll find that I am. And I'm sure you don't mean really that goodness, if one could attain it, makes one unhappy."

"Yes, I do," said Mrs. Wilkins. "Our sort of goodness does. We have attained it, and we are unhappy. There are miserable sorts of goodness and happy sorts—the sort we'll have at the mediaeval castle, for instance, is the happy sort."

"That is, supposing we go there," said Mrs. Arbuthnot restrainingly. She felt that Mrs. Wilkins needed holding on to. "After all, we've only written just to ask. Anybody may do that. I think it quite likely we shall find the conditions impossible, and even if they were not, probably by to-morrow we shall not want to go."

"I see us there," was Mrs. Wilkins's answer to that.

All this was very unbalancing. Mrs. Arbuthnot, as she presently splashed though the dripping streets on her way to a meeting she was to speak at, was in an unusually disturbed condition of mind. She had, she hoped, shown herself very calm to Mrs. Wilkins, very practical and sober, concealing her own excitement. But she was really extraordinarily moved, and she felt happy, and she felt guilty, and she felt afraid, and she had all the feelings, though this she did not know, of a woman who was come away from a secret meeting with her lover. That, indeed, was what she looked like when she arrived late on her platform; she, the open-browed, looked almost furtive as her eyes fell on the staring wooden faces waiting to hear her try and persuade them to contribute to the alleviation of the urgent needs of the Hampstead poor, each one convinced that they needed contributions themselves. She looked as though she were hiding something discreditable but delightful. Certainly her customary clear expression of candor was not there, and its place was taken by a kind of suppressed and frightened pleasedness, which would have led a more worldly-minded audience to the instant conviction of recent and probably impassioned lovemaking.

Beauty, beauty, beauty . . . the words kept ringing in her ears as she stood on the platform talking of sad things to the sparsely attended meeting. She had never been to Italy. Was that really what her nest-egg was to be spent on after all? Though she couldn't approve of the way Mrs. Wilkins was introducing the idea of predestination into her immediate future, just as if she had no choice, just as if to struggle, or even to reflect, were useless, it yet influenced her. Mrs. Wilkins's eyes had been the eyes of a seer. Some people were like that, Mrs. Arbuthnot knew; and if Mrs. Wilkins had actually seen her at the mediaeval castle it did seem probable that struggling would be a waste of time. Still, to spend her nest-egg on self-indulgence— The origin of this egg had been corrupt, but she had at least supposed its end was to be creditable. Was she to deflect it from its intended destination, which alone had appeared to justify her keeping it, and spend it on giving herself pleasure?

Mrs. Arbuthnot spoke on and on, so much practiced in the kind of speech that she could have said it all in her sleep, and at the end of the meeting, her eyes dazzled by her secret visions, she hardly noticed that nobody was moved in any way whatever, least of all in the way of contributions.

But the vicar noticed. The vicar was disappointed. Usually his good friend and supporter Mrs. Arbuthnot succeeded better than this. And, what was even more unusual, she appeared, he observed, not even to mind.

"I can't imagine," he said to her as they parted, speaking irritably, for he was irritated both by the audience and by her, "what these people are coming to. Nothing seems to move them."

"Perhaps they need a holiday," suggested Mrs. Arbuthnot; an unsatisfactory, a queer reply, the vicar thought.

"In February?" he called after her sarcastically.

"Oh no—not till April," said Mrs. Arbuthnot over her shoulder.

"Very odd," thought the vicar. "Very odd indeed." And he went home and was not perhaps quite Christian to his wife.

That night in her prayers Mrs. Arbuthnot asked for guidance. She felt she ought really to ask, straight out and roundly, that the mediaeval castle should already have been taken by some one else and the whole thing thus be settled, but her courage failed her. Suppose her prayer were to be answered? No; she couldn't ask it; she couldn't risk it. And after all—she almost pointed this out to God—if she spent her present nest-egg on a holiday she could quite soon accumulate another. Frederick pressed money on her; and it would only mean, while she rolled up a second egg, that for a time her contributions to the parish charities would be less. And then it could be the next nest-egg whose original corruption would be purged away by the use to which it was finally put.

For Mrs. Arbuthnot, who had no money of her own, was obliged to live on the proceeds of Frederick's activities, and her very nest-egg was the fruit, posthumously ripened, of ancient sin. The way Frederick made his living was one of the standing distresses of her life. He wrote immensely popular memoirs, regularly, every year, of the mistresses of kings. There were in history numerous kings who had had mistresses, and there were still more numerous mistresses who had had kings; so that he had been able to publish a book of memoirs during each year of his married life, and even so there were greater further piles of these ladies waiting to be dealt with. Mrs. Arbuthnot was helpless. Whether she liked it or not, she was obliged to live on the proceeds. He gave her a dreadful sofa once, after the success of his Du Barri memoir, with swollen cushions and soft, receptive lap, and it seemed to her a miserable thing that there, in her very home, should flaunt this re-incarnation of a dead old French sinner.

Simply good, convinced that morality is the basis of happiness, the fact that she and Frederick should draw their sustenance from guilt, however much purged by the passage of centuries, was one of the secret reasons of her sadness. The more the memoired lady had forgotten herself, the more his book about her was read and the more free-handed he was to his wife; and all that he gave her was spent, after adding slightly to her nest-egg— for she did hope and believe that some day people would cease to want to read of wickedness, and then Frederick would need supporting—on helping the poor. The parish flourished because, to take a handful at random, of the ill-behavior of the ladies Du Barri, Montespan, Pompadour, Ninon de l'Enclos, and even of learned Maintenon. The poor were the filter through which the money was passed, to come out, Mrs. Arbuthnot hoped, purified. She could do no more. She had tried in days gone by to think the situation out, to discover the exact right course for her to take, but had found it, as she had found Frederick, too difficult, and had left it, as she had left Frederick, to God. Nothing of this money was spent on her house or dress; those remained, except for the great soft sofa, austere. It was the poor who profited. Their very boots were stout with sins. But how difficult it had been. Mrs. Arbuthnot, groping for guidance, prayed about it to exhaustion. Ought she perhaps to refuse to touch the money, to avoid it as she would have avoided the sins which were its source? But then what about the parish's boots? She asked the vicar what he thought, and through much delicate language, evasive and cautious, it did finally appear that he was for the boots.

At least she had persuaded Frederick, when first he began his terrible successful career—he only began it after their marriage; when she married him he had been a blameless official attached to the library of the British Museum—to publish the memoirs under another name, so that she was not publicly branded. Hampstead read the books with glee, and had no idea that their writer lived in its midst. Frederick was almost unknown, even by sight, in Hampstead. He never went to any of its gatherings. Whatever it was he did in the way of recreation was done in London, but he never spoke of what he did or whom he saw; he might have been perfectly friendless for any mention he ever made of friends to his wife. Only the vicar knew where the money for the parish came from, and he regarded it, he told Mrs. Arbuthnot, as a matter of honour not to mention it.

And at least her little house was not haunted by the loose lived ladies, for Frederick did his work away from home. He had two rooms near the

British Museum, which was the scene of his exhumations, and there he went every morning, and he came back long after his wife was asleep. Sometimes he did not come back at all. Sometimes she did not see him for several days together. Then he would suddenly appear at breakfast, having let himself in with his latchkey the night before, very jovial and good-natured and free-handed and glad if she would allow him to give her something—a well-fed man, contented with the world; a jolly, full-blooded, satisfied man. And she was always gentle, and anxious that his coffee should be as he liked it.

He seemed very happy. Life, she often thought, however much one tabulated was yet a mystery. There were always some people it was impossible to place. Frederick was one of them. He didn't seem to bear the remotest resemblance to the original Frederick. He didn't seem to have the least need of any of the things he used to say were so important and beautiful—love, home, complete communion of thoughts, complete immersion in each other's interests. After those early painful attempts to hold him up to the point from which they had hand in hand so splendidly started, attempts in which she herself had got terribly hurt and the Frederick she supposed she had married was mangled out of recognition, she hung him up finally by her bedside as the chief subject of her prayers, and left him, except for those, entirely to God. She had loved Frederick too deeply to be able now to do anything but pray for him. He had no idea that he never went out of the house without her blessing going with him too, hovering, like a little echo of finished love, round that once dear head. She didn't dare think of him as he used to be, as he had seemed to her to be in those marvelous first days of their love-making, of their marriage. Her child had died; she had nothing, nobody of her own to lavish herself on. The poor became her children, and God the object of her love. What could be happier than such a life, she sometimes asked herself; but her face, and particularly her eyes, continued sad.

"Perhaps when we're old . . . perhaps when we are both quite old . . ." she would think wistfully.

Chapter 3

The owner of the mediaeval castle was an Englishman, a Mr. Briggs, who was in London at the moment and wrote that it had beds enough for eight people, exclusive of servants, three sitting-rooms, battlements, dungeons, and electric light. The rent was £60 for the month, the servants' wages were extra, and he wanted references—he wanted assurances that the second half of his rent would be paid, the first half being paid in advance, and he wanted assurances of respectability from a solicitor, or a doctor, or a clergyman. He was very polite in his letter, explaining that his desire for references was what was usual and should be regarded as a mere formality.

Mrs. Arbuthnot and Mrs. Wilkins had not thought of references, and they had not dreamed a rent could be so high. In their minds had floated sums like three guineas a week; or less, seeing that the place was small and old.

Sixty pounds for a single month.

It staggered them.

Before Mrs. Arbuthnot's eyes rose up boots: endless vistas, all the stout boots that sixty pounds would buy; and besides the rent there would be the servants' wages and the food, and the railway journeys out and home. While as for references, these did indeed seem a stumbling-block; it did seem impossible to give any without making their plan more public than they had intended.

They had both—even Mrs. Arbuthnot, lured for once away from perfect candour by the realization of the great saving of trouble and criticism an imperfect explanation would produce—they had both thought it would be a good plan to give out, each to her own circle, their circles being luckily distinct, that each was going to stay with a friend who had a house in Italy. It would be true as far as it went— Mrs. Wilkins asserted that it would be quite true, but Mrs. Arbuthnot thought it wouldn't be quite—and it was the only way, Mrs. Wilkins said, to keep Mellersh even approximately quiet. To spend any of her money just on the mere getting to Italy would cause him indignation; what he would say if he knew she was renting part of a mediaeval castle on her own account Mrs. Wilkins preferred not to think. It would take him days to say it all; and this although it was her very own money, and not a penny of it had ever been his.

"But I expect," she said, "your husband is just the same. I expect all husbands are alike in the long run."

Mrs. Arbuthnot said nothing, because her reason for not wanting Frederick to know was the exactly opposite one—Frederick would by only too pleased for her to go, he would not mind it in the very least; indeed, he would hail such a manifestation of self-indulgence and worldliness with an amusement that would hurt, and urge her to have a good time and not to hurry home with a crushing detachment. Far better, she thought, to be missed by Mellersh than to be sped by Frederick. To be missed, to be needed, from whatever motive, was, she thought, better than the complete loneliness of not being missed or needed at all.

She therefore said nothing, and allowed Mrs. Wilkins to leap at her conclusions unchecked. But they did, both of them, for a whole day feel that the only thing to be done was to renounce the mediaeval castle; and it was in arriving at this bitter decision that they really realized how acute had been their longing for it.

Then Mrs. Arbuthnot, whose mind was trained in the finding of ways out of difficulties, found a way out of the reference difficulty; and simultaneously Mrs. Wilkins had a vision revealing to her how to reduce the rent.

Mrs. Arbuthnot's plan was simple, and completely successful. She took the whole of the rent in person to the owner, drawing it out of her Savings Bank—again she looked furtive and apologetic, as if the clerk must know the money was wanted for purposes of self-indulgence—and, going up with the six ten pound notes in her hand-bag to the address near the Brompton Oratory where the owner lived, presented them to him, waiving her right to pay only half. And when he saw her, and her parted hair and soft dark eyes and sober apparel, and heard her grave voice, he told her not to bother about writing round for those references.

"It'll be all right," he said, scribbling a receipt for the rent. "Do sit down, won't you? Nasty day, isn't it? You'll find the old castle has lots of sunshine, whatever else it hasn't got. Husband going?"

Mrs. Arbuthnot, unused to anything but candour, looked troubled at this question and began to murmur inarticulately, and the owner at once concluded that she was a widow—a war one, of course, for other widows were old—and that he had been a fool not to guess it.

"Oh, I'm sorry," he said, turning red right up to his fair hair.
"I didn't mean—h'm, h'm, h'm—"

He ran his eye over the receipt he had written. "Yes, I think that's all right," he said, getting up and giving it to her. "Now," he added, taking the six notes she held out and smiling, for Mrs. Arbuthnot was agreeable to look at, "I'm richer, and you're happier. I've got money, and you've got San Salvatore. I wonder got which is best."

"I think you know," said Mrs. Arbuthnot with her sweet smile.

He laughed and opened the door for her. It was a pity the interview was over. He would have liked to ask her to lunch with him. She made him think of his mother, of his nurse, of all things kind and comforting, besides having the attraction of not being his mother or his nurse.

"I hope you'll like the old place," he said, holding her hand a minute at the door. The very feel of her hand, even through its glove, was reassuring; it was the sort of hand, he thought, that children would like to hold in the dark. "In April, you know, it's simply a mass of flowers. And then there's the sea. You must wear white. You'll fit in very well. There are several portraits of you there."

"Portraits?"

"Madonnas, you know. There's one on the stairs really exactly like you."

Mrs. Arbuthnot smiled and said good-bye and thanked him. Without the least trouble and at once she had got him placed in his proper category: he was an artist and of an effervescent temperament.

She shook hands and left, and he wished she hadn't. After she was gone he supposed that he ought to have asked for those references, if only because she would think him so unbusiness-like not to, but he could as soon have insisted on references from a saint in a nimbus as from that grave, sweet lady.

Rose Arbuthnot.

Her letter, making the appointment, lay on the table.

Pretty name.

That difficulty, then, was overcome. But there still remained the other one, the really annihilating effect of the expense on the nest-eggs, and especially on Mrs. Wilkins's, which was in size, compared with Mrs. Arbuthnot's, as the egg of the plover to that of the duck; and this in its turn was overcome by the vision vouchsafed to Mrs. Wilkins, revealing to her the steps to be taken for its overcoming. Having got San Salvatore—the beautiful, the religious name, fascinated them—they in their turn would advertise in the Agony Column of The Times, and would inquire after two more ladies, of similar desires to their own, to join them and share the expenses.

At once the strain of the nest-eggs would be reduced from half to a quarter. Mrs. Wilkins was prepared to fling her entire egg into the adventure, but she realized that if it were to cost even sixpence over her ninety pounds her position would be terrible. Imagine going to Mellersh and saying, "I owe." It would be awful enough if some day circumstances forced her to say, "I have no nest-egg," but at least she would be supported in such a case by the knowledge that the egg had been her own. She therefore, though prepared to fling her last penny into the adventure, was not prepared to fling into it a single farthing that was not demonstrably her own; and she felt that if her share of the rent was reduced to fifteen pounds only, she would have a safe margin for the other expenses. Also they might economise very much on food—gather olives off their own trees and eat them, for instance, and perhaps catch fish.

Of course, as they pointed out to each other, they could reduce the rent to an almost negligible sum by increasing the number of sharers; they could have six more ladies instead of two if they wanted to, seeing that there were eight beds. But supposing the eight beds were distributed in couples in four rooms, it would not be altogether what they wanted, to find themselves shut up at night with a stranger. Besides they thought that perhaps having so many would not be quite so peaceful. After all, they were going to San Salvatore for peace and rest and joy, and six more ladies, especially if they got into one's bedroom, might a little interfere with that.

However, there seemed to be only two ladies in England at that moment who had any wish to join them, for they had only two answers to their advertisement.

"Well, we only want two," said Mrs. Wilkins, quickly recovering, for she had imagined a great rush.

"I think a choice would have been a good thing," said Mrs. Arbuthnot.
"You mean because then we needn't have had Lady Caroline Dester."

"I didn't say that," gently protested Mrs. Arbuthnot.

"We needn't have her," said Mrs. Wilkins. "Just one more person would help us a great deal with the rent. We're not obliged to have two."

"But why should we not have her? She seems really quite what we want."

"Yes—she does from her letter," said Mrs. Wilkins doubtfully.

She felt she would be terribly shy of Lady Caroline. Incredible as it may seem, seeing how they get into everything, Mrs. Wilkins had never come across any members of the aristocracy.

They interviewed Lady Caroline, and they interviewed the other applicant, a Mrs. Fisher.

Lady Caroline came to the club in Shaftesbury Avenue, and appeared to be wholly taken up by one great longing, a longing to get away from everybody she had ever known. When she saw the club, and Mrs. Arbuthnot, and Mrs. Wilkins, she was sure that here was exactly what she wanted. She would be in Italy—a place she adored; she would not be in hotels—places she loathed; she would not be staying with friends—persons she disliked; and she would be in the company of strangers who would never mention a single person she knew, for the simple reason that they had not, could not have, and would not come across them. She asked a few questions about the fourth woman, and was satisfied with the answers. Mrs. Fisher, of Prince of Wales Terrace. A widow. She too would be unacquainted with any of her friends. Lady Caroline did not even know where Prince of Wales Terrace was.

"It's in London," said Mrs. Arbuthnot.

"Is it?" said Lady Caroline.

It all seemed most restful.

Mrs. Fisher was unable to come to the club because, she explained by letter, she could not walk without a stick; therefore Mrs. Arbuthnot and Mrs. Wilkins went to her.

"But if she can't come to the club how can she go to Italy?" wondered Mrs. Wilkins, aloud.

"We shall hear that from her own lips," said Mrs. Arbuthnot.

From Mrs. Fisher's lips they merely heard, in reply to delicate questioning, that sitting in trains was not walking about; and they knew that already. Except for the stick, however, she appeared to be a most desirable fourth— quiet, educated, elderly. She was much older than they or Lady Caroline— Lady Caroline had informed them she was twenty-eight—but not so old as to have ceased to be active-minded. She was very respectable indeed, and still wore a complete suit of black though her husband had died, she told them, eleven years before. Her house was full of signed photographs of illustrious Victorian dead, all of whom she said she had known when she was little. Her father had been an eminent critic, and in his house she had seen practically everybody who was anybody in letters and art. Carlyle had scowled at her; Matthew Arnold had held her on his knee; Tennyson had sonorously rallied her on the length of her pig-tail. She animatedly showed them the photographs, hung everywhere on her walls, pointing out the signatures with her stick, and she neither gave any information about her own husband nor asked for any about the husbands of her visitors; which was the greatest comfort. Indeed, she seemed to think that they also were widows, for on inquiring who the fourth lady was to be, and being told it was a Lady Caroline Dester, she said, "Is she a widow too?" And on their explaining that she was not, because she had not yet been married, observed with abstracted amiability, "All in good time."

But Mrs. Fisher's very abstractedness—and she seemed to be absorbed chiefly in the interesting people she used to know and in their memorial photographs, and quite a good part of the interview was taken up by reminiscent anecdote of Carlyle, Meredith, Matthew Arnold, Tennyson, and a host of others—her very abstractedness was a recommendation. She only asked, she said, to be allowed to sit quiet in the sun and remember. That was all Mrs. Arbuthnot and Mrs. Wilkins asked of their sharers. It was their idea of a perfect sharer that she should sit quiet in the sun and remember, rousing herself on Saturday evenings sufficiently to pay her share. Mrs. Fisher was very fond, too, she said, of flowers, and once when she was spending a week-end with her father at Box Hill—

"Who lived at Box Hill?" interrupted Mrs. Wilkins, who hung on Mrs. Fisher's reminiscences, intensely excited by meeting somebody who had actually been familiar with all the really and truly and undoubtedly great— actually seen them, heard them talking, touched them.

Mrs. Fisher looked at her over the top of her glasses in some surprise. Mrs. Wilkins, in her eagerness to tear the heart out quickly of Mrs. Fisher's reminiscences, afraid that at any moment Mrs. Arbuthnot would take her away and she wouldn't have heard half, had already interrupted several times with questions which appeared ignorant to Mrs. Fisher.

"Meredith of course," said Mrs. Fisher rather shortly. "I remember a particular week-end"—she continued. "My father often took me, but I always remember this week-end particularly—"

"Did you know Keats?" eagerly interrupted Mrs. Wilkins.

Mrs. Fisher, after a pause, said with sub-acid reserve that she had been unacquainted with both Keats and Shakespeare.

"Oh of course—how ridiculous of me!" cried Mrs. Wilkins, flushing scarlet. "It's because"—she floundered—"it's because the immortals somehow still seem alive, don't they—as if they were here, going to walk into the room in another minute—and one forgets they are dead. In fact one knows perfectly well that they're not dead—not nearly so dead as you and I even now," she assured Mrs. Fisher, who observed her over the top of her glasses.

"I thought I saw Keats the other day," Mrs. Wilkins incoherently proceeded, driven on by Mrs. Fisher's look over the top of her glasses. "In Hampstead—crossing the road in front of that house—you know—the house where he lived—"

Mrs. Arbuthnot said they must be going.

Mrs. Fisher did nothing to prevent them.

"I really thought I saw him," protested Mrs. Wilkins, appealing for belief first to one and then to the other while waves of colour passed over her face, and totally unable to stop because of Mrs. Fisher's glasses and the steady eyes looking at her over their tops. "I believe I did see him—he was dressed in a—"

Even Mrs. Arbuthnot looked at her now, and in her gentlest voice said they would be late for lunch.

It was at this point that Mrs. Fisher asked for references. She had no wish to find herself shut up for four weeks with somebody who saw things. It is true that there were three sitting-rooms, besides the garden and the battlements at San Salvatore, so that there would be opportunities of withdrawal from Mrs. Wilkins; but it would be disagreeable to Mrs. Fisher, for instance, if Mrs. Wilkins were suddenly to assert that she saw Mr. Fisher. Mr. Fisher was dead; let him remain so. She had no wish to be told he was walking about the garden. The only reference she really wanted, for she was much too old and firmly seated in her place in the world for questionable associates to matter to her, was one with regard to Mrs. Wilkins's health. Was her health quite normal? Was she an ordinary, everyday, sensible woman? Mrs. Fisher felt that if she were given even one address she would be able to find out what she needed. So she asked for references, and her visitors appeared to be so much taken aback—Mrs. Wilkins, indeed, was instantly sobered—that she added, "It is usual."

Mrs. Wilkins found her speech first. "But," she said "aren't we the ones who ought to ask for some from you?"

And this seemed to Mrs. Arbuthnot too the right attitude. Surely it was they who were taking Mrs. Fisher into their party, and not Mrs. Fisher who was taking them into it?

For answer Mrs. Fisher, leaning on her stick, went to the writing-table and in a firm hand wrote down three names and offered them to Mrs. Wilkins, and the names were so respectable, more, they were so momentous, they were so nearly august, that just to read them was enough. The President of the Royal Academy, the Archbishop of Canterbury, and the Governor of the Bank of England—who would dare disturb such personages in their meditations with inquires as to whether a female friend of theirs was all she should be?

"They have know me since I was little," said Mrs. Fisher— everybody seemed to have known Mrs. Fisher since or when she was little.

"I don't think references are nice things at all between—between ordinary decent women," burst out Mrs. Wilkins, made courageous by being, as she felt, at bay; for she very well knew that the only reference she could give without getting into trouble was Shoolbred, and she had little confidence in that, as it would be entirely based on Mellersh's fish. "We're not business people. We needn't distrust each other—"

And Mrs. Arbuthnot said, with a dignity that yet was sweet, "I'm afraid references do bring an atmosphere into our holiday plan that isn't quite what we want, and I don't think we'll take yours up or give you any ourselves. So that I suppose you won't wish to join us."

And she held out her hand in good-bye.

Then Mrs. Fisher, her gaze diverted to Mrs. Arbuthnot, who inspired trust and liking even in Tube officials, felt that she would be idiotic to lose the opportunity of being in Italy in the particular conditions offered, and that she and this calm-browed woman between them would certainly be able to curb the other one when she had her attacks. So she said, taking Mrs. Arbuthnot's offered hand, "Very well. I waive references."

She waived references.

The two as they walked to the station in Kensington High Street could not help thinking that this way of putting it was lofty. Even Mrs. Arbuthnot, spendthrift of excuses for lapses, thought Mrs. Fisher might have used other words; and Mrs. Wilkins, by the time she got to the station, and the walk and the struggle on the crowded pavement with other people's umbrellas had warmed her blood, actually suggested waiving Mrs. Fisher.

"If there is any waiving to be done, do let us be the ones who waive," she said eagerly.

But Mrs. Arbuthnot, as usual, held on to Mrs. Wilkins; and presently, having cooled down in the train, Mrs. Wilkins announced that at San Salvatore Mrs. Fisher would find her level. "I see her finding her level there," she said, her eyes very bright.

Whereupon Mrs. Arbuthnot, sitting with her quiet hands folded, turned over in her mind how best she could help Mrs. Wilkins not to see quite so much; or at least, if she must see, to see in silence.

Chapter 4

It had been arranged that Mrs. Arbuthnot and Mrs. Wilkins, traveling together, should arrive at San Salvatore on the evening of March 31st—the owner, who told them how to get there, appreciated their disinclination to begin their time in it on April 1st—and Lady Caroline and Mrs. Fisher, as yet unacquainted and therefore under no obligations to bore each other on the journey, for only towards the end would they find out by a process of sifting who they were, were to arrive on the morning of April 2nd. In this way everything would be got nicely ready for the two who seemed, in spite of the equality of the sharing, yet to have something about them of guests.

There were disagreeable incidents towards the end of March, when Mrs. Wilkins, her heart in her mouth and her face a mixture of guilt, terror and determination, told her husband that she had been invited to Italy, and he declined to believe it. Of course he declined to believe it. Nobody had ever invited his wife to Italy before. There was no precedent. He required proofs. The only proof was Mrs. Arbuthnot, and Mrs. Wilkins had produced her; but after what entreaties, what passionate persuading! Mrs. Arbuthnot had not imagined she would have to face Mr. Wilkins and say things to him that were short of the truth, and it brought home to her what she had for some time suspected, that she was slipping more and more away from God.

Indeed, the whole of March was filled with unpleasant, anxious moments. It was an uneasy month. Mrs. Arbuthnot's conscience, made super-sensitive by years of pampering, could not reconcile what she was doing with its own high standard of what was right. It gave her little peace. It nudged her at her prayers. It punctuated her entreaties for divine guidance with disconcerting questions, such as, "Are you not a hypocrite? Do you really mean that? Would you not, frankly, be disappointed if that prayer were granted?"

The prolonged wet, raw weather was on the side too of her conscience, producing far more sickness than usual among the poor. They had bronchitis; they had fevers; there was no end to the distress. And here she was going off, spending precious money on going off, simply and solely to be happy. One woman. One woman being happy, and these piteous multitudes . . .

She was unable to look the vicar in the face. He did not know, nobody knew, what she was going to do, and from the very beginning she was unable to look anybody in the face. She excused herself from making speeches appealing for money. How could she stand up and ask people for money when she herself was spending so much on her own selfish pleasure? Nor did it help her or quiet her that, having actually told Frederick, in her desire to make up for what she was squandering, that she would be grateful if he would let her have some money, he instantly gave her a cheque for £100. He asked no questions. She was scarlet. He looked at her a moment and then looked away. It was a relief to Frederick that she should take some money. She gave it all immediately to the organization she worked with, and found herself more tangled in doubts than ever.

Mrs. Wilkins, on the contrary, had no doubts. She was quite certain that it was a most proper thing to have a holiday, and altogether right and beautiful to spend one's own hard-collected savings on being happy.

"Think how much nicer we shall be when we come back," she said to Mrs. Arbuthnot, encouraging that pale lady.
No, Mrs. Wilkins had no doubts, but she had fears; and March was for her too an anxious month, with the unconscious Mr. Wilkins coming back daily to his dinner and eating his fish in the silence of imagined security.

Also things happened so awkwardly. It really is astonishing, how awkwardly they happen. Mrs. Wilkins, who was very careful all this month to give Mellersh only the food he liked, buying it and hovering over its cooking with a zeal more than common, succeeded so well the Mellersh was pleased; definitely pleased; so much pleased that he began to think that he might, after all, have married the right wife instead of, as he had frequently suspected, the wrong one. The result was that on the third Sunday in the month—Mrs. Wilkins had made up her trembling mind that on the fourth Sunday, there being five in that March and it being on the fifth of them that she and Mrs. Arbuthnot were to start, she would tell Mellersh of her invitation—on the third Sunday, then, after a very well-cooked lunch in which the Yorkshire pudding had melted in his mouth and the apricot tart had been so perfect that he ate it all, Mellersh, smoking his cigar by the brightly burning fire the while hail gusts banged on the window, said "I am thinking of taking you to Italy for Easter." And paused for her astounded and grateful ecstasy.

None came. The silence in the room, except for the hail hitting the windows and the gay roar of the fire, was complete. Mrs. Wilkins could not speak. She was dumbfounded. The next Sunday was the day she had meant to break her news to him, and she had not yet even prepared the form of words in which she would break it.

Mr. Wilkins, who had not been abroad since before the war, and was noticing with increasing disgust, as week followed week of wind and rain, the peculiar persistent vileness of the weather, and slowly conceived a desire to get away from England for Easter. He was doing very well in his business. He could afford a trip. Switzerland was useless in April. There was a familiar sound about Easter in Italy. To Italy he would go; and as it would cause comment if he did not take his wife, take her he must— besides, she would be useful; a second person was always useful in a country whose language one did not speak for holding things, for waiting with the luggage.

He had expected an explosion of gratitude and excitement. The absence of it was incredible. She could not, he concluded, have heard. Probably she was absorbed in some foolish day-dream. It was regrettable how childish she remained.

He turned his head—their chairs were in front of the fire—and looked at her. She was staring straight into the fire, and it was no doubt the fire that made her face so red.

"I am thinking," he repeated, raising his clear, cultivated voice and speaking with acerbity, for inattention at such a moment was deplorable, "of taking you to Italy for Easter. Did you not hear me?"

Yes, she had heard him, and she had been wondering at the extraordinary coincidence—really most extraordinary—she was just going to tell him how—how she had been invited—a friend had invited her—Easter, too— Easter was in April, wasn't it?—-her friend had a— had a house there.

In fact Mrs. Wilkins, driven by terror, guilt and surprise, had been more incoherent if possible than usual.

It was a dreadful afternoon. Mellersh, profoundly indignant, besides having his intended treat coming back on him like a blessing to roost, cross-examined her with the utmost severity. He demanded that she refuse the invitation. He demanded that, since she had so outrageously accepted it without consulting him, she should write and cancel her acceptance. Finding himself up against an unsuspected, shocking rock of obstinacy in her, he then declined to believe she had been invited to Italy at all. He declined to believe in this Mrs. Arbuthnot, of whom till that moment he had never heard; and it was only when the gentle creature was brought round—with such difficulty, with such a desire on her part to throw the whole thing up rather than tell Mr. Wilkins less than the truth—and herself endorsed his wife's statements that he was able to give them credence. He could not but believe Mrs. Arbuthnot. She produced the precise effect on him that she did on Tube officials. She hardly needed to say anything. But that made no difference to her conscience, which knew and would not let her forget that she had given him an incomplete impression. "Do you," asked her conscience, "see any real difference between an incomplete impression and a completely stated lie? God sees none."

The remainder of March was a confused bad dream. Both Mrs. Arbuthnot and Mrs. Wilkins were shattered; try as they would not to, both felt extraordinarily guilty; and when on the morning of the 30th they did finally get off there was no exhilaration about the departure, no holiday feeling at all.

"We've been too good—much too good," Mrs. Wilkins kept on murmuring as they walked up and down the platform at Victoria, having arrived there an hour before they need have, "and that's why we feel as though we're doing wrong. We're brow-beaten—we're not any longer real human beings. Real human beings aren't ever as good as we've been. Oh"—she clenched her thin hands—"to think that we ought to be so happy now, here on the very station, actually starting, and we're not, and it's being spoilt for us just simply because we've spoilt them! What have we done—what have we done, I should like to know," she inquired of Mrs. Arbuthnot indignantly, "except for once want to go away by ourselves and have a little rest from them?"

Mrs. Arbuthnot, patiently pacing, did not ask who she meant by them, because she knew. Mrs. Wilkins meant their husbands, persisting in her assumption that Frederick was as indignant as Mellersh over the departure of his wife, whereas Frederick did not even know his wife had gone.

Mrs. Arbuthnot, always silent about him, had said nothing of this to Mrs. Wilkins. Frederick went too deep into her heart for her to talk about him. He was having an extra bout of work finishing another of those dreadful books, and had been away practically continually the last few weeks, and was away when she left. Why should she tell him beforehand? Sure as she so miserably was that he would have no objection to anything she did, she merely wrote him a note and put it on the hall-table ready for him if and when he should come home. She said she was going for a month's holiday as she needed a rest and she had not had one for so long, and that Gladys, the efficient parlourmaid, had orders to see to his comforts. She did not say where she was going; there was no reason why she should; he would not be interested, he would not care.

The day was wretched, blustering and wet; the crossing was atrocious, and they were very sick. But after having been very sick, just to arrive at Calais and not be sick was happiness, and it was there that the real splendour of what they were doing first began to warm their benumbed spirits. It got hold of Mrs. Wilkins first, and spread from her like a rose-coloured flame over her pale companion. Mellersh at Calais, where they restored themselves with soles because of Mrs. Wilkins's desire to eat a sole Mellersh wasn't having—Mellersh at Calais had already begun to dwindle and seem less important. None of the French porters knew him; not a single official at Calais cared a fig for Mellersh. In Paris there was no time to think of him because their train was late and they only just caught the Turin train at the Gare de Lyons; and by the afternoon of the next day when they got into Italy, England, Frederick, Mellersh, the vicar, the poor, Hampstead, the club, Shoolbred, everybody and everything, the whole inflamed sore dreariness, had faded to the dimness of a dream.

Chapter 5

It was cloudy in Italy, which surprised them. They had expected brilliant
sunshine. But never mind: it was Italy, and the very clouds looked fat.
Neither of them had ever been there before. Both gazed out of the windows
with rapt faces. The hours flew as long as it was daylight, and after that
there was the excitement of getting nearer, getting quite near, getting there.
At Genoa it had begun to rain— Genoa! Imagine actually being at Genoa,
seeing its name written up in the station just like any other name—at Nervi
it was pouring, and when at last towards midnight, for again the train was
late, they got to Mezzago, the rain was coming down in what seemed solid
sheets. But it was Italy. Nothing it did could be bad. The very rain was
different— straight rain, falling properly on to one's umbrella; not that
violently blowing English stuff that got in everywhere. And it did leave
off; and when it did, behold the earth would be strewn with roses.

Mr. Briggs, San Salvatore's owner, had said, "You get out at Mezzago, and
then you drive." But he had forgotten what he amply knew, that trains in
Italy are sometimes late, and he had imagined his tenants arriving at
Mezzago at eight o'clock and finding a string of flys to choose from.

The train was four hours late, and when Mrs. Arbuthnot and Mrs. Wilkins
scrambled down the ladder-like high steps of their carriage into the black
downpour, their skirts sweeping off great pools of sooty wet because their
hands were full of suit-cases, if it had not been for the vigilance of
Domenico, the gardener at San Salvatore, they would have found nothing
for them to drive in. All ordinary flys had long since gone home.
Domenico, foreseeing this, had sent his aunt's fly, driven by her son his
cousin; and his aunt and her fly lived in Castagneto, the village crouching
at the feet of San Salvatore, and therefore, however late the train was, the
fly would not dare come home without containing that which it had been
sent to fetch.

Domenico's cousin's name was Beppo, and he presently emerged out of the
dark where Mrs. Arbuthnot and Mrs. Wilkins stood, uncertain what to do
next after the train had gone on, for they could see no porter and they
thought from the feel of it that they were standing not so much on a
platform as in the middle of the permanent way.

Beppo, who had been searching for them, emerged from the dark with a
kind of pounce and talked Italian to them vociferously. Beppo was a most
respectable young man, but he did not look as if he were, especially not in
the dark, and he had a dripping hat slouched over one eye. They did not

like the way he seized their suit-cases. He could not be, they thought, a porter. However, they presently from out of his streaming talk discerned the words San Salvatore, and after that they kept on saying them to him, for it was the only Italian they knew, as they hurried after him, unwilling to lose sight of their suit-cases, stumbling across rails and through puddles out to where in the road a small, high fly stood.

Its hood was up, and its horse was in an attitude of thought. They climbed in, and the minute they were in—Mrs. Wilkins, indeed, could hardly be called in—the horse awoke with a start from its reverie and immediately began going home rapidly; without Beppo; without the suit-cases.

Beppo darted after him, making the night ring with his shouts, and caught the hanging reins just in time. He explained proudly, and as it seemed to him with perfect clearness, that the horse always did that, being a fine animal full of corn and blood, and cared for by him, Beppo, as if he were his own son, and the ladies must be alarmed—he had noticed they were clutching each other; but clear, and loud, and profuse of words though he was, they only looked at him blankly.

He went on talking, however, while he piled the suit-cases up round them, sure that sooner or later they must understand him, especially as he was careful to talk very loud and illustrate everything he said with the simplest elucidatory gestures, but they both continued only to look at him. They both, he noticed sympathetically, had white faces, fatigued faces, and they both had big eyes, fatigued eyes. They were beautiful ladies, he thought, and their eyes, looking at him over the tops of the suit-cases watching his every movement—there were no trunks, only numbers of suit-cases—were like the eyes of the Mother of God. The only thing the ladies said, and they repeated it at regular intervals, even after they had started, gently prodding him as he sat on his box to call his attention to it, was, "San Salvatore?"

And each time he answered vociferously, encouragingly, "Si, si— San Salvatore."
"We don't know of course if he's taking us there," said Mrs. Arbuthnot at last in a low voice, after they had been driving as it seemed to them a long while, and had got off the paving-stones of the sleep-shrouded town and were out on a winding road with what they could just see was a low wall on their left beyond which was a great black emptiness and the sound of the sea. On their right was something close and steep and high and black— rocks, they whispered to each other; huge rocks.

They felt very uncomfortable. It was so late. It was so dark.

The road was so lonely. Suppose a wheel came off. Suppose they met Fascisti, or the opposite of Fascisti. How sorry they were now that they had not slept at Genoa and come on the next morning in daylight. "But that would have been the first of April," said Mrs. Wilkins, in a low voice.

"It is that now," said Mrs. Arbuthnot beneath her breath.

"So it is," murmured Mrs. Wilkins.

They were silent.

Beppo turned round on his box—a disquieting habit already noticed, for surely his horse ought to be carefully watched—and again addressed them with what he was convinced was lucidity—no patois, and the clearest explanatory movements.

How much they wished their mothers had made them learn Italian when they were little. If only now they could have said, "Please sit round the right way and look after the horse." They did not even know what horse was in Italian. It was contemptible to be so ignorant.

In their anxiety, for the road twisted round great jutting rocks, and on their left was only the low wall to keep them out of the sea should anything happen, they too began to gesticulate, waving their hands at Beppo, pointing ahead. They wanted him to turn round again and face his horse, that was all. He thought they wanted him to drive faster; and there followed a terrifying ten minutes during which, as he supposed, he was gratifying them. He was proud of his horse, and it could go very fast. He rose in his seat, the whip cracked, the horse rushed forward, the rocks leaped towards them, the little fly swayed, the suit-cases heaved, Mrs. Arbuthnot and Mrs. Wilkins clung. In this way they continued, swaying, heaving, clattering, clinging, till at a point near Castagneto there was a rise in the road, and on reaching the foot of the rise the horse, who knew every inch of the way, stopped suddenly, throwing everything in the fly into a heap, and then proceeded up at the slowest of walks.

Beppo twisted himself round to receive their admiration, laughing with pride in his horse.

There was no answering laugh from the beautiful ladies. Their eyes, fixed on him, seemed bigger than ever, and their faces against the black of the night showed milky.

But here at least, once they were up the slope, were houses. The rocks left off, and there were houses; the low wall left off, and there were houses; the sea shrunk away, and the sound of it ceased, and the loneliness of the road was finished. No lights anywhere, of course, nobody to see them pass; and yet Beppo, when the houses began, after looking over his shoulder and shouting "Castagneto" at the ladies, once more stood up and cracked his whip and once more made his horse dash forward.

"We shall be there in a minute," Mrs. Arbuthnot said to herself, holding on.

"We shall soon stop now," Mrs. Wilkins said to herself, holding on. They said nothing aloud, because nothing would have been heard above the whip-cracking and the wheel-clattering and the boisterous inciting noises Beppo was making at his horse.

Anxiously they strained their eyes for any sight of the beginning of San Salvatore.

They had supposed and hoped that after a reasonable amount of village a mediaeval archway would loom upon them, and through it they would drive into a garden and draw up at an open, welcoming door, with light streaming from it and those servants standing in it who, according to the advertisement, remained.

Instead the fly suddenly stopped.

Peering out they could see they were still in the village street, with small dark houses each side; and Beppo, throwing the reins over the horse's back as if completely confident this time that he would not go any farther, got down off his box. At the same moment, springing as it seemed out of nothing, a man and several half-grown boys appeared on each side of the fly and began dragging out the suit-cases.

"No, no—San Salvatore, San Salvatore"—exclaimed Mrs. Wilkins, trying to hold on to what suit-cases she could.

"Si, si—San Salvatore," they all shouted, pulling.

"This can't be San Salvatore," said Mrs. Wilkins, turning to Mrs. Arbuthnot, who sat quite still watching her suit-cases being taken from her with the same patience she applied to lesser evils. She knew she could do nothing if these men were wicked men determined to have her suit-cases.

"I don't think it can be," she admitted, and could not refrain from a moment's wonder at the ways of God. Had she really been brought here, she and poor Mrs. Wilkins, after so much trouble in arranging it, so much difficulty and worry, along such devious paths of prevarication and deceit, only to be—

She checked her thoughts, and gently said to Mrs. Wilkins, while the ragged youths disappeared with the suit-cases into the night and the man with the lantern helped Beppo pull the rug off her, that they were both in God's hands; and for the first time on hearing this, Mrs. Wilkins was afraid.

There was nothing for it but to get out. Useless to try to go on sitting in the fly repeating San Salvatore. Every time they said it, and their voices each time were fainter, Beppo and the other man merely echoed it in a series of loud shouts. If only they had learned Italian when they were little. If only they could have said, "We wish to be driven to the door." But they did not even know what door was in Italian. Such ignorance was not only contemptible, it was, they now saw, definitely dangerous. Useless, however, to lament it now. Useless to put off whatever it was that was going to happen to them by trying to go on sitting in the fly. They therefore got out.

The two men opened their umbrellas for them and handed them to them. From this they received a faint encouragement, because they could not believe that if these men were wicked they would pause to open umbrellas. The man with the lantern then made signs to them to follow him, talking loud and quickly, and Beppo, they noticed, remained behind. Ought they to pay him? Not, they thought, if they were going to be robbed and perhaps murdered. Surely on such an occasion one did not pay. Besides, he had not after all brought them to San Salvatore. Where they had got to was evidently somewhere else. Also, he did not show the least wish to be paid; he let them go away into the night with no clamour at all. This, they could not help thinking, was a bad sign. He asked for nothing because presently he was to get so much.

They came to some steps. The road ended abruptly in a church and some descending steps. The man held the lantern low for them to see the steps.

"San Salvatore?" said Mrs. Wilkins once again, very faintly, before committing herself to the steps. It was useless to mention it now, of course, but she could not go down steps in complete silence. No mediaeval castle, she was sure, was ever built at the bottom of steps.

Again, however, came the echoing shout—"Si, si—San Salvatore."

They descended gingerly, holding up their skirts just as if they would be wanting them another time and had not in all probability finished with skirts for ever.

The steps ended in a steeply sloping path with flat stone slabs down the middle. They slipped a good deal on these wet slabs, and the man with the lantern, talking loud and quickly, held them up. His way of holding them up was polite.

"Perhaps," said Mrs. Wilkins in a low voice to Mrs. Arbuthnot,
"It is all right after all."
"We're in God's hands," said Mrs. Arbuthnot again; and again Mrs. Wilkins was afraid.
They reached the bottom of the sloping path, and the light of the lantern flickered over an open space with houses round three sides. The sea was the fourth side, lazily washing backwards and forwards on pebbles.

"San Salvatore," said the man pointing with his lantern to a black mass curved round the water like an arm flung about it.

They strained their eyes. They saw the black mass, and on the top of it a light.

"San Salvatore?" they both repeated incredulously, for where were the suitcases, and why had they been forced to get out of the fly?

"Si, si—San Salvatore."

They went along what seemed to be a quay, right on the edge of the water. There was not even a low wall here—nothing to prevent the man with the lantern tipping them in if he wanted to. He did not, however, tip them in. Perhaps it was all right after all, Mrs. Wilkins again suggested to Mrs. Arbuthnot on noticing this, who this time was herself beginning to think that it might be, and said no more about God's hands.

The flicker of the lantern danced along, reflected in the wet pavement of the quay. Out to the left, in the darkness and evidently at the end of a jetty, was a red light. They came to an archway with a heavy iron gate. The man with the lantern pushed the gate open. This time they went up steps instead of down, and at the top of them was a little path that wound upwards among flowers. They could not see the flowers, but the whole place was evidently full of them.

It here dawned on Mrs. Wilkins that perhaps the reason why the fly had not driven them up to the door was that there was no road, only a footpath. That also would explain the disappearance of the suit-cases. She began to feel confident that they would find their suit-cases waiting for them when they got up to the top. San Salvatore was, it seemed, on the top of a hill, as a mediaeval castle should be. At a turn of the path they saw above them, much nearer now and shining more brightly, the light they had seen from the quay. She told Mrs. Arbuthnot of her dawning belief, and Mrs. Arbuthnot agreed that it was very likely a true one.

Once more, but this time in a tone of real hopefulness, Mrs. Wilkins said, pointing upwards at the black outline against the only slightly less black sky, "San Salvatore?" And once more, but this time comfortingly, encouragingly, came back the assurance, "Si, si—San Salvatore."

They crossed a little bridge, over what was apparently a ravine, and then came a flat bit with long grass at the sides and more flowers. They felt the grass flicking wet against their stockings, and the invisible flowers were everywhere. Then up again through trees, along a zigzag path with the smell all the way of the flowers they could not see. The warm rain was bringing out all the sweetness. Higher and higher they went in this sweet darkness, and the red light on the jetty dropped farther and farther below them.

The path wound round to the other side of what appeared to be a little peninsula; the jetty and the red light disappeared; across the emptiness on their left were distant lights.

"Mezzago," said the man, waving his lantern at the lights.

"Si, si," they answered, for they had by now learned si, si. Upon which the man congratulated them in a great flow of polite words, not one of which they understood, on their magnificent Italian; for this was Domenico, the vigilant and accomplished gardener of San Salvatore, the prop and stay of the establishment, the resourceful, the gifted, the eloquent, the courteous, the intelligent Domenico. Only they did not know that yet; and he did in the dark, and even sometimes in the light, look, with his knife-sharp swarthy features and swift, panther movements, very like somebody wicked.

They passed along another flat bit of path, with a black shape like a high wall towering above them on their right, and then the path went up again under trellises, and trailing sprays of scented things caught at them and shook raindrops on them, and the light of the lantern flickered over lilies, and then came a flight of ancient steps worn with centuries, and then another iron gate, and then they were inside, though still climbing a twisting flight of stone steps with old walls on either side like the walls of dungeons, and with a vaulted roof.

At the top was a wrought-iron door, and through it shone a flood of electric light.

"Ecco," said Domenico, lithely running up the last few steps ahead and pushing the door open.

And there they were, arrived; and it was San Salvatore; and their suit-cases were waiting for them; and they had not been murdered.

They looked at each other's white faces and blinking eyes very solemnly.

It was a great, a wonderful moment. Here they were, in their mediaeval castle at last. Their feet touched its stones.

Mrs. Wilkins put her arm round Mrs. Arbuthnot's neck and kissed her.

"The first thing to happen in this house," she said softly, solemnly, "shall be a kiss."

"Dear Lotty," said Mrs. Arbuthnot.

"Dear Rose," said Mrs. Wilkins, her eyes brimming with gladness.

Domenico was delighted. He liked to see beautiful ladies kiss. He made them a most appreciative speech of welcome, and they stood arm in arm, holding each other up, for they were very tired, blinking smilingly at him, and not understanding a word.

Chapter 6

When Mrs. Wilkins woke next morning she lay in bed a few minutes before getting up and opening the shutters. What would she see out of her window? A shining world, or a world of rain? But it would be beautiful; whatever it was would be beautiful.

She was in a little bedroom with bare white walls and a stone floor and sparse old furniture. The beds—there were two—were made of iron, enameled black and painted with bunches of gay flowers. She lay putting off the great moment of going to the window as one puts off opening a precious letter, gloating over it. She had no idea what time it was; she had forgotten to wind up her watch ever since, centuries ago, she last went to bed in Hampstead. No sounds were to be heard in the house, so she supposed it was very early, yet she felt as if she had slept a long while—so completely rested, so perfectly content. She lay with her arms clasped round her head thinking how happy she was, her lips curved upwards in a delighted smile. In bed by herself: adorable condition. She had not been in a bed without Mellersh once now for five whole years; and the cool roominess of it, the freedom of one's movements, the sense of recklessness, of audacity, in giving the blankets a pull if one wanted to, or twitching the pillows more comfortably! It was like the discovery of an entirely new joy.

Mrs. Wilkins longed to get up and open the shutters, but where she was was really so very delicious. She gave a sigh of contentment, and went on lying there looking round her, taking in everything in her room, her own little room, her very own to arrange just as she pleased for this one blessed month, her room bought with her own savings, the fruit of her careful denials, whose door she could bolt if she wanted to, and nobody had the right to come in. It was such a strange little room, so different from any she had known, and so sweet. It was like a cell. Except for the two beds, it suggested a happy austerity. "And the name of the chamber," she thought, quoting and smiling round at it, "was Peace."

Well, this was delicious, to lie there thinking how happy she was, but outside those shutters it was more delicious still. She jumped up, pulled on her slippers, for there was nothing on the stone floor but one small rug, ran to the window and threw open the shutters.

"Oh!" cried Mrs. Wilkins.

All the radiance of April in Italy lay gathered together at her feet. The sun poured in on her. The sea lay asleep in it, hardly stirring. Across the bay the lovely mountains, exquisitely different in colour, were asleep too in the light; and underneath her window, at the bottom of the flower-starred grass slope from which the wall of the castle rose up, was a great cypress, cutting through the delicate blues and violets and rose-colours of the mountains and the sea like a great black sword.

She stared. Such beauty; and she there to see it. Such beauty; and she alive to feel it. Her face was bathed in light. Lovely scents came up to the window and caressed her. A tiny breeze gently lifted her hair. Far out in the bay a cluster of almost motionless fishing boats hovered like a flock of white birds on the tranquil sea. How beautiful, how beautiful. Not to have died before this . . . to have been allowed to see, breathe, feel this. . . . She stared, her lips parted. Happy? Poor, ordinary, everyday word. But what could one say, how could one describe it? It was as though she could hardly stay inside herself, it was as though she were too small to hold so much of joy, it was as though she were washed through with light. And how astonishing to feel this sheer bliss, for here she was, not doing and not going to do a single unselfish thing, not going to do a thing she didn't want to do. According to everybody she had ever come across she ought at least to have twinges. She had not one twinge. Something was wrong somewhere. Wonderful that at home she should have been so good, so terribly good, and merely felt tormented. Twinges of every sort had there been her portion; aches, hurts, discouragements, and she the whole time being steadily unselfish. Now she had taken off all her goodness and left it behind her like a heap in rain-sodden clothes, and she only felt joy. She was naked of goodness, and was rejoicing in being naked. She was stripped, and exulting. And there, away in the dim mugginess of Hampstead, was Mellersh being angry.

She tried to visualize Mellersh, she tried to see him having breakfast and thinking bitter things about her; and lo, Mellersh himself began to shimmer, became rose-colour, became delicate violet, became an enchanting blue, became formless, became iridescent. Actually Mellersh, after quivering a minute, was lost in light.

"Well," thought Mrs. Wilkins, staring, as it were, after him. How extraordinary not to be able to visualize Mellersh; and she who used to know every feature, every expression of his by heart. She simply could not see him as he was. She could only see him resolved into beauty, melted into harmony with everything else. The familiar words of the General Thanksgiving came quite naturally into her mind, and she found herself blessing God for her creation, preservation, and all the blessings of this life, but above all for His inestimable Love; out loud; in a burst of acknowledgment. While Mellersh, at that moment angrily pulling on his boots before going out into the dripping streets, was indeed thinking bitter things about her.

She began to dress, choosing clean white clothes in honour of the summer's day, unpacking her suit-cases, tidying her adorable little room. She moved about with quick, purposeful steps, her long thin body held up straight, her small face, so much puckered at home with effort and fear, smoothed out. All she had been and done before this morning, all she had felt and worried about, was gone. Each of her worries behaved as the image of Mellersh had behaved, and dissolved into colour and light. And she noticed things she had not noticed for years—when she was doing her hair in front of the glass she noticed it, and thought, "Why, what pretty stuff." For years she had forgotten she had such a thing as hair, plaiting it in the evening and unplaiting it in the morning with the same hurry and indifference with which she laced and unlaced her shoes. Now she suddenly saw it, and she twisted it round her fingers before the glass, and was glad it was so pretty. Mellersh couldn't have seen it either, for he had never said a word about it. Well, when she got home she would draw his attention to it. "Mellersh," she would say, "look at my hair. Aren't you pleased you've got a wife with hair like curly honey?"

She laughed. She had never said anything like that to Mellersh yet, and the idea of it amused her. But why had she not? Oh yes—she used to be afraid of him. Funny to be afraid of anybody; and especially of one's husband, whom one saw in his more simplified moments, such as asleep, and not breathing properly through his nose.

When she was ready she opened her door to go across to see if Rose, who had been put the night before by a sleepy maidservant into a cell opposite, were awake. She would say good-morning to her, and then she would run down and stay with that cypress tree till breakfast was ready, and after breakfast she wouldn't so much as look out of a window till she had helped Rose get everything ready for Lady Caroline and Mrs. Fisher. There was much to be done that day, settling in, arranging the rooms; she mustn't leave Rose to do it alone. They would make it all so lovely for the two to come, have such an entrancing vision ready for them of little cells bright with flowers. She remembered she had wanted Lady Caroline not to come; fancy wanting to shut some one out of heaven because she thought she would be shy of her! And as though it mattered if she were, and as though she would be anything so self-conscious as shy. Besides, what a reason. She could not accuse herself of goodness over that. And she remembered she had wanted not to have Mrs. Fisher either, because she had seemed lofty. How funny of her. So funny to worry about such little things, making them important.

The bedrooms and two of the sitting-rooms at San Salvatore were on the top floor, and opened into a roomy hall with a wide glass window at the north end. San Salvatore was rich in small gardens in different parts and on different levels. The garden this window looked down on was made on the highest part of the walls, and could only be reached through the corresponding spacious hall on the floor below. When Mrs. Wilkins came out of her room this window stood wide open, and beyond it in the sun was a Judas tree in full flower. There was no sign of anybody, no sound of voices or feet. Tubs of arum lilies stood about on the stone floor, and on a table flamed a huge bunch of fierce nasturtiums. Spacious, flowery, silent, with the wide window at the end opening into the garden, and the Judas tree absurdly beautiful in the sunshine, it seemed to Mrs. Wilkins, arrested on her way across to Mrs. Arbuthnot, too good to be true. Was she really going to live in this for a whole month? Up to now she had had to take what beauty she could as she went along, snatching at little bits of it when she came across it—a patch of daisies on a fine day in a Hampstead field, a flash of sunset between two chimney pots. She had never been in definitely, completely beautiful places. She had never been even in a venerable house; and such a thing as a profusion of flowers in her rooms was unattainable to her. Sometimes in the spring she had bought six tulips at Shoolbred's, unable to resist them, conscious that Mellersh if he knew what they had cost would think it inexcusable; but they had soon died, and then there were no more. As for the Judas tree, she hadn't an idea what it was, and gazed at it out there against the sky with the rapt expression of one who sees a heavenly vision.

Mrs. Arbuthnot, coming out of her room, found her there like that, standing in the middle of the hall staring.

"Now what does she think she sees now?" thought Mrs. Arbuthnot.

"We are in God's hands," said Mrs. Wilkins, turning to her, speaking with extreme conviction.

"Oh!" said Mrs. Arbuthnot quickly, her face, which had been covered with smiles when she came out of her room, falling. "Why, what has happened?"

For Mrs. Arbuthnot had woken up with such a delightful feeling of security, of relief, and she did not want to find she had not after all escaped from the need of refuge. She had not even dreamed of Frederick. For the first time in years she had been spared the nightly dream that he was with her, that they were heart to heart, and its miserable awakening. She had slept like a baby, and had woken up confident; she had found there was nothing she wished to say in her morning prayer, except Thank you. It was disconcerting to be told she was after all in God's hands.

"I hope nothing has happened?" she asked anxiously.

Mrs. Wilkins looked at her a moment, and laughed. "How funny," she said, kissing her.

"What is funny?" asked Mrs. Arbuthnot, her face clearing because Mrs. Wilkins laughed.
"We are. This is. Everything. It's all so wonderful. It's so funny and so adorable that we should be in it. I daresay when we finally reach heaven— the one they talk about so much—we shan't find it a bit more beautiful."

Mrs. Arbuthnot relaxed to smiling security again. "Isn't it divine?" she said.

"Were you ever, ever in your life so happy?" asked Mrs. Wilkins, catching her by the arm.

"No," said Mrs. Arbuthnot. Nor had she been; not ever; not even in her first love-days with Frederick. Because always pain had been close at hand in that other happiness, ready to torture with doubts, to torture even with the very excess of her love; while this was the simple happiness of complete harmony with her surroundings, the happiness that asks for nothing, that just accepts, just breathes, just is.

"Let's go and look at that tree close," said Mrs. Wilkins. "I don't believe it can only be a tree."

And arm in arm they went along the hall, and their husbands would not have known them their faces were so young with eagerness, and together they stood at the open window, and when their eyes, having feasted on the marvelous pink thing, wandered farther among the beauties of the garden, they saw sitting on the low wall at the east edge of it, gazing out over the bay, her feet in lilies, Lady Caroline.

They were astonished. They said nothing in their astonishment, but stood quite still, arm in arm, staring down at her.

She too had on a white frock, and her head was bare. They had had no idea that day in London, when her hat was down to her nose and her furs were up to her ears, that she was so pretty. They had merely thought her different from the other women in the club, and so had the other women themselves, and so had all the waitresses, eyeing her sideways and eyeing her again as they passed the corner where she sat talking; but they had had no idea she was so pretty. She was exceedingly pretty. Everything about her was very much that which it was. Her fair hair was very fair, her lovely grey eyes were very lovely and grey, her dark eyelashes were very dark, her white skin was very white, her red mouth was very red. She was extravagantly slender— the merest thread of a girl, though not without little curves beneath her thin frock where little curves should be. She was looking out across the bay, and was sharply defined against the background of empty blue. She was full in the sun. Her feet dangled among the leaves and flowers of the lilies just as if it did not matter that they should be bent or bruised.

"She ought to have a headache," whispered Mrs. Arbuthnot at last, "sitting there in the sun like that."

"She ought to have a hat," whispered Mrs. Wilkins.

"She is treading on lilies."

"But they're hers as much as ours."

"Only one-fourth of them."

Lady Caroline turned her head. She looked up at them a moment, surprised to see them so much younger than they had seemed that day at the club, and so much less unattractive. Indeed, they were really almost quite attractive, if any one could ever be really quite attractive in the wrong clothes. Her eyes, swiftly glancing over them, took in every inch of each of them in the half second before she smiled and waved her hand and called out Good-morning. There was nothing, she saw at once to be hoped for in the way of interest from their clothes. She did not consciously think this, for she was having a violent reaction against beautiful clothes and the slavery they impose on one, her experience being that the instant one had got them they took one in hand and gave one no peace till they had been everywhere and been seen by everybody. You didn't take your clothes to parties; they took you. It was quite a mistake to think that a woman, a really well-dressed woman, wore out her clothes; it was the clothes that wore out the woman—dragging her about at all hours of the day and night.

No wonder men stayed younger longer. Just new trousers couldn't excite them. She couldn't suppose that even the newest trousers ever behaved like that, taking the bit between their teeth. Her images were disorderly, but she thought as she chose, she used what images she like. As she got off the wall and came towards the window, it seemed a restful thing to know she was going to spend an entire month with people in dresses made as she dimly remembered dresses used to be made five summers ago.

"I got here yesterday morning," she said, looking up at them and smiling. She really was bewitching. She had everything, even a dimple.

"It's a great pity," said Mrs. Arbuthnot, smiling back, "because we were going to choose the nicest room for you."

"Oh, but I've done that," said Lady Caroline. "At least, I think it's the nicest. It looks two ways—I adore a room that looks two ways, don't you? Over the sea to the west, and over this Judas tree to the north."

"And we had meant to make it pretty for you with flowers," said Mrs. Wilkins.
"Oh, Domenico did that. I told him to directly I got here. He's the gardener. He's wonderful."

"It's a good thing, of course," said Mrs. Arbuthnot a little hesitatingly, "to be independent, and to know exactly what one wants."

"Yes, it saves trouble," agreed Lady Caroline.

"But one shouldn't be so independent," said Mrs. Wilkins, "as to leave no opportunity for other people to exercise their benevolences on one."

Lady Caroline, who had been looking at Mrs. Arbuthnot, now looked at Mrs. Wilkins. That day at the queer club she had had merely a blurred impression of Mrs. Wilkins, for it was the other one who did all the talking, and her impression had been of somebody so shy, so awkward that it was best to take no notice of her. She had not even been able to say good-bye properly, doing it in an agony, turning red, turning damp. Therefore she now looked at her in some surprise; and she was still more surprised when Mrs. Wilkins added, gazing at her with the most obvious sincere admiration, speaking indeed with a conviction that refused to remain unuttered, "I didn't realize you were so pretty."

She stared at Mrs. Wilkins. She was not usually told this quite so immediately and roundly. Abundantly as she was used to it— impossible not to be after twenty-eight solid years—it surprised her to be told it with such bluntness, and by a woman.

"It's very kind of you to think so," she said.

"Why, you're very lovely," said Mrs. Wilkins. "Quite, quite lovely."

"I hope," said Mrs. Arbuthnot pleasantly, "you make the most of it."

Lady Caroline then stared at Mrs. Arbuthnot. "Oh yes," she said. "I make the most of it. I've been doing that ever since I can remember."

"Because," said Mrs. Arbuthnot, smiling and raising a warning forefinger, "it won't last."

Then Lady Caroline began to be afraid these two were originals. If so, she would be bored. Nothing bored her so much as people who insisted on being original, who came and buttonholed her and kept her waiting while they were being original. And the one who admired her— it would be tiresome if she dogged her about in order to look at her. What she wanted of this holiday was complete escape from all she had had before, she wanted the rest of complete contrast. Being admired, being dogged, wasn't contrast, it was repetition; and as for originals, to find herself shut up with two on the top of a precipitous hill in a medieval castle built for the express purpose of preventing easy goings out and in, would not, she was afraid, be especially restful. Perhaps she had better be a little less encouraging. They had seemed such timid creatures, even the dark one—she couldn't remember their names—that day at the club, that she had felt it quite safe to be very friendly. Here they had come out of their shells; already; indeed, at once. There was no sign of timidity about either of them here. If they had got out of their shells so immediately, at the very first contact, unless she checked them they would soon begin to press upon her, and then good-bye to her dream of thirty restful, silent days, lying unmolested in the sun, getting her feathers smooth again, not being spoken to, not waited on, not grabbed at and monopolized, but just recovering from the fatigue, the deep and melancholy fatigue, of the too much.

Besides, there was Mrs. Fisher. She too must be checked. Lady Caroline had started two days earlier than had been arranged for two reasons: first, because she wished to arrive before the others in order to pick out the room or rooms she preferred, and second, because she judged it likely that otherwise she would have to travel with Mrs. Fisher. She did not want to travel with Mrs. Fisher. She did not want to arrive with Mrs. Fisher. She saw no reason whatever why for a single moment she should have to have anything at all to do with Mrs. Fisher.

But unfortunately Mrs. Fisher also was filled with a desire to get to San Salvatore first and pick out the room or rooms she preferred, and she and Lady Caroline had after all traveled together. As early as Calais they began to suspect it; in Paris they feared it; at Modane they knew it; at Mezzago they concealed it, driving out to Castagneto in two separate flys, the nose of the one almost touching the back of the other the whole way. But when the road suddenly left off at the church and the steps, further evasion was impossible; and faced by this abrupt and difficult finish to their journey there was nothing for it but to amalgamate.

Because of Mrs. Fisher's stick Lady Caroline had to see about everything. Mrs. Fisher's intentions, she explained from her fly when the situation had become plain to her, were active, but her stick prevented their being carried out. The two drivers told Lady Caroline boys would have to carry the luggage up to the castle, and she went in search of some, while Mrs. Fisher waited in the fly because of her stick. Mrs. Fisher could speak Italian, but only, she explained, the Italian of Dante, which Matthew Arnold used to read with her when she was a girl, and she thought this might be above the heads of boys. Therefore Lady Caroline, who spoke ordinary Italian very well, was obviously the one to go and do things.

"I am in your hands," said Mrs. Fisher, sitting firmly in her fly. "You must please regard me as merely an old woman with a stick."

And presently, down the steps and cobbles to the piazza, and along the quay, and up the zigzag path, Lady Caroline found herself as much obliged to walk slowly with Mrs. Fisher as if she were her own grandmother.

"It's my stick," Mrs. Fisher complacently remarked at intervals.

And when they rested at those bends of the zigzag path where seats were, and Lady Caroline, who would have liked to run on and get to the top quickly, was forced in common humanity to remain with Mrs. Fisher because of her stick, Mrs. Fisher told her how she had been on a zigzag path once with Tennyson.

"Isn't his cricket wonderful?" said Lady Caroline absently.

"The Tennyson," said Mrs. Fisher, turning her head and observing her a moment over her spectacles.

"Isn't he?" said Lady Caroline.

"And it was a path, too," Mrs. Fisher went on severely, "curiously like this. No eucalyptus tree, of course, but otherwise curiously like this. And at one of the bends he turned and said to me—I see him now turning and saying to me—"

Yes, Mrs. Fisher would have to be checked. And so would these two up at the window. She had better begin at once. She was sorry she had got off the wall. All she need have done was to have waved her hand, and waited till they came down and out into the garden to her.

So she ignored Mrs. Arbuthnot's remark and raised forefinger, and said with marked coldness—at least, she tried to make it sound marked— that she supposed they would be going to breakfast, and that she had had hers; but it was her fate that however coldly she sent forth her words they came out sounding quite warm and agreeable. That was because she had a sympathetic and delightful voice, due entirely to some special formation of her throat and the roof of her mouth, and having nothing whatever to do with what she was feeling. Nobody in consequence ever believed they were being snubbed. It was most tiresome. And if she stared icily it did not look icy at all, because her eyes, lovely to begin with, had the added loveliness of very long, soft, dark eyelashes. No icy stare could come out of eyes like that; it got caught and lost in the soft eyelashes, and the persons stared at merely thought they were being regarded with a flattering and exquisite attentiveness. And if ever she was out of humour or definitely cross— and who would not be sometimes in such a world?—-she only looked so pathetic that people all rushed to comfort her, if possible by means of kissing. It was more than tiresome, it was maddening. Nature was determined that she should look and sound angelic. She could never be disagreeable or rude without being completely misunderstood.

"I had my breakfast in my room," she said, trying her utmost to sound curt. "Perhaps I'll see you later."

And she nodded, and went back to where she had been sitting on the wall, with the lilies being nice and cool round her feet.

Chapter 7

Their eyes followed her admiringly. They had no idea they had been snubbed. It was a disappointment, of course, to find she had forestalled them and that they were not to have the happiness of preparing for her, of watching her face when she arrived and first saw everything, but there was till Mrs. Fisher. They would concentrate on Mrs. Fisher, and would watch her face instead; only, like everybody else, they would have preferred to watch Lady Caroline's.

Perhaps, then, as Lady Caroline had talked of breakfast, they had better begin by going and having it, for there was too much to be done that day to spend any more time gazing at the scenery—servants to be interviewed, the house to be gone through and examined, and finally Mrs. Fisher's room to be got ready and adorned.

They waved their hands gaily at Lady Caroline, who seemed absorbed in what she saw and took no notice, and turning away found the maidservant of the night before had come up silently behind them in cloth slippers with string soles.

She was Francesca, the elderly parlour-maid, who had been with the owner, he had said, for years, and whose presence made inventories unnecessary; and after wishing them good-morning and hoping they had slept well, she told them breakfast was ready in the dining-room on the floor below, and if they would follow her she would lead.

They did not understand a single word of the very many in which Francesca succeeded in clothing this simple information, but they followed her, for it at least was clear that they were to follow, and going down the stairs, and along the broad hall like the one above except for glass doors at the end instead of a window opening into the garden, they were shown into the dining-room; where, sitting at the head of the table having her breakfast, was Mrs. Fisher.

This time they exclaimed. Even Mrs. Arbuthnot exclaimed, though her exclamation was only "Oh."

Mrs. Wilkins exclaimed at greater length. "Why, but it's like having the bread taken out of one's mouth!" exclaimed Mrs. Wilkins.

"How do you do," said Mrs. Fisher. "I can't get up because of my stick." And she stretched out her hand across the table.

They advanced and shook it.

"We had no idea you were here," said Mrs. Arbuthnot.

"Yes," said Mrs. Fisher, resuming her breakfast. "Yes. I am here." And with composure she removed the top of her egg.

"It's a great disappointment," said Mrs. Wilkins. "We had meant to give you such a welcome."

This was the one, Mrs. Fisher remembered, briefly glancing at her, who when she came to Prince of Wales Terrace said she had seen Keats. She must be careful with this one—curb her from the beginning.

She therefore ignored Mrs. Wilkins and said gravely, with a downward face of impenetrable calm bent on her egg, "Yes. I arrived yesterday with Lady Caroline."

"It's really dreadful," said Mrs. Wilkins, exactly as if she had not been ignored. "There's nobody left to get anything ready for now. I feel thwarted. I feel as if the bread had been taken out of my mouth just when I was going to be happy swallowing it."

"Where will you sit?" asked Mrs. Fisher of Mrs. Arbuthnot—markedly of Mrs. Arbuthnot; the comparison with the bread seemed to her most unpleasant.

"Oh, thank you—" said Mrs. Arbuthnot, sitting down rather suddenly next to her.

There were only two places she could sit down in, the places laid on either side of Mrs. Fisher. She therefore sat down in one, and Mrs. Wilkins sat down opposite her in the other.

Mrs. Fisher was at the head of the table. Round her was grouped the coffee and the tea. Of course they were all sharing San Salvatore equally, but it was she herself and Lotty, Mrs. Arbuthnot mildly reflected, who had found it, who had had the work of getting it, who had chosen to admit Mrs. Fisher into it. Without them, she could not help thinking, Mrs. Fisher would not have been there. Morally Mrs. Fisher was a guest. There was no hostess in this party, but supposing there had been a hostess it would not have been Mrs. Fisher, nor Lady Caroline, it would have been either herself or Lotty.

Mrs. Arbuthnot could not help feeling this as she sat down, and Mrs. Fisher, the hand which Ruskin had wrung suspended over the pots before her, inquired, "Tea or coffee?" She could not help feeling it even more definitely when Mrs. Fisher touched a small gong on the table beside her as though she had been used to that gong and that table ever since she was little, and, on Francesca's appearing, bade her in the language of Dante bring more milk. There was a curious air about Mrs. Fisher, thought Mrs. Arbuthnot, of being in possession; and if she herself had not been so happy she would have perhaps minded.

Mrs. Wilkins noticed it too, but it only made her discursive brain think of cuckoos. She would no doubt immediately have begun to talk of cuckoos, incoherently, unrestrainably and deplorably, if she had been in the condition of nerves and shyness she was in last time she saw Mrs. Fisher. But happiness had done away with shyness—she was very serene; she could control her conversation; she did not have, horrified, to listen to herself saying things she had no idea of saying when she began; she was quite at her ease, and completely natural. The disappointment of not going to be able to prepare a welcome for Mrs. Fisher had evaporated at once, for it was impossible to go on being disappointed in heaven. Nor did she mind her behaving as hostess. What did it matter? You did not mind things in heaven. She and Mrs. Arbuthnot, therefore, sat down more willingly than they otherwise would have done, one on either side of Mrs. Fisher, and the sun, pouring through the two windows facing east across the bay, flooded the room, and there was an open door leading into the garden, and the garden was full of many lovely things, especially freesias.

The delicate and delicious fragrance of the freesias came in through the door and floated round Mrs. Wilkins's enraptured nostrils. Freesias in London were quite beyond her. Occasionally she went into a shop and asked what they cost, so as just to have an excuse for lifting up a bunch and smelling them, well knowing that it was something awful like a shilling for about three flowers. Here they were everywhere— bursting out of every corner and carpeting the rose beds. Imagine it— having freesias to pick in armsful if you wanted to, and with glorious sunshine flooding the room, and in your summer frock, and its being only the first of April!

"I suppose you realize, don't you, that we've got to heaven?" she said, beaming at Mrs. Fisher with all the familiarity of a fellow-angel.

"They are considerably younger than I had supposed," thought Mrs. Fisher, "and not nearly so plain." And she mused a moment, while she took no notice of Mrs. Wilkins's exuberance, on their instant and agitated refusal that day at Prince of Wales Terrace to have anything to do with the giving or the taking of references.

Nothing could affect her, of course; nothing that anybody did. She was far too solidly seated in respectability. At her back stood massively in a tremendous row those three great names she had offered, and they were not the only ones she could turn to for support and countenance. Even if these young women—she had no grounds for believing the one out in the garden to be really Lady Caroline Dester, she had merely been told she was—even if these young women should all turn out to be what Browning used to call—how well she remembered his amusing and delightful way of putting things—Fly-by-Nights, what could it possibly, or in any way matter to her? Let them fly by night if they wished. One was not sixty-five for nothing. In any case there would only be four weeks of it, at the end of which she would see no more of them. And in the meanwhile there were plenty of places where she could sit quietly away from them and remember. Also there was her own sitting-room, a charming room, all honey-coloured furniture and pictures, with windows to the sea towards Genoa, and a door opening on to the battlements. The house possessed two sitting-rooms, and she explained to that pretty creature Lady Caroline—certainly a pretty creature, whatever else she was; Tennyson would have enjoyed taking her for blows on the downs—who had seemed inclined to appropriate the honey-colored one, that she needed some little refuge entirely to herself because of her stick.

"Nobody wants to see an old woman hobbling about everywhere," she had said. "I shall be quite content to spend much of my time by myself in here or sitting out on these convenient battlements."

And she had a very nice bedroom, too; it looked two ways, across the bay in the morning sun—she liked the morning sun—and onto the garden. There were only two of these bedrooms with cross-views in the house, she and Lady Caroline had discovered, and they were by far the airiest. They each had two beds in them, and she and Lady Caroline had had the extra beds taken out at once and put into two of the other rooms. In this way there was much more space and comfort. Lady Caroline, indeed, had turned hers into a bed-sitting-room, with the sofa out of the bigger drawing-room and the writing-table and the most comfortable chair, but she herself had not had to do that because she had her own sitting-room, equipped with what was necessary. Lady Caroline had thought at first of taking the bigger sitting-room entirely for her own, because the dining-room on the floor below could quite well be used between meals to sit in by the two others, and was a very pleasant room with nice chairs, but she had not liked the bigger sitting-room's shape—it was a round room in the tower, with deep slit windows pierced through the massive walls, and a domed and ribbed ceiling arranged to look like an open umbrella, and it seemed a little dark. Undoubtedly Lady Caroline had cast covetous glances at the honey-coloured room, and if she Mrs. Fisher, had been less firm would have installed herself in it. Which would have been absurd.

"I hope," said Mrs. Arbuthnot, smilingly making an attempt to convey to Mrs. Fisher that though she, Mrs. Fisher, might not be exactly a guest she certainly was not in the very least a hostess, "your room is comfortable."

"Quite," said Mrs. Fisher. "Will you have some more coffee?"

"No, thank you. Will you?"

"No, thank you. There were two beds in my bedroom, filling it up unnecessarily, and I had one taken out. It has made it much more convenient."

"Oh that's why I've got two beds in my room!" exclaimed Mrs. Wilkins, illuminated; the second bed in her little cell had seemed an unnatural and inappropriate object from the moment she saw it.

"I gave no directions," said Mrs. Fisher, addressing Mrs. Arbuthnot, "I merely asked Francesca to remove it."
"I have two in my room as well," said Mrs. Arbuthnot.

"Your second one must be Lady Caroline's. She had hers removed too," said Mrs. Fisher. "It seems foolish to have more beds in a room than there are occupiers."

"But we haven't got husbands here either," said Mrs. Wilkins, "and I don't see any use in extra beds in one's room if one hasn't got husbands to put in them. Can't we have them taken away too?"

"Beds," said Mrs. Fisher coldly, "cannot be removed from one room after another. They must remain somewhere."

Mrs. Wilkins's remarks seemed to Mrs. Fisher persistently unfortunate. Each time she opened her mouth she said something best left unsaid. Loose talk about husbands had never in Mrs. Fisher's circle been encouraged. In the 'eighties, when she chiefly flourished, husbands were taken seriously, as the only real obstacles to sin. Beds too, if they had to be mentioned, were approached with caution; and a decent reserve prevented them and husbands ever being spoken of in the same breath.

She turned more markedly than ever to Mrs. Arbuthnot. "Do let me give you a little more coffee," she said.

"No, thank you. But won't you have some more?"

"No indeed. I never have more than two cups at breakfast. Would you like an orange?"

"No thank you. Would you?"

"No, I don't eat fruit at breakfast. It is an American fashion which I am too old now to adopt. Have you had all you want?"

"Quite. Have you?"

Mrs. Fisher paused before replying. Was this a habit, this trick of answering a simple question with the same question? If so it must be curbed, for no one could live for four weeks in any real comfort with somebody who had a habit.

She glanced at Mrs. Arbuthnot, and her parted hair and gentle brow reassured her. No; it was accident, not habit, that had produced those echoes. She could as soon imagine a dove having tiresome habits as Mrs. Arbuthnot. Considering her, she thought what a splendid wife she would have been for poor Carlyle. So much better than that horrid clever Jane. She would have soothed him.

"Then shall we go?" she suggested.

"Let me help you up," said Mrs. Arbuthnot, all consideration.

"Oh, thank you—I can manage perfectly. It's only sometimes that my stick prevents me—"

Mrs. Fisher got up quite easily; Mrs. Arbuthnot had hovered over her for nothing.

"I'm going to have one of these gorgeous oranges," said Mrs. Wilkins, staying where she was and reaching across to a black bowl piled with them. "Rose, how can you resist them. Look—have this one.

Do have this beauty—" And she held out a big one.

"No, I'm going to see to my duties," said Mrs. Arbuthnot, moving towards the door. "You'll forgive me for leaving you, won't you," she added politely to Mrs. Fisher.

Mrs. Fisher moved towards the door too; quite easily; almost quickly; her stick did not hinder her at all. She had no intention of being left with Mrs. Wilkins.

"What time would you like to have lunch?" Mrs. Arbuthnot asked her, trying to keep her head as at least a non-guest, if not precisely a hostess, above water.

"Lunch," said Mrs. Fisher, "is at half-past twelve."

"You shall have it at half-past twelve then," said Mrs. Arbuthnot. "I'll tell the cook. It will be a great struggle," she continued, smiling, "but I've brought a little dictionary—"

"The cook," said Mrs. Fisher, "knows."

"Oh?" said Mrs. Arbuthnot.

"Lady Caroline has already told her," said Mrs. Fisher.

"Oh?" said Mrs. Arbuthnot.

"Yes. Lady Caroline speaks the kind of Italian cooks understand.
I am prevented going into the kitchen because of my stick. And even if
I were able to go, I fear I shouldn't be understood."
"But—" began Mrs. Arbuthnot.

"But it's too wonderful," Mrs. Wilkins finished for her from the table, delighted with these unexpected simplifications in her and Rose's lives. "Why, we've got positively nothing to do here, either of us, except just be happy. You wouldn't believe," she said, turning her head and speaking straight to Mrs. Fisher, portions of orange in either hand, "how terribly good Rose and I have been for years without stopping, and how much now we need a perfect rest."

And Mrs. Fisher, going without answering her out the room, said to herself, "She must, she shall be curbed."

Chapter 8

Presently, when Mrs. Wilkins and Mrs. Arbuthnot, unhampered by any duties, wandered out and down the worn stone steps and under the pergola into the lower garden, Mrs. Wilkins said to Mrs. Arbuthnot, who seemed pensive, "Don't you see that if somebody else does the ordering it frees us?"

Mrs. Arbuthnot said she did see, but nevertheless she thought it rather silly to have everything taken out of their hands.

"I love things to be taken out of my hands," said Mrs. Wilkins.

"But we found San Salvatore," said Mrs. Arbuthnot, "and it is rather silly that Mrs. Fisher should behave as if it belonged only to her."

"What is rather silly," said Mrs. Wilkins with much serenity, "is to mind. I can't see the least point in being in authority at the price of one's liberty."

Mrs. Arbuthnot said nothing to that for two reasons—first, because she was struck by the remarkable and growing calm of the hitherto incoherent and excited Lotty, and secondly because what she was looking at was so very beautiful.

All down the stone steps on either side were periwinkles in full flower, and she could now see what it was that had caught at her the night before and brushed, wet and scented, across her face. It was wistaria. Wistaria and sunshine . . . she remembered the advertisement. Here indeed were both in profusion. The wistaria was tumbling over itself in its excess of life, its prodigality of flowering; and where the pergola ended the sun blazed on scarlet geraniums, bushes of them, and nasturtiums in great heaps, and marigolds so brilliant that they seemed to be burning, and red and pink snapdragons, all outdoing each other in bright, fierce colour. The ground behind these flaming things dropped away in terraces to the sea, each terrace a little orchard, where among the olives grew vines on trellises, and fig-trees, and peach-trees, and cherry-trees. The cherry-trees and peach-trees were in blossom—lovely showers of white and deep rose-colour among the trembling delicacy of the olives; the fig-leaves were just big enough to smell of figs, the vine-buds were only beginning to show. And beneath these trees were groups of blue and purple irises, and bushes of lavender, and grey, sharp cactuses, and the grass was thick with dandelions and daisies, and right down at the bottom was the sea. Colour seemed flung down anyhow, anywhere; every sort of colour, piled up in heaps, pouring along in rivers—the periwinkles looked exactly as if they were being poured down each side of the steps—and flowers that grow only in borders in England, proud flowers keeping themselves to themselves over there, such as the great blue irises and the lavender, were being jostled by small, shining common things like dandelions and daisies and the white bells of the wild onion, and only seemed the better and the more exuberant for it.

They stood looking at this crowd of loveliness, this happy jumble, in silence. No, it didn't matter what Mrs. Fisher did; not here; not in such beauty. Mrs. Arbuthnot's discomposure melted out of her. In the warmth and light of what she was looking at, of what to her was a manifestation, and entirely new side of God, how could one be discomposed? If only Frederick were with her, seeing it too, seeing as he would have seen it when first they were lovers, in the days when he saw what she saw and loved what she loved. . .

She sighed.

"You mustn't sigh in heaven," said Mrs. Wilkins. "One doesn't."

"I was thinking how one longs to share this with those one loves," said Mrs. Arbuthnot.

"You mustn't long in heaven," said Mrs. Wilkins. "You're supposed to be quite complete there. And it is heaven, isn't it, Rose? See how everything has been let in together—the dandelions and the irises, the vulgar and the superior, me and Mrs. Fisher—all welcome, all mixed up anyhow, and all so visibly happy and enjoying ourselves."

"Mrs. Fisher doesn't seem happy—not visibly, anyhow," said Mrs. Arbuthnot, smiling.
"She'll begin soon, you'll see."

Mrs. Arbuthnot said she didn't believe that after a certain age people began anything.

Mrs. Wilkins said she was sure no one, however old and tough, could resist the effects of perfect beauty. Before many days, perhaps only hours, they would see Mrs. Fisher bursting out into every kind of exuberance. "I'm quite sure," said Mrs. Wilkins, "that we've got to heaven, and once Mrs. Fisher realizes that that's where she is, she's bound to be different. You'll see. She'll leave off being ossified, and go all soft and able to stretch, and we shall get quite—why, I shouldn't be surprised if we get quite fond of her."

The idea of Mrs. Fisher bursting out into anything, she who seemed so particularly firmly fixed inside her buttons, made Mrs. Arbuthnot laugh. She condoned Lotty's loose way of talking of heaven, because in such a place, on such a morning, condonation was in the very air. Besides, what an excuse there was.

And Lady Caroline, sitting where they had left her before breakfast on the wall, peeped over when she heard laughter, and saw them standing on the path below, and thought what a mercy it was they were laughing down there and had not come up and done it round her. She disliked jokes at all times, but in the morning she hated them; especially close up; especially crowding in her ears. She hoped the originals were on their way out for a walk, and not on their way back from one. They were laughing more and more. What could they possibly find to laugh at?

She looked down on the tops of their heads with a very serious face, for the thought of spending a month with laughers was a grave one, and they, as though they felt her eyes, turned suddenly and looked up.

The dreadful geniality of those women. . .

She shrank away from their smiles and wavings, but she could not shrink out of sight without falling into the lilies. She neither smiled nor waved back, and turning her eyes to the more distant mountains surveyed them carefully till the two, tired of waving, moved away along the path and turned the corner and disappeared.

This time they both did notice that they had been met with, at least, unresponsiveness.

"If we weren't in heaven," said Mrs. Wilkins serenely, "I should say we had been snubbed, but as nobody snubs anybody there of course we can't have been."

"Perhaps she is unhappy," said Mrs. Arbuthnot.

"Whatever it is she is she'll get over it here," said Mrs. Wilkins with conviction.
"We must try and help her," said Mrs. Arbuthnot.

"Oh, but nobody helps anybody in heaven. That's finished with.

You don't try to be, or do. You simply are."

Well, Mrs. Arbuthnot wouldn't go into that—not here, not to-day. The vicar, she knew, would have called Lotty's talk levity, if not profanity. How old he seemed from here; an old, old vicar.

They left the path, and clambered down the olive terraces, down and down, to where at the bottom the warm, sleepy sea heaved gently among the rocks. There a pine-tree grew close to the water, and they sat under it, and a few yards away was a fishing-boat lying motionless and green-bellied on the water. The ripples of the sea made little gurgling noises at their feet. They screwed up their eyes to be able to look into the blaze of light beyond the shade of their tree. The hot smell from the pine-needles and from the cushions of wild thyme that padded the spaces between the rocks, and sometimes a smell of pure honey from a clump of warm irises up behind them in the sun, puffed across their faces. Very soon Mrs. Wilkins took her shoes and stockings off, and let her feet hang in the water. After watching her a minute Mrs. Arbuthnot did the same. Their happiness was then complete. Their husbands would not have known them. They left off talking. They ceased to mention heaven. They were just cups of acceptance.

Meanwhile Lady Caroline, on her wall, was considering her position. The garden on the top of the wall was a delicious garden, but its situation made it insecure and exposed to interruptions. At any moment the others might come and want to use it, because both the hall and the dining-room had doors opening straight into it. Perhaps, thought Lady Caroline, she could arrange that it should be solely hers. Mrs. Fisher had the battlements, delightful with flowers, and a watch-tower all to herself, besides having snatched the one really nice room in the house. There were plenty of places the originals could go to—she had herself seen at least two other little gardens, while the hill the castle stood on was itself a garden, with walks and seats. Why should not this one spot be kept exclusively for her? She liked it; she liked it best of all. It had the Judas tree and an umbrella pine, it had the freesias and the lilies, it had a tamarisk beginning to flush pink, it had the convenient low wall to sit on, it had from each of its three sides the most amazing views—to the east the bay and mountains, to the north the village across the tranquil clear green water of the little harbour and the hills dotted with white houses and orange groves, and to the west was the thin thread of land by which San Salvatore was tied to the mainland, and then the open sea and the coast line beyond Genoa reaching away into the blue dimness of France. Yes, she would say she wanted to have this entirely to herself. How obviously sensible if each of them had their own special place to sit in apart. It was essential to her comfort that she should be able to be apart, left alone, not talked to. The others ought to like it best too. Why herd? One had enough of that in England, with one's relations and friends—oh, the numbers of them!—pressing on one continually. Having successfully escaped them for four weeks why continue, and with persons having no earthly claim on one, to herd?

She lit a cigarette. She began to feel secure. Those two had gone for a walk. There was no sign of Mrs. Fisher. How very pleasant this was.

Somebody came out through the glass doors, just as she was drawing a deep breath of security. Surely it couldn't be Mrs. Fisher, wanting to sit with her? Mrs. Fisher had her battlements. She ought to stay on them, having snatched them. It would be too tiresome if she wouldn't, and wanted not only to have them and her sitting-room but to establish herself in this garden as well.

No; it wasn't Mrs. Fisher, it was the cook.

She frowned. Was she going to have to go on ordering the food? Surely one or other of those two waving women would do that now. The cook, who had been waiting in increasing agitation in the kitchen, watching the clock getting nearer to lunch—time while she still was without knowledge of what lunch was to consist of, had gone at last to Mrs. Fisher, who had immediately waved her away. She then wandered about the house seeking a mistress, any mistress, who would tell her what to cook, and finding none; and at last, directed by Francesca, who always knew where everybody was, came out to Lady Caroline.

Dominica had provided this cook. She was Costanza, the sister of that one of his cousins who kept a restaurant down on the piazza. She helped her brother in his cooking when she had no other job, and knew every sort of fat, mysterious Italian dish such as the workmen of Castagneto, who crowded the restaurant at midday, and the inhabitants of Mezzago when they came over on Sundays, loved to eat. She was a fleshless spinster of fifty, grey-haired, nimble, rich of speech, and thought Lady Caroline more beautiful than anyone she had ever seen; and so did Domenico; and so did the boy Giuseppe who helped Domenico and was, besides, his nephew; and so did the girl Angela who helped Francesca and was, besides, Domenico's niece; and so did Francesca herself. Domenico and Francesca, the only two who had seen them, thought the two ladies who arrived last very beautiful, but compared to the fair young lady who arrived first they were as candles to the electric light that had lately been installed, and as the tin tubs in the bedrooms to the wonderful new bathroom their master had had arranged on his last visit.

Lady Caroline scowled at the cook. The scowl, as usual, was transformed on the way into what appeared to be an intent and beautiful gravity, and Costanza threw up her hands and took the saints aloud to witness that here was the very picture of the Mother of God.

Lady Caroline asked her crossly what she wanted, and Costanza's head went on one side with delight at the sheer music of her voice. She said, after waiting a moment in case the music was going to continue, for she didn't wish to miss any of it, that she wanted orders; she had been to the Signorina's mother, but in vain.

"She is not my mother," repudiated Lady Caroline angrily; and her anger sounded like the regretful wail of a melodious orphan.

Costanza poured forth pity. She too, she explained, had no mother—

Lady Caroline interrupted with the curt information that her mother was alive and in London.

Costanza praised God and the saints that the young lady did not yet know what it was like to be without a mother. Quickly enough did misfortunes overtake one; no doubt the young lady already had a husband.

"No," said Lady Caroline icily. Worse than jokes in the morning did she hate the idea of husbands. And everybody was always trying to press them on her—all her relations, all her friends, all the evening papers. After all, she could only marry one, anyhow; but you would think from the way everybody talked, and especially those persons who wanted to be husbands, that she could marry at least a dozen.

Her soft, pathetic "No" made Costanza, who was standing close to her, well with sympathy.

"Poor little one," said Costanza, moved actually to pat her encouragingly on the shoulder, "take hope. There is still time."

"For lunch," said Lady Caroline freezingly, marveling as she spoke that she should be patted, she who had taken so much trouble to come to a place, remote and hidden, where she could be sure that among other things of a like oppressive nature pattings also were not, "we will have—"

Costanza became business-like. She interrupted with suggestions, and her suggestions were all admirable and all expensive.

Lady Caroline did not know they were expensive, and fell in with them at once. They sounded very nice. Every sort of young vegetables and fruits came into them, and much butter and a great deal of cream and incredible numbers of eggs. Costanza said enthusiastically at the end, as a tribute to this acquiescence, that of the many ladies and gentlemen she had worked for on temporary jobs such as this she preferred the English ladies and gentlemen. She more than preferred them—they roused devotion in her. For they knew what to order; they did not skimp; they refrained from grinding down the faces of the poor.

From this Lady Caroline concluded that she had been extravagant, and promptly countermanded the cream.

Costanza's face fell, for she had a cousin who had a cow, and the cream was to have come from them both.

"And perhaps we had better not have chickens," said Lady Caroline.
Costanza's face fell more, for her brother at the restaurant kept chickens in his back-yard, and many of them were ready for killing.

"Also do not order strawberries till I have consulted with the other ladies," said Lady Caroline, remembering that it was only the first of April, and that perhaps people who lived in Hampstead might be poor; indeed, must be poor, or why live in Hampstead? "It is not I who am mistress here."

"Is it the old one?" asked Costanza, her face very long.

"No," said Lady Caroline.

"Which of the other two ladies is it?"

"Neither," said Lady Caroline.

Then Costanza's smiles returned, for the young lady was having fun with her and making jokes. She told her so, in her friendly Italian way, and was genuinely delighted.

"I never make jokes," said Lady Caroline briefly. "You had better go, or lunch will certainly not be ready by half-past twelve."

And these curt words came out sounding so sweet that Costanza felt as if kind compliments were being paid her, and forgot her disappointment about the cream and the chickens, and went away all gratitude and smiles.

"This," thought Lady Caroline, "will never do. I haven't come here to housekeep, and I won't."

She called Costanza back. Costanza came running. The sound of her name in that voice enchanted her.

"I have ordered the lunch for to-day," said Lady Caroline, with the serious angel face that was hers when she was annoyed, "and I have also ordered the dinner, but from now on you will go to one of the other ladies for orders. I give no more."

The idea that she would go on giving orders was too absurd. She never gave orders at home. Nobody there dreamed of asking her to do anything. That such a very tiresome activity should be thrust upon her here, simply because she happened to be able to talk Italian, was ridiculous. Let the originals give orders if Mrs. Fisher refused to. Mrs. Fisher, of course, was the one Nature intended for such a purpose. She had the very air of a competent housekeeper. Her clothes were the clothes of a housekeeper, and so was the way she did her hair.

Having delivered herself of her ultimatum with an acerbity that turned sweet on the way, and accompanied it by a peremptory gesture of dismissal that had the grace and loving-kindness of a benediction, it was annoying that Costanza should only stand still with her head on one side gazing at her in obvious delight.

"Oh, go away!" exclaimed Lady Caroline in English, suddenly exasperated.

There had been a fly in her bedroom that morning which had stuck just as Costanza was sticking; only one, but it might have been a myriad it was so tiresome from daylight on. It was determined to settle on her face, and she was determined it should not. Its persistence was uncanny. It woke her, and would not let her go to sleep again. She hit at it, and it eluded her without fuss or effort and with an almost visible blandness, and she had only hit herself. It came back again instantly, and with a loud buzz alighted on her cheek. She hit at it again and hurt herself, while it skimmed gracefully away. She lost her temper, and sat up in bed and waited, watching to hit at it and kill it. She kept on hitting at it at last with fury and with all her strength, as if it were a real enemy deliberately trying to madden her; and it elegantly skimmed in and out of her blows, not even angry, to be back again the next instant. It succeeded every time in getting on to her face, and was quite indifferent how often it was driven away. That was why she had dressed and come out so early. Francesca had already been told to put a net over her bed, for she was not going to allow herself to be annoyed twice like that. People were exactly like flies. She wished there were nets for keeping them off too. She hit at them with words and frowns, and like the fly they slipped between her blows and were untouched. Worse than the fly, they seemed unaware that she had even tried to hit them. The fly at least did for a moment go away. With human beings the only way to get rid of them was to go away herself. That was what, so tired, she had done this April; and having got here, having got close up to the details of life at San Salvatore, it appeared that here, too, she was not to be let alone.

Viewed from London there had seemed to be no details. San Salvatore from there seemed to be an empty, a delicious blank. Yet, after only twenty-four hours of it, she was discovering that it was not a blank at all, and that she was having to ward off as actively as ever. Already she had been much stuck to. Mrs. Fisher had stuck nearly the whole of the day before, and this morning there had been no peace, not ten minutes uninterruptedly alone.

Costanza of course had finally to go because she had to cook, but hardly had she gone before Domenico came. He came to water and tie up. That was natural, since he was the gardener, but he watered and tied up all the things that were nearest to her; he hovered closer and closer; he watered to excess; he tied plants that were as straight and steady as arrows. Well, at least he was a man, and therefore not quite so annoying, and his smiling good-morning was received with an answering smile; upon which Domenico forgot his family, his wife, his mother, his grown-up children and all his duties, and only wanted to kiss the young lady's feet.

He could not do that, unfortunately, but he could talk while he worked, and talk he did; voluminously; pouring out every kind of information, illustrating what he said with gestures so lively that he had to put down the watering-pot, and thus delay the end of the watering.

Lady Caroline bore it for a time but presently was unable to bear it, and as he would not go, and she could not tell him to, seeing that he was engaged in his proper work, once again it was she who had to.

She got off the wall and moved to the other side of the garden, where in a wooden shed were some comfortable low cane chairs. All she wanted was to turn one of these round with its back to Domenico and its front to the sea towards Genoa. Such a little thing to want. One would have thought she might have been allowed to do that unmolested. But he, who watched her every movement, when he saw her approaching the chairs darted after her and seized one and asked to be told where to put it.

Would she never get away from being waited on, being made comfortable, being asked where she wanted things put, having to say thank you? She was short with Domenico, who instantly concluded the sun had given her a headache, and ran in and fetched her a sunshade and a cushion and a footstool, and was skilful, and was wonderful, and was one of Nature's gentlemen.

She shut her eyes in a heavy resignation. She could not be unkind to Domenico. She could not get up and walk indoors as she would have done if it had been one of the others. Domenico was intelligent and very competent. She had at once discovered that it was he who really ran the house, who really did everything. And his manners were definitely delightful, and he undoubtedly was a charming person. It was only that she did so much long to be let alone. If only, only she could be left quite quiet for this one month, she felt that she might perhaps make something of herself after all.

She kept her eyes shut, because then he would think she wanted to sleep and would go away.

Domenico's romantic Italian soul melted within him at the sight, for having her eyes shut was extraordinarily becoming to her. He stood entranced, quite still, and she thought he had stolen away, so she opened them again.

No; there he was, staring at her. Even he. There was no getting away from being stared at.

"I have a headache," she said, shutting them again.

"It is the sun," said Domenico, "and sitting on the wall without a hat."

"I wish to sleep."

"Si signorina," he said sympathetically; and went softly away.

She opened her eyes with a sigh of relief. The gentle closing of the glass doors showed her that he had not only gone quite away but had shut her out in the garden so that she should be undisturbed. Now perhaps she would be alone till lunch-time.

It was very curious, and no one in the world could have been more surprised than she herself, but she wanted to think. She had never wanted to do that before. Everything else that it is possible to do without too much inconvenience she had either wanted to do or had done at one period or another of her life, but not before had she wanted to think. She had come to San Salvatore with the single intention of lying comatose for four weeks in the sun, somewhere where her parents and friends were not, lapped in forgetfulness, stirring herself only to be fed, and she had not been there more than a few hours when this strange new desire took hold of her.

There had been wonderful stars the evening before, and she had gone out into the top garden after dinner, leaving Mrs. Fisher alone over her nuts and wine, and, sitting on the wall at the place where the lilies crowded their ghost heads, she had looked out into the gulf of the night, and it had suddenly seemed as if her life had been a noise all about nothing.

She had been intensely surprised. She knew stars and darkness did produce unusual emotions because, in others, she had seen them being produced, but they had not before done it in herself. A noise all about nothing. Could she be quite well? She had wondered. For a long while past she had been aware that her life was a noise, but it had seemed to be very much about something; a noise, indeed, about so much that she felt she must get out of earshot for a little or she would be completely, and perhaps permanently, deafened. But suppose it was only a noise about nothing?

She had not had a question like that in her mind before. It had made her feel lonely. She wanted to be alone, but not lonely. That was very different; that was something that ached and hurt dreadfully right inside one. It was what one dreaded most. It was what made one go to so many parties; and lately even the parties had seemed once or twice not to be a perfectly certain protection. Was it possible that loneliness had nothing to do with circumstances, but only with the way one met them? Perhaps, she had thought, she had better go to bed. She couldn't be very well.

She went to bed; and in the morning, after she had escaped the fly and had her breakfast and got out again into the garden, there was this same feeling again, and in broad daylight. Once more she had that really rather disgusting suspicion that her life till now had not only been loud but empty. Well, if that were so, and if her first twenty-eight years—the best ones—had gone just in meaningless noise, she had better stop a moment and look round her; pause, as they said in tiresome novels, and consider. She hadn't got many sets of twenty-eight years. One more would see her growing very like Mrs. Fisher. Two more— She averted her eyes.

Her mother would have been concerned if she had known. Her mother doted. Her father would have been concerned too, for he also doted. Everybody doted. And when, melodiously obstinate, she had insisted on going off to entomb herself in Italy for a whole month with queer people she had got out of an advertisement, refusing even to take her maid, the only explanation her friends could imagine was that poor Scrap—such was her name among them—had overdone it and was feeling a little nervy.

Her mother had been distressed at her departure. It was such an odd thing to do, such a sign of disappointment. She encouraged the general idea of the verge of a nervous breakdown. If she could have seen her adored Scrap, more delightful to look upon than any other mother's daughter had ever yet been, the object of her utmost pride, the source of all her fondest hopes, sitting staring at the empty noonday Mediterranean considering her three possible sets of twenty-eight years, she would have been miserable. To go away alone was bad; to think was worse. No good could come out of the thinking of a beautiful young woman. Complications could come out of it in profusion, but no good. The thinking of the beautiful was bound to result in hesitations, in reluctances, in unhappiness all round. And here, if she could have seen her, sat her Scrap thinking quite hard. And such things. Such old things. Things nobody ever began to think till they were at least forty.

Chapter 9

That one of the two sitting-rooms which Mrs. Fisher had taken for her own was a room of charm and character. She surveyed it with satisfaction on going into it after breakfast, and was glad it was hers. It had a tiled floor, and walls the colour of pale honey, and inlaid furniture the colour of amber, and mellow books, many in ivory or lemon-coloured covers. There was a big window overlooking the sea towards Genoa, and a glass door through which she could proceed out on to the battlements and walk along past the quaint and attractive watch-tower, in itself a room with chairs and a writing table, to where on the other side of the tower the battlements ended in a marble seat, and one could see the western bay and the point round which began the Gulf of Spezia. Her south view, between these two stretches of sea, was another hill, higher than San Salvatore, the last of the little peninsula, with the bland turrets of a smaller and uninhabited castle on the top, on which the setting sun still shone when everything else was sunk in shadow. Yes, she was very comfortably established here; and receptacles—Mrs. Fisher did not examine their nature closely, but they seemed to be small stone troughs, or perhaps little sarcophagi— ringed round the battlements with flowers.

These battlements, she thought, considering them, would have been a perfect place for her to pace up and down gently in moments when she least felt the need of her stick, or to sit in on the marble seat, having first put a cushion on it, if there had not unfortunately been a second glass door opening on to them, destroying their complete privacy, spoiling her feeling that the place was only for her. The second door belonged to the round drawing-room, which both she and Lady Caroline had rejected as too dark. That room would probably be sat in by the women from Hampstead, and she was afraid they would not confine themselves to sitting in it, but would come out through the glass door and invade her battlements. This would ruin the battlements. It would ruin them as far as she was concerned if they were to be overrun; or even if, not actually overrun, they were liable to be raked by the eyes of persons inside the room. No one could be perfectly at ease if they were being watched and knew it. What she wanted, what she surely had a right to, was privacy. She had no wish to intrude on the others; why then should they intrude on her? And she could always relax her privacy if, when she became better acquainted with her companions, she should think it worth while, but she doubted whether any of the three would so develop as to make her think it worth while.

Hardly anything was really worth while, reflected Mrs. Fisher, except the past. It was astonishing, it was simply amazing, the superiority of the past to the present. Those friends of hers in London, solid persons of her own age, knew the same past that she knew, could talk about it with her, could compare it as she did with the tinkling present, and in remembering great men forget for a moment the trivial and barren young people who still, in spite of the war, seemed to litter the world in such numbers. She had not come away from these friends, these conversable ripe friends, in order to spend her time in Italy chatting with three persons of another generation and defective experience; she had come away merely to avoid the treacheries of a London April. It was true what she had told the two who came to Prince of Wales Terrace, that all she wished to do at San Salvatore was to sit by herself in the sun and remember. They knew this, for she had told them. It had been plainly expressed and clearly understood. Therefore she had a right to expect them to stay inside the round drawing-room and not to emerge interruptingly on to her battlements.

But would they? The doubt spoilt her morning. It was only towards lunch-time that she saw a way to be quite safe, and ringing for Francesca, bade her, in slow and majestic Italian, shut the shutters of the glass door of the round drawing-room, and then, going with her into the room, which had become darker than ever in consequence, but also, Mrs. Fisher observed to Francesca, who was being voluble, would because of this very darkness remain agreeably cool, and after all there were the numerous slit-windows in the walls to let in light and it was nothing to do with her if they did not let it in, she directed the placing of a cabinet of curios across the door on its inside.

This would discourage egress.

Then she rang for Domenico, and caused him to move one of the flower-filled sarcophagi across the door on its outside.

This would discourage ingress.

"No one," said Domenico, hesitating, "will be able to use the door."

"No one," said Mrs. Fisher firmly, "will wish to."

She then retired to her sitting-room, and from a chair placed where she could look straight on to them, gazed at her battlements, secured to her now completely, with calm pleasure.

Being here, she reflected placidly, was much cheaper than being in an hotel and, if she could keep off the others, immeasurably more agreeable. She was paying for her rooms—extremely pleasant rooms, now that she was arranged in them—£3 a week, which came to about eight shillings a day, battlements, watch-tower and all. Where else abroad could she live as well for so little, and have as many baths as she like, for eight shillings a day? Of course she did not yet know what her food would cost, but she would insist on carefulness over that, though she would also insist on its being carefulness combined with excellence. The two were perfectly compatible if the caterer took pains. The servants' wages, she had ascertained, were negligible, owing to the advantageous exchange, so that there was only the food to cause her anxiety. If she saw signs of extravagance she would propose that they each hand over a reasonable sum every week to Lady Caroline which should cover the bills, any of it that was not used to be returned, and if it were exceeded the loss to be borne by the caterer.

Mrs. Fisher was well off and had the desire for comforts proper to her age, but she disliked expenses. So well off was she that, had she so chosen, she could have lived in an opulent part of London and driven from it and to it in a Rolls-Royce. She had no such wish. It needed more vitality than went with true comfort to deal with a house in an opulent spot and a Rolls-Royce. Worries attended such possessions, worries of every kind, crowned by bills. In the sober gloom of Prince of Wales Terrace she could obscurely enjoy inexpensive yet real comfort, without being snatched at by predatory men-servants or collectors for charities, and a taxi stand was at the end of the road. Her annual outlay was small. The house was inherited. Death had furnished it for her. She trod in the dining-room on the Turkey carpet of her fathers; she regulated her day by the excellent black marble clock on the mantelpiece which she remembered from childhood; her walls were entirely covered by the photographs her illustrious deceased friends had given either herself or her father, with their own handwriting across the lower parts of their bodies, and the windows, shrouded by the maroon curtains of all her life, were decorated besides with the selfsame aquariums to which she owed her first lessons in sealore, and in which still swam slowly the goldfishes of her youth.

Were they the same goldfish? She did not know. Perhaps, like carp, they outlived everybody. Perhaps, on the other hand, behind the deep-sea vegetation provided for them at the bottom, they had from time to time as the years went by withdrawn and replaced themselves. Were they or were they not, she sometimes wondered, contemplating them between the courses of her solitary means, the same goldfish that had that day been there when Carlyle—how well she remembered it—angrily strode up to them in the middle of some argument with her father that had grown heated, and striking the glass smartly with his fist had put them to flight, shouting as they fled, "Och, ye deaf devils! Och, ye lucky deaf devils! Ye can't hear anything of the blasted, blethering, doddering, glaikit fool-stuff yer maister talks, can ye?" Or words to that effect.

Dear, great-souled Carlyle. Such natural gushings forth; such true freshness; such real grandeur. Rugged, if you will—yes, undoubtedly sometimes rugged, and startling in a drawing-room, but magnificent. Who was there now to put beside him? Who was there to mention in the same breath? Her father, than whom no one had had more flair, said: "Thomas is immortal." And here was this generation, this generation of puniness, raising its little voice in doubts, or, still worse, not giving itself the trouble to raise it at all, not—it was incredible, but it had been thus reported to her—even reading him. Mrs. Fisher did not read him either, but that was different. She had read him; she had certainly read him. Of course she had read him. There was Teufelsdröck—she quite well remembered a tailor called Teufelsdröck. So like Carlyle to call him that. Yes, she must have read him, though naturally details escaped her.

The gong sounded. Lost in reminiscence Mrs. Fisher had forgotten time, and hastened to her bedroom to wash her hands and smoothe her hair. She did not wish to be late and set a bad example, and perhaps find her seat at the head of the table taken. One could put no trust in the manners of the younger generation; especially not in those of that Mrs. Wilkins.

She was, however, the first to arrive in the dining-room. Francesca in a white apron stood ready with an enormous dish of smoking hot, glistening macaroni, but nobody was there to eat it.

Mrs. Fisher sat down, looking stern. Lax, lax.

"Serve me," she said to Francesca, who showed a disposition to wait for the others.

Francesca served her. Of the party she liked Mrs. Fisher least, in fact she did not like her at all. She was the only one of the four ladies who had not yet smiled. True she was old, true she was unbeautiful, true she therefore had no reason to smile, but kind ladies smiled, reason or no. They smiled, not because they were happy but because they wished to make happy. This one of the four ladies could not then, Francesca decided, be kind; so she handed her the macaroni, being unable to hide any of her feelings, morosely.

It was very well cooked, but Mrs. Fisher had never cared for maccaroni, especially not this long, worm-shaped variety. She found it difficult to eat—slippery, wriggling off her fork, making her look, she felt, undignified when, having got it as she supposed into her mouth, ends of it yet hung out. Always, too, when she ate it she was reminded of Mr. Fisher. He had during their married life behaved very much like maccaroni. He had slipped, he had wriggled, he had made her feel undignified, and when at last she had got him safe, as she thought, there had invariably been little bits of him that still, as it were, hung out.

Francesca from the sideboard watched Mrs. Fisher's way with macaroni gloomily, and her gloom deepened when she saw her at last take her knife to it and chop it small.

Mrs. Fisher really did not know how else to get hold of the stuff. She was aware that knives in this connection were improper, but one did finally lose patience. Maccaroni was never allowed to appear on her table in London. Apart from its tiresomeness she did not even like it, and she would tell Lady Caroline not to order it again. Years of practice, reflected Mrs. Fisher, chopping it up, years of actual living in Italy, would be necessary to learn the exact trick. Browning managed maccaroni wonderfully. She remembered watching him one day when he came to lunch with her father, and a dish of it had been ordered as a compliment to his connection with Italy. Fascinating, the way it went in. No chasing round the plate, no slidings off the fork, no subsequent protrusions of loose ends—just one dig, one whisk, one thrust, one gulp, and lo, yet another poet had been nourished.

"Shall I go and seek the young lady?" asked Francesca, unable any longer to look on a good maccaroni being cut with a knife.

Mrs. Fisher came out of her reminiscent reflections with difficulty. "She knows lunch is at half-past twelve," she said. "They all know."

"She may be asleep," said Francesca. "The other ladies are further away, but this one is not far away."

"Beat the gong again then," said Mrs. Fisher.

What manners, she thought; what, what manners. It was not an hotel, and considerations were due. She must say she was surprised at Mrs. Arbuthnot, who had not looked like somebody unpunctual. Lady Caroline, too—she had seemed amiable and courteous, whatever else she might be. From the other one, of course, she expected nothing.

Francesca fetched the gong, and took it out into the garden and advanced, beating it as she advanced, close up to Lady Caroline, who, still stretched in her low chair, waited till she had done, and then turned her head and in the sweetest tones poured forth what appeared to be music but was really invective.

Francesca did not recognize the liquid flow as invective; how was she to, when it came out sounding like that? And with her face all smiles, for she could not but smile when she looked at this young lady, she told her the maccaroni was getting cold.

"When I do not come to meals it is because I do not wish to come to meals," said the irritated Scrap, "and you will not in future disturb me."

"Is she ill?" asked Francesca, sympathetic but unable to stop smiling. Never, never had she seen hair so beautiful. Like pure flax; like the hair of northern babes. On such a little head only blessing could rest, on such a little head the nimbus of the holiest saints could fitly be placed.

Scrap shut her eyes and refused to answer. In this she was injudicious, for its effect was to convince Francesca, who hurried away full of concern to tell Mrs. Fisher, that she was indisposed. And Mrs. Fisher, being prevented, she explained, from going out to Lady Caroline herself because of her stick, sent the two others instead, who had come in at that moment heated and breathless and full of excuses, while she herself proceeded to the next course, which was a very well-made omelette, bursting most agreeably at both its ends with young green peas.

"Serve me," she directed Francesca, who again showed a disposition to wait for the others.

"Oh, why won't they leave me alone?" Scrap asked herself when she heard more scrunchings on the little pebbles which took the place of grass, and therefore knew some one else was approaching.

She kept her eyes tight shut this time. Why should she go in to lunch if she didn't want to? This wasn't a private house; she was in no way tangled up in duties towards a tiresome hostess. For all practical purposes San Salvatore was an hotel, and she ought to be let alone to eat or not to eat exactly as if she really had been in an hotel.

But the unfortunate Scrap could not just sit still and close her eyes without rousing that desire to stroke and pet in her beholders with which she was only too familiar. Even the cook had patted her. And now a gentle hand—how well she knew and how much she dreaded gentle hands—was placed on her forehead.

"I'm afraid you're not well," said a voice that was not Mrs. Fisher's, and therefore must belong to one of the originals. "I have a headache," murmured Scrap. Perhaps it was best to say that; perhaps it was the shortest cut to peace.

"I'm so sorry," said Mrs. Arbuthnot softly, for it was her hand being gentle.

"And I," said Scrap to herself, "who thought if I came here I would escape mothers."

"Don't you think some tea would do you good?" asked Mrs. Arbuthnot tenderly. "Tea? The idea was abhorrent to Scrap. In this heat to be drinking tea in the middle of the day. . .

"No," she murmured.

"I expect what would really be best for her," said another voice, "is to be left quiet."

How sensible, thought Scrap; and raised the eye-lashes of one eye just enough to peep through and see who was speaking.

It was the freckled original. The dark one, then, was the one with the hand. The freckled one rose in her esteem.

"But I can't bear to think of you with a headache and nothing being done for it," said Mrs. Arbuthnot. "Would a cup of strong black coffee—?"

Scrap said no more. She waited, motionless and dumb, till Mrs. Arbuthnot should remove her hand. After all, she couldn't stand there all day, and when she went away she would have to take her hand with her.

"I do think," said the freckled one, "that she wants nothing except quiet."

And perhaps the freckled one pulled the one with the hand by the sleeve, for the hold on Scrap's forehead relaxed, and after a minute's silence, during which no doubt she was being contemplated—she was always being contemplated—the footsteps began to scrunch the pebbles again, and grew fainter, and were gone.

"Lady Caroline has a headache," said Mrs. Arbuthnot, re-entering the dining-room and sitting down in her place next to Mrs. Fisher. "I can't persuade her to have even a little tea, or some black coffee. Do you know what aspirin is in Italian?"

"The proper remedy for headaches," said Mrs. Fisher firmly, "is castor oil."

"But she hasn't got a headache," said Mrs. Wilkins.

"Carlyle," said Mrs. Fisher, who had finished her omelette and had leisure, while she waited for the next course, to talk, "suffered at one period terribly from headaches, and he constantly took castor oil as a remedy. He took it, I should say, almost to excess, and called it, I remember, in his interesting way the oil of sorrow. My father said it coloured for a time his whole attitude to life, his whole philosophy. But that was because he took too much. What Lady Caroline wants is one dose, and one only. It is a mistake to keep on taking castor oil."

"Do you know the Italian for it?" asked Mrs. Arbuthnot.

"Ah, that I'm afraid I don't. However, she would know. You can ask her."

"But she hasn't got a headache," repeated Mrs. Wilkins, who was struggling with the maccaroni. "She only wants to be let alone."

They both looked at her. The word shovel crossed Mrs. Fisher's mind in connection with Mrs. Wilkins's actions at that moment.

"Then why should she say she has?" asked Mrs. Arbuthnot.

"Because she is still trying to be polite. Soon she won't try, when the place has got more into her—she'll really be it. Without trying. Naturally."

"Lotty, you see," explained Mrs. Arbuthnot, smiling to Mrs. Fisher, who sat waiting with a stony patience for her next course, delayed because Mrs. Wilkins would go on trying to eat the maccaroni, which must be less worth eating than ever now that it was cold; "Lotty, you see, has a theory about this place—"

But Mrs. Fisher had no wish to hear any theory of Mrs. Wilkins's.

"I am sure I don't know," she interrupted, looking severely at Mrs. Wilkins, "why you should assume Lady Caroline is not telling the truth."

"I don't assume—I know." said Mrs. Wilkins.

"And pray how do you know?" asked Mrs. Fisher icily, for Mrs. Wilkins was actually helping herself to more maccaroni, offered her officiously and unnecessarily a second time by Francesca.

"When I was out there just now I saw inside her."

Well, Mrs. Fisher wasn't going to say anything to that; she wasn't going to trouble to reply to downright idiocy. Instead she sharply rapped the little table-gong by her side, though there was Francesca standing at the sideboard, and said, for she would wait no longer for her next course, "Serve me."

And Francesca—it must have been wilful—offered her the maccaroni again.

Chapter 10

There was no way of getting into or out of the top garden at San Salvatore except through the two glass doors, unfortunately side by side, of the dining-room and the hall. A person in the garden who wished to escape unseen could not, for the person to be escaped from could be met on the way. It was a small, oblong garden, and concealment was impossible. What trees there were—the Judas tree, the tamarisk, the umbrella-pine—grew close to the low parapets. Rose bushes gave no real cover; one step to right or left of them, and the person wishing to be private was discovered. Only the north-west corner was a little place jutting out from the great wall, a kind of excrescence or loop, no doubt used in the old distrustful days for observation, where it was possible to sit really unseen, because between it and the house was a thick clump of daphne.

Scrap, after glancing round to see that no one was looking, got up and carried her chair into this place, stealing away as carefully on tiptoe as those steal whose purpose is sin. There was another excrescence on the walls just like it at the north-east corner, but this, though the view from it was almost more beautiful, for from it you could see the bay and the lovely mountains behind Mezzago, was exposed. No bushes grew near it, nor had it any shade. The north-west loop then was where she would sit, and she settled into it, and nestling her head in her cushion and putting her feet comfortably on the parapet, from whence they appeared to the villagers on the piazza below as two white doves, thought that now indeed she would be safe.

Mrs. Fisher found her there, guided by the smell of her cigarette. The incautious Scrap had not thought of that. Mrs. Fisher did not smoke herself, and all the more distinctly could she smell the smoke of others. The virile smell met her directly she went out into the garden from the dining-room after lunch in order to have her coffee. She had bidden Francesca set the coffee in the shade of the house just outside the glass door, and when Mrs. Wilkins, seeing a table being carried there, reminded her, very officiously and tactlessly Mrs. Fisher considered, that Lady Caroline wanted to be alone, she retorted—and with what propriety—that the garden was for everybody.

Into it accordingly she went, and was immediately aware that Lady Caroline was smoking. She said to herself, "These modern young women," and proceeded to find her; her stick, now that lunch was over, being no longer the hindrance to action that it was before her meal had been securely, as Browning once said—surely it was Browning? Yes, she remembered how much diverted she had been—roped in.

Nobody diverted her now, reflected Mrs. Fisher, making straight for the clump of daphne; the world had grown very dull, and had entirely lost its sense of humour. Probably they still had their jokes, these people—in fact she knew they did, for Punch still went on; but how differently it went on, and what jokes. Thackeray, in his inimitable way, would have made mincemeat of this generation. Of how much it needed the tonic properties of that astringent pen it was of course unaware. It no longer even held him—at least, so she had been informed—in any particular esteem. Well, she could not give it eyes to see and ears to hear and a heart to understand, but she could and would give it, represented and united in the form of Lady Caroline, a good dose of honest medicine.

"I hear you are not well," she said, standing in the narrow entrance of the loop and looking down with the inflexible face of one who is determined to do good at the motionless and apparently sleeping Scrap.

Mrs. Fisher had a deep voice, very like a man's, for she had been overtaken by that strange masculinity that sometimes pursues a woman during the last laps of her life.

Scrap tried to pretend that she was asleep, but if she had been her cigarette would not have been held in her fingers but would have been lying on the ground.

She forgot this. Mrs. Fisher did not, and coming inside the loop, sat down on a narrow stone seat built out of the wall. For a little she could sit on it; for a little, till the chill began to penetrate.

She contemplated the figure before her. Undoubtedly a pretty creature, and one that would have had a success at Farringford. Strange how easily even the greatest men were moved by exteriors. She had seen with her own eyes Tennyson turn away from everybody—turn, positively, his back on a crowd of eminent people assembled to do him honour, and withdraw to the window with a young person nobody had ever heard of, who had been brought there by accident and whose one and only merit—if it be a merit, that which is conferred by chance—was beauty. Beauty! All over before you can turn round. An affair, one might almost say, of minutes. Well, while it lasted it did seem able to do what it liked with men. Even husbands were not immune. There had been passages in the life of Mr. Fisher . . .

"I expect the journey has upset you," she said in her deep voice.

"What you want is a good dose of some simple medicine. I shall ask Domenico if there is such a thing in the village as castor oil."
Scrap opened her eyes and looked straight at Mrs. Fisher.

"Ah," said Mrs. Fisher, "I knew you were not asleep. If you had been you would have let your cigarette fall to the ground."

"Waste," said Mrs. Fisher. "I don't like smoking for women, but I still less like waste."
"What does one do with people like this?" Scrap asked herself, her eyes fixed on Mrs. Fisher in what felt to her an indignant stare but appeared to Mrs. Fisher as really charming docility.

"Now you'll take my advice," said Mrs. Fisher, touched, "and not neglect what may very well turn into an illness. We are in Italy, you know, and one has to be careful. You ought, to begin with, to go to bed."

"I never go to bed," snapped Scrap; and it sounded as moving, as forlorn, as that line spoken years and years ago by an actress playing the part of Poor Jo in dramatized version of Bleak House—"I'm always moving on," said Poor Jo in this play, urged to do so by a policeman; and Mrs. Fisher, then a girl, had laid her head on the red velvet parapet of the front row of the dress circle and wept aloud.

It was wonderful, Scrap's voice. It had given her, in the ten years since she came out, all the triumphs that intelligence and wit can have, because it made whatever she said seem memorable. She ought, with a throat formation like that, to have been a singer, but in every kind of music Scrap was dumb except this one music of the speaking voice; and what a fascination, what a spell lay in that. Such was the liveliness of her face and the beauty of her colouring that there was not a man into whose eyes at the sight of her there did not leap a flame of intensest interest; but, when he heard her voice, the flame in that man's eyes was caught and fixed. It was the same with every man, educated and uneducated, old, young, desirable themselves or undesirable, men of her own world and bus-conductors, generals and Tommies—during the war she had had a perplexing time— bishops equally with vergers—round about her confirmation startling occurrences had taken place—wholesome and unwholesome, rich and penniless, brilliant or idiotic; and it made no difference at all what they were, or how long and securely married: into the eyes of every one of them, when they saw her, leapt this flame, and when they heard her it stayed there.

Scrap had had enough of this look. It only led to difficulties. At first it had delighted her. She had been excited, triumphant. To be apparently incapable of doing or saying the wrong thing, to be applauded, listened to, petted, adored wherever she went, and when she came home to find nothing there either but the most indulgent proud fondness—why, how extremely pleasant. And so easy, too. No preparation necessary for this achievement, no hard work, nothing to learn. She need take no trouble. She had only to appear, and presently say something.

But gradually experiences gathered round her. After all, she had to take trouble, she had to make efforts, because, she discovered with astonishment and rage, she had to defend herself. That look, that leaping look, meant that she was going to be grabbed at. Some of those who had it were more humble than others, especially if they were young, but they all, according to their several ability, grabbed; and she who had entered the world so jauntily, with her head in the air and the completest confidence in anybody whose hair was grey, began to distrust, and then to dislike, and soon to shrink away from, and presently to be indignant. Sometimes it was just as if she didn't belong to herself, wasn't her own at all, but was regarded as a universal thing, a sort of beauty-of-all-work. Really men . . . And she found herself involved in queer vague quarrels, being curiously hated. Really women . . . And when the war came, and she flung herself into it along with everybody else, it finished her. Really generals . . .

The war finished Scrap. It killed the one man she felt safe with, whom she would have married, and it finally disgusted her with love. Since then she had been embittered. She was struggling as angrily in the sweet stuff of life as a wasp got caught in honey. Just as desperately did she try to unstick her wings. It gave her no pleasure to outdo other women; she didn't want their tiresome men. What could one do with men when one had got them? None of them would talk to her of anything but the things of love, and how foolish and fatiguing that became after a bit. It was as though a healthy person with a normal hunger was given nothing whatever to eat but sugar. Love, love . . . the very word made her want to slap somebody. "Why should I love you? Why should I?" she would ask amazed sometimes when somebody was trying—somebody was always trying—to propose to her. But she never got a real answer, only further incoherence.

A deep cynicism took hold of the unhappy Scrap. Her inside grew hoary with disillusionment, while her gracious and charming outside continued to make the world more beautiful. What had the future in it for her? She would not be able, after such a preparation, to take hold of it. She was fit for nothing; she had wasted all this time being beautiful. Presently she wouldn't be beautiful, and what then? Scrap didn't know what then, it appalled her to wonder even. Tired as she was of being conspicuous she was at least used to that, she had never known anything else; and to become inconspicuous, to fade, to grow shabby and dim, would probably be most painful. And once she began, what years and years of it there would be! Imagine, thought Scrap, having most of one's life at the wrong end. Imagine being old for two or three times as long as being young. Stupid, stupid. Everything was stupid. There wasn't a thing she wanted to do. There were thousands of things she didn't want to do. Avoidance, silence, invisibility, if possible unconsciousness—these negations were all she asked for a moment; and here, even here, she was not allowed a minute's peace, and this absurd woman must come pretending, merely because she wanted to exercise power and make her go to bed and make her—hideous—drink castor oil, that she thought she was ill.

"I'm sure," said Mrs. Fisher, who felt the cold of the stone beginning to come through and knew she could not sit much longer, "you'll do what is reasonable. Your mother would wish—have you a mother?"

A faint wonder came into Scrap's eyes. Have you a mother? If ever anybody had a mother it was Scrap. It had not occurred to her that there could be people who had never heard of her mother. She was one of the major marchionesses—there being, as no one knew better than Scrap, marchionesses and marchionesses—and had held high positions at Court. Her father, too, in his day had been most prominent. His day was a little over, poor dear, because in the war he had made some important mistakes, and besides he was now grown old; still, there he was, an excessively well-known person. How restful, how extraordinarily restful to have found some one who had never heard of any of her lot, or at least had not yet connected her with them.

She began to like Mrs. Fisher. Perhaps the originals didn't know anything about her either. When she first wrote to them and signed her name, that great name of Dester which twisted in and out of English history like a bloody thread, for its bearers constantly killed, she had taken it for granted that they would know who she was; and at the interview of Shaftesbury Avenue she was sure they did know, because they hadn't asked, as they otherwise would have, for references.

Scrap began to cheer up. If nobody at San Salvatore had ever heard of her, if for a whole month she could shed herself, get right away from everything connected with herself, be allowed really to forget the clinging and the clogging and all the noise, why, perhaps she might make something of herself after all. She might really think; really clear up her mind; really come to some conclusion.

"What I want to do here," she said, leaning forward in her chair and clasping her hands round her knees and looking up at Mrs. Fisher, whose seat was higher than hers, almost with animation, so much pleased was she that Mrs. Fisher knew nothing about her, "is to come to a conclusion. That's all. It isn't much to want, is it? Just that."

She gazed at Mrs. Fisher, and thought that almost any conclusion would do; the great thing was to get hold of something, catch something tight, cease to drift.

Mrs. Fisher's little eyes surveyed her. "I should say," she said, "that what a young woman like you wants is a husband and children."

"Well, that's one of the things I'm going to consider," said Scrap amiably. "But I don't think it would be a conclusion."
"And meanwhile," said Mrs. Fisher, getting up, for the cold of the stone was now through, "I shouldn't trouble my head if I were you with considerings and conclusions. Women's heads weren't made for thinking, I assure you. I should go to bed and get well."

"I am well," said Scrap.

"Then why did you send a message that you were ill?"

"I didn't."

"Then I've had all the trouble of coming out here for nothing."

"But wouldn't you prefer coming out and finding me well than coming out and finding me ill?" asked Scrap, smiling.

Even Mrs. Fisher was caught by the smile.

"Well, you're a pretty creature," she said forgivingly. "It's a pity you weren't born fifty years ago. My friends would have liked looking at you."

"I'm very glad I wasn't," said Scrap. "I dislike being looked at."

"Absurd," said Mrs. Fisher, growing stern again. "That's what you are made for, young women like you. For what else, pray? And I assure you that if my friends had looked at you, you would have been looked at by some very great people."

"I dislike very great people," said Scrap, frowning. There had been an incident quite recently—really potentates. . .

"What I dislike," said Mrs. Fisher, now as cold as that stone she had got up from, "is the pose of the modern young woman. It seems to me pitiful, positively pitiful, in its silliness."

And, her stick crunching the pebbles, she walked away.

"That's all right," Scrap said to herself, dropping back into her comfortable position with her head in the cushion and her feet on the parapet; if only people would go away she didn't in the least mind why they went.

"Don't you think darling Scrap is growing a little, just a little, peculiar?" her mother had asked her father a short time before that latest peculiarity of the flight to San Salvatore, uncomfortably struck by the very odd things Scrap said and the way she had taken to slinking out of reach whenever she could and avoiding everybody except —such a sign of age—quite young men, almost boys.

"Eh? What? Peculiar? Well, let her be peculiar if she likes. A woman with her looks can be any damned thing she pleases," was the infatuated answer.

"I do let her," said her mother meekly; and indeed if she did not, what difference would it make?

Mrs. Fisher was sorry she had bothered about Lady Caroline. She went along the hall towards her private sitting-room, and her stick as she went struck the stone floor with a vigour in harmony with her feelings. Sheer silliness, these poses. She had no patience with them. Unable to be or do anything of themselves, the young of the present generation tried to achieve a reputation for cleverness by decrying all that was obviously great and obviously good and by praising everything, however obviously bad, that was different. Apes, thought Mrs. Fisher, roused. Apes. Apes. And in her sitting-room she found more apes, or what seemed to her in her present mood more, for there was Mrs. Arbuthnot placidly drinking coffee, while at the writing-table, the writing-table she already looked upon as sacred, using her pen, her own pen brought for her hand alone from Prince of Wales Terrace, sat Mrs. Wilkins writing; at the table; in her room; with her pen.

"Isn't this a delightful place?" said Mrs. Arbuthnot cordially. "We have just discovered it."

"I'm writing to Mellersh," said Mrs. Wilkins, turning her head and also cordially—as though, Mrs. Fisher thought, she cared a straw who she was writing to and anyhow knew who the person she called Mellersh was. "He'll want to know," said Mrs. Wilkins, optimism induced by her surroundings, "that I've got here safely."

Chapter 11

The sweet smells that were everywhere in San Salvatore were alone enough to produce concord. They came into the sitting-room from the flowers on the battlements, and met the ones from the flowers inside the room, and almost, thought Mrs. Wilkins, could be seen greeting each other with a holy kiss. Who could be angry in the middle of such gentlenesses? Who could be acquisitive, selfish, in the old rasped London way, in the presence of this bounteous beauty?

Yet Mrs. Fisher seemed to be all three of these things.

There was so much beauty, so much more than enough for every one, that it did appear to be a vain activity to try and make a corner in it.

Yet Mrs. Fisher was trying to make a corner in it, and had railed off a portion for her exclusive use.

Well, she would get over that presently; she would get over it inevitably, Mrs. Wilkins was sure, after a day or two in the extraordinary atmosphere of peace in that place.

Meanwhile she obviously hadn't even begun to get over it. She stood looking at her and Rose with an expression that appeared to be one of anger. Anger. Fancy. Silly old nerve-racked London feelings, thought Mrs. Wilkins, whose eyes saw the room full of kisses, and everybody in it being kissed, Mrs. Fisher as copiously as she herself and Rose.

"You don't like us being in here," said Mrs. Wilkins, getting up and at once, after her manner, fixing on the truth. "Why?"

"I should have thought," said Mrs. Fisher leaning on her stick, "you could have seen that it is my room."

"You mean because of the photographs," said Mrs. Wilkins.

Mrs. Arbuthnot, who was a little red and surprised, got up too.

"And the notepaper," said Mrs. Fisher. "Notepaper with my London address on it. That pen—"

She pointed. It was still in Mrs. Wilkins's hand.

"Is yours. I'm very sorry," said Mrs. Wilkins, laying it on the table. And she added smiling, that it had just been writing some very amiable things.

"But why," asked Mrs. Arbuthnot, who found herself unable to acquiesce in Mrs. Fisher's arrangements without at least a gentle struggle, "ought we not to be here? It's a sitting-room."

"There is another one," said Mrs. Fisher. "You and your friend cannot sit in two rooms at once, and if I have no wish to disturb you in yours I am unable to see why you should wish to disturb me in mine."

"But why—" began Mrs. Arbuthnot again.

"It's quite natural," Mrs. Wilkins interrupted, for Rose was looking stubborn; and turning to Mrs. Fisher she said that although sharing things with friends was pleasant she could understand that Mrs. Fisher, still steeped in the Prince of Wales Terrace attitude to life, did not yet want to, but that she would get rid of that after a bit and feel quite different. "Soon you'll want us to share," said Mrs. Wilkins reassuringly. "Why, you may even get so far as asking me to use your pen if you knew I hadn't got one."

Mrs. Fisher was moved almost beyond control by this speech. To have a ramshackle young woman from Hampstead patting her on the back as it were, in breezy certitude that quite soon she would improve, stirred her more deeply than anything had stirred her since her first discovery that Mr. Fisher was not what he seemed. Mrs. Wilkins must certainly be curbed. But how? There was a curious imperviousness about her. At that moment, for instance, she was smiling as pleasantly and with as unclouded a face as if she were saying nothing in the least impertinent. Would she know she was being curbed? If she didn't know, if she were too tough to feel it, then what? Nothing, except avoidance; except, precisely, one's own private sitting-room.

"I'm an old woman," said Mrs. Fisher, "and I need a room to myself. I cannot get about, because of my stick. As I cannot get about I have to sit. Why should I not sit quietly and undisturbed, as I told you in London I intended to? If people are to come in and out all day long, chattering and leaving doors open, you will have broken the agreement, which was that I was to be quiet."

"But we haven't the least wish—" began Mrs. Arbuthnot, who was again cut short by Mrs. Wilkins.

"We're only too glad," said Mrs. Wilkins, "for you to have this room if it makes you happy. We didn't know about it, that's all. We wouldn't have come in if we had—not till you invited us, anyhow. I expect," she finished looking down cheerfully at Mrs. Fisher, "you soon will." And picking up her letter she took Mrs. Arbuthnot's hand and drew her towards the door.

Mrs. Arbuthnot did not want to go. She, the mildest of women, was filled with a curious and surely unchristian desire to stay and fight. Not, of course, really, nor even with any definitely aggressive words. No; she only wanted to reason with Mrs. Fisher, and to reason patiently. But she did feel that something ought to be said, and that she ought not to allow herself to be rated and turned out as if she were a schoolgirl caught in ill behaviour by Authority.

Mrs. Wilkins, however, drew her firmly to and through the door, and once again Rose wondered at Lotty, at her balance, her sweet and equable temper—she who in England had been such a thing of gusts. From the moment they got into Italy it was Lotty who seemed the elder. She certainly was very happy; blissful, in fact. Did happiness so completely protect one? Did it make one so untouchable, so wise? Rose was happy herself, but not anything like so happy. Evidently not, for not only did she want to fight Mrs. Fisher but she wanted something else, something more than this lovely place, something to complete it; she wanted Frederick. For the first time in her life she was surrounded by perfect beauty, and her one thought was to show it to him, to share it with him. She wanted Frederick. She yearned for Frederick. Ah, if only, only Frederick . . .

"Poor old thing," said Mrs. Wilkins, shutting the door gently on Mrs. Fisher and her triumph. "Fancy on a day like this."
"She's a very rude old thing," said Mrs. Arbuthnot.

"She'll get over that. I'm sorry we chose just her room to go and sit in."

"It's much the nicest," said Mrs. Arbuthnot. "And it isn't hers."

"Oh but there are lots of other places, and she's such a poor old thing. Let her have the room. Whatever does it matter?"

And Mrs. Wilkins said she was going down to the village to find out where the post-office was and post her letter to Mellersh, and would Rose go too.

"I've been thinking about Mellersh," said Mrs. Wilkins as they walked, one behind the other, down the narrow zigzag path up which they had climbed in the rain the night before.

She went first. Mrs. Arbuthnot, quite naturally now, followed. In England it had been the other way about—Lotty, timid, hesitating, except when she burst out so awkwardly, getting behind the calm and reasonable Rose whenever she could.

"I've been thinking about Mellersh," repeated Mrs. Wilkins over her shoulder, as Rose seemed not to have heard.

"Have you?" said Rose, a faint distaste in her voice, for her experiences with Mellersh had not been of a kind to make her enjoy remembering him. She had deceived Mellersh; therefore she didn't like him. She was unconscious that this was the reason of her dislike, and thought it was that there didn't seem to be much, if any, of the grace of god about him. And yet how wrong to feel that, she rebuked herself, and how presumptuous. No doubt Lotty's husband was far, far nearer to God than she herself was ever likely to be. Still, she didn't like him.

"I've been a mean dog," said Mrs. Wilkins.

"A what?" asked Mrs. Arbuthnot, incredulous of her hearing.

"All this coming away and leaving him in that dreary place while I rollick in heaven. He had planned to take me to Italy for Easter himself. Did I tell you?"

"No," said Mrs. Arbuthnot; and indeed she had discouraged talk about husbands. Whenever Lotty had begun to blurt out things she had swiftly changed the conversation. One husband led to another, in conversation as well as in life, she felt, and she could not, she would not, talk of Frederick. Beyond the bare fact that he was there, he had not been mentioned. Mellersh had had to be mentioned, because of his obstructiveness, but she had carefully kept him from overflowing outside the limits of necessity.

"Well, he did," said Mrs. Wilkins. "He had never done such a thing in his life before, and I was horrified. Fancy—just as I had planned to come to it myself."

She paused on the path and looked up at Rose.

"Yes," said Rose, trying to think of something else to talk about.

"Now you see why I say I've been a mean dog. He had planned a holiday in Italy with me, and I had planned a holiday in Italy leaving him at home. I think," she went on, her eyes fixed on Rose's face, "Mellersh has every reason to be both angry and hurt."

Mrs. Arbuthnot was astonished. The extraordinary quickness with which, hour by hour, under her very eyes, Lotty became more selfless, disconcerted her. She was turning into something surprisingly like a saint. Here she was now being affectionate about Mellersh—Mellersh, who only that morning, while they hung their feet into the sea, had seemed a mere iridescence, Lotty had told her, a thing of gauze. That was only that morning; and by the time they had had lunch Lotty had developed so far as to have got him solid enough again to write to, and to write to at length. And now, a few minutes later, she was announcing that he had every reason to be angry with her and hurt, and that she herself had been—the language was unusual, but it did express real penitence—a mean dog.

Rose stared at her astonished. If she went on like this, soon a nimbus might be expected round her head, was there already, if one didn't know it was the sun through the tree-trunks catching her sandy hair.

A great desire to love and be friends, to love everybody, to be friends with everybody, seemed to be invading Lotty—a desire for sheer goodness. Rose's own experience was that goodness, the state of being good, was only reached with difficulty and pain. It took a long time to get to it; in fact one never did get to it, or, if for a flashing instant one did, it was only for a flashing instant. Desperate perseverance was needed to struggle along its path, and all the way was dotted with doubts. Lotty simply flew along. She had certainly, thought Rose, not got rid of her impetuousness. It had merely taken another direction. She was now impetuously becoming a saint. Could one really attain goodness so violently? Wouldn't there be an equally violent reaction?

"I shouldn't," said Rose with caution, looking down into Lotty's bright eyes—the path was steep, so that Lotty was well below her—"I shouldn't be sure of that too quickly."

"But I am sure of it, and I've written and told him so."

Rose stared. "Why, but only this morning—" she began.

"It's all in this," interrupted Lotty, tapping the envelope and looking pleased.

"What—everything?"

"You mean about the advertisement and my savings being spent? Oh no—not yet. But I'll tell him all that when he comes."

"When he comes?" repeated Rose.

"I've invited him to come and stay with us."

Rose could only go on staring.

"It's the least I could do. Besides—look at this." Lotty waived her hand. "Disgusting not to share it. I was a mean dog to go off and leave him, but no dog I've every heard of was ever as mean as I'd be if I didn't try and persuade Mellersh to come out and enjoy this too. It's barest decency that he should have some of the fun out of my nest-egg. After all, he has housed me and fed me for years. One shouldn't be churlish."

"But—do you think he'll come?

"Oh, I hope so," said Lotty with the utmost earnestness; and added, "Poor lamb."

At that Rose felt she would like to sit down. Mellersh a poor lamb? That same Mellersh who a few hours before was mere shimmer? There was a seat at the bend of the path, and Rose went to it and sat down. She wished to get her breath, gain time. If she had time she might perhaps be able to catch up the leaping Lotty, and perhaps be able to stop her before she committed herself to what she probably presently would be sorry for. Mellersh at San Salvatore? Mellersh, from whom Lotty had taken such pains so recently to escape?

"I see him here," said Lotty, as if in answer to her thoughts.

Rose looked at her with real concern: for every time Lotty said in that convinced voice, "I see," what she saw came true. Then it was to be supposed that Mr. Wilkins too would presently come true.

"I wish," said Rose anxiously, "I understood you."

"Don't try," said Lotty, smiling.

"But I must, because I love you."

"Dear Rose," said Lotty, swiftly bending down and kissing her.

"You're so quick," said Rose. "I can't follow your developments.
I can't keep touch. It was what happened with Freder—"
She broke off and looked frightened.

"The whole idea of our coming here," she went on again, as Lotty didn't
seem to have noticed, "was to get away, wasn't it? Well, we've got away.
And now, after only a single day of it, you want to write to the very
people—"

She stopped.

"The very people we were getting away from," finished Lotty.
"It's quite true. It seems idiotically illogical. But I'm so happy,
I'm so well, I feel so fearfully wholesome. This place—why, it makes
me feel flooded with love."
And she stared down at Rose in a kind of radiant surprise.

Rose was silent a moment. Then she said, "And do you think it will have
the same effect on Mr. Wilkins?"

Lotty laughed. "I don't know," she said. "But even if it doesn't, there's
enough love about to flood fifty Mr. Wilkinses, as you call him. The great
thing is to have lots of love about. I don't see," she went on, "at least I don't
see here, though I did at home, that it matters who loves as long as
somebody does. I was a stingy beast at home, and used to measure and
count. I had a queer obsession about justice. As though justice mattered. As
though justice can really be distinguished from vengeance. It's only love
that's any good. At home I wouldn't love Mellersh unless he loved me
back, exactly as much, absolute fairness. Did you ever. And as he didn't,
neither did I, and the aridity of that house! The aridity . . ."

Rose said nothing. She was bewildered by Lotty. One odd effect of San
Salvatore on her rapidly developing friend was her sudden free use of
robust words. She had not used them in Hampstead. Beast and dog were
more robust than Hampstead cared about. In words, too, Lotty had come
unchained.

But how she wished, oh how Rose wished, that she too could write to her
husband and say "Come." The Wilkins ménage, however pompous

Mellersh might be, and he had seemed to Rose pompous, was on a healthier, more natural footing than hers. Lotty could write to Mellersh and would get an answer. She couldn't write to Frederick, for only too well did she know he wouldn't answer. At least, he might answer—a hurried scribble, showing how much bored he was at doing it, with perfunctory thanks for her letter. But that would be worse than no answer at all; for his handwriting, her name on an envelope addressed by him, stabbed her heart. Too acutely did it bring back the letters of their beginnings together, the letters from him so desolate with separation, so aching with love and longing. To see apparently one of these very same letters arrive, and open it to find:

Dear Rose—Thanks for letter. Glad you're having a good time. Don't hurry back. Say if you want any money. Everything going splendidly here—

    Yours, Frederick.

—no, it couldn't be borne.

"I don't think I'll come down to the village with you to-day," she said, looking up at Lotty with eyes suddenly gone dim. "I think I want to think."

"All right," said Lotty, at once starting off briskly down the path. "But don't think too long," she called back over her shoulder. "Write and invite him at once."

"Invite whom?" asked Rose, startled.

"Your husband."

Chapter 12

At the evening meal, which was the first time the whole four sat round the dining-room table together, Scrap appeared.

She appeared quite punctually, and in one of those wrappers or tea-gowns which are sometimes described as ravishing. This one really was ravishing. It certainly ravished Mrs. Wilkins, who could not take her eyes off the enchanting figure opposite. It was a shell-pink garment, and clung to the adorable Scrap as though it, too, loved her.

"What a beautiful dress!" exclaimed Mrs. Wilkins eagerly.

"What—this old rag?" said Scrap, glancing down at it as if to see which one she had got on. "I've had it a hundred years." And she concentrated on her soup.

"You must be very cold in it," said Mrs. Fisher, thin-lipped; for it showed a great deal of Scrap—the whole of her arms, for instance, and even where it covered her up it was so thin that you still saw her.

"Who—me?" said Scrap, looking up a moment. "Oh, no."

And she continued her soup.

"You mustn't catch a chill, you know," said Mrs. Arbuthnot, feeling that such loveliness must at all costs be preserved unharmed. "There's a great difference here when the sun goes down."

"I'm quite warm," said Scrap, industriously eating her soup.

"You look as if you had nothing at all on underneath," said Mrs. Fisher.
"I haven't. At least, hardly anything," said Scrap, finishing her soup.

"How every imprudent," said Mrs. Fisher, "and how highly improper."

Whereupon Scrap stared at her.

Mrs. Fisher had arrived at dinner feeling friendly towards Lady Caroline. She at least had not intruded into her room and sat at her table and written with her pen. She did, Mrs. Fisher had supposed, know how to behave. Now it appeared that she did not know, for was this behaving, to come dressed—no, undressed—like that to a meal? Such behaviour was not only exceedingly improper but also most inconsiderate, for the indelicate creature would certainly catch a chill, and then infect the entire party. Mrs. Fisher had a great objection to other people's chills. They were always the fruit of folly; and then they were handed on to her, who had done nothing at all to deserve them.

"Bird-brained," though Mrs. Fisher, sternly contemplating Lady Caroline. "Not an idea in her head except vanity."
"But there are no men here," said Mrs. Wilkins, "so how can it be improper? Have you noticed," she inquired of Mrs. Fisher, who endeavoured to pretend she did not hear, "How difficult it is to be improper without men?"

Mrs. Fisher neither answered her not looked at her; but Scrap looked at her, and did that with her mouth which in any other mouth would have been a fain grin. Seen from without, across the bowl of nasturtiums, it was the most beautiful of brief and dimpled smiles.

She had a very alive sort of face, that one, thought Scrap, observing Mrs. Wilkins with a dawn of interest. It was rather like a field of corn swept by lights and shadows. Both she and the dark one, Scrap noticed, had changed their clothes, but only in order to put on silk jumpers. The same amount of trouble would have been enough to dress them properly, reflected Scrap. Naturally they looked like nothing on earth in the jumpers. It didn't matter what Mrs. Fisher wore; indeed, the only thing for her, short of plumes and ermine, was what she did wear. But these others were quite young still, and quite attractive. They really definitely had faces. How different life would be for them if they made the most of themselves instead of the least. And yet—Scrap was suddenly bored, and turned away her thoughts and absently ate toast. What did it matter? If you did make the most of yourself, you only collected people round you who ended by wanting to grab.

"I've had the most wonderful day," began Mrs. Wilkins, her eyes shining.

Scrap lowered hers. "Oh," she thought, "she's going to gush."

"As though anybody were interested in her day," thought Mrs. Fisher, lowering hers also.
In fact, whenever Mrs. Wilkins spoke Mrs. Fisher deliberately cast down her eyes. Thus would she mark her disapproval. Besides, it seemed the only safe thing to do with her eyes, for no one could tell what the uncurbed creature would say next. That which she had just said, for instance, about

men—addressed too, to her—what could she mean? Better not conjecture, thought Mrs. Fisher; and her eyes, though cast down, yet saw Lady Caroline stretch out her hand to the Chianti flask and fill her glass again.

Again. She had done it once already, and the fish was only just going out of the room. Mrs. Fisher could see that the other respectable member of the party, Mrs. Arbuthnot, was noticing it too. Mrs. Arbuthnot was, she hoped and believed, respectable and well-meaning. It is true she also had invaded her sitting-room, but no doubt she had been dragged there by the other one, and Mrs. Fisher had little if anything against Mrs. Arbuthnot, and observed with approval that she only drank water. That was as it should be. So, indeed, to give her her dues, did the freckled one; and very right at their age. She herself drank wine, but with what moderation: one meal, one glass. And she was sixty-five, and might properly, and even beneficially, have had at least two.

"That," she said to Lady Caroline, cutting right across what Mrs. Wilkins was telling them about her wonderful day and indicating the wine-glass, "is very bad for you."

Lady Caroline, however, could not have heard, for she continued to sip, her elbow on the table, and listen to what Mrs. Wilkins was saying.

And what was it she was saying? She had invited somebody to come and stay? A man?

Mrs. Fisher could not credit her ears. Yet it evidently was a man, for she spoke of the person as he.

Suddenly and for the first time—but then this was most important—Mrs. Fisher addressed Mrs. Wilkins directly. She was sixty-five, and cared very little what sorts of women she happened to be with for a month, but if the women were to be mixed with men it was a different proposition altogether. She was not going to be made a cat's-paw of. She had not come out there to sanction by her presence what used in her day to be called fast behaviour. Nothing had been said at the interview in London about men; if there had been she would have declined, of course to come.

"What is his name?" asked Mrs. Fisher, abruptly interposing.

Mrs. Wilkins turned to her with a slight surprise. "Wilkins," she said.

"Wilkins?"

"Yes,"

"Your name?"

"And his."

"A relation?"

"Not blood."

"A connection?"

"A husband."

Mrs. Fisher once more cast down her eyes. She could not talk to Mrs. Wilkins. There was something about the things she said. . . "A husband." Suggesting one of many. Always that unseemly twist to everything. Why could she not say "My husband"? Besides, Mrs. Fisher had, she herself knew not for what reason, taken both the Hampstead young women for widows. War ones. There had been an absence of mention of husbands at the interview which would not, she considered, be natural if such persons did after all exist. And if a husband was not a relation, who was? "Not blood." What a way to talk. Why, a husband was the first of all relations. How well she remembered Ruskin—no, it was not Ruskin, it was the Bible that said a man should leave his father and mother and cleave only to his wife; showing that she became by marriage an even more than blood relation. And if the husband's father and mother were to be nothing to him compared to his wife, how much less than nothing ought the wife's father and mother be to her compared to her husband. She herself had been unable to leave her father and mother in order to cleave to Mr. Fisher because they were no longer, when she married, alive, but she certainly would have left them if they had been there to leave. Not blood, indeed. Silly talk.

The dinner was very good. Succulence succeeded succulence. Costanza had determined to do as she chose in the matter of cream and eggs the first week, and see what happened at the end of it when the bills had to be paid. Her experience of the English was that they were quiet about bills. They were shy of words. They believed readily. Besides, who was the mistress here? In the absence of a definite one, it occurred to Costanza that she might as well be the mistress herself. So she did as she chose about the dinner, and it was very good.

The four, however, were so much preoccupied by their own conversation that they ate it without noticing how good it was. Even Mrs. Fisher, she who in such matters was manly, did not notice. The entire excellent cooking was to her as though it were not; which shows how much she must have been stirred.

She was stirred. It was that Mrs. Wilkins. She was enough to stir anybody. And she was undoubtedly encouraged by Lady Caroline, who, in her turn, was no doubt influenced by the Chianti.

Mrs. Fisher was very glad there were no men present, for they certainly would have been foolish about Lady Caroline. She was precisely the sort of young woman to unbalance them; especially, Mrs. Fisher recognized, at that moment. Perhaps it was the Chianti momentarily intensifying her personality, but she was undeniably most attractive; and there were few things Mrs. Fisher disliked more than having to look on while sensible, intelligent men, who the moment before were talking seriously and interestingly about real matters, became merely foolish and simpering— she had seen them actually simpering—just because in walked a bit of bird-brained beauty. Even Mr. Gladstone, that great wise statesman, whose hand had once rested for an unforgettable moment solemnly on her head, would have, she felt, on perceiving Lady Caroline left off talking sense and horribly embarked on badinage.

"You see," Mrs. Wilkins said—a silly trick that, with which she mostly began her sentences; Mrs. Fisher each time wished to say, "Pardon me—I do not see, I hear"—but why trouble?—"You see," said Mrs. Wilkins, leaning across towards Lady Caroline, "we arranged, didn't we, in London that if any of us wanted to we could each invite one guest. So now I'm doing it."

"I don't remember that," said Mrs. Fisher, her eyes on her plate.

"Oh yes, we did—didn't we, Rose?"

"Yes—I remember," said Lady Caroline. "Only it seemed so incredible that one could ever want to. One's whole idea was to get away from one's friends."

"And one's husbands."

Again that unseemly plural. But how altogether unseemly, thought Mrs.

Fisher. Such implications. Mrs. Arbuthnot clearly thought so too, for she had turned red.

"And family affection," said Lady Caroline—or was it the Chianti speaking? Surely it was the Chianti.

"And the want of family affection," said Mrs. Wilkins—what a light she was throwing on her home life and real character.

"That wouldn't be so bad," said Lady Caroline. "I'd stay with that. It would give one room."

"Oh no, no—it's dreadful," cried Mrs. Wilkins. "It's as if one had no clothes on."

"But I like that," said Lady Caroline.

"Really—" said Mrs. Fisher.

"It's a divine feeling, getting rid of things," said Lady Caroline, who was talking altogether to Mrs. Wilkins and paid no attention to the other two.

"Oh, but in a bitter wind to have nothing on and know there never will be anything on and you going to get colder and colder till at last you die of it—that's what it was like, living with somebody who didn't love one."

These confidences, thought Mrs. Fisher . . . and no excuse whatever for Mrs. Wilkins, who was making them entirely on plain water. Mrs. Arbuthnot, judging from her face, quite shared Mrs. Fisher's disapproval; she was fidgeting.

"But didn't he?" asked Lady Caroline—every bit as shamelessly unreticent as Mrs. Wilkins.

"Mellersh? He showed no signs of it."

"Delicious," murmured Lady Caroline.

"Really—" said Mrs. Fisher.

"I didn't think it was at all delicious. I was miserable. And now, since I've been here, I simply stare at myself being miserable. As miserable as that. And about Mellersh."

"You mean he wasn't worth it."

"Really—" said Mrs. Fisher.

"No, I don't. I mean I've suddenly got well."

Lady Caroline, slowly twisting the stem of her glass in her fingers, scrutinized the lit-up face opposite.

"And now I'm well I find I can't sit here and gloat all to myself. I can't be happy, shutting him out. I must share. I understand exactly what the Blessed Damozel felt like."

"What was the Blessed Damozel?" asked Scrap.

"Really—" said Mrs. Fisher; and with such emphasis this time that Lady Caroline turned to her.

"Ought I to know?" she asked. "I don't know any natural history.
It sounds like a bird."
"It is a poem," said Mrs. Fisher with extraordinary frost.

"Oh," said Scrap.

"I'll lend it to you," said Mrs. Wilkins, over whose face laughter rippled.

"No," said Scrap.

"And its author," said Mrs. Fisher icily, "though not perhaps quite what one would have wished him to be, was frequently at my father's table."

"What a bore for you," said Scrap. "That's what mother's always doing—inviting authors. I hate authors. I wouldn't mind them so much if they didn't write books. Go on about Mellersh," she said, turning to Mrs. Wilkins.

"Really—" said Mrs. Fisher.

"All those empty beds," said Mrs. Wilkins.

"What empty beds?" asked Scrap.

"The ones in this house. Why, of course they each ought to have somebody happy inside them. Eight beds, and only four people. It's dreadful, dreadful to be so greedy and keep everything just for oneself. I want Rose to ask her husband out too. You and Mrs. Fisher haven't got husbands, but why not give some friend a glorious time?"

Rose bit her lip. She turned red, she turned pale. If only Lotty would keep quiet, she thought. It was all very well to have suddenly become a saint and want to love everybody, but need she be so tactless? Rose felt that all her poor sore places were being danced on. If only Lotty would keep quiet . . .

And Mrs. Fisher, with even greater frostiness than that with which she had received Lady Caroline's ignorance of the Blessed Damozel, said, "There is only one unoccupied bedroom in this house."

"Only one?" echoed Mrs. Wilkins, astonished. "Then who are in all the others?"

"We are," said Mrs. Fisher.

"But we're not in all the bedrooms. There must be at least six. That leaves two over, and the owner told us there were eight beds— didn't he Rose?"

"There are six bedrooms," said Mrs. Fisher; for both she and Lady Caroline had thoroughly searched the house on arriving, in order to see which part of it they would be most comfortable in, and they both knew that there were six bedrooms, two of which were very small, and in one of these small ones Francesca slept in the company of a chair and a chest of drawers, and the other, similarly furnished, was empty.

Mrs. Wilkins and Mrs. Arbuthnot had hardly looked at the house, having spent most of their time out-of-doors gaping at the scenery, and had, in the agitated inattentiveness of their minds when first they began negotiating for San Salvatore, got into their heads that the eight beds of which the owner spoke were the same as eight bedrooms; which they were not. There were indeed eight beds, but four of them were in Mrs. Wilkins's and Mrs. Arbuthnot's rooms.

"There are six bedrooms," repeated Mrs. Fisher. "We have four, Francesca has the fifth, and the sixth is empty."
"So that," said Scrap, "However kind we feel we would be if we could, we can't. Isn't it fortunate?"

"But then there's only room for one?" said Mrs. Wilkins, looking round at the three faces.

"Yes—and you've got him," said Scrap.

Mrs. Wilkins was taken aback. This question of the beds was unexpected. In inviting Mellersh she had intended to put him in one of the four spare-rooms that she imagined were there. When there were plenty of rooms and enough servants there was no reason why they should, as they did in their small, two-servanted house at home, share the same one. Love, even universal love, the kind of love with which she felt herself flooded, should not be tried. Much patience and self-effacement were needed for successful married sleep. Placidity; a steady faith; these too were needed. She was sure she would be much fonder of Mellersh, and he not mind her nearly so much, if they were not shut up together at night, if in the morning they could meet with the cheery affection of friends between whom lies no shadow of differences about the window or the washing arrangements, or of absurd little choked-down resentments at something that had seemed to one of them unfair. Her happiness, she felt, and her ability to be friends with everybody, was the result of her sudden new freedom and its peace. Would there be that sense of freedom, that peace, after a night shut up with Mellersh? Would she be able in the morning to be full towards him, as she was at that moment full, of nothing at all but loving-kindness? After all, she hadn't been very long in heaven. Suppose she hadn't been in it long enough for her to have become fixed in blandness? And only that morning what an extraordinary joy it had been to find herself alone when she woke, and able to pull the bed-clothes any way she liked!

Francesca had to nudge her. She was so much absorbed that she did not notice the pudding.

"If," thought Mrs. Wilkins, distractedly helping herself, "I share my room with Mellersh I risk losing all I now feel about him. If on the other hand I put him in the one spare-room, I prevent Mrs. Fisher and Lady Caroline from giving somebody a treat. True they don't seem to want to at present, but at any moment in this place one or the other of them may be seized with a desire to make somebody happy, and then they wouldn't be able to because of Mellersh."

"What a problem," she said aloud, her eyebrows puckered.

"What is?" asked Scrap.

"Where to put Mellersh."

Scrap stared. "Why, isn't one room enough for him?" she asked.

"Oh yes, quite. But then there won't be any room left at all— any room for somebody you may want to invite."

"I shan't want to," said Scrap.

"Or you," said Mrs. Wilkins to Mrs. Fisher. "Rose, of course, doesn't count. I'm sure she would like sharing her room with her husband. It's written all over her."

"Really—" said Mrs. Fisher.

"Really what?" asked Mrs. Wilkins, turning hopefully to her, for she thought the word this time was the preliminary to a helpful suggestion.

It was not. It stood by itself. It was, as before, mere frost.

Challenged, however, Mrs. Fisher did fasten it on to a sentence. "Really am I to understand," she asked, "that you propose to reserve the one spare-room for the exclusive use of your own family?"

"He isn't my own family," said Mrs. Wilkins. "He's my husband.
You see—"
"I see nothing," Mrs. Fisher could not this time refrain from interrupting— for what an intolerable trick. "At the most I hear, and that reluctantly."

But Mrs. Wilkins, as impervious to rebuke as Mrs. Fisher had feared, immediately repeated the tiresome formula and launched out into a long and excessively indelicate speech about the best place for the person she called Mellersh to sleep in.

Mellersh—Mrs. Fisher, remembering the Thomases and Johns and Alfreds and Roberts of her day, plain names that yet had all become glorious, thought it sheer affection to be christened Mellersh—was, it seemed, Mrs. Wilkins's husband, and therefore his place was clearly indicated. Why this talk? She herself, as if foreseeing his arrival, had had a second bed put in Mrs. Wilkins's room. There were certain things in life which were never talked about but only done. Most things connected with husbands were not talked about; and to have a whole dinner-table taken up with a discussion as to where one of them should sleep was an affront to the decencies. How and where husbands slept should be known only to their wives. Sometimes it was not known to them, and then the marriage had less happy moments; but these moments were not talked about either; the decencies continued to be preserved. At least, it was so in her day. To have to hear whether Mr. Wilkins should or should not sleep with Mrs. Wilkins, and the reasons why he should and the reasons why he shouldn't, was both uninteresting and indelicate.

She might have succeeded in imposing propriety and changing the conversation if it had not been for Lady Caroline. Lady Caroline encouraged Mrs. Wilkins, and threw herself into the discussion with every bit as much unreserve as Mrs. Wilkins herself. No doubt she was impelled on this occasion by Chianti, but whatever the reason there it was. And, characteristically, Lady Caroline was all for Mr. Wilkins being given the solitary spare-room. She took that for granted. Any other arrangement would be impossible, she said; her expression was, Barbarous. Had she never read her Bible, Mrs. Fisher was tempted to inquire—And they two shall be one flesh? Clearly also, then, one room. But Mrs. Fisher did not inquire. She did not care even to allude to such texts to some one unmarried.

However, there was one way she could force Mr. Wilkins into his proper place and save the situation: she could say she herself intended to invite a friend. It was her right. They had all said so. Apart from propriety, it was monstrous that Mrs. Wilkins should want to monopolise the one spare-room, when in her own room was everything necessary for her husband. Perhaps she really would invite somebody— not invite, but suggest coming. There was Kate Lumley, for instance. Kate could perfectly afford to come and pay her share; and she was of her own period and knew, and had known, most of the people she herself knew and had known. Kate, of course, had only been on the fringe; she used to be asked only to the big parties, not to the small ones, and she still was only on the fringe. There were some people who never got off the fringe, and Kate was one. Often, however, such people were more permanently agreeable to be with than the others, in that they remained grateful.

Yes; she might really consider Kate. The poor soul had never married, but then everybody could not expect to marry, and she was quite comfortably off—not too comfortably, but just comfortably enough to pay her own expenses if she came and yet be grateful. Yes; Kate was the solution. If she came, at one stroke, Mrs. Fisher saw, would the Wilkinses be regularized and Mrs. Wilkins be prevented from having more than her share of the rooms. Also, Mrs. Fisher would save herself from isolation; spiritual isolation. She desired physical isolation between meals, but she disliked that isolation which is of the spirit. Such isolation would, she feared, certainly be hers with these three alien-minded young women. Even Mrs. Arbuthnot was, owing to her friendship with Mrs. Wilkins, necessarily alien-minded. In Kate she would have a support. Kate, without intruding on her sitting-room, for Kate was tractable, would be there at meals to support her.

Mrs. Fisher said nothing at the moment; but presently in the drawing-room, when they were gathered round the wood fire—she had discovered there was no fireplace in her own sitting-room, and therefore she would after all be forced, so long as the evenings remained cool, to spend them in the other room—presently, while Francesca was handing coffee round and Lady Caroline was poisoning the air with smoke, Mrs. Wilkins, looking relieved and pleased, said: "Well, if nobody really wants that room, and wouldn't use it anyhow, I shall be very glad if Mellersh may have it."

"Of course he must have it," said Lady Caroline.

Then Mrs. Fisher spoke.

"I have a friend," she said in her deep voice; and sudden silence fell upon the others.

"Kate Lumley," said Mrs. Fisher.

Nobody spoke.

"Perhaps," continued Mrs. Fisher, addressing Lady Caroline, "you know her?"

No, Lady Caroline did not know Kate Lumley; and Mrs. Fisher, without asking the others if they did, for she was sure they knew no one, proceeded. "I wish to invite her to join me," said Mrs. Fisher.

Complete silence.

Then Scrap said, turning to Mrs. Wilkins, "That settles Mellersh, then."

"It settles the question of Mr. Wilkins," said Mrs. Fisher, "although I am unable to understand that there should ever have been a question, in the only way that is right."

"I'm afraid you're in for it, then," said Lady Caroline, again to Mrs. Wilkins. "Unless," she added, "he can't come."

But Mrs. Wilkins, her brow perturbed—for suppose after all she were not yet quite stable in heaven?—could only say, a little uneasily, "I see him here."

Chapter 13

The uneventful days—only outwardly uneventful—slipped by in floods of sunshine, and the servants, watching the four ladies, came to the conclusion there was very little life in them.

To the servants San Salvatore seemed asleep. No one came to tea, nor did the ladies go anywhere to tea. Other tenants in other springs had been far more active. There had been stir and enterprise; the boat had been used; excursions had been made; Beppo's fly was ordered; people from Mezzago came over and spent the day; the house rang with voices; even sometimes champagne had been drunk. Life was varied, life was interesting. But this? What was this? The servants were not even scolded. They were left completely to themselves. They yawned.

Perplexing, too, was the entire absence of gentlemen. How could gentlemen keep away from so much beauty? For, added up, and even after the subtraction of the old one, the three younger ladies produced a formidable total of that which gentlemen usually sought.

Also the evident desire of each lady to spend long hours separated from the other ladies puzzled the servants. The result was a deathly stillness in the house, except at meal-times. It might have been as empty as it had been all the winter, for any sounds of life there were. The old lady sat in her room, alone; the dark-eyed lady wandered off alone, loitering, so Domenico told them, who sometimes came across her in the course of his duties, incomprehensibly among the rocks; the very beautiful fair lady lay in her low chair in the top garden, alone; the less, but still beautiful fair lady went up the hills and stayed up them for hours, alone; and every day the sun blazed slowly round the house, and disappeared at evening into the sea, and nothing at all had happened.

The servants yawned.

Yet the four visitors, while their bodies sat—that was Mrs. Fisher's—or lay—that was Lady Caroline's—or loitered—that was Mrs. Arbuthnot's—or went in solitude up into the hills—that was Mrs. Wilkins's—were anything but torpid really. Their minds were unusually busy. Even at night their minds were busy, and the dreams they had were clear, thin, quick things, entirely different from the heavy dreams of home. There was that in the atmosphere of San Salvatore which produced active-mindedness in all except the natives. They, as before, whatever the beauty around them, whatever the prodigal seasons did, remained immune from thoughts other than those they were accustomed to. All their lives they had seen, year by year, the amazing recurrent spectacle of April in the gardens, and custom had made it invisible to them. They were as blind to it, as unconscious of it, as Domenico's dog asleep in the sun.

The visitors could not be blind to it—it was too arresting after London in a particularly wet and gloomy March. Suddenly to be transported to that place where the air was so still that it held its breath, where the light was so golden that the most ordinary things were transfigured—to be transported into that delicate warmth, that caressing fragrance, and to have the old grey castle as the setting, and, in the distance, the serene clear hills of Perugini's backgrounds, was an astonishing contrast. Even Lady Caroline, used all her life to beauty, who had been everywhere and seen everything, felt the surprise of it. It was, that year, a particularly wonderful spring, and of all the months at San Salvatore April, if the weather was fine, was best. May scorched and withered; March was restless, and could be hard and cold in its brightness; but April came along softly like a blessing, and if it were a fine April it was so beautiful that it was impossible not to feel different, not to feel stirred and touched.

Mrs. Wilkins, we have seen, responded to it instantly. She, so to speak, at once flung off all her garments and dived straight into glory, unhesitatingly, with a cry of rapture.

Mrs. Arbuthnot was stirred and touched, but differently. She had odd sensations—presently to be described.

Mrs. Fisher, being old, was of a closer, more impermeable texture, and offered more resistance; but she too had odd sensations, also in their place to be described.

Lady Caroline, already amply acquainted with beautiful houses and climates, to whom they could not come quite with the same surprise, yet was very nearly as quick to react as Mrs. Wilkins. The place had an almost instantaneous influence on her as well, and of one part of this influence she was aware: it had made her, beginning on the very first evening, want to think, and acted on her curiously like a conscience. What this conscience seemed to press upon her notice with an insistence that startled her—Lady Caroline hesitated to accept the word, but it would keep on coming into her head—was that she was tawdry.

She must think that out.

The morning after the first dinner together, she woke up in a condition of regret that she should have been so talkative to Mrs. Wilkins the night before. What had made her be, she wondered. Now, of course, Mrs. Wilkins would want to grab, she would want to be inseparable; and the thought of a grabbing and an inseparableness that should last four weeks made Scrap's spirit swoon within her. No doubt the encouraged Mrs. Wilkins would be lurking in the top garden waiting to waylay her when she went out, and would hail her with morning cheerfulness. How much she hated being hailed with morning cheerfulness—or indeed, hailed at all. She oughtn't to have encouraged Mrs. Wilkins the night before. Fatal to encourage. It was bad enough not to encourage, for just sitting there and saying nothing seemed usually to involve her, but actively to encourage was suicidal. What on earth had made her? Now she would have to waste all the precious time, the precious, lovely time for thinking in, for getting square with herself, in shaking Mrs. Wilkins off.

With great caution and on the tips of her toes, balancing herself carefully lest the pebbles should scrunch, she stole out when she was dressed to her corner; but the garden was empty. No shaking off was necessary. Neither Mrs. Wilkins nor anybody else was to be seen. She had it entirely to herself. Except for Domenico, who presently came and hovered, watering his plants, again especially all the plants that were nearest her, no one came out at all; and when, after a long while of following up thoughts which seemed to escape her just as she had got them, and dropping off exhausted to sleep in the intervals of this chase, she felt hungry and looked at her watch and saw that it was past three, she realized that nobody had even bothered to call her in to lunch. So that, Scrap could not but remark, if any one was shaken off it was she herself.

Well, but how delightful, and how very new. Now she would really be able to think, uninterruptedly. Delicious to be forgotten.

Still, she was hungry; and Mrs. Wilkins, after that excessive friendliness the night before, might at least have told her lunch was ready. And she had really been excessively friendly—so nice about Mellersh's sleeping arrangements, wanting him to have the spare-room and all. She wasn't usually interested in arrangements, in fact she wasn't ever interested in them; so that Scrap considered she might be said almost to have gone out of her way to be agreeable to Mrs. Wilkins. And, in return, Mrs. Wilkins didn't even bother whether or not she had any lunch.

Fortunately, though she was hungry, she didn't mind missing a meal. Life was full of meals. They took up an enormous proportion of one's time; and

Mrs. Fisher was, she was afraid, one of those persons who at meals linger. Twice now had she dined with Mrs. Fisher, and each time she had been difficult at the end to dislodge, lingering on slowly cracking innumerable nuts and slowly drinking a glass of wine that seemed as if it would never be finished. Probably it would be a good thing to make a habit of missing lunch, and as it was quite easy to have tea brought out to her, and as she breakfasted in her room, only once a day would she have to sit at the dining-room table and endure the nuts.

Scrap burrowed her head comfortably in the cushions, and with her feet crossed on the low parapet gave herself up to more thought. She said to herself, as she had said at intervals throughout the morning: Now I'm going to think. But, never having thought out anything in her life, it was difficult. Extraordinary how one's attention wouldn't stay fixed; extraordinary how one's mind slipped sideways. Settling herself down to a review of her past as a preliminary to the consideration of her future, and hunting in it to begin with for any justification of that distressing word tawdry, the next thing she knew was that she wasn't thinking about this at all, but had somehow switched on to Mr. Wilkins.

Well, Mr. Wilkins was quite easy to think about, though not pleasant. She viewed his approach with misgivings. For not only was it a profound and unexpected bore to have a man added to the party, and a man, too, of the kind she was sure Mr. Wilkins must be, but she was afraid—and her fear was the result of a drearily unvarying experience —that he might wish to hang about her.

This possibility had evidently not yet occurred to Mrs. Wilkins, and it was not one to which she could very well draw her attention; not, that is, without being too fatuous to live. She tried to hope that Mr. Wilkins would be a wonderful exception to the dreadful rule. If only he were, she would be so much obliged to him that she believed she might really quite like him.

But—she had misgivings. Suppose he hung about her so that she was driven from her lovely top garden; suppose the light in Mrs. Wilkins's funny, flickering face was blown out. Scrap felt she would particularly dislike this to happen to Mrs. Wilkins's face, yet she had never in her life met any wives, not any at all, who had been able to understand that she didn't in the least want their husbands. Often she had met wives who didn't want their husbands either, but that made them none the less indignant if they thought somebody else did, and none the less sure, when they saw them hanging round Scrap, that she was trying to get them. Trying to get them! The bare thought, the bare recollection of these situations, filled her with a boredom so extreme that it instantly sent her to sleep again.

When she woke up she went on with Mr. Wilkins.

Now if, thought Scrap, Mr. Wilkins were not an exception and behaved in the usual way, would Mrs. Wilkins understand, or would it just simply spoil her holiday? She seemed quick, but would she be quick about just this? She seemed to understand and see inside one, but would she understand and see inside one when it came to Mr. Wilkins?

The experienced Scrap was full of doubts. She shifted her feet on the parapet; she jerked a cushion straight. Perhaps she had better try and explain to Mrs. Wilkins, during the days still remaining before the arrival—explain in a general way, rather vague and talking at large—her attitude towards such things. She might also expound to her her peculiar dislike of people's husbands, and her profound craving to be, at least for this one month, let alone.

But Scrap had her doubts about this too. Such talk meant a certain familiarity, meant embarking on a friendship with Mrs. Wilkins; and if, after having embarked on it and faced the peril it contained of too much Mrs. Wilkins, Mr. Wilkins should turn out to be artful—and people did get very artful when they were set on anything—and manage after all to slip through into the top garden, Mrs. Wilkins might easily believe she had been taken in, and that she, Scrap, was deceitful. Deceitful! And about Mr. Wilkins. Wives were really pathetic.

At half-past four she heard sounds of saucers on the other side of the daphne bushes. Was tea being sent out to her?

No; the sounds came no closer, they stopped near the house. Tea was to be in the garden, in her garden. Scrap considered she might at least have been asked if she minded being disturbed. They all knew she sat there.

Perhaps some one would bring hers to her in her corner.

No; nobody brought anything.

Well, she was too hungry not to go and have it with the others to-day, but she would give Francesca strict orders for the future.

She got up, and walked with that slow grace which was another of her outrageous number of attractions towards the sounds of tea. She was conscious not only of being very hungry but of wanting to talk to Mrs. Wilkins again. Mrs. Wilkins had not grabbed, she had left her quite free all day in spite of the rapprochement the night before. Of course she was an original, and put on a silk jumper for dinner, but she hadn't grabbed. This was a great thing. Scrap went towards the tea-table quite looking forward to Mrs. Wilkins; and when she came in sight of it she saw only Mrs. Fisher and Mrs. Arbuthnot.

Mrs. Fisher was pouring out the tea, and Mrs. Arbuthnot was offering Mrs. Fisher macaroons. Every time Mrs. Fisher offered Mrs. Arbuthnot anything—her cup, or milk, or sugar—Mrs. Arbuthnot offered her macaroons—pressed them on her with an odd assiduousness, almost with obstinacy. Was it a game? Scrap wondered, sitting down and seizing a macaroon.

"Where is Mrs. Wilkins?" asked Scrap.

They did not know. At least, Mrs. Arbuthnot, on Scrap's inquiry, did not know; Mrs. Fisher's face, at the name, became elaborately uninterested.

It appeared that Mrs. Wilkins had not been seen since breakfast. Mrs. Arbuthnot thought she had probably gone for a picnic. Scrap missed her. She ate the enormous macaroons, the best and biggest she had ever come across, in silence. Tea without Mrs. Wilkins was dull; and Mrs. Arbuthnot had that fatal flavour of motherliness about her, of wanting to pet one, to make one very comfortable, coaxing one to eat— coaxing her, who was already so frankly, so even excessively, eating— that seemed to have dogged Scrap's steps through life. Couldn't people leave one alone? She was perfectly able to eat what she wanted uncited. She tried to quench Mrs. Arbuthnot's zeal by being short with her. Useless. The shortness was not apparent. It remained, as all Scrap's evil feelings remained, covered up by the impenetrable veil of her loveliness.

Mrs. Fisher sat monumentally, and took no notice of either of them. She had had a curious day, and was a little worried. She had been quite alone, for none of the three had come to lunch, and none of them had taken the trouble to let her know they were not coming; and Mrs. Arbuthnot, drifting casually into tea, had behaved oddly till Lady Caroline joined them and distracted her attention.

Mrs. Fisher was prepared not to dislike Mrs. Arbuthnot, whose parted hair and mild expression seemed very decent and womanly, but she certainly had habits that were difficult to like. Her habit of instantly echoing any offer made her of food and drink, of throwing the offer back on one, as it were, was not somehow what one expected of her. "Will you have some more tea?" was surely a question to which the answer was simply yes or no; but Mrs. Arbuthnot persisted in the trick she had exhibited the day before at breakfast, of adding to her yes or no the words, "Will you?" She had done it again that morning at breakfast and here she was doing it at tea—the two meals at which Mrs. Fisher presided and poured out. Why did she do it? Mrs. Fisher failed to understand.

But this was not what was worrying her; this was merely by the way. What was worrying her was that she had been quite unable that day to settle to anything, and had done nothing but wander restlessly from her sitting-room to her battlements and back again. It had been a wasted day, and how much she disliked waste. She had tried to read, and she had tried to write to Kate Lumley; but no—a few words read, a few lines written, and up she got again and went out on to the battlements and stared at the sea.

It did not matter that the letter to Kate Lumley should not be written. There was time enough for that. Let the others suppose her coming was definitely fixed. All the better. So would Mr. Wilkins be kept out of the spare-room and put where he belonged. Kate would keep. She could be held in reserve. Kate in reserve was just as potent as Kate in actuality, and there were points about Kate in reserve which might be missing from Kate in actuality. For instance, if Mrs. Fisher were going to be restless, she would rather Kate were not there to see. There was a want of dignity about restlessness, about trotting backwards and forwards. But it did matter that she could not read a sentence of any of her great dead friends' writings; no, not even of Browning's, who had been so much in Italy, nor of Ruskin's, whose Stones of Venice she had brought with her to re-read so nearly on the very spot; nor even a sentence of a really interesting book like the one she had found in her sitting-room about the home life of the German Emperor, poor man—written in the nineties, when he had not yet begun to be more sinned against than sinning, which was, she was firmly convinced, what was the matter with him now, and full of exciting things about his birth and his right arm and accoucheurs—without having to put it down and go and stare at the sea.

Reading was very important; the proper exercise and development of one's mind was a paramount duty. How could one read if one were constantly trotting in and out? Curious, this restlessness. Was she going to be ill? No, she felt well; indeed, unusually well, and she went in and out quite quickly—trotted, in fact—and without her stick. Very odd that she shouldn't be able to sit still, she thought, frowning across the tops of some purple hyacinths at the Gulf of Spezia glittering beyond a headland; very odd that she, who walked so slowly, with such dependence on her stick, should suddenly trot.

It would be interesting to talk to some one about it, she felt. Not to Kate—to a stranger. Kate would only look at her and suggest a cup of tea. Kate always suggested cups of tea. Besides, Kate had a flat face. That Mrs. Wilkins, now—annoying as she was, loose-tongued as she was, impertinent, objectionable, would probably understand, and perhaps know what was making her be like this. But she could say nothing to Mrs. Wilkins. She was the last person to whom one would admit sensations. Dignity alone forbade it. Confide in Mrs. Wilkins? Never.

And Mrs. Arbuthnot, while she wistfully mothered the obstructive Scrap at tea, felt too that she had had a curious day. Like Mrs. Fisher's, it had been active, but, unlike Mrs. Fisher's, only active in mind. Her body had been quite still; her mind had not been still at all, it had been excessively active. For years she had taken care to have no time to think. Her scheduled life in the parish had prevented memories and desires from intruding on her. That day they had crowded. She went back to tea feeling dejected, and that she should feel dejected in such a place with everything about her to make her rejoice, only dejected her the more. But how could she rejoice alone? How could anybody rejoice and enjoy and appreciate, really appreciate, alone? Except Lotty. Lotty seemed able to. She had gone off down the hill directly after breakfast, alone yet obviously rejoicing, for she had not suggested that Rose should go too, and she was singing as she went.

Rose had spent the day by herself, sitting with her hands clasping her knees, staring straight in front of her. What she was staring at were the grey swords of the agaves, and, on their tall stalks, the pale irises that grew in the remote place she had found, while beyond them, between the grey leaves and the blue flowers, she saw the sea. The place she had found was a hidden corner where the sun-baked stones were padded with thyme, and nobody was likely to come. It was out of sight and sound of the house; it was off any path; it was near the end of the promontory. She sat so quiet that presently lizards darted over her feet, and some tiny birds like finches, frightened away at first, came back again and flitted among the bushes round her just as if she hadn't been there. How beautiful it was. And what was the good of it with no one there, no one who loved being with one, who belonged to one, to whom one could say, "Look." And wouldn't one say, "Look—dearest?" Yes, one would say dearest; and the sweet word, just to say it to somebody who loved one, would make one happy.

She sat quite still, staring straight in front of her. Strange that in this place she did not want to pray. She who had prayed so constantly at home didn't seem able to do it here at all. The first morning she had merely thrown up a brief thank you to heaven on getting out of bed, and had gone straight to the window to see what everything looked like—thrown up the thank you as carelessly as a ball, and thought no more about it. That morning, remembering this and ashamed, she had knelt down with determination; but perhaps determination was bad for prayers, for she had been unable to think of a thing to say. And as for her bedtime prayers, on neither of the nights had she said a single one. She had forgotten them. She had been so much absorbed in other thoughts that she had forgotten them; and, once in bed, she was asleep and whirling along among bright, thin swift dreams before she had so much time as to stretch herself out.

What had come over her? Why had she let go the anchor of prayer? And she had difficulty, too, in remembering her poor, in remembering even that there were such things as poor. Holidays, of course, were good, and were recognized by everybody as good, but ought they so completely to blot out, to make such havoc of, the realities? Perhaps it was healthy to forget her poor; with all the greater gusto would she go back to them. But it couldn't be healthy to forget her prayers, and still less could it be healthy not to mind.

Rose did not mind. She knew she did not mind. And, even worse, she knew she did not mind not minding. In this place she was indifferent to both the things that had filled her life and made it seem as if it were happy for years. Well, if only she could rejoice in her wonderful new surroundings, have that much at least to set against the indifference, the letting go—but she could not. She had no work; she did not pray; she was left empty.

Lotty had spoilt her day that day, as she had spoilt her day the day before— Lotty, with her invitation to her husband, with her suggestion that she too should invite hers. Having flung Frederick into her mind again the day before, Lotty had left her; for the whole afternoon she had left her alone with her thoughts. Since then they had been all of Frederick. Where at Hampstead he came to her only in her dreams, here he left her dreams free and was with her during the day instead. And again that morning, as she was struggling not to think of him, Lotty had asked her, just before disappearing singing down the path, if she had written yet and invited him, and again he was flung into her mind and she wasn't able to get him out.

How could she invite him? It had gone on so long, their estrangement, such years; she would hardly know what words to use; and besides, he would not come. Why should he come? He didn't care about being with her. What could they talk about? Between them was the barrier of his work and her religion. She could not—how could she, believing as she did in purity, in responsibility for the effect of one's actions on others—bear his work, bear living by it; and he she knew, had at first resented and then been merely bored by her religion. He had let her slip away; he had given her up; he no longer minded; he accepted her religion indifferently, as a settled fact. Both it and she—Rose's mind, becoming more luminous in the clear light of April at San Salvatore, suddenly saw the truth—bored him.

Naturally when she saw this, when that morning it flashed upon her for the first time, she did not like it; she liked it so little that for a space the whole beauty of Italy was blotted out. What was to be done about it? She could not give up believing in good and not liking evil, and it must be evil to live entirely on the proceeds of adulteries, however dead and distinguished they were. Besides, if she did, if she sacrificed her whole past, her bringing up, her work for the last ten years, would she bore him less? Rose felt right down at her very roots that if you have once thoroughly bored somebody it is next to impossible to unbore him. Once a bore always a bore— certainly, she thought, to the person originally bored.

Then, thought she, looking out to sea through eyes grown misty, better cling to her religion. It was better—she hardly noticed the reprehensibleness of her thought—than nothing. But oh, she wanted to cling to something tangible, to love something living, something that one could hold against one's heart, that one could see and touch and do things for. If her poor baby hadn't died . . . babies didn't get bored with one, it took them a long while to grow up and find one out. And perhaps one's baby never did find one out; perhaps one would always be to it, however old and bearded it grew, somebody special, somebody different from every one else, and if for no other reason, precious in that one could never be repeated.

Sitting with dim eyes looking out to sea she felt an extraordinary yearning to hold something of her very own tight to her bosom. Rose was slender, and as reserved in figure as in character, yet she felt a queer sensation of—how could she describe it?—bosom. There was something about San Salvatore that made her feel all bosom. She wanted to gather to her bosom, to comfort and protect, soothing the dear head that should lie on it with softest strokings and murmurs of love. Frederick, Frederick's child—come to her, pillowed on her, because they were unhappy, because they had been hurt. . . They would need her then, if they had been hurt; they would let themselves be loved then, if they were unhappy.

Well, the child was gone, would never come now; but perhaps Frederick—some day—when he was old and tired . . .
Such were Mrs. Arbuthnot's reflections and emotions that first day at San Salvatore by herself. She went back to tea dejected as she had not been for years. San Salvatore had taken her carefully built-up semblance of happiness away from her, and given her nothing in exchange. Yes—it had given her yearnings in exchange, this ache and longing, this queer feeling of bosom; but that was worse than nothing. And she who had learned balance, who never at home was irritated but always able to be kind, could not, even in her dejection, that afternoon endure Mrs. Fisher's assumption of the position as hostess at tea.

One would have supposed that such a little thing would not have touched her, but it did. Was her nature changing? Was she to be not only thrown back on long-stifled yearnings after Frederick, but also turned into somebody who wanted to fight over little things? After tea, when both Mrs. Fisher and Lady Caroline had disappeared again—it was quite evident that nobody wanted her—she was more dejected than ever, overwhelmed by the discrepancy between the splendour outside her, the warm, teeming beauty and self-sufficiency of nature, and the blank emptiness of her heart.

Then came Lotty, back to dinner, incredibly more freckled, exuding the sunshine she had been collecting all day, talking, laughing, being tactless, being unwise, being without reticence; and Lady Caroline, so quiet at tea, woke up to animation, and Mrs. Fisher was not so noticeable, and Rose was beginning to revive a little, for Lotty's spirits were contagious as she described the delights of her day, a day which might easily to any one else have had nothing in it but a very long and very hot walk and sandwiches, when she suddenly said catching Rose's eye, "Letter gone?"

Rose flushed. This tactlessness . . .

"What letter?" asked Scrap, interested. Both her elbows were on the table and her chin was supported in her hands, for the nut-stage had been reached, and there was nothing for it but to wait in as comfortable as position as possible till Mrs. Fisher had finished cracking.

"Asking her husband here," said Lotty.

Mrs. Fisher looked up. Another husband? Was there to be no end to them? Nor was this one, then, a widow either; but her husband was no doubt a decent, respectable man, following a decent, respectable calling. She had little hope of Mr. Wilkins; so little, that she had refrained from inquiring what he did.

"Has it?" persisted Lotty, as Rose said nothing.

"No," said Rose.

"Oh, well—to-morrow then," said Lotty.

Rose wanted to say No again to this. Lotty would have in her place, and would, besides, have expounded all her reasons. But she could not turn herself inside out like that and invite any and everybody to come and look. How was it that Lotty, who saw so many things, didn't see stuck on her heart, and seeing keep quiet about it, the sore place that was Frederick?

"Who is your husband?" asked Mrs. Fisher, carefully adjusting another nut between the crackers.

"Who should he be," said Rose quickly, roused at once by Mrs. Fisher to irritation, "except Mr. Arbuthnot?"
"I mean, of course, what is Mr. Arbuthnot?"

And Rose, gone painfully red at this, said after a tiny pause, "My husband."
Naturally, Mrs. Fisher was incensed. She couldn't have believed it of this one, with her decent hair and gentle voice, that she too should be impertinent.

Chapter 14

That first week the wistaria began to fade, and the flowers of the Judas-tree and peach-trees fell off and carpeted the ground with rose-colour. Then all the freesias disappeared, and the irises grew scarce. And then, while these were clearing themselves away, the double banksia roses came out, and the big summer roses suddenly flaunted gorgeously on the walls and trellises. Fortune's Yellow was one of them; a very beautiful rose. Presently the tamarisk and the daphnes were at their best, and the lilies at their tallest. By the end of the week the fig-trees were giving shade, the plum-blossom was out among the olives, the modest weigelias appeared in their fresh pink clothes, and on the rocks sprawled masses of thick-leaved, star-shaped flowers, some vivid purple and some a clear, pale lemon.

By the end of the week, too, Mr. Wilkins arrived; even as his wife had foreseen he would, so he did. And there were signs almost of eagerness about his acceptance of her suggestion, for he had not waited to write a letter in answer to hers, but had telegraphed.

That, surely, was eager. It showed, Scrap thought, a definite wish for reunion; and watching his wife's happy face, and aware of her desire that Mellersh should enjoy his holiday, she told herself that he would be a very unusual fool should he waste his time bothering about anybody else. "If he isn't nice to her," Scrap thought, "he shall be taken to the battlements and tipped over." For, by the end of the week, she and Mrs. Wilkins had become Caroline and Lotty to each other, and were friends.

Mrs. Wilkins had always been friends, but Scrap had struggled not to be. She had tried hard to be cautious, but how difficult was caution with Mrs. Wilkins! Free herself from every vestige of it, she was so entirely unreserved, so completely expansive, that soon Scrap, almost before she knew what she was doing, was being unreserved too. And nobody could be more unreserved than Scrap, once she let herself go.

The only difficulty about Lotty was that she was nearly always somewhere else. You couldn't catch her; you couldn't pin her down to come and talk. Scrap's fears that she would grab seemed grotesque in retrospect. Why, there was no grab in her. At dinner and after dinner were the only times one really saw her. All day long she was invisible, and would come back in the late afternoon looking a perfect sight, her hair full of bits of moss, and her freckles worse than ever. Perhaps she was making the most of her time before Mellersh arrived to do all the things she wanted to do, and meant to devote herself afterwards to going about with him, tidy and in her best clothes.

Scrap watched her, interested in spite of herself, because it seemed so extraordinary to be as happy as all that on so little. San Salvatore was beautiful, and the weather was divine; but scenery and weather had never been enough for Scrap, and how could they be enough for somebody who would have to leave them quite soon and go back to life in Hampstead? Also, there was the imminence of Mellersh, of that Mellersh from whom Lotty had so lately run. It was all very well to feel one ought to share, and to make a beau geste and do it, but the beaux gestes Scrap had known hadn't made anybody happy. Nobody really liked being the object of one, and it always meant an effort on the part of the maker. Still, she had to admit there was no effort about Lotty; it was quite plain that everything she did and said was effortless, and that she was just simply, completely happy.

And so Mrs. Wilkins was; for her doubts as to whether she had had time to become steady enough in serenity to go on being serene in Mellersh's company when she had it uninterruptedly right round the clock, had gone by the middle of the week, and she felt that nothing now could shake her. She was ready for anything. She was firmly grafted, rooted, built into heaven. Whatever Mellersh said or did, she would not budge an inch out of heaven, would not rouse herself a single instant to come outside it and be cross. On the contrary, she was going to pull him up into it beside her, and they would sit comfortably together, suffused in light, and laugh at how much afraid of him she used to be in Hampstead, and at how deceitful her afraidness had made her. But he wouldn't need much pulling. He would come in quite naturally after a day or two, irresistibly wafted on the scented breezes of that divine air; and there he would sit arrayed in stars, thought Mrs. Wilkins, in whose mind, among much other débris, floated occasional bright shreds of poetry. She laughed to herself a little at the picture of Mellersh, that top-hatted, black-coated, respectable family solicitor, arrayed in stars, but she laughed affectionately, almost with a maternal pride in how splendid he would look in such fine clothes. "Poor lamb," she murmured to herself affectionately. And added, "What he wants is a thorough airing."

This was during the first half of the week. By the beginning of the last half, at the end of which Mr. Wilkins arrived, she left off even assuring herself that she was unshakeable, that she was permeated beyond altering by the atmosphere, she no longer thought of it or noticed it; she took it for granted. If one may say so, and she certainly said so, not only to herself but also to Lady Caroline, she had found her celestial legs.

Contrary to Mrs. Fisher's idea of the seemly—but of course contrary; what else would one expect of Mrs. Wilkins?—she did not go to meet her husband at Messago, but merely walked down to the point where Beppo's fly would leave him and his luggage in the street of Castagneto. Mrs. Fisher disliked the arrival of Mr. Wilkins, and was sure that anybody who could have married Mrs. Wilkins must be at least of an injudicious disposition, but a husband, whatever his disposition, should be properly met. Mr. Fisher had always been properly met. Never once in his married life had he gone unmet at a station, nor had he ever not been seen off. These observances, these courtesies, strengthened the bonds of marriage, and made the husband feel he could rely on his wife's being always there. Always being there was the essential secret for a wife. What would have become of Mr. Fisher if she had neglected to act on this principle she preferred not to think. Enough things became of him as it was; for whatever one's care in stopping up, married life yet seemed to contain chinks.

But Mrs. Wilkins took no pains. She just walked down the hill singing— Mrs. Fisher could hear her—and picked up her husband in the street as casually as if he were a pin. The three others, still in bed, for it was not nearly time to get up, heard her as she passed beneath their windows down the zigzag path to meet Mr. Wilkins, who was coming by the morning train, and Scrap smiled, and Rose sighed, and Mrs. Fisher rang her bell and desired Francesca to bring her her breakfast in her room. All three had breakfast that day in their rooms, moved by a common instinct to take cover.

Scrap always breakfasted in bed, but she had the same instinct for cover, and during breakfast she made plans for spending the whole day where she was. Perhaps, though, it wouldn't be as necessary that day as the next. That day, Scrap calculated, Mellersh would be provided for. He would want to have a bath, and having a bath at San Salvatore was an elaborate business, a real adventure if one had a hot one in the bathroom, and it took a lot of time. It involved the attendance of the entire staff—Domenico and the boy Giuseppe coaxing the patent stove to burn, restraining it when it burnt too fiercely, using the bellows to it when it threatened to go out, relighting it when it did go out; Francesca anxiously hovering over the tap regulating its trickle, because if it were turned on too full the water instantly ran cold, and if not full enough the stove blew up inside and mysteriously flooded the house; and Costanza and Angela running up and down bringing pails of hot water from the kitchen to eke out what the tap did.

This bath had been put in lately, and was at once the pride and the terror of the servants. It was very patent. Nobody quite understood it. There were long printed instructions as to its right treatment hanging on the wall, in which the word pericoloso recurred. When Mrs. Fisher, proceeding on her arrival to the bathroom, saw this word, she went back to her room again and ordered a sponge-bath instead; and when the others found what using the bathroom meant, and how reluctant the servants were to leave them alone with the stove, and how Francesca positively refused to, and stayed with her back turned watching the tap, and how the remaining servants waited anxiously outside the door till the bather came safely out again, they too had sponge-baths brought into their rooms instead.

Mr. Wilkins, however, was a man, and would be sure to want a big bath. Having it, Scrap calculated, would keep him busy for a long while. Then he would unpack, and then, after his night in the train, he would probably sleep till the evening. So would he be provided for the whole of that day, and not be let loose on them till dinner.

Therefore Scrap came to the conclusion she would be quite safe in the garden that day, and got up as usual after breakfast, and dawdled as usual through her dressing, listening with a slight cocked ear to the sounds of Mr. Wilkins's arrival, of his luggage being carried into Lotty's room on the other side of the landing, of his educated voice as he inquired of Lotty, first, "Do I give this fellow anything?" and immediately afterwards, "Can I have a hot bath?"—of Lotty's voice cheerfully assuring him that he needn't give the fellow anything because he was the gardener, and that yes, he could have a hot bath; and soon after this the landing was filled with the familiar noises of wood being brought, of water being brought, of feet running, of tongues vociferating—-in fact, with the preparation of the bath.

Scrap finished dressing, and then loitered at her window, waiting till she should hear Mr. Wilkins go into the bathroom. When he was safely there she would slip out and settle herself in her garden and resume her inquiries into the probable meaning of her life. She was getting on with her inquiries. She dozed much less frequently, and was beginning to be inclined to agree that tawdry was the word to apply to her past. Also she was afraid that her future looked black.

There—she could hear Mr. Wilkins's educated voice again. Lotty's door had opened, and he was coming out of it asking his way to the bathroom.

"It's where you see the crowd," Lotty's voice answered—still a cheerful voice, Scrap was glad to notice.

His steps went along the landing, and Lotty's steps seemed to go downstairs, and then there seemed to be a brief altercation at the bathroom door—hardly so much an altercation as a chorus of vociferations on one side and wordless determination, Scrap judged, to have a bath by oneself on the other.

Mr. Wilkins knew no Italian, and the expression pericoloso left him precisely as it found him—or would have if he had seen it, but naturally he took no notice of the printed matter on the wall. He firmly closed the door on the servants, resisting Domenico, who tried to the last to press through, and locked himself in as a man should for his bath, judicially considering, as he made his simple preparations for getting in, the singular standard of behaviour of these foreigners who, both male and female, apparently wished to stay with him while he bathed. In Finland, he had heard, the female natives not only were present on such occasions but actually washed the bath-taking traveler. He had not heard, however, that this was true too of Italy, which somehow seemed much nearer civilization— perhaps because one went there, and did not go to Finland.

Impartially examining this reflection, and carefully balancing the claims to civilization of Italy and Finland, Mr. Wilkins got into the bath and turned off the tap. Naturally he turned off the tap. It was what one did. But on the instructions, printed in red letters, was a paragraph saying that the tap should not be turned off as long as there was still fire in the stove. It should be left on—not much on, but on—until the fire was quite out; otherwise, and here again was the word pericoloso, the stove would blow up.

Mr. Wilkins got into the bath, turned off the tap, and the stove blew up, exactly as the printed instructions said it would. It blew up, fortunately, only in its inside, but it blew up with a terrific noise, and Mr. Wilkins leapt out of the bath and rushed to the door, and only the instinct born of years of training made him snatch up a towel as he rushed.

Scrap, half-way across the landing on her way out of doors, heard the explosion.

"Good heavens," she thought, remembering the instruction, "there goes Mr. Wilkins!"

And she ran toward the head of the stairs to call the servants, and as she ran, out ran Mr. Wilkins clutching his towel, and they ran into each other.

"That damned bath!" cried Mr. Wilkins, imperfectly concealed in his towel, his shoulders exposed at one end and his legs at the other, and Lady Caroline Dester, to meet whom he had swallowed all his anger with his wife and come out to Italy.

For Lotty in her letter had told him who was at San Salvatore besides herself and Mrs. Arbuthnot, and Mr. Wilkins at once had perceived that this was an opportunity which might never recur. Lotty had merely said, "There are two other women here, Mrs. Fisher and Lady Caroline Dester," but that was enough. He knew all about the Droitwiches, their wealth, their connections, their place in history, and the power they had, should they choose to exert it, of making yet another solicitor happy by adding him to those they already employed. Some people employed one solicitor for one branch of their affairs, and another for another. The affairs of the Droitwiches must have many branches. He had also heard—for it was, he considered, part of his business to hear, and having heard to remember—of the beauty of their only daughter. Even if the Droitwiches themselves did not need his services, their daughter might. Beauty led one into strange situations; advice could never come amiss. And should none of them, neither parents nor daughter nor any of their brilliant sons, need him in his professional capacity, it yet was obviously a most valuable acquaintance to make. It opened up vistas. It swelled with possibilities. He might go on living in Hampstead for years, and not again come across such another chance.

Directly his wife's letter reached him he telegraphed and packed. This was business. He was not a man to lose time when it came to business; nor was he a man to jeopardize a chance by neglecting to be amiable. He met his wife perfectly amiably, aware that amiability under such circumstances was wisdom. Besides, he actually felt amiable—very. For once, Lotty was really helping him. He kissed her affectionately on getting out of Beppo's fly, and was afraid she must have got up extremely early; he made no complaints of the steepness of the walk up; he told her pleasantly of his journey, and when called upon, obediently admired the views. It was all neatly mapped out in his mind, what he was going to do that first day— have a shave, have a bath, put on clean clothes, sleep a while, and then would come lunch and the introduction to Lady Caroline.

In the train he had selected the words of his greeting, going over them with care—some slight expression of his gratification in meeting one of whom he, in common with the whole world, had heard—but of course put delicately, very delicately; some slight reference to her distinguished parents and the part her family had played in the history of England— made, of course, with proper tact; a sentence or two about her eldest brother Lord Winchcombe, who had won his V.C. in the late war under circumstances which could only cause—he might or might not add this—every Englishman's heart to beat higher than ever with pride, and the first steps towards what might well be the turning-point in his career would have been taken.

And here he was . . . no, it was too terrible, what could be more terrible? Only a towel on, water running off his legs, and that exclamation. He knew at once the lady was Lady Caroline—the minute the exclamation was out he knew it. Rarely did Mr. Wilkins use that word, and never, never in the presence of a lady or a client. While as for the towel—why had he come? Why had he not stayed in Hampstead? It would be impossible to live this down.

But Mr. Wilkins was reckoning without Scrap. She, indeed, screwed up her face at the first flash of him on her astonished sight in an enormous effort not to laugh, and having choked the laughter down and got her face serious again, she said as composedly as if he had had all his clothes on, "How do you do."

What perfect tact. Mr. Wilkins could have worshipped her. This exquisite ignoring. Blue blood, of course, coming out.

Overwhelmed with gratitude he took her offered hand and said "How do you do," in his turn, and merely to repeat the ordinary words seemed magically to restore the situation to the normal. Indeed, he was so much relieved, and it was so natural to be shaking hands, to be conventionally greeting, that he forgot he had only a towel on and his professional manner came back to him. He forgot what he was looking like, but he did not forget that this was Lady Caroline Dester, the lady he had come all the way to Italy to see, and he did not forget that it was in her face, her lovely and important face, that he had flung his terrible exclamation. He must at once entreat her forgiveness. To say such a word to a lady—to any lady, but of all ladies to just this one . . .

"I'm afraid I used unpardonable language," began Mr. Wilkins very earnestly, as earnestly and ceremoniously as if he had had his clothes on.

"I thought it most appropriate," said Scrap, who was used to damns.

Mr. Wilkins was incredibly relieved and soothed by this answer. No offence, then, taken. Blue blood again. Only blue blood could afford such a liberal, such an understanding attitude.

"It is Lady Caroline Dester, is it not, to whom I am speaking?" he asked, his voice sounding even more carefully cultivated than usual, for he had to restrain too much pleasure, too much relief, too much of the joy of the pardoned and the shriven from getting into it.

"Yes," said Scrap; and for the life of her she couldn't help smiling. She couldn't help it. She hadn't meant to smile at Mr. Wilkins, not ever; but really he looked—and then his voice was the top of the rest of him, oblivious of the towel and his legs, and talking just like a church.

"Allow me to introduce myself," said Mr. Wilkins, with the ceremony of the drawing-room. "My name is Mellersh-Wilkins."

And he instinctively held out his hand a second time at the words.

"I thought perhaps it was," said Scrap, a second time having hers shaken and a second time unable not to smile.

He was about to proceed to the first of the graceful tributes he had prepared in the train, oblivious, as he could not see himself, that he was without his clothes, when the servants came running up the stairs and, simultaneously, Mrs. Fisher appeared in the doorway of her sitting-room. For all this had happened very quickly, and the servants away in the kitchen, and Mrs. Fisher pacing her battlements, had not had time on hearing the noise to appear before the second handshake.

The servants when they heard the dreaded noise knew at once what had happened, and rushed straight into the bathroom to try and staunch the flood, taking no notice of the figure on the landing in the towel, but Mrs. Fisher did not know what the noise could be, and coming out of her room to inquire stood rooted on the door-sill.

It was enough to root anybody. Lady Caroline shaking hands with what evidently, if he had had clothes on, would have been Mrs. Wilkins's husband, and both of them conversing just as if—

Then Scrap became aware of Mrs. Fisher. She turned to her at once. "Do let me," she said gracefully, "introduce Mr. Mellersh-Wilkins. He has just come. This," she added, turning to Mr. Wilkins, "is Mrs. Fisher."

And Mr. Wilkins, nothing if not courteous, reacted at once to the conventional formula. First he bowed to the elderly lady in the doorway, then he crossed over to her, his wet feet leaving footprints as he went, and having got to her he politely held out his hand.

"It is a pleasure," said Mr. Wilkins in his carefully modulated voice, "to meet a friend of my wife's."

Scrap melted away down into the garden.

Chapter 15

The strange effect of this incident was that when they met that evening at dinner both Mrs. Fisher and Lady Caroline had a singular feeling of secret understanding with Mr. Wilkins. He could not be to them as other men. He could not be to them as he would have been if they had met him in his clothes. There was a sense of broken ice; they felt at once intimate and indulgent; almost they felt to him as nurses do—as those feel who have assisted either patients or young children at their baths. They were acquainted with Mr. Wilkins's legs.

What Mrs. Fisher said to him that morning in her first shock will never be known, but what Mr. Wilkins said to her in reply, when reminded by what she was saying of his condition, was so handsome in its apology, so proper in its confusion, that she had ended by being quite sorry for him and completely placated. After all, it was an accident, and nobody could help accidents. And when she saw him next at dinner, dressed, polished, spotless as to linen and sleek as to hair, she felt this singular sensation of a secret understanding with him and, added to it, of a kind of almost personal pride in his appearance, now that he was dressed, which presently extended in some subtle way to an almost personal pride in everything he said.

There was no doubt whatever in Mrs. Fisher's mind that a man was infinitely preferable as a companion to a woman. Mr. Wilkins's presence and conversation at once raised the standard of the dinner-table from that of a bear garden—yes, a bear garden—to that of a civilized social gathering. He talked as men talk, about interesting subjects, and, though most courteous to Lady Caroline, showed no traces of dissolving into simpers and idiocy whenever he addressed her. He was, indeed, precisely as courteous to Mrs. Fisher herself; and when for the first time at that table politics were introduced, he listened to her with the proper seriousness on her exhibiting a desire to speak, and treated her opinions with the attention they deserved. He appeared to think much as she did about Lloyd George, and in regard to literature he was equally sound. In fact there was real conversation, and he liked nuts. How he could have married Mrs. Wilkins was a mystery.

Lotty, for her part, looked on with round eyes. She had expected Mellersh to take at least two days before he got to this stage, but the San Salvatore spell had worked instantly. It was not only that he was pleasant at dinner, for she had always seen him pleasant at dinners with other people, but he had been pleasant all day privately—so pleasant that he had complimented her on her looks while she was brushing out her hair, and kissed her.

Kissed her! And it was neither good-morning nor good-night.

Well, this being so, she would put off telling him the truth about her nest-egg, and about Rose not being his hostess after all, till next day. Pity to spoil things. She had been going to blurt it out as soon as he had had a rest, but it did seem a pity to disturb such a very beautiful frame of mind as that of Mellersh this first day. Let him too get more firmly fixed in heaven. Once fixed he wouldn't mind anything.

Her face sparkled with delight at the instantaneous effect of San Salvatore. Even the catastrophe of the bath, of which she had been told when she came in from the garden, had not shaken him. Of course all that he had needed was a holiday. What a brute she had been to him when he wanted to take her himself to Italy. But this arrangement, as it happened, was ever so much better, though not through any merit of hers. She talked and laughed gaily, not a shred of fear of him left in her, and even when she said, struck by his spotlessness, that he looked so clean that one could eat one's dinner off him, and Scrap laughed, Mellersh laughed too. He would have minded that at home, supposing that at home she had had the spirit to say it.

It was a successful evening. Scrap, whenever she looked at Mr. Wilkins, saw him in his towel, dripping water, and felt indulgent. Mrs. Fisher was delighted with him. Rose was a dignified hostess in Mr. Wilkins's eyes, quiet and dignified, and he admired the way she waived her right to preside at the head of the table—as a graceful compliment, of course, to Mrs. Fisher's age. Mrs. Arbuthnot was, opined Mr. Wilkins, naturally retiring. She was the most retiring of the three ladies. He had met her before dinner alone for a moment in the drawing-room, and had expressed in appropriate language his sense of her kindness in wishing him to join her party, and she had been retiring. Was she shy? Probably. She had blushed, and murmured as if in deprecation, and then the others had come in. At dinner she talked least. He would, of course, become better acquainted with her during the next few days, and it would be a pleasure, he was sure.

Meanwhile Lady Caroline was all and more than all Mr. Wilkins had imagined, and had received his speeches, worked in skillfully between the courses, graciously; Mrs. Fisher was the exact old lady he had been hoping to come across all his professional life; and Lotty had not only immensely improved, but was obviously au mieux—Mr. Wilkins knew what was necessary in French—with Lady Caroline. He had been much tormented during the day by the thought of how he had stood conversing with Lady Caroline forgetful of his not being dressed, and had at last written her a note most deeply apologizing, and beseeching her to overlook his amazing, his incomprehensible obliviousness, to which she had replied in pencil on the back of the envelop, "Don't worry." And he had obeyed her commands, and had put it from him. The result was he was now in great contentment. Before going to sleep that night he pinched his wife's ear. She was amazed. These endearments . . .

What is more, the morning brought no relapse in Mr. Wilkins, and he kept up to his high level through out the day, in spite of its being the first day of the second week, and therefore pay day.

It being pay day precipitated Lotty's confession, which she had, when it came to the point, been inclined to put off a little longer. She was not afraid, she dared anything, but Mellersh was in such an admirable humour—why risk clouding it just yet? When, however, soon after breakfast Costanza appeared with a pile of very dirty little bits of paper covered with sums in pencil, and having knocked at Mrs. Fisher's door and been sent away, and at Lady Caroline's door and been sent away, and at Rose's door and had no answer because Rose had gone out, she waylaid Lotty, who was showing Mellersh over the house, and pointed to the bits of paper and talked very rapidly and loud, and shrugged her shoulders a great deal, and kept on pointing at the bits of paper, Lotty remembered that a week had passed without anybody paying anything to anyone, and that the moment had come to settle up.

"Does this good lady want something?" inquired Mr. Wilkins mellifluously.

"Money," said Lotty.

"Money?"

"It's the housekeeping bills."

"Well, you have nothing to do with those," said Mr. Wilkins serenely.

"Oh yes, I have—"

And the confession was precipitated.

It was wonderful how Mellersh took it. One would have imagined that his sole idea about the nest-egg had always been that it should be lavished on just this. He did not, as he would have done at home, cross-examine her; he accepted everything as it came pouring out, about her fibs and all, and when she had finished and said, "You have every right to be angry, I think, but I hope you won't be and will forgive me instead," he merely asked, "What can be more beneficial than such a holiday?"

Whereupon she put her arm through his and held it tight and said, "Oh, Mellersh, you really are too sweet!"—her face red with pride in him.

That he should so quickly assimilate the atmosphere, that he should at once become nothing but kindness, showed surely what a real affinity he had with good and beautiful things. He belonged quite naturally in this place of heavenly calm. He was—extraordinary how she had misjudged him—by nature a child of light. Fancy not minding the dreadful fibs she had gone in for before leaving home; fancy passing even those over without comment. Wonderful. Yet not wonderful, for wasn't he in heaven? In heaven nobody minded any of those done-with things, one didn't even trouble to forgive and forget, one was much too happy. She pressed his arm tight in her gratitude and appreciation; and though he did not withdraw his, neither did he respond to her pressure. Mr. Wilkins was of a cool habit, and rarely had any real wish to press.

Meanwhile, Costanza, perceiving that she had lost the Wilkinses' ear had gone back to Mrs. Fisher, who at least understood Italian, besides being clearly in the servants' eyes the one of the party marked down by age and appearance to pay the bills; and to her, while Mrs. Fisher put the final touches to her toilette, for she was preparing, by means of putting on a hat and veil and feather boa and gloves, to go for her first stroll in the lower garden—positively her first since her arrival—she explained that unless she was given money to pay the last week's bills the shops of Castagneto would refuse credit for the current week's food. Not even credit would they give, affirmed Costanza, who had been spending a great deal and was anxious to pay all her relations what was owed them and also to find out how her mistresses took it, for that day's meals. Soon it would be the hour of colazione, and how could there be colazione without meat, without fish, without eggs, without—

Mrs. Fisher took the bills out of her hand and looked at the total; and she was so much astonished by its size, so much horrified by the extravagance to which it testified, that she sat down at her writing-table to go into the thing thoroughly.

Costanza had a very bad half-hour. She had not supposed it was in the English to be so mercenary. And then la Vecchia, as she was called in the kitchen, knew so much Italian, and with a doggedness that filled Costanza with shame on her behalf, for such conduct was the last one expected from the noble English, she went through item after item, requiring and persisting till she got them, explanations.

There were no explanations, except that Costanza had had one glorious week of doing exactly as she chose, of splendid unbridled licence, and that this was the result.

Costanza, having no explanations, wept. It was miserable to think she would have to cook from now on under watchfulness, under suspicion; and what would her relations say when they found the orders they received were whittled down? They would say she had no influence; they would despise her.

Costanza wept, but Mrs. Fisher was unmoved. In slow and splendid Italian, with the roll of the cantos of the Inferno, she informed her that she would pay no bills till the following week, and that meanwhile the food was to be precisely as good as ever, and at a quarter the cost.

Costanza threw up her hands.

Next week, proceeded Mrs. Fisher unmoved, if she found this had been so she would pay the whole. Otherwise—she paused; for what she would do otherwise she did not know herself. But she paused and looked impenetrable, majestic and menacing, and Costanza was cowed.

Then Mrs. Fisher, having dismissed her with a gesture, went in search of Lady Caroline to complain. She had been under the impression that Lady Caroline ordered the meals and therefore was responsible for the prices, but now it appeared that the cook had been left to do exactly as she pleased ever since they got there, which of course was simply disgraceful.

Scrap was not in her bedroom, but the room, on Mrs. Fisher's opening the door, for she suspected her of being in it and only pretending not to hear the knock, was still flowerlike from her presence.

"Scent," sniffed Mrs. Fisher, shutting it again; and she wished Carlyle could have had five minutes' straight talk with this young woman. And yet—perhaps even he—

She went downstairs to go into the garden in search of her, and in the hall encountered Mr. Wilkins. He had his hat on, and was lighting a cigar.

Indulgent as Mrs. Fisher felt towards Mr. Wilkins, and peculiarly and even mystically related after the previous morning's encounter, she yet could not like a cigar in the house. Out of doors she endured it, but it was not necessary, when out of doors was such a big place, to indulge the habit indoors. Even Mr. Fisher, who had been, she should say, a man originally tenacious of habits, had quite soon after marriage got out of this one.

However, Mr. Wilkins, snatching off his hat on seeing her, instantly threw the cigar away. He threw it into the water a great jar of arum lilies presumably contain, and Mrs. Fisher, aware of the value men attach to their newly-lit cigars, could not but be impressed by this immediate and magnificent amende honorable.

But the cigar did not reach the water. It got caught in the lilies, and smoked on by itself among them, a strange and depraved-looking object.

"Where are you going to, my prett—" began Mr. Wilkins, advancing towards Mrs. Fisher; but he broke off just in time.

Was it morning spirits impelling him to address Mrs. Fisher in the terms of a nursery rhyme? He wasn't even aware that he knew the thing. Most strange. What could have put it, at such a moment, into his self-possessed head? He felt great respect for Mrs. Fisher, and would not for the world have insulted her by addressing her as a maid, pretty or otherwise. He wished to stand well with her. She was a woman of parts, and also, he suspected, of property. At breakfast they had been most pleasant together, and he had been struck by her apparent intimacy with well-known persons. Victorians, of course; but it was restful to talk about them after the strain of his brother-in-law's Georgian parties on Hampstead Heath. He and she were getting on famously, he felt. She already showed all the symptoms of presently wishing to become a client. Not for the world would he offend her. He turned a little cold at the narrowness of his escape.

She had not, however, noticed.

"You are going out," he said very politely, all readiness should she confirm his assumption to accompany her.

"I want to find Lady Caroline," said Mrs. Fisher, going towards the glass door leading into the top garden.

"An agreeable quest," remarked Mr. Wilkins, "May I assist in the search? Allow me—" he added, opening the door for her.

"She usually sits over in that corner behind the bushes," said Mrs. Fisher. "And I don't know about it being an agreeable quest. She has been letting the bills run up in the most terrible fashion, and needs a good scolding."

"Lady Caroline?" said Mr. Wilkins, unable to follow such an attitude. "What has Lady Caroline, if I may inquire, to do with the bills here?"

"The housekeeping was left to her, and as we all share alike it ought to have been a matter of honour with her—"

"But—Lady Caroline housekeeping for the party here? A party which includes my wife? My dear lady, you render me speechless. Do you not know she is the daughter of the Droitwiches?"

"Oh, is that who she is," said Mrs. Fisher, scrunching heavily over the pebbles towards the hidden corner. "Well, that accounts for it. The muddle that man Droitwich made in his department in the war was a national scandal. It amounted to misappropriation of the public funds."

"But it is impossible, I assure you, to expect the daughter of the Droitwiches—" began Mr. Wilkins earnestly.

"The Droitwiches," interrupted Mrs. Fisher, "are neither here nor there. Duties undertaken should be performed. I don't intend my money to be squandered for the sake of any Droitwiches."

A headstrong old lady. Perhaps not so easy to deal with as he had hoped. But how wealthy. Only the consciousness of great wealth would make her snap her fingers in this manner at the Droitwiches. Lotty, on being questioned, had been vague about her circumstances, and had described her house as a mausoleum with gold-fish swimming about in it; but now he was sure she was more than very well off. Still, he wished he had not joined her at this moment, for he had no sort of desire to be present at such a spectacle as the scolding of Lady Caroline Dester.

Again, however, he was reckoning without Scrap. Whatever she felt when she looked up and beheld Mr. Wilkins discovering her corner on the very first morning, nothing but angelicness appeared on her face. She took her feet off the parapet on Mrs. Fisher's sitting down on it, and listening gravely to her opening remarks as to her not having any money to fling about in reckless and uncontrolled household expenditure, interrupted her flow by pulling one of the cushions from behind her head and offering it to her.

"Sit on this," said Scrap, holding it out. "You'll be more comfortable."

Mr. Wilkins leapt to relieve her of it.

"Oh, thanks," said Mrs. Fisher, interrupted.

It was difficult to get into the swing again. Mr. Wilkins inserted the cushion solicitously between the slightly raised Mrs. Fisher and the stone of the parapet, and again she had to say "Thanks." It was interrupted. Besides, Lady Caroline said nothing in her defence; she only looked at her, and listened with the face of an attentive angel.

It seemed to Mr. Wilkins that it must be difficult to scold a Dester who looked like that and so exquisitely said nothing. Mrs. Fisher, he was glad to see, gradually found it difficult herself, for her severity slackened, and she ended by saying lamely, "You ought to have told me you were not doing it."

"I didn't know you thought I was," said the lovely voice.

"I would now like to know," said Mrs. Fisher, "what you propose to do for the rest of the time here."

"Nothing," said Scrap, smiling.

"Nothing? Do you mean to say—"

"If I may be allowed, ladies," interposed Mr. Wilkins in his suavest professional manner, "to make a suggestion"—they both looked at him, and remembering him as they first saw him felt indulgent— "I would advise you not to spoil a delightful holiday with worries over housekeeping."

"Exactly," said Mrs. Fisher. "It is what I intend to avoid."

"Most sensible," said Mr. Wilkins. "Why not, then," he continued, "allow the cook—an excellent cook, by the way—so much a head per diem"—Mr. Wilkins knew what was necessary in Latin—"and tell her that for this sum she must cater for you, and not only cater but cater as well as ever? One could easily reckon it out. The charges of a moderate hotel, for instance, would do as a basis, halved, or perhaps even quartered."

"And this week that has just passed?" asked Mrs. Fisher. "The terrible bills of this first week? What about them?"

"They shall be my present to San Salvatore," said Scrap, who didn't like the idea of Lotty's nest-egg being reduced so much beyond what she was prepared for.

There was a silence. The ground was cut from under Mrs. Fisher's feet.

"Of course if you choose to throw your money about—" she said at last, disapproving but immensely relieved, while Mr. Wilkins was rapt in the contemplation of the precious qualities of blue blood. This readiness, for instance, not to trouble about money, this free-handedness—it was not only what one admired in others, admired in others perhaps more than anything else, but it was extraordinarily useful to the professional classes. When met with it should be encouraged by warmth of reception. Mrs. Fisher was not warm. She accepted—from which he deduced that with her wealth went closeness—but she accepted grudgingly. Presents were presents, and one did not look them in this manner in the mouth, he felt; and if Lady Caroline found her pleasure in presenting his wife and Mrs. Fisher with their entire food for a week, it was their part to accept gracefully. One should not discourage gifts.

On behalf of his wife, then, Mr. Wilkins expressed what she would wish to express, and remarking to Lady Caroline—with a touch of lightness, for so should gifts be accepted in order to avoid embarrassing the donor—that she had in that case been his wife's hostess since her arrival, he turned almost gaily to Mrs. Fisher and pointed out that she and his wife must now jointly write Lady Caroline the customary latter of thanks for hospitality. "A Collins," said Mr. Wilkins, who knew what was necessary in literature. "I prefer the name Collins for such a letter to either that of Board and Lodging or Bread and Butter. Let us call it a Collins."

Scrap smiled, and held out her cigarette case. Mrs. Fisher could not help being mollified. A way out of waste was going to be found, thanks to Mr. Wilkins, and she hated waste quite as much as having to pay for it; also a way was found out of housekeeping. For a moment she had thought that if everybody tried to force her into housekeeping on her brief holiday by their own indifference (Lady Caroline), or inability to speak Italian (the other two), she would have to send for Kate Lumley after all. Kate could do it. Kate and she had learnt Italian together. Kate would only be allowed to come on condition that she did do it.

But this was much better, this way of Mr. Wilkins's. Really a most superior man. There was nothing like an intelligent, not too young man for profitable and pleasurable companionship. And when she got up, the business for which she had come being settled, and said she now intended to take a little stroll before lunch, Mr. Wilkins did not stay with Lady Caroline, as most of the men she had known would, she was afraid, have wanted to—he asked to be permitted to go and stroll with her; so that he evidently definitely preferred conversation to faces. A sensible, companionable man. A clever, well-read man. A man of the world. A man. She was very glad indeed she had not written to Kate the other day. What did she want with Kate? She had found a better companion.

But Mr. Wilkins did not go with Mrs. Fisher because of her conversation, but because, when she got up and he got up because she got up, intending merely to bow her out of the recess, Lady Caroline had put her feet up on the parapet again, and arranging her head sideways in the cushions had shut her eyes.

The daughter of the Droitwiches desired to go to sleep.

It was not for him, by remaining, to prevent her.

Chapter 16

And so the second week began, and all was harmony. The arrival of Mr. Wilkins, instead of, as three of the party had feared and the fourth had only been protected from fearing by her burning faith in the effect on him of San Salvatore, disturbing such harmony as there was, increased it. He fitted in. He was determined to please, and he did please. He was most amiable to his wife—not only in public, which she was used to, but in private, when he certainly wouldn't have been if he hadn't wanted to. He did want to. He was so much obliged to her, so much pleased with her, for making him acquainted with Lady Caroline, that he felt really fond of her. Also proud; for there must be, he reflected, a good deal more in her than he had supposed, for Lady Caroline to have become so intimate with her and so affectionate. And the more he treated her as though she were really very nice, the more Lotty expanded and became really very nice, and the more he, affected in his turn, became really very nice himself; so that they went round and round, not in a vicious but in a highly virtuous circle.

Positively, for him, Mellersh petted her. There was at no time much pet in Mellersh, because he was by nature a cool man; yet such was the influence on him of, as Lotty supposed, San Salvatore, that in this second week he sometimes pinched both her ears, one after the other, instead of only one; and Lotty, marveling at such rapidly developing affectionateness, wondered what he would do, should he continue at this rate, in the third week, when her supply of ears would have come to an end.

He was particularly nice about the washstand, and genuinely desirous of not taking up too much of the space in the small bedroom. Quick to respond, Lotty was even more desirous not to be in his way; and the room became the scene of many an affectionate combat de générosité, each of which left them more pleased with each other than ever. He did not again have a bath in the bathroom, though it was mended and ready for him, but got up and went down every morning to the sea, and in spite of the cool nights making the water cold early had his dip as a man should, and came up to breakfast rubbing his hands and feeling, as he told Mrs. Fisher, prepared for anything.

Lotty's belief in the irresistible influence of the heavenly atmosphere of San Salvatore being thus obviously justified, and Mr. Wilkins, whom Rose knew as alarming and Scrap had pictured as icily unkind, being so evidently a changed man, both Rose and Scrap began to think there might after all be something in what Lotty insisted on, and that San Salvatore did work purgingly on the character.

They were the more inclined to think so in that they too felt a working going on inside themselves: they felt more cleared, both of them, that second week—Scrap in her thoughts, many of which were now quite nice thoughts, real amiable ones about her parents and relations, with a glimmer in them of recognition of the extraordinary benefits she had received at the hands of—what? Fate? Providence?—anyhow of something, and of how, having received them, she had misused them by failing to be happy; and Rose in her bosom, which though it still yearned, yearned to some purpose, for she was reaching the conclusion that merely inactively to yearn was no use at all, and that she must either by some means stop her yearning or give it at least a chance— remote, but still a chance—of being quieted by writing to Frederick and asking him to come out.

If Mr. Wilkins could be changed, thought Rose, why not Frederick? How wonderful it would be, how too wonderful, if the place worked on him too and were able to make them even a little understand each other, even a little be friends. Rose, so far had loosening and disintegration gone on in her character, now was beginning to think her obstinate strait-lacedness about his books and her austere absorption in good works had been foolish and perhaps even wrong. He was her husband, and she had frightened him away. She had frightened love away, precious love, and that couldn't be good. Was not Lotty right when she said the other day that nothing at all except love mattered? Nothing certainly seemed much use unless it was built up on love. But once frightened away, could it ever come back? Yes, it might in that beauty, it might in the atmosphere of happiness Lotty and San Salvatore seemed between them to spread round like some divine infection.

She had, however, to get him there first, and he certainly couldn't be got there if she didn't write and tell him where she was.

She would write. She must write; for if she did there was at least a chance of his coming, and if she didn't there was manifestly none. And then, once here in this loveliness, with everything so soft and kind and sweet all round, it would be easier to tell him, to try and explain, to ask for something different, for at least an attempt at something different in their lives in the future, instead of the blankness of separation, the cold—oh, the cold—of nothing at all but the great windiness of faith, the great bleakness of works. Why, one person in the world, one single person belonging to one, of one's very own, to talk to, to take care of, to love, to be interested in, was worth more than all the speeches on platforms and the compliments of chairmen in the world. It was also worth more—Rose couldn't help it, the thought would come—than all the prayers.

These thoughts were not head thoughts, like Scrap's, who was altogether free from yearnings, but bosom thoughts. They lodged in the bosom; it was in the bosom that Rose ached, and felt so dreadfully lonely. And when her courage failed her, as it did on most days, and it seemed impossible to write to Frederick, she would look at Mr. Wilkins and revive.

There he was, a changed man. There he was, going into that small, uncomfortable room every night, that room whose proximities had been Lotty's only misgiving, and coming out of it in the morning, and Lotty coming out of it too, both of them as unclouded and as nice to each other as when they went in. And hadn't he, so critical at home, Lotty had told her, of the least thing going wrong, emerged from the bath catastrophe as untouched in spirit as Shadrach, Meshach and Abednego were untouched in body when they emerged from the fire? Miracles were happening in this place. If they could happen to Mr. Wilkins, why not to Frederick?

She got up quickly. Yes, she would write. She would go and write to him at once.

But suppose—

She paused. Suppose he didn't answer. Suppose he didn't even answer.

And she sat down again to think a little longer.

In these hesitations did Rose spend most of the second week.

Then there was Mrs. Fisher. Her restlessness increased that second week. It increased to such an extent that she might just as well not have had her private sitting-room at all, for she could no longer sit. Not for ten minutes together could Mrs. Fisher sit. And added to the restlessness, as the days of the second week proceeded on their way, she had a curious sensation, which worried her, of rising sap. She knew the feeling, because she had sometimes had it in childhood in specially swift springs, when the lilacs and the syringes seemed to rush out into blossom in a single night, but it was strange to have it again after over fifty years. She would have liked to remark on the sensation to some one, but she was ashamed. It was such an absurd sensation at her age. Yet oftener and oftener, and every day more and more, did Mrs. Fisher have a ridiculous feeling as if she were presently going to burgeon.

Sternly she tried to frown the unseemly sensation down. Burgeon, indeed. She had heard of dried staffs, pieces of mere dead wood, suddenly putting forth fresh leaves, but only in legend. She was not in legend. She knew perfectly what was due to herself. Dignity demanded that she should have nothing to do with fresh leaves at her age; and yet there it was—the feeling that presently, that at any moment now, she might crop out all green.

Mrs. Fisher was upset. There were many things she disliked more than anything else, and one was when the elderly imagined they felt young and behaved accordingly. Of course they only imagined it, they were only deceiving themselves; but how deplorable were the results. She herself had grown old as people should grow old—steadily and firmly. No interruptions, no belated after-glows and spasmodic returns. If, after all these years, she were now going to be deluded into some sort of unsuitable breaking-out, how humiliating.

Indeed she was thankful, that second week, that Kate Lumley was not there. It would be most unpleasant, should anything different occur in her behaviour, to have Kate looking on. Kate had known her all her life. She felt she could let herself go—here Mrs. Fisher frowned at the book she was vainly trying to concentrate on, for where did that expression come from?—much less painfully before strangers than before an old friend. Old friends, reflected Mrs. Fisher, who hoped she was reading, compare one constantly with what one used to be. They are always doing it if one develops. They are surprised at development. They hark back; they expect motionlessness after, say, fifty, to the end of one's days.

That, thought Mrs. Fisher, her eyes going steadily line by line down the page and not a word of it getting through into her consciousness, is foolish of friends. It is condemning one to a premature death. One should continue (of course with dignity) to develop, however old one may be. She had nothing against developing, against further ripeness, because as long as one was alive one was not dead—obviously, decided Mrs. Fisher, and development, change, ripening, were life. What she would dislike would be unripening, going back to something green. She would dislike it intensely; and this is what she felt she was on the brink of doing.

Naturally it made her very uneasy, and only in constant movement could she find distraction. Increasingly restless and no longer able to confine herself to her battlements, she wandered more and more frequently, and also aimlessly, in and out of the top garden, to the growing surprise of Scrap, especially when she found that all Mrs. Fisher did was to stare for a few minutes at the view, pick a few dead leaves off the rose-bushes, and go away again.

In Mr. Wilkins's conversation she found temporary relief, but though he joined her whenever he could he was not always there, for he spread his attentions judiciously among the three ladies, and when he was somewhere else she had to face and manage her thoughts as best she could by herself. Perhaps it was the excess of light and colour at San Salvatore which made every other place seem dark and black; and Prince of Wales Terrace did seem a very dark black spot to have to go back to —a dark, narrow street, and her house dark and narrow as the street, with nothing really living or young in it. The goldfish could hardly be called living, or at most not more than half living, and were certainly not young, and except for them there were only the maids, and they were dusty old things.

Dusty old things. Mrs. Fisher paused in her thoughts, arrested by the strange expression. Where had it come from? How was it possible for it to come at all? It might have been one of Mrs. Wilkins's, in its levity, its almost slang. Perhaps it was one of hers, and she had heard her say it and unconsciously caught it from her.

If so, this was both serious and disgusting. That the foolish creature should penetrate into Mrs. Fisher's very mind and establish her personality there, the personality which was still, in spite of the harmony apparently existing between her and her intelligent husband, so alien to Mrs. Fisher's own, so far removed from what she understood and liked, and infect her with her undesirable phrases, was most disturbing. Never in her life before had such a sentence come into Mrs. Fisher's head. Never in her life before had she thought of her maids, or of anybody else, as dusty old things. Her maids were not dusty old things; they were most respectable, neat women, who were allowed the use of the bathroom every Saturday night. Elderly, certainly, but then so was she, so was her house, so was her furniture, so were her goldfish. They were all elderly, as they should be, together. But there was a great difference between being elderly and being a dusty old thing.

How true it was what Ruskin said, that evil communications corrupt good manners. But did Ruskin say it? On second thoughts she was not sure, but it was just the sort of thing he would have said if he had said it, and in any case it was true. Merely hearing Mrs. Wilkins's evil communications at meals—she did not listen, she avoided listening, yet it was evident she had heard—those communications which, in that they so often were at once vulgar, indelicate and profane, and always, she was sorry to say, laughed at by Lady Caroline, must be classed as evil, was spoiling her own mental manners. Soon she might not only think but say. How terrible that would be. If that were the form her breaking-out was going to take, the form of unseemly speech, Mrs. Fisher was afraid she would hardly with any degree of composure be able to bear it.

At this stage Mrs. Fisher wished more than ever that she were able to talk over her strange feelings with some one who would understand. There was, however, no one who would understand except Mrs. Wilkins herself. She would. She would know at once, Mrs. Fisher was sure, what she felt like. But this was impossible. It would be as abject as begging the very microbe that was infecting one for protection against its disease.

She continued, accordingly, to bear her sensations in silence, and was driven by them into that frequent aimless appearing in the top garden which presently roused even Scrap's attention.

Scrap had noticed it, and vaguely wondered at it, for some time before Mr. Wilkins inquired of her one morning as he arranged her cushions for her— he had established the daily assisting of Lady Caroline into her chair as his special privilege—whether there was anything the matter with Mrs. Fisher.

At that moment Mrs. Fisher was standing by the eastern parapet, shading her eyes and carefully scrutinizing the distant white houses of Mezzago. They could see her through the branches of the daphnes.

"I don't know," said Scrap.

"She is a lady, I take it," said Mr. Wilkins, "who would be unlikely to have anything on her mind?"

"I should imagine so," said Scrap, smiling.

"If she has, and her restlessness appears to suggest it, I should be more than glad to assist her with advice."

"I am sure you would be most kind."

"Of course she has her own legal adviser, but he is not on the spot. I am. And a lawyer on the spot," said Mr. Wilkins, who endeavoured to make his conversation when he talked to Lady Caroline light, aware that one must be light with young ladies, "is worth two in—we won't be ordinary and complete the proverb, but say London."

"You should ask her."

"Ask her if she needs assistance? Would you advise it? Would it not be a little—a little delicate to touch on such a question, the question whether or no a lady has something on her mind?"

"Perhaps she will tell you if you go and talk to her. I think it must be lonely to be Mrs. Fisher."

"You are all thoughtfulness and consideration," declared Mr. Wilkins, wishing, for the first time in his life, that he were a foreigner so that he might respectfully kiss her hand on withdrawing to go obediently and relieve Mrs. Fisher's loneliness.

It was wonderful what a variety of exits from her corner Scrap contrived for Mr. Wilkins. Each morning she found a different one, which sent him off pleased after he had arranged her cushions for her. She allowed him to arrange the cushions because she instantly had discovered, the very first five minutes of the very first evening, that her fears lest he should cling to her and stare in dreadful admiration were baseless. Mr. Wilkins did not admire like that. It was not only, she instinctively felt, not in him, but if it had been he would not have dared to in her case. He was all respectfulness. She could direct his movements in regard to herself with the raising of an eyelash. His one concern was to obey. She had been prepared to like him if he would only be so obliging as not to admire her, and she did like him. She did not forget his moving defencelessness the first morning in his towel, and he amused her, and he was kind to Lotty. It is true she liked him most when he wasn't there, but then she usually liked everybody most when they weren't there. Certainly he did seem to be one of those men, rare in her experience, who never looked at a woman from the predatory angle. The comfort of this, the simplification it brought into the relations of the party, was immense. From this point of view Mr. Wilkins was simply ideal; he was unique and precious. Whenever she thought of him, and was perhaps inclined to dwell on the aspects of him that were a little boring, she remembered this and murmured, "But what a treasure."

Indeed it was Mr. Wilkins's one aim during his stay at San Salvatore to be a treasure. At all costs the three ladies who were not his wife must like him and trust him. Then presently when trouble arose in their lives—and in what lives did not trouble sooner or later arise?—they would recollect how reliable he was and how sympathetic, and turn to him for advice. Ladies with something on their minds were exactly what he wanted. Lady Caroline, he judged, had nothing on hers at the moment, but so much beauty—for he could not but see what was evident—must have had its difficulties in the past and would have more of them before it had done. In the past he had not been at hand; in the future he hoped to be. And meanwhile the behaviour of Mrs. Fisher, the next in importance of the ladies from the professional point of view, showed definite promise. It was almost certain that Mrs. Fisher had something on her mind. He had been observing her attentively, and it was almost certain.

With the third, with Mrs. Arbuthnot, he had up to this made least headway, for she was so very retiring and quiet. But might not this very retiringness, this tendency to avoid the others and spend her time alone, indicate that she too was troubled? If so, he was her man. He would cultivate her. He would follow her and sit with her, and encourage her to tell him about herself. Arbuthnot, he understood from Lotty, was a British Museum official—nothing specially important at present, but Mr. Wilkins regarded it as his business to know all sorts and kinds. Besides, there was promotion. Arbuthnot, promoted, might become very much worth while.

As for Lotty, she was charming. She really had all the qualities he had credited her with during his courtship, and they had been, it appeared, merely in abeyance since. His early impressions of her were now being endorsed by the affection and even admiration Lady Caroline showed for her. Lady Caroline Dester was the last person, he was sure, to be mistaken on such a subject. Her knowledge of the world, her constant association with only the best, must make her quite unerring. Lotty was evidently, then, that which before marriage he had believed her to be—she was valuable. She certainly had been most valuable in introducing him to Lady Caroline and Mrs. Fisher. A man in his profession could be immensely helped by a clever and attractive wife. Why had she not been attractive sooner? Why this sudden flowering?

Mr. Wilkins began too to believe there was something peculiar, as Lotty had almost at once informed him, in the atmosphere of San Salvatore. It promoted expansion. It brought out dormant qualities. And feeling more and more pleased, and even charmed, by his wife, and very content with the progress he was making with the two others, and hopeful of progress to be made with the retiring third, Mr. Wilkins could not remember ever having had such an agreeable holiday. The only thing that might perhaps be bettered was the way they would call him Mr. Wilkins. Nobody said Mr. Mellersh-Wilkins. Yet he had introduced himself to Lady Caroline—he flinched a little on remembering the circumstances—as Mellersh-Wilkins.

Still, this was a small matter, not enough to worry about. He would be foolish if in such a place and such society he worried about anything. He was not even worrying about what the holiday was costing, and had made up his mind to pay not only his own expenses but his wife's as well, and surprise her at the end by presenting her with her nest-egg as intact as when she started; and just the knowledge that he was preparing a happy surprise for her made him feel warmer than ever towards her.

In fact Mr. Wilkins, who had begun by being consciously and according to plan on his best behaviour, remained on it unconsciously, and with no effort at all.

And meanwhile the beautiful golden days were dropping gently from the second week one by one, equal in beauty with those of the first, and the scent of beanfields in flower on the hillside behind the village came across to San Salvatore whenever the air moved. In the garden that second week the poet's eyed narcissus disappeared out the long grass at the edge of the zigzag path, and wild gladiolus, slender and rose-coloured, came in their stead, white pinks bloomed in the borders, filing the whole place with their smoky-sweet smell, and a bush nobody had noticed burst into glory and fragrance, and it was a purple lilac bush. Such a jumble of spring and summer was not to be believed in, except by those who dwelt in those gardens. Everything seemed to be out together—all the things crowded into one month which in England are spread penuriously over six. Even primroses were found one day by Mrs. Wilkins in a cold corner up in the hills; and when she brought them down to the geraniums and heliotrope of San Salvatore they looked quite shy.

Chapter 17

On the first day of the third week Rose wrote to Frederick.

In case she should again hesitate and not post the letter, she gave it to Domenico to post; for if she did not write now there would be no time left at all. Half the month at San Salvatore was over. Even if Frederick started directly he got the letter, which of course he wouldn't be able to do, what with packing and passport, besides not being in a hurry to come, he couldn't arrive for five days.

Having done it, Rose wished she hadn't. He wouldn't come. He wouldn't bother to answer. And if he did answer, it would just be giving some reason which was not true, and about being too busy to get away; and all that had been got by writing to him would be that she would be more unhappy than before.

What things one did when one was idle. This resurrection of Frederick, or rather this attempt to resurrect him, what was it but the result of having nothing whatever to do? She wished she had never come away on a holiday. What did she want with holidays? Work was her salvation; work was the only thing that protected one, that kept one steady and one's values true. At home in Hampstead, absorbed and busy, she had managed to get over Frederick, thinking of him latterly only with the gentle melancholy with which one thinks of some one once loved but long since dead; and now this place, idleness in this soft place, had thrown her back to the wretched state she had climbed so carefully out of years ago. Why, if Frederick did come she would only bore him. Hadn't she seen in a flash quite soon after getting to San Salvatore that that was really what kept him away from her? And why should she suppose that now, after such a long estrangement, she would be able not to bore him, be able to do anything but stand before him like a tongue-tied idiot, with all the fingers of her spirit turned into thumbs? Besides, what a hopeless position, to have as it were to beseech: Please wait a little—please don't be impatient—I think perhaps I shan't be a bore presently.

A thousand times a day Rose wished she had let Frederick alone. Lotty, who asked her every evening whether she had sent her letter yet, exclaimed with delight when the answer at last was yes, and threw her arms round her. "Now we shall be completely happy!" cried the enthusiastic Lotty.

But nothing seemed less certain to Rose, and her expression became more and more the expression of one who has something on her mind.

Mr. Wilkins, wanting to find out what it was, strolled in the sun in his Panama hat, and began to meet her accidentally.

"I did not know," said Mr. Wilkins the first time, courteously raising his hat, "that you too liked this particular spot." And he sat down beside her.

In the afternoon she chose another spot; and she had not been in it half an hour before Mr. Wilkins, lightly swinging his cane, came round the corner.

"We are destined to meet in our rambles," said Mr. Wilkins pleasantly. And he sat down beside her.

Mr. Wilkins was very kind, and she had, she saw, misjudged him in Hampstead, and this was the real man, ripened like fruit by the beneficent sun of San Salvatore, but Rose did want to be alone. Still, she was grateful to him for proving to her that though she might bore Frederick she did not bore everybody; if she had, he would not have sat talking to her on each occasion till it was time to go in. True he bored her, but that wasn't anything like so dreadful as if she bored him. Then indeed her vanity would have been sadly ruffled. For now that Rose was not able to say her prayers she was being assailed by every sort of weakness: vanity, sensitiveness, irritability, pugnacity —strange, unfamiliar devils to have coming crowding on one and taking possession of one's swept and empty heart. She had never been vain or irritable or pugnacious in her life before. Could it be that San Salvatore was capable of opposite effects, and the same sun that ripened Mr. Wilkins made her go acid?

The next morning, so as to be sure of being alone, she went down, while Mr. Wilkins was still lingering pleasantly with Mrs. Fisher over breakfast, to the rocks by the water's edge where she and Lotty had sat the first day. Frederick by now had got her letter. To-day, if he were like Mr. Wilkins, she might get a telegram from him.

She tried to silence the absurd hope by jeering at it. Yet—if Mr. Wilkins had telegraphed, why not Frederick? The spell of San Salvatore lurked even, it seemed, in notepaper. Lotty had not dreamed of getting a telegram, and when she came in at lunch-time there it was. It would be too wonderful if when she went back at lunch-time she found one there for her too. . .

Rose clasped her hands tight round her knees. How passionately she longed to be important to somebody again—not important on platforms, not important as an asset in an organization, but privately important, just to one other person, quite privately, nobody else to know or notice. It didn't seem much to ask in a world so crowded with people, just to have one of them, only one out of all the millions, to oneself. Somebody who needed one, who thought of one, who was eager to come to one—oh, oh how dreadfully one wanted to be precious!

All the morning she sat beneath the pine-tree by the sea. Nobody came near her. The great hours passed slowly; they seemed enormous. But she wouldn't go up before lunch, she would give the telegram time to arrive. . .

That day Scrap, egged on by Lotty's persuasions and also thinking that perhaps she had sat long enough, had arisen from her chair and cushions and gone off with Lotty and sandwiches up into the hills till evening. Mr. Wilkins, who wished to go with them, stayed on Lady Caroline's advice with Mrs. Fisher in order to cheer her solitude, and though he left off cheering her about eleven to go and look for Mrs. Arbuthnot, so as for a space to cheer her too, thus dividing himself impartially between these solitary ladies, he came back again presently mopping his forehead and continued with Mrs. Fisher where he had left off, for this time Mrs. Arbuthnot had hidden successfully. There was a telegram, too, for her he noticed when he came in. Pity he did not know where she was.

"Ought we to open it?" he said to Mrs. Fisher.

"No," said Mrs. Fisher.

"It may require an answer."

"I don't approve of tampering with other people's correspondence."

"Tampering! My dear lady—"

Mr. Wilkins was shocked. Such a word. Tampering. He had the greatest possible esteem for Mrs. Fisher, but he did at times find her a little difficult. She liked him, he was sure, and she was in a fair way, he felt, to become a client, but he feared she would be a headstrong and secretive client. She was certainly secretive, for though he had been skilful and sympathetic for a whole week, she had as yet given him no inkling of what was so evidently worrying her.

"Poor old thing," said Lotty, on his asking her if she perhaps could throw light on Mrs. Fisher's troubles. "She hasn't got love."

"Love?" Mr. Wilkins could only echo, genuinely scandalized. "But surely, my dear—at her age—"

"Any love," said Lotty.

That very morning he had asked his wife, for he now sought and respected her opinion, if she could tell him what was the matter with Mrs. Arbuthnot, for she too, though he had done his best to thaw her into confidence, had remained persistently retiring.

"She wants her husband," said Lotty.

"Ah," said Mr. Wilkins, a new light shed on Mrs. Arbuthnot's shy and modest melancholy. And he added, "Very proper."

And Lotty said, smiling at him, "One does."

And Mr. Wilkins said, smiling at her, "Does one?"

And Lotty said, smiling at him, "Of course."

And Mr. Wilkins, much pleased with her, though it was still quite early in the day, a time when caresses are sluggish, pinched her ear.

Just before half-past twelve Rose came slowly up through the pergola and between the camellias ranged on either side of the old stone steps. The rivulets of periwinkles that flowed down them when first she arrived were gone, and now there were these bushes, incredibly rosetted. Pink, white, red, striped—she fingered and smelt them one after the other, so as not to get to her disappointment too quickly. As long as she hadn't seen for herself, seen the table in the hall quite empty except for its bowl of flowers, she still could hope, she still could have the joy of imagining the telegram lying on it waiting for her. But there is no smell in a camellia, as Mr. Wilkins, who was standing in the doorway on the look-out for her and knew what was necessary in horticulture, reminded her.

She started at his voice and looked up.

"A telegram has come for you," said Mr. Wilkins.

She stared at him, her mouth open.

"I searched for you everywhere, but failed—"

Of course. She knew it. She had been sure of it all the time. Bright and burning, Youth in that instant flashed down again on Rose. She flew up the steps, red as the camellia she had just been fingering, and was in the hall and tearing open the telegram before Mr. Wilkins had finished his sentence. Why, but if things could happen like this— why, but there was no end to—why, she and Frederick—they were going to be—again—at last—

"No bad news, I trust?" said Mr. Wilkins who had followed her, for when she had read the telegram she stood staring at it and her face went slowly white. Curious to watch how her face went slowly white.

She turned and looked at Mr. Wilkins as if trying to remember him.

"Oh no. On the contrary—"

She managed to smile. "I'm going to have a visitor," she said, holding out the telegram; and when he had taken it she walked away towards the dining-room, murmuring something about lunch being ready.

Mr. Wilkins read the telegram. It had been sent that morning from Mezzago, and was:

Am passing through on way to Rome. May I pay my respects this afternoon?

Thomas Briggs.

Why should such a telegram make the interesting lady turn pale?
For her pallor on reading it had been so striking as to convince Mr. Wilkins she was receiving a blow.
"Who is Thomas Briggs?" he asked, following her into the dining-room.

She looked at him vaguely. "Who is—?" she repeated, getting her thoughts together again.

"Thomas Briggs."

"Oh. Yes. He is the owner. This is his house. He is very nice.
He is coming this afternoon."
Thomas Briggs was at that very moment coming. He was jogging along the road between Mezzago and Castagneto in a fly, sincerely hoping that the

dark-eyed lady would grasp that all he wanted was to see her, and not at all to see if his house were still there. He felt that an owner of delicacy did not intrude on a tenant. But—he had been thinking so much of her since that day. Rose Arbuthnot. Such a pretty name. And such a pretty creature— mild, milky, mothery in the best sense; the best sense being that she wasn't his mother and couldn't have been if she had tried, for parents were the only things impossible to have younger than oneself. Also, he was passing so near. It seemed absurd not just to look in and see if she were comfortable. He longed to see her in his house. He longed to see it as her background, to see her sitting in his chairs, drinking out of his cups, using all his things. Did she put the big crimson brocade cushion in the drawing-room behind her little dark head? Her hair and the whiteness of her skin would look lovely against it. Had she seen the portrait of herself on the stairs? He wondered if she liked it. He would explain it to her. If she didn't paint, and she had said nothing to suggest it, she wouldn't perhaps notice how exactly the moulding of the eyebrows and the slight hollow of the cheek—

He told the fly to wait in Castagneto, and crossed the piazza, hailed by children and dogs, who all knew him and sprang up suddenly from nowhere, and walking quickly up the zigzag path, for he was an active young man not much more than thirty, he pulled the ancient chain that rang the bell, and waited decorously on the proper side of the open door to be allowed to come in.

At the sight of him Francesca flung up every bit of her that would fling up—eyebrows, eyelids, and hands, and volubly assured him that all was in perfect order and that she was doing her duty.

"Of course, of course," said Briggs, cutting her short. "No one doubts it."

And he asked her to take in his card to her mistress.

"Which mistress?" asked Francesca.

"Which mistress?"

"There are four," said Francesca, scenting an irregularity on the part of the tenants, for her master looked surprised; and she felt pleased, for life was dull and irregularities helped it along at least a little.

"Four?" he repeated surprised. "Well, take it to the lot then," he said, recovering himself, for he noticed her expression.

Coffee was being drunk in the top garden in the shade of the umbrella pine. Only Mrs. Fisher and Mr. Wilkins were drinking it, for Mrs. Arbuthnot, after eating nothing and being completely silent during lunch, had disappeared immediately afterwards.

While Francesca went away into the garden with his card, her master stood examining the picture on the staircase of that Madonna by an early Italian painter, name unknown, picked up by him at Orvieto, who was so much like his tenant. It really was remarkable, the likeness. Of course his tenant that day in London had had her hat on, but he was pretty sure her hair grew just like that off her forehead. The expression of the eyes, grave and sweet, was exactly the same. He rejoiced to think that he would always have her portrait.

He looked up at the sound of footsteps, and there she was, coming down the stairs just as he had imagined her in that place, dressed in white.

She was astonished to see him so soon. She had supposed he would come about tea-time, and till then she had meant to sit somewhere out of doors where she could be by herself.

He watched her coming down the stairs with the utmost eager interest. In a moment she would be level with her portrait.

"It really is extraordinary," said Briggs.

"How do you do," said Rose, intent only on a decent show of welcome.

She did not welcome him. He was here, she felt, the telegram bitter in her heart, instead of Frederick, doing what she had longed Frederick would do, taking his place.

"Just stand still a moment—"

She obeyed automatically.

"Yes—quite astonishing. Do you mind taking off your hat?"

Rose, surprised, took it off obediently.

"Yes—I thought so—I just wanted to make sure. And look—have you noticed—"

He began to make odd swift passes with his hand over the face in the picture, measuring it, looking from it to her.

Rose's surprise became amusement, and she could not help smiling. "Have you come to compare me with my original?" she asked. "You do see how extraordinarily alike—"

"I didn't know I looked so solemn."

"You don't. Not now. You did a minute ago, quite as solemn. Oh yes—how do you do," he finished suddenly, noticing her outstretched hand. And he laughed and shook it, flushing—a trick of his—to the roots of his hair.

Francesca came back. "The Signora Fisher," she said, "will be pleased to see Him."

"Who is the Signora Fisher?" he asked Rose.

"One of the four who are sharing your house."

"Then there are four of you?"

"Yes. My friend and I found we couldn't afford it by ourselves."

"Oh, I say—" began Briggs in confusion, for he would best have liked Rose Arbuthnot—pretty name—not to have to afford anything, but to stay at San Salvatore as long as she liked as his guest.

"Mrs. Fisher is having coffee in the top garden," said Rose. "I'll take you to her and introduce you." "I don't want to go. You've got your hat on, so you were going for a walk. Mayn't I come too? I'd immensely like being shown round by you."

"But Mrs. Fisher is waiting for you."

"Won't she keep?"

"Yes," said Rose, with the smile that had so much attracted him the first day. "I think she will keep quite well till tea."

"Do you speak Italian?"

"No," said Rose. "Why?"

On that he turned to Francesca, and told her at a great rate, for in Italian he was glib, to go back to the Signora in the top garden and tell her he had encountered his old friend the Signora Arbuthnot, and was going for a walk with her and would present himself to her later.

"Do you invite me to tea?" he asked Rose, when Francesca had gone.

"Of course. It's your house."

"It isn't. It's yours."

"Till Monday week," she smiled.

"Come and show me all the views," he said eagerly; and it was plain, even to the self-depreciatory Rose, that she did not bore Mr. Briggs.

Chapter 18

They had a very pleasant walk, with a great deal of sitting down in warm, thyme-fragrant corners, and if anything could have helped Rose to recover from the bitter disappointment of the morning it would have been the company and conversation of Mr. Briggs. He did help her to recover, and the same process took place as that which Lotty had undergone with her husband, and the more Mr. Briggs thought Rose charming the more charming she became.

Briggs was a man incapable of concealments, who never lost time if he could help it. They had not got to the end of the headland where the lighthouse is—Briggs asked her to show him the lighthouse, because the path to it, he knew, was wide enough for two to walk abreast and fairly level—before he had told her of the impression she made on him in London.

Since even the most religious, sober women like to know they have made an impression, particularly the kind that has nothing to do with character or merits, Rose was pleased. Being pleased, she smiled. Smiling, she was more attractive than ever. Colour came into her cheeks, and brightness into her eyes. She heard herself saying things that really sounded quite interesting and even amusing. If Frederick were listening now, she thought, perhaps he would see that she couldn't after all be such a hopeless bore; for here was a man, nice-looking, young, and surely clever—he seemed clever, and she hoped he was, for then the compliment would be still greater— who was evidently quite happy to spend the afternoon just talking to her.

And indeed Mr. Briggs seemed very much interested. He wanted to hear all about everything she had been doing from the moment she got there. He asked her if she had seen this, that, and the other in the house, what she liked best, which room she had, if she were comfortable, if Francesca was behaving, if Domenico took care of her, and whether she didn't enjoy using the yellow sitting-room—the one that got all the sun and looked out towards Genoa.

Rose was ashamed how little she had noticed in the house, and how few of the things he spoke of as curious or beautiful in it she had even seen. Swamped in thought of Frederick, she appeared to have lived in San Salvatore blindly, and more than half the time had gone, and what had been the good of it? She might just as well have been sitting hankering on Hampstead Heath. No, she mightn't; through all her hankerings she had been conscious that she was at least in the very heart of beauty; and indeed it was this beauty, this longing to share it, that had first started her off hankering.

Mr. Briggs, however, was too much alive for her to be able to spare any attention at this moment for Frederick, and she praised the servants in answer to his questions, and praised the yellow sitting-room without telling him she had only been in it once and then was ignominiously ejected, and she told him she knew hardly anything about art and curiosities, but thought perhaps if somebody would tell her about them she would know more, and she said she had spent every day since her arrival out-of-doors, because out-of-doors there was so very wonderful and different from anything she had ever seen.

Briggs walked by her side along his paths that were yet so happily for the moment her paths, and felt all the innocent glows of family life. He was an orphan and an only child, and had a warm, domestic disposition. He would have adored a sister and spoilt a mother, and was beginning at this time to think of marrying; for though he had been very happy with his various loves, each of whom, contrary to the usual experience, turned ultimately into his devoted friend, he was fond of children and thought he had perhaps now got to the age of settling if he did not wish to be too old by the time his eldest son was twenty. San Salvatore had latterly seemed a little forlorn. He fancied it echoed when he walked about it. He had felt lonely there; so lonely that he had preferred this year to miss out a spring and let it. It wanted a wife in it. It wanted that final touch of warmth and beauty, for he never thought of his wife except in terms of warmth and beauty—she would of course be beautiful and kind. It amused him how much in love with this vague wife he was already.

At such a rate was he making friends with the lady with the sweet name as he walked along the path towards the lighthouse, that he was sure presently he would be telling her everything about himself and his past doings and his future hopes; and the thought of such a swiftly developing confidence made him laugh.

"Why are you laughing?" she asked, looking at him and smiling.

"It's so like coming home," he said.

"But it is coming home for you to come here."

"I mean really like coming home. To one's—one's family. I never had a family. I'm an orphan."

"Oh, are you?" said Rose with the proper sympathy. "I hope you've not been one very long. No—I don't mean I hope you have been one very long. No—I don't know what I mean, except that I'm sorry."

He laughed again. "Oh I'm used to it. I haven't anybody. No sisters or brothers."

"Then you're an only child," she observed intelligently.

"Yes. And there's something about you that's exactly my idea of a—of a family."

She was amused.

"So—cosy," he said, looking at her and searching for a word.

"You wouldn't think so if you saw my house in Hampstead," she said, a vision of that austere and hard-seated dwelling presenting itself to her mind, with nothing soft in it except the shunned and neglected Du Barri sofa. No wonder, she thought, for a moment clear-brained, that Frederick avoided it. There was nothing cosy about his family.

"I don't believe any place you lived in could be anything but exactly like you," he said.

"You're not going to pretend San Salvatore is like me?"

"Indeed I do pretend it. Surely you admit that it is beautiful?"

He said several things like that. She enjoyed her walk. She could not recollect any walk so pleasant since her courting days.

She came back to tea, bringing Mr. Briggs, and looking quite different, Mr. Wilkins noticed, from what she had looked till then. Trouble here, trouble here, thought Mr. Wilkins, mentally rubbing his professional hands. He could see himself being called in presently to advise. On the one hand there was Arbuthnot, on the other hand here was Briggs. Trouble brewing, trouble sooner or later. But why had Briggs's telegram acted on the lady like a blow? If she had turned pale from excess of joy, then trouble was nearer than he had supposed. She was not pale now; she was more like her name than he had yet seen her. Well, he was the man for trouble. He regretted, of course, that people should get into it, but being in he was their man.

And Mr. Wilkins, invigorated by these thoughts, his career being very precious to him, proceeded to assist in doing the honours to Mr. Briggs, both in his quality of sharer in the temporary ownership of San Salvatore and of probable helper out of difficulties, with great hospitality, and pointed out the various features of the place to him, and led him to the parapet and showed him Mezzago across the bay.

Mrs. Fisher too was gracious. This was this young man's house. He was a man of property. She liked property, and she liked men of property. Also there seemed a peculiar merit in being a man of property so young. Inheritance, of course; and inheritance was more respectable than acquisition. It did indicate fathers; and in an age where most people appeared neither to have them nor to want them she liked this too.

Accordingly it was a pleasant meal, with everybody amiable and pleased. Briggs thought Mrs. Fisher a dear old lady, and showed he thought so; and again the magic worked, and she became a dear old lady. She developed benignity with him, and a kind of benignity which was almost playful— actually before tea was over including in some observation she made him the words "My dear boy."

Strange words in Mrs. Fisher's mouth. It is doubtful whether in her life she had used them before. Rose was astonished. Now nice people really were. When would she leave off making mistakes about them? She hadn't suspected this side of Mrs. Fisher, and she began to wonder whether those other sides of her with which alone she was acquainted had not perhaps after all been the effect of her own militant and irritating behaviour. Probably they were. How horrid, then, she must have been. She felt very penitent when she saw Mrs. Fisher beneath her eyes blossoming out into real amiability the moment some one came along who was charming to her, and she could have sunk into the ground with shame when Mrs. Fisher presently laughed, and she realized by the shock it gave her that the sound was entirely new. Not once before had she or any one else there heard Mrs. Fisher laugh. What an indictment of the lot of them! For they had all laughed, the others, some more and some less, at one time or another since their arrival, and only Mrs. Fisher had not. Clearly, since she could enjoy herself as she was now enjoying herself, she had not enjoyed herself before. Nobody had cared whether she did or not, except perhaps Lotty. Yes; Lotty had cared, and had wanted her to be happy; but Lotty seemed to produce a bad effect on Mrs. Fisher, while as for Rose herself she had never been with her for five minutes without wanting, really wanting, to provoke and oppose her.

How very horrid she had been. She had behaved unpardonably. Her penitence showed itself in a shy and deferential solicitude towards Mrs. Fisher which made the observant Briggs think her still more angelic, and wish for a moment that he were an old lady himself in order to be behaved to by Rose Arbuthnot just like that. There was evidently no end, he thought, to the things she could do sweetly. He would even not mind taking medicine, really nasty medicine, if it were Rose Arbuthnot bending over him with the dose.

She felt his bright blue eyes, the brighter because he was so sunburnt, fixed on her with a twinkle in them, and smiling asked him what he was thinking about.

But he couldn't very well tell her that, he said; and added,
"Some day."
"Trouble, trouble," thought Mr. Wilkins at this, again mentally rubbing his hands. "Well, I'm their man."

"I'm sure," said Mrs. Fisher benignly, "you have no thoughts we may not hear."

"I'm sure," said Briggs, "I would be telling you every one of my secrets in a week."

"You would be telling somebody very safe, then," said Mrs. Fisher benevolently—just such a son would she have liked to have had. "And in return," she went on, "I daresay I would tell you mine."

"Ah no," said Mr. Wilkins, adapting himself to this tone of easy badinage, "I must protest. I really must. I have a prior claim, I am the older friend. I have known Mrs. Fisher ten days, and you, Briggs, have not yet known her one. I assert my right to be told her secrets first. That is," he added, bowing gallantly, "if she has any—which I beg leave to doubt."

"Oh, haven't I!" exclaimed Mrs. Fisher, thinking of those green leaves. That she should exclaim at all was surprising, but that she should do it with gaiety was miraculous. Rose could only watch her in wonder.

"Then I shall worm them out," said Briggs with equal gaiety.

"They won't need much worming out," said Mrs. Fisher. "My difficulty is to keep them from bursting out."

It might have been Lotty talking. Mr. Wilkins adjusted the single eyeglass he carried with him for occasions like this, and examined Mrs. Fisher carefully. Rose looked on, unable not to smile too since Mrs. Fisher seemed so much amused, though Rose did not quite know why, and her smile was a little uncertain, for Mrs. Fisher amused was a new sight, not without its awe-inspiring aspects, and had to be got accustomed to.

What Mrs. Fisher was thinking was how much surprised they would be if she told them of her very odd and exciting sensation of going to come out all over buds. They would think she was an extremely silly old woman, and so would she have thought as lately as two days ago; but the bud idea was becoming familiar to her, she was more apprivoisée now, as dear Matthew Arnold used to say, and though it would undoubtedly be best if one's appearance and sensations matched, yet supposing they did not—and one couldn't have everything—was it not better to feel young somewhere rather than old everywhere? Time enough to be old everywhere again, inside as well as out, when she got back to her sarcophagus in Prince of Wales Terrace.

Yet it is probable that without the arrival of Briggs Mrs. Fisher would have gone on secretly fermenting in her shell. The others only knew her as severe. It would have been more than her dignity could bear suddenly to relax—especially towards the three young women. But now came the stranger Briggs, a stranger who at once took to her as no young man had taken to her in her life, and it was the coming of Briggs and his real and manifest appreciation—for just such a grandmother, thought Briggs, hungry for home life and its concomitants, would he have liked to have— that released Mrs. Fisher from her shell; and here she was at last, as Lotty had predicted, pleased, good-humoured and benevolent.

Lotty, coming back half an hour later from her picnic, and following the sound of voices into the top garden in the hope of still finding tea, saw at once what had happened, for Mrs. Fisher at that very moment was laughing.

"She's burst her cocoon," thought Lotty; and swift as she was in all her movements, and impulsive, and also without any sense of propriety to worry and delay her, she bent over the back of Mrs. Fisher's chair and kissed her.

"Good gracious!" cried Mrs. Fisher, starting violently, for such a thing had not happened to her since Mr. Fisher's earlier days, and then only gingerly. This kiss was a real kiss, and rested on Mrs. Fisher's cheek a moment with a strange, soft sweetness.

When she saw whose it was, a deep flush spread over her face. Mrs. Wilkins kissing her and the kiss feeling so affectionate. . . Even if she had wanted to she could not in the presence of the appreciative Mr. Briggs resume her cast-off severity and begin rebuking again; but she did not want to. Was it possible Mrs. Wilkins liked her— had liked her all this time, while she had been so much disliking her herself? A queer little trickle of warmth filtered through the frozen defences of Mrs. Fisher's heart. Somebody young kissing her—somebody young wanting to kiss her. . . Very much flushed, she watched the strange creature, apparently quite unconscious she had done anything extraordinary, shaking hands with Mr. Briggs, on her husband's introducing him, and immediately embarking on the friendliest conversation with him, exactly as if she had known him all her life. What a strange creature; what a very strange creature. It was natural, she being so strange, that one should have, perhaps, misjudged her. . .

"I'm sure you want some tea," said Briggs with eager hospitality to Lotty. He thought her delightful,—freckles, picnic-untidiness and all. Just such a sister would he—

"This is cold," he said, feeling the teapot. "I'll tell
Francesca to make you some fresh—"
He broke off and blushed. "Aren't I forgetting myself," he said, laughing and looking round at them.

"Very natural, very natural," Mr. Wilkins reassured him.

"I'll go and tell Francesca," said Rose, getting up.

"No, no," said Briggs. "Don't go away." And he put his hands to his mouth and shouted.

"Francesca!" shouted Briggs.

She came running. No summons in their experience had been answered by her with such celerity.

"'Her Master's voice,'" remarked Mr. Wilkins; aptly, he considered.

"Make fresh tea," ordered Briggs in Italian. "Quick—quick—" And then remembering himself he blushed again, and begged everybody's pardon.

"Very natural, very natural," Mr. Wilkins reassured him.

Briggs then explained to Lotty what he had explained twice already, once to Rose and once to the other two, that he was on his way to Rome and thought he would get out at Mezzago and just look in to see if they were comfortable and continue his journey the next day, staying the night in an hotel at Mezzago.

"But how ridiculous," said Lotty. "Of course you must stay here. It's your house. There's Kate Lumley's room," she added, turning to Mrs. Fisher. "You wouldn't mind Mr. Briggs having it for one night? Kate Lumley isn't in it, you know," she said turning to Briggs again and laughing.
And Mrs. Fisher to her immense surprise laughed too. She knew that any other time this remark would have struck her as excessively unseemly, and yet now she only thought it funny.

No indeed, she assured Briggs, Kate Lumley was not in that room. Very fortunately, for she was an excessively wide person and the room was excessively narrow. Kate Lumley might get into it, but that was about all. Once in, she would fit it so tightly that probably she would never be able to get out again. It was entirely at Mr. Briggs's disposal, and she hoped he would do nothing so absurd as go to an hotel—he, the owner of the whole place.

Rose listened to this speech wide-eyed with amazement. Mrs. Fisher laughed very much as she made it. Lotty laughed very much too, and at the end of it bent down and kissed her again—kissed her several times.

"So you see, my dear boy," said Mrs. Fisher, "you must stay here and give us all a great deal of pleasure."

"A great deal indeed," corroborated Mr. Wilkins heartily.

"A very great deal," repeated Mrs. Fisher, looking exactly like a pleased mother.

"Do," said Rose, on Briggs's turning inquiringly to her.

"How kind of you all," he said, his face broad with smiles. "I'd love to be a guest here. What a new sensation. And with three such—"

He broke off and looked round. "I say," he asked, "oughtn't I to have a fourth hostess? Francesca said she had four mistresses."

"Yes. There's Lady Caroline," said Lotty.

"Then hadn't we better find out first if she invites me too?"

"Oh, but she's sure—" began Lotty.

"The daughter of the Droitwiches, Briggs," said Mr. Wilkins, "is not likely to be wanting in the proper hospitable impulses."

"The daughter of the—" repeated Briggs; but he stopped dead, for there in the doorway was the daughter of the Droitwiches herself; or rather, coming towards him out of the dark doorway into the brightness of the sunset, was that which he had not in his life yet seen but only dreamed of, his ideal of absolute loveliness.

Chapter 19

And then when she spoke . . . what chance was there for poor
Briggs? He was undone. All Scrap said was, "How do you do," on Mr.
Wilkins presenting him, but it was enough; it undid Briggs.
From a cheerful, chatty, happy young man, overflowing with life and
friendliness, he became silent, solemn, and with little beads on his temples.
Also he became clumsy, dropping the teaspoon as he handed her her cup,
mismanaging the macaroons, so that one rolled on the ground. His eyes
could not keep off the enchanting face for a moment; and when Mr.
Wilkins, elucidating him, for he failed to elucidate himself, informed Lady
Caroline that in Mr. Briggs she beheld the owner of San Salvatore, who
was on his way to Rome, but had got out at Mezzago, etc. etc., and that the
other three ladies had invited him to spend the night in what was to all
intents and purposes his own house rather than an hotel, and Mr. Briggs
was only waiting for the seal of her approval to this invitation, she being
the fourth hostess—when Mr. Wilkins, balancing his sentences and being
admirably clear and enjoying the sound of his own cultured voice,
explained the position in this manner to Lady Caroline, Briggs sat and said
never a word.

A deep melancholy invaded Scrap. The symptoms of the incipient grabber
were all there and only too familiar, and she knew that if Briggs stayed her
rest-cure might be regarded as over.

Then Kate Lumley occurred to her. She caught at Kate as at a straw.

"It would have been delightful," she said, faintly smiling at Briggs—she
could not in decency not smile, at least a little, but even a little betrayed the
dimple, and Briggs's eyes became more fixed than ever—"I'm only
wondering if there is room."

"Yes, there is," said Lotty. "There's Kate Lumley's room."

"I thought," said Scrap to Mrs. Fisher, and it seemed to Briggs that he had
never heard music till now, "your friend was expected immediately."

"Oh, no," said Mrs. Fisher—with an odd placidness, Scrap thought.

"Miss Lumley," said Mr. Wilkins, "—or should I," he inquired of
Mrs. Fisher, "say Mrs.?"
"Nobody has ever married Kate," said Mrs. Fisher complacently.

"Quite so. Miss Lumley does not arrive to-day in any case, Lady Caroline, and Mr. Briggs has—unfortunately, if I may say so—to continue his journey to-morrow, so that his staying would in no way interfere with Miss Lumley's possible movements."

"Then of course I join in the invitation," said Scrap, with what was to Briggs the most divine cordiality.

He stammered something, flushing scarlet, and Scrap thought, "Oh," and turned her head away; but that merely made Briggs acquainted with her profile, and if there existed anything more lovely than Scrap's full face it was her profile.

Well, it was only for this one afternoon and evening. He would leave, no doubt, the first thing in the morning. It took hours to get to Rome. Awful if he hung on till the night train. She had a feeling that the principal express to Rome passed through at night. Why hadn't that woman Kate Lumley arrived yet? She had forgotten all about her, but now she remembered she was to have been invited a fortnight ago. What had become of her? This man, once let in, would come and see her in London, would haunt the places she was likely to go to. He had the makings, her experienced eye could see, of a passionately persistent grabber.

"If," thought Mr. Wilkins, observing Briggs's face and sudden silence, "any understanding existed between this young fellow and Mrs. Arbuthnot, there is now going to be trouble. Trouble of a different nature from the kind I feared, in which Arbuthnot would have played a leading part, in fact the part of petitioner, but trouble that may need help and advice none the less for its not being publicly scandalous. Briggs, impelled by his passions and her beauty, will aspire to the daughter of the Droitwiches. She, naturally and properly, will repel him. Mrs. Arbuthnot, left in the cold, will be upset and show it. Arbuthnot, on his arrival will find his wife in enigmatic tears. Inquiring into their cause, he will be met with an icy reserve. More trouble may then be expected, and in me they will seek and find their adviser. When Lotty said Mrs. Arbuthnot wanted her husband, she was wrong. What Mrs. Arbuthnot wants is Briggs, and it looks uncommonly as if she were not going to get him. Well, I'm their man."

"Where are your things, Mr. Briggs?" asked Mrs. Fisher, her voice round with motherliness. "Oughtn't they to be fetched?" For the sun was nearly in the sea now, and the sweet-smelling April dampness that followed immediately on its disappearance was beginning to steal into the garden.

Briggs started. "My things?" he repeated. "Oh yes—I must fetch them.

They're in Mezzago. I'll send Domenico. My fly is waiting in the village. He can go back in it. I'll go and tell him."

He got up. To whom was he talking? To Mrs. Fisher, ostensibly, yet his eyes were fixed on Scrap, who said nothing and looked at no one.

Then, recollecting himself, he stammered, "I'm awfully sorry—I keep on forgetting—I'll go down and fetch them myself."

"We can easily send Domenico," said Rose; and at her gentle voice he turned his head.

Why, there was his friend, the sweet-named lady—but how had she not in this short interval changed! Was it the failing light making her so colourless, so vague-featured, so dim, so much like a ghost? A nice good ghost, of course, and still with a pretty name, but only a ghost.

He turned from her to Scrap again, and forgot Rose Arbuthnot's existence. How was it possible for him to bother about anybody or anything else in this first moment of being face to face with his dream come true?

Briggs had not supposed or hoped that any one as beautiful as his dream of beauty existed. He had never till now met even an approximation. Pretty women, charming women by the score he had met and properly appreciated, but never the real, the godlike thing itself. He used to think "If ever I saw a perfectly beautiful woman I should die"; and though, having now met what to his ideas was a perfectly beautiful woman, he did not die, he became very nearly as incapable of managing his own affairs as if he had.

The others were obliged to arrange everything for him. By questions they extracted from him that his luggage was in the station cloakroom at Mezzago, and they sent for Domenico, and, urged and prompted by everybody except Scrap, who sat in silence and looked at no one, Briggs was induced to give him the necessary instructions for going back in the fly and bringing out his things.

It was a sad sight to see the collapse of Briggs. Everybody noticed it, even Rose.

"Upon my word," thought Mrs. Fisher, "the way one pretty face can turn a delightful man into an idiot is past all patience."

And feeling the air getting chilly, and the sight of the enthralled Briggs painful, she went in to order his room to be got ready, regretting now that she had pressed the poor boy to stay. She had forgotten Lady Caroline's kill-joy face for the moment, and the more completely owing to the absence of any ill effects produced by it on Mr. Wilkins. Poor boy. Such a charming boy too, left to himself. It was true she could not accuse Lady Caroline of not leaving him to himself, for she was taking no notice of him at all, but that did not help. Exactly like foolish moths did men, in other respects intelligent, flutter round the impassive lighted candle of a pretty face. She had seen them doing it. She had looked on only too often. Almost she laid a mother hand on Briggs's fair head as she passed him. Poor boy.

Then Scrap, having finished her cigarette, got up and went indoors too. She saw no reason why she should sit there in order to gratify Mr. Briggs's desire to stare. She would have liked to stay out longer, to go to her corner behind the daphne bushes and look at the sunset sky and watch the lights coming out one by one in the village below and smell the sweet moistness of the evening, but if she did Mr. Briggs would certainly follow her.

The old familiar tyranny had begun again. Her holiday of peace and liberation was interrupted—perhaps over, for who knew if he would go away, after all, to-morrow? He might leave the house, driven out of it by Kate Lumley, but that was nothing to prevent his taking rooms in the village and coming up every day. This tyranny of one person over another! And she was so miserably constructed that she wouldn't even be able to frown him down without being misunderstood.

Scrap, who loved this time of the evening in her corner, felt indignant with Mr. Briggs who was doing her out of it, and she turned her back on the garden and him and went towards the house without a look or a word. But Briggs, when he realized her intention, leapt to his feet, snatched chairs which were not in her way out of it, kicked a footstool which was not in her path on one side, hurried to the door, which stood wide open, in order to hold it open, and followed her through it, walking by her side along the hall.

What was to be done with Mr. Briggs? Well, it was his hall; she couldn't prevent his walking along it.

"I hope," he said, not able while walking to take his eyes off her, so that he knocked against several things he would otherwise have avoided—the corner of a bookcase, an ancient carved cupboard, the table with the flowers on it, shaking the water over—"that you are quite comfortable here? If you're not I'll—I'll flay them alive."

His voice vibrated. What was to be done with Mr. Briggs? She could of course stay in her room the whole time, say she was ill, not appear at dinner; but again, the tyranny of this . . .

"I'm very comfortable indeed," said Scrap.

"If I had dreamed you were coming—" he began.

"It's a wonderful old place," said Scrap, doing her utmost to sound detached and forbidding, but with little hope of success.

The kitchen was on this floor, and passing its door, which was open a crack, they were observed by the servants, whose thoughts, communicated to each other by looks, may be roughly reproduced by such rude symbols as Aha and Oho—symbols which represented and included their appreciation of the inevitable, their foreknowledge of the inevitable, and their complete understanding and approval.

"Are you going upstairs?" asked Briggs, as she paused at the foot of them.

"Yes."

"Which room do you sit in? The drawing-room, or the small yellow room?"

"In my own room."

So then he couldn't go up with her; so then all he could do was to wait till she came out again.

He longed to ask her which was her own room—it thrilled him to hear her call any room in his house her own room—that he might picture her in it. He longed to know if by any happy chance it was his room, for ever after to be filled with her wonder; but he didn't dare. He would find that out later from some one else—Francesca, anybody.

"Then I shan't see you again till dinner?"

"Dinner is at eight," was Scrap's evasive answer as she went upstairs.

He watched her go.

She passed the Madonna, the portrait of Rose Arbuthnot, and the dark-eyed figure he had thought so sweet seemed to turn pale, to shrivel into insignificance as she passed.

She turned the bend of the stairs, and the setting sun, shining through the west window a moment on her face, turned her to glory.

She disappeared, and the sun went out too, and the stairs were dark and empty.

He listened till her footsteps were silent, trying to tell from the sound of the shutting door which room she had gone into, then wandered aimlessly away through the hall again, and found himself back in the top garden.

Scrap from her window saw him there. She saw Lotty and Rose sitting on the end parapet, where she would have liked to have been, and she saw Mr. Wilkins buttonholing Briggs and evidently telling him the story of the oleander tree in the middle of the garden.

Briggs was listening with a patience she thought rather nice, seeing that it was his oleander and his own father's story. She knew Mr. Wilkins was telling him the story by his gestures. Domenico had told it her soon after her arrival, and he had also told Mrs. Fisher, who had told Mr. Wilkins. Mrs. Fisher thought highly of this story, and often spoke of it. It was about a cherrywood walking-stick. Briggs's father had thrust this stick into the ground at that spot, and said to Domenico's father, who was then the gardener, "Here we will have an oleander." And Briggs's father left the stick in the ground as a reminder to Domenico's father, and presently— how long afterwards nobody remembered—the stick began to sprout, and it was an oleander.

There stood poor Mr. Briggs being told all about it, and listening to the story he must have known from infancy with patience.

Probably he was thinking of something else. She was afraid he was. How unfortunate, how extremely unfortunate, the determination that seized people to get hold of and engulf other people. If only they could be induced to stand more on their own feet. Why couldn't Mr. Briggs be more like Lotty, who never wanted anything of anybody, but was complete in herself and respected other people's completeness? One loved being with Lotty. With her one was free, and yet befriended. Mr. Briggs looked so really nice, too. She thought she might like him if only he wouldn't so excessively like her.

Scrap felt melancholy. Here she was shut up in her bedroom, which was stuffy from the afternoon sun that had been pouring into it, instead of out in the cool garden, and all because of Mr. Briggs.

Intolerably tyranny, she thought, flaring up. She wouldn't endure it; she would go out all the same; she would run downstairs while Mr. Wilkins— really that man was a treasure—held Mr. Briggs down telling him about the oleander, and get out of the house by the front door, and take cover in the shadows of the zigzag path. Nobody could see her there; nobody would think of looking for her there.

She snatched up a wrap, for she did not mean to come back for a long while, perhaps not even to dinner—it would be all Mr. Briggs's fault if she went dinnerless and hungry—and with another glance out of the window to see if she were still safe, she stole out and got away to the sheltering trees of the zigzag path, and there sat down on one of the seats placed at each bend to assist the upward journey of those who were breathless.

Ah, this was lovely, thought Scrap with a sigh of relief. How cool. How good it smelt. She could see the quiet water of the little harbour through the pine trunks, and the lights coming out in the houses on the other side, and all round her the green dusk was splashed by the rose-pink of the gladioluses in the grass and the white of the crowding daisies.

Ah, this was lovely. So still. Nothing moving—not a leaf, not a stalk. The only sound was a dog barking, far away somewhere up on the hills, or when the door of the little restaurant in the piazza below was opened and there was a burst of voices, silenced again immediately by the swinging to of the door.

She drew in a deep breath of pleasure. Ah, this was—

Her deep breath was arrested in the middle. What was that?

She leaned forward listening, her body tense.

Footsteps. On the zigzag path. Briggs. Finding her out.

Should she run?

No—the footsteps were coming up, not down. Some one from the village.

Perhaps Angelo, with provisions.

She relaxed again. But the steps were not the steps of Angelo, that swift and springy youth; they were slow and considered, and they kept on pausing.

"Some one who isn't used to hills," thought Scrap.

The idea of going back to the house did not occur to her. She was afraid of nothing in life except love. Brigands or murderers as such held no terrors for the daughter of the Droitwiches; she only would have been afraid of them if they left off being brigands and murderers and began instead to try and make love.

The next moment the footsteps turned the corner of her bit of path, and stood still.

"Getting his wind," thought Scrap, not looking round.

Then as he—from the sounds of the steps she took them to belong to a man—did not move, she turned her head, and beheld with astonishment a person she had seen a good deal of lately in London, the well-known writer of amusing memoirs, Mr. Ferdinand Arundel.

She stared. Nothing in the way of being followed surprised her any more, but that he should have discovered where she was surprised her. Her mother had promised faithfully to tell no one.

"You?" she said, feeling betrayed. "Here?"

He came up to her and took off his hat. His forehead beneath the hat was wet with the beads of unaccustomed climbing. He looked ashamed and entreating, like a guilty but devoted dog.

"You must forgive me," he said. "Lady Droitwich told me where you were, and as I happened to be passing through on my way to Rome I thought I would get out at Mezzago and just look in and see how you were."

"But—didn't my mother tell you I was doing a rest-cure?"

"Yes. She did. And that's why I haven't intruded on you earlier in the day. I thought you would probably sleep all day, and wake up about now so as to be fed."

"But—"

"I know. I've got nothing to say in excuse. I couldn't help myself."

"This," thought Scrap, "comes of mother insisting on having authors to lunch, and me being so much more amiable in appearance than I really am."

She had been amiable to Ferdinand Arundel; she liked him—or rather she did not dislike him. He seemed a jovial, simple man, and had the eyes of a nice dog. Also, though it was evident that he admired her, he had not in London grabbed. There he had merely been a good-natured, harmless person of entertaining conversation, who helped to make luncheons agreeable. Now it appeared that he too was a grabber. Fancy following her out there—daring to. Nobody else had. Perhaps her mother had given him the address because she considered him so absolutely harmless, and thought he might be useful and see her home.

Well, whatever he was he couldn't possibly give her the trouble an active young man like Mr. Briggs might give her. Mr. Briggs, infatuated, would be reckless, she felt, would stick at nothing, would lose his head publicly. She could imagine Mr. Briggs doing things with rope-ladders, and singing all night under her window—being really difficult and uncomfortable. Mr. Arundel hadn't the figure for any kind of recklessness. He had lived too long and too well. She was sure he couldn't sing, and wouldn't want to. He must be at least forty. How many good dinners could not a man have eaten by the time he was forty? And if during that time instead of taking exercise he had sat writing books, he would quite naturally acquire the figure Mr. Arundel had in fact acquired—the figure rather for conversation than adventure.

Scrap, who had become melancholy at the sight of Briggs, became philosophical at the sight of Arundel. Here he was. She couldn't send him away till after dinner. He must be nourished.

This being so, she had better make the best of it, and do that with a good grace which anyhow wasn't to be avoided. Besides, he would be a temporary shelter from Mr. Briggs. She was at least acquainted with Ferdinand Arundel, and could hear news from him of her mother and her friends, and such talk would put up a defensive barrier at dinner between herself and the approaches of the other one. And it was only for one dinner, and he couldn't eat her.

She therefore prepared herself for friendliness. "I'm to be fed," she said, ignoring his last remark, "at eight, and you must come up and be fed too. Sit down and get cool and tell me how everybody is."

"May I really dine with you? In these travelling things?" he said, wiping his forehead before sitting down beside her.

She was too lovely to be true, he thought. Just to look at her for an hour, just to hear her voice, was enough reward for his journey and his fears.

"Of course. I suppose you've left your fly in the village, and will be going on from Mezzago by the night train."

"Or stay in Mezzago in an hotel and go on to-morrow. But tell me," he said, gazing at the adorable profile, "about yourself. London has been extraordinarily dull and empty. Lady Droitwich said you were with people here she didn't know. I hope they've been kind to you? You look—well, as if your cure had done everything a cure should."

"They've been very kind," said Scrap. "I got them out of an advertisement."

"An advertisement?"

"It's a good way, I find, to get friends. I'm fonder of one of these than I've been of anybody in years."

"Really? Who is it?"

"You shall guess which of them it is when you see them. Tell me about mother. When did you see her last? We arranged not to write to each other unless there was something special. I wanted to have a month that was perfectly blank."

"And now I've come and interrupted. I can't tell you how ashamed I am—both of having done it and of not having been able to help it."
"Oh, but," said Scrap quickly, for he could not have come on a better day, when up there waiting and watching for her was, she knew, the enamoured Briggs, "I'm really very glad indeed to see you. Tell me about mother."

Chapter 20

Scrap wanted to know so much about her mother that Arundel had presently to invent. He would talk about anything she wished if only he might be with her for a while and see her and hear her, but he knew very little of the Droitwiches and their friends really—beyond meeting them at those bigger functions where literature is also represented, and amusing them at luncheons and dinners, he knew very little of them really. To them he had always remained Mr. Arundel; no one called him Ferdinand; and he only knew the gossip also available to the evening papers and the frequenters of clubs. But he was, however, good at inventing; and as soon as he had come to an end of first-hand knowledge, in order to answer her inquires and keep her there to himself he proceeded to invent. It was quite easy to fasten some of the entertaining things he was constantly thinking on to other people and pretend they were theirs. Scrap, who had that affection for her parents which warms in absence, was athirst for news, and became more and more interested by the news he gradually imparted.

At first it was ordinary news. He had met her mother here, and seen her there. She looked very well; she said so and so. But presently the things Lady Droitwich had said took on an unusual quality: they became amusing.

"Mother said that?" Scrap interrupted, surprised.

And presently Lady Droitwich began to do amusing things as well as say them.

"Mother did that?" Scrap inquired, wide-eyed.

Arundel warmed to his work. He fathered some of the most entertaining ideas he had lately had on to Lady Droitwich, and also any charming funny things that had been done—or might have been done, for he could imagine almost anything.

Scrap's eyes grew round with wonder and affectionate pride in her mother. Why, but how funny—-fancy mother. What an old darling. Did she really do that? How perfectly adorable of her. And did she really say—but how wonderful of her to think of it. What sort of a face did Lloyd George make?

She laughed and laughed, and had a great longing to hug her mother, and the time flew, and it grew quite dusk, and it grew nearly dark, and Mr. Arundel still went on amusing her, and it was a quarter to eight before she suddenly remembered dinner.

"Oh, good heavens!" she exclaimed, jumping up.

"Yes. It's late," said Arundel.

"I'll go on quickly and send the maid to you. I must run, or
I'll never be ready in time—"
And she was gone up the path with the swiftness of a young, slender deer.

Arundel followed. He did not wish to arrive too hot, so had to go slowly.
Fortunately he was near the top, and Francesca came down the pergola to
pilot him indoors, and having shown him where he could wash she put him
in the empty drawing-room to cool himself by the crackling wood fire.

He got as far away from the fire as he could, and stood in one of the deep
window-recesses looking out at the distant lights of Mezzago. The
drawing-room door was open, and the house was quiet with the hush that
precedes dinner, when the inhabitants are all shut up in their rooms
dressing. Briggs in his room was throwing away spoilt tie after spoilt tie;
Scrap in hers was hurrying into a black frock with a vague notion that Mr.
Briggs wouldn't be able to see her so clearly in black; Mrs. Fisher was
fastening the lace shawl, which nightly transformed her day dress into her
evening dress, with the brooch Ruskin had given her on her marriage,
formed of two pearl lilies tied together by a blue enamel ribbon on which
was written in gold letters Esto perpetua; Mr. Wilkins was sitting on the
edge of his bed brushing his wife's hair— thus far in this third week had he
progressed in demonstrativeness— while she, for her part, sitting on a chair
in front of him, put his studs in a clean shirt; and Rose, ready dressed, sat at
her window considering her day.

Rose was quite aware of what had happened to Mr. Briggs. If she had had
any difficulty about it, Lotty would have removed it by the frank comments
she made while she and Rose sat together after tea on the wall. Lotty was
delighted at more love being introduced into San Salvatore, even if it were
only one-sided, and said that when once Rose's husband was there she
didn't suppose, now that Mrs. Fisher too had at last come unglued—Rose
protested at the expression, and Lotty retorted that it was in Keats—there
would be another place in the world more swarming with happiness than
San Salvatore.

"Your husband," said Lotty, swinging her feet, "might be here quite soon,
perhaps to-morrow evening if he starts at once, and there'll be a glorious
final few days before we all go home refreshed for life. I don't believe any

of us will ever be the same again—and I wouldn't be a bit surprised if Caroline doesn't end by getting fond of the young man Briggs. It's in the air. You have to get fond of people here."

Rose sat at her window thinking of these things. Lotty's optimism . . . yet it had been justified by Mr. Wilkins; and look, too, at Mrs. Fisher. If only it would come true as well about Frederick! For Rose, who between lunch and tea had left off thinking about Frederick, was now, between tea and dinner, thinking of him harder than ever.

It has been funny and delightful, that little interlude of admiration, but of course it couldn't go on once Caroline appeared. Rose knew her place. She could see as well as any one the unusually, the unique loveliness of Lady Caroline. How warm, though, things like admiration and appreciation made one feel, how capable of really deserving them, how different, how glowing. They seemed to quicken unsuspected faculties into life. She was sure she had been a thoroughly amusing woman between lunch and tea, and a pretty one too. She was quite certain she had been pretty; she saw it in Mr. Briggs's eyes as clearly as in a looking-glass. For a brief space, she thought, she had been like a torpid fly brought back to gay buzzing by the lighting of a fire in a wintry room. She still buzzed, she still tingled, just at the remembrance. What fun it had been, having an admirer even for that little while. No wonder people liked admirers. They seemed, in some strange way, to make one come alive.

Although it was all over she still glowed with it and felt more exhilarated, more optimistic, more as Lotty probably constantly felt, than she had done since she was a girl. She dressed with care, though she knew Mr. Briggs would no longer see her, but it gave her pleasure to see how pretty, while she was about it, she could make herself look; and very nearly she stuck a crimson camellia in her hair down by her ear. She did hold it there for a minute, and it looked almost sinfully attractive and was exactly the colour of her mouth, but she took it out again with a smile and a sigh and put it in the proper place for flowers, which is water. She mustn't be silly, she thought. Think of the poor. Soon she would be back with them again, and what would a camellia behind her ear seem like then? Simply fantastic.

But on one thing she was determined: the first thing she would do when she got home would be to have it out with Frederick. If he didn't come to San Salvatore that is what she would do—the very first thing. Long ago she ought to have done this, but always she had been handicapped, when she tried to, by being so dreadfully fond of him and so much afraid that fresh wounds were going to be given her wretched, soft heart. But now let him wound her as much as he chose, as much as he possibly could, she would still have it out with him. Not that he ever intentionally wounded her; she knew he never meant to, she knew he often had no idea of having done it. For a person who wrote books, thought Rose, Frederick didn't seem to have much imagination. Anyhow, she said to herself, getting up from the dressing-table, things couldn't go on like this. She would have it out with him. This separate life, this freezing loneliness, she had had enough of it. Why shouldn't she too be happy? Why on earth—the energetic expression matched her mood of rebelliousness—shouldn't she too be loved and allowed to love?

She looked at her little clock. Still ten minutes before dinner.
Tired of staying in her bedroom she thought she would go on to Mrs. Fisher's battlements, which would be empty at this hour, and watch the moon rise out of the sea.
She went into the deserted upper hall with this intention, but was attracted on her way along it by the firelight shining through the open door of the drawing-room.

How gay it looked. The fire transformed the room. A dark, ugly room in the daytime, it was transformed just as she had been transformed by the warmth of—no, she wouldn't be silly; she would think of the poor; the thought of them always brought her down to sobriety at once.

She peeped in. Firelight and flowers; and outside the deep slits of windows hung the blue curtain of the night. How pretty. What a sweet place San Salvatore was. And that gorgeous lilac on the table— she must go and put her face in it . . .

But she never got to the lilac. She went one step towards it, and then stood still, for she had seen the figure looking out of the window in the farthest corner, and it was Frederick.

All the blood in Rose's body rushed to her heart and seemed to stop its beating.

She stood quite still. He had not heard her. He did not turn round. She stood looking at him. The miracle had happened, and he had come.

She stood holding her breath. So he needed her, for he had come instantly. So he too must have been thinking, longing . . .

Her heart, which had seemed to stop beating, was suffocating her now, the way it raced along. Frederick did love her then—he must love her, or why had he come? Something, perhaps her absence, had made him turn to her, want her . . . and now the understanding she had made up her mind to have with him would be quite—would be quite—easy—

Her thoughts wouldn't go on. Her mind stammered. She couldn't think. She could only see and feel. She didn't know how it had happened. It was a miracle. God could do miracles. God had done this one. God could—God could—could—

Her mind stammered again, and broke off.

"Frederick—" she tried to say; but no sound came, or if it did the crackling of the fire covered it up.

She must go nearer. She began to creep towards him—softly, softly.

He did not move. He had not heard.

She stole nearer and nearer, and the fire crackled and he heard nothing.

She stopped a moment, unable to breathe. She was afraid.
Suppose he—suppose he—oh, but he had come, he had come.
She went on again, close up to him, and her heart beat so loud that she thought he must hear it. And couldn't he feel—didn't he know—

"Frederick," she whispered, hardly able even to whisper, choked by the beating of her heart.

He spun round on his heels.

"Rose!" he exclaimed, staring blankly.

But she did not see his stare, for her arms were round his neck, and her cheek was against his, and she was murmuring, her lips on his ear, "I knew you would come—in my very heart I always, always knew you would come—"

Chapter 21

Now Frederick was not the man to hurt anything if he could help it; besides, he was completely bewildered. Not only was his wife here —here, of all places in the world—but she was clinging to him as she had not clung for years, and murmuring love, and welcoming him. If she welcomed him she must have been expecting him. Strange as this was, it was the only thing in the situation which was evident—that, and the softness of her cheek against his, and the long-forgotten sweet smell of her.

Frederick was bewildered. But not being the man to hurt anything if he could help it he too put his arms round her, and having put them round her he also kissed her; and presently he was kissing her almost as tenderly as she was kissing him; and presently he was kissing her quite as tenderly; and again presently he was kissing her more tenderly, and just as if he had never left off.

He was bewildered, but he still could kiss. It seemed curiously natural to be doing it. It made him feel as if he were thirty again instead of forty, and Rose were his Rose of twenty, the Rose he had so much adored before she began to weigh what he did with her idea of right, and the balance went against him, and she had turned strange, and stony, and more and more shocked, and oh, so lamentable. He couldn't get at her in those days at all; she wouldn't, she couldn't understand. She kept on referring everything to what she called God's eyes—in God's eyes it couldn't be right, it wasn't right. Her miserable face—whatever her principles did for her they didn't make her happy—her little miserable face, twisted with effort to be patient, had been at last more than he could bear to see, and he had kept away as much as he could. She never ought to have been the daughter of a low-church rector—narrow devil; she was quite unfitted to stand up against such an upbringing.

What had happened, why she was here, why she was his Rose again, passed his comprehension; and meanwhile, and until such time as he understood, he still could kiss. In fact he could not stop kissing; and it was he now who began to murmur, to say love things in her ear under the hair that smelt so sweet and tickled him just as he remembered it used to tickle him.

And as he held her close to his heart and her arms were soft round his neck, he felt stealing over him a delicious sense of—at first he didn't know what it was, this delicate, pervading warmth, and then he recognized it as security. Yes; security. No need now to be ashamed of his figure, and to make jokes about it so as to forestall other people's and show he didn't mind it; no need now to be ashamed of getting hot going up hills, or to torment himself with pictures of how he probably appeared to beautiful young women—how middle-aged, how absurd in his inability to keep away from them. Rose cared nothing for such things. With her he was safe. To her he was her lover, as he used to be; and she would never notice or mind any of the ignoble changes that getting older had made in him and would go on making more and more.

Frederick continued, therefore, with greater and greater warmth and growing delight to kiss his wife, and the mere holding of her in his arms caused him to forget everything else. How could he, for instance, remember or think of Lady Caroline, to mention only one of the complications with which his situation bristled, when here was his sweet wife, miraculously restored to him, whispering with her cheek against his in the dearest, most romantic words how much she loved him, how terribly she had missed him? He did for one brief instant, for even in moments of love there were brief instants of lucid thought, recognize the immense power of the woman present and being actually held compared to that of the woman, however beautiful, who is somewhere else, but that is as far as he got towards remembering Scrap; no farther. She was like a dream, fleeing before the morning light.

"When did you start?" murmured Rose, her mouth on his ear. She couldn't let him go; not even to talk she couldn't let him go.

"Yesterday morning," murmured Frederick, holding her close. He couldn't let her go either.

"Oh—the very instant then," murmured Rose.

This was cryptic, but Frederick said, "Yes, the very instant," and kissed her neck.

"How quickly my letter got to you," murmured Rose, whose eyes were shut in the excess of her happiness.

"Didn't it," said Frederick, who felt like shutting his eyes himself.

So there had been a letter. Soon, no doubt, light would be vouchsafed him, and meanwhile this was so strangely, touchingly sweet, this holding his Rose to his heart again after all the years, that he couldn't bother to try to guess anything. Oh, he had been happy during these years, because it was not in him to be unhappy; besides, how many interests life had had to offer him, how many friends, how much success, how many women only too willing to help him to blot out the thought of the altered, petrified, pitiful little wife at home who wouldn't spend his money, who was appalled by his books, who drifted away and away from him, and always if he tried to have it out with her asked him with patient obstinacy what he thought the things he wrote and lived by looked in the eyes of God. "No one," she said once, "should ever write a book God wouldn't like to read. That is the test, Frederick." And he had laughed hysterically, burst into a great shriek of laughter, and rushed out of the house, away from her solemn little face—away from her pathetic, solemn little face. . .

But this Rose was his youth again, the best part of his life, the part of it that had had all the visions in it and all the hopes. How they had dreamed together, he and she, before he struck that vein of memoirs; how they had planned, and laughed and loved. They had lived for a while in the very heart of poetry. After the happy days came the happy nights, the happy, happy nights, with her asleep close against his heart, with her when he woke in the morning still close against his heart, for they hardly moved in their deep, happy sleep. It was wonderful to have it all come back to him at the touch of her, at the feel of her face against his—wonderful that she should be able to give him back his youth.

"Sweetheart—sweetheart," he murmured, overcome by remembrance, clinging to her now in his turn.

"Beloved husband," she breathed—the bliss of it—the sheer bliss . . .

Briggs, coming in a few minutes before the gong went on the chance that Lady Caroline might be there, was much astonished. He had supposed Rose Arbuthnot was a widow, and he still supposed it; so that he was much astonished.

"Well I'm damned," thought Briggs, quite clearly and distinctly, for the shock of what he saw in the window startled him so much that for a moment he was shaken free of his own confused absorption.

Aloud he said, very red, "Oh I say—I beg your pardon"—and then stood hesitating, and wondering whether he oughtn't to go back to his bedroom again.

If he had said nothing they would not have noticed he was there, but when he begged their pardon Rose turned and looked at him as one looks who is trying to remember, and Frederick looked at him too without at first quite seeing him.

They didn't seem, thought Briggs, to mind or to be at all embarrassed. He couldn't be her brother; no brother ever brought that look into a woman's face. It was very awkward. If they didn't mind, he did. It upset him to come across his Madonna forgetting herself.

"Is this one of your friends?" Frederick was able after an instant to ask Rose, who made no attempt to introduce the young man standing awkwardly in front of them but continued to gaze at him with a kind of abstracted, radiant goodwill.

"It's Mr. Briggs," said Rose, recognizing him. "This is my husband," she added.

And Briggs, shaking hands, just had time to think how surprising it was to have a husband when you were a widow before the gong sounded, and Lady Caroline would be there in a minute, and he ceased to be able to think at all, and merely became a thing with its eyes fixed on the door.

Through the door immediately entered, in what seemed to him an endless procession, first Mrs. Fisher, very stately in her evening lace shawl and brooch, who when she saw him at once relaxed into smiles and benignity, only to stiffen, however, when she caught sight of the stranger; then Mr. Wilkins, cleaner and neater and more carefully dressed and brushed than any man on earth; and then, tying something hurriedly as she came, Mrs. Wilkins; and then nobody.

Lady Caroline was late. Where was she? Had she heard the gong? Oughtn't it to be beaten again? Suppose she didn't come to dinner after all. . .

Briggs went cold.

"Introduce me," said Frederick on Mrs. Fisher's entrance, touching Rose's elbow.

"My husband," said Rose, holding him by the hand, her face exquisite.

"This," thought Mrs. Fisher, "must now be the last of the husbands, unless Lady Caroline produces one from up her sleeve."

But she received him graciously, for he certainly looked exactly like a husband, not at all like one of those people who go about abroad pretending they are husbands when they are not, and said she supposed he had come to accompany his wife home at the end of the month, and remarked that now the house would be completely full. "So that," she added, smiling at Briggs, "we shall at last really be getting our money's worth."

Briggs grinned automatically, because he was just able to realize that somebody was being playful with him, but he had not heard her and he did not look at her. Not only were his eyes fixed on the door but his whole body was concentrated on it.

Introduced in his turn, Mr. Wilkins was most hospitable and called Frederick "sir."

"Well, sir," said Mr. Wilkins heartily, "here we are, here we are"—and having gripped his hand with an understanding that only wasn't mutual because Arbuthnot did not yet know what he was in for in the way of trouble, he looked at him as a man should, squarely in the eyes, and allowed his look to convey as plainly as a look can that in him would be found staunchness, integrity, reliability—in fact a friend in need. Mrs. Arbuthnot was very much flushed, Mr. Wilkins noticed. He had not seen her flushed like that before. "Well, I'm their man," he thought.

Lotty's greeting was effusive. It was done with both hands.
"Didn't I tell you?" she laughed to Rose over her shoulder while Frederick was shaking her hands in both his.
"What did you tell her?" asked Frederick, in order to say something. The way they were all welcoming him was confusing. They had evidently all expected him, not only Rose.

The sandy but agreeable young woman didn't answer his question, but looked extraordinarily pleased to see him. Why should she be extraordinarily pleased to see him?

"What a delightful place this is," said Frederick, confused, and making the first remark that occurred to him.

"It's a tub of love," said the sandy young woman earnestly; which confused him more than ever.

And his confusion became excessive at the next words he heard— spoken, these, by the old lady, who said: "We won't wait. Lady Caroline is always late"—for he only then, on hearing her name, really and properly remembered Lady Caroline, and the thought of her confused him to excess.

He went into the dining-room like a man in a dream. He had come out to this place to see Lady Caroline, and had told her so. He had even told her in his fatuousness—it was true, but how fatuous—that he hadn't been able to help coming. She didn't know he was married. She thought his name was Arundel. Everybody in London thought his name was Arundel. He had used it and written under it so long that he almost thought it was himself. In the short time since she had left him on the seat in the garden, where he told her he had come because he couldn't help it, he had found Rose again, had passionately embraced and been embraced, and had forgotten Lady Caroline. It would be an extraordinary piece of good fortune if Lady Caroline's being late meant she was tired or bored and would not come to dinner at all. Then he could—no, he couldn't. He turned a deeper red even than usual, he being a man of full habit and red anyhow, at the thought of such cowardice. No, he couldn't go away after dinner and catch his train and disappear to Rome; not unless, that is, Rose came with him. But even so, what a running away. No, he couldn't.

When they got to the dining-room Mrs. Fisher went to the head of the table—was this Mrs. Fisher's house? He asked himself. He didn't know; he didn't know anything—and Rose, who in her earlier day of defying Mrs. Fisher had taken the other end as her place, for after all no one could say by looking at a table which was its top and which its bottom, led Frederick to the seat next to her. If only, he thought, he could have been alone with Rose; just five minutes more alone with Rose, so that he could have asked her—

But probably he wouldn't have asked her anything, and only gone on kissing her.

He looked round. The sandy young woman was telling the man they called Briggs to go and sit beside Mrs. Fisher—was the house, then, the sandy young woman's and not Mrs. Fisher's? He didn't know; he didn't know anything—and she herself sat down on Rose's other side, so that she was opposite him, Frederick, and next to the genial man who had said "Here we are," when it was only too evident that there they were indeed.

Next to Frederick, and between him and Briggs, was an empty chair: Lady Caroline's. No more than Lady Caroline knew of the presence in Frederick's life of Rose was Rose aware of the presence in Frederick's life of Lady Caroline. What would each think? He didn't know; he didn't know anything. Yes, he did know something, and that was that his wife had made it up with him—suddenly, miraculously, unaccountably, and divinely. Beyond that he knew nothing. The situation was one with which he felt he could not cope. It must lead him whither it would. He could only drift.

In silence Frederick ate his soup, and the eyes, the large expressive eyes of the young woman opposite, were on him, he could feel, with a growing look in them of inquiry. They were, he could see, very intelligent and attractive eyes, and full, apart from the inquiry of goodwill. Probably she thought he ought to talk—but if she knew everything she wouldn't think so. Briggs didn't talk either. Briggs seemed uneasy. What was the matter with Briggs? And Rose too didn't talk, but then that was natural. She never had been a talker. She had the loveliest expression on her face. How long would it be on it after Lady Caroline's entrance? He didn't know; he didn't know anything.

But the genial man on Mrs. Fisher's left was talking enough for everybody. That fellow ought to have been a parson. Pulpits were the place for a voice like his; it would get him a bishopric in six months. He was explaining to Briggs, who shuffled about in his seat—why did Briggs shuffle about in his seat?—that he must have come out by the same train as Arbuthnot, and when Briggs, who said nothing, wriggled in apparent dissent, he undertook to prove it to him, and did prove it to him in long clear sentences.

"Who's the man with the voice?" Frederick asked Rose in a whisper; and the young woman opposite, whose ears appeared to have the quickness of hearing of wild creatures, answered, "He's my husband."

"Then by all the rules," said Frederick pleasantly, pulling himself together, "you oughtn't to be sitting next to him."

"But I want to. I like sitting next to him. I didn't before I came here."

Frederick could think of nothing to say to this, so he only smiled generally.

"It's this place," she said, nodding at him. "It makes one understand. You've no idea what a lot you'll understand before you've done here."

"I'm sure I hope so," said Frederick with real fervour.

The soup was taken away, and the fish was brought. Briggs, on the other side of the empty chair, seemed more uneasy than ever. What was the matter with Briggs? Didn't he like fish?

Frederick wondered what Briggs would do in the way of fidgets if he were in his own situation. Frederick kept on wiping his moustache, and was not able to look up from his plate, but that was as much as he showed of what he was feeling.

Though he didn't look up he felt the eyes of the young woman opposite raking him like searchlights, and Rose's eyes were on him too, he knew, but they rested on him unquestioningly, beautifully, like a benediction. How long would they go on doing that once Lady Caroline was there? He didn't know; he didn't know anything.

He wiped his moustache for the twentieth unnecessary time, and could not quite keep his hand steady, and the young woman opposite saw his hand not being quite steady, and her eyes raked him persistently. Why did her eyes rake him persistently? He didn't know; he didn't know anything.

Then Briggs leapt to his feet. What was the matter with Briggs?
Oh—yes—quite: she had come.
Frederick wiped his moustache and got up too. He was in for it now. Absurd, fantastic situation. Well, whatever happened he could only drift— drift, and look like an ass to Lady Caroline, the most absolute as well as deceitful ass—an ass who was also a reptile, for she might well think he had been mocking her out in the garden when he said, no doubt in a shaking voice—fool and ass—that he had come because he couldn't help it; while as for what he would look like to his Rose—when Lady Caroline introduced him to her—when Lady Caroline introduced him as her friend whom she had invited in to dinner—well, God alone knew that.

He, therefore, as he got up wiped his moustache for the last time before the catastrophe.

But he was reckoning without Scrap.

That accomplished and experienced young woman slipped into the chair Briggs was holding for her, and on Lotty's leaning across eagerly, and saying before any one else could get a word in, "Just fancy, Caroline, how quickly Rose's husband has got here!" turned to him without so much as the faintest shadow of surprise on her face, and held out her hand, and smiled like a young angel, and said, "and me late your very first evening."

The daughter of the Droitwiches. . .

Chapter 22

That evening was the evening of the full moon. The garden was an enchanted place where all the flowers seemed white. The lilies, the daphnes, the orange-blossom, the white stocks, the white pinks, the white roses—you could see these as plainly as in the day-time; but the coloured flowers existed only as fragrance.

The three younger women sat on the low wall at the end of the top garden after dinner, Rose a little apart from the others, and watched the enormous moon moving slowly over the place where Shelley had lived his last months just on a hundred years before. The sea quivered along the path of the moon. The stars winked and trembled. The mountains were misty blue outlines, with little clusters of lights shining through from little clusters of homes. In the garden the plants stood quite still, straight and unstirred by the smallest ruffle of air. Through the glass doors the dining-room, with its candle-lit table and brilliant flowers—nasturtiums and marigolds that night—glowed like some magic cave of colour, and the three men smoking round it looked strangely animated figures seen from the silence, the huge cool calm of outside.

Mrs. Fisher had gone to the drawing-room and the fire. Scrap and Lotty, their faces upturned to the sky, said very little and in whispers. Rose said nothing. Her face too was upturned. She was looking at the umbrella pine, which had been smitten into something glorious, silhouetted against stars. Every now and then Scrap's eyes lingered on Rose; so did Lotty's. For Rose was lovely. Anywhere at that moment, among all the well-known beauties, she would have been lovely. Nobody could have put her in the shade, blown out her light that evening; she was too evidently shining.

Lotty bent close to Scrap's ear, and whispered. "Love," she whispered.

Scrap nodded. "Yes," she said, under her breath.

She was obliged to admit it. You only had to look at Rose to know that here was Love.

"There's nothing like it," whispered Lotty.

Scrap was silent.

"It's a great thing," whispered Lotty after a pause, during which they both watched Rose's upturned face, "to get on with one's loving. Perhaps you can tell me of anything else in the world that works such wonders."

But Scrap couldn't tell her; and if she could have, what a night to begin arguing in. This was a night for—

She pulled herself up. Love again. It was everywhere. There was no getting away from it. She had come to this place to get away from it, and here was everybody in its different stages. Even Mrs. Fisher seemed to have been brushed by one of the many feathers of Love's wing, and at dinner was different—full of concern because Mr. Briggs wouldn't eat, and her face when she turned to him all soft with motherliness.

Scrap looked up at the pine-tree motionless among stars. Beauty made you love, and love made you beautiful. . .

She pulled her wrap closer round her with a gesture of defence, of keeping out and off. She didn't want to grow sentimental. Difficult not to, here; the marvelous night stole in through all one's chinks, and brought in with it, whether one wanted them or not, enormous feelings—feelings one couldn't manage, great things about death and time and waste; glorious and devastating things, magnificent and bleak, at once rapture and terror and immense, heart-cleaving longing. She felt small and dreadfully alone. She felt uncovered and defenceless. Instinctively she pulled her wrap closer. With this thing of chiffon she tired to protect herself from the eternities.

"I suppose," whispered Lotty, "Rose's husband seems to you just an ordinary, good-natured, middle-aged man."

Scrap brought her gaze down from the stars and looked at Lotty a moment while she focused her mind again.

"Just a rather red, rather round man," whispered Lotty.

Scrap bowed her head.

"He isn't," whispered Lotty. "Rose sees through all that. That's mere trimmings. She sees what we can't see, because she loves him."

Always love.

Scrap got up, and winding herself very tightly in her wrap moved away to her day corner, and sat down there alone on the wall and looked out across the other sea, the sea where the sun had gone down, the sea with the far-away dim shadow stretching into it which was France.

Yes, love worked wonders, and Mr. Arundel—she couldn't at once get used to his other name—was to Rose Love itself; but it also worked inverted wonders, it didn't invariably, as she well knew, transfigure people into saints and angels. Grievously indeed did it sometimes do the opposite. She had had it in her life applied to her to excess. If it had let her alone, if it had at least been moderate and infrequent, she might, she thought, have turned out a quite decent, generous-minded, kindly, human being. And what was she, thanks to this love Lotty talked so much about? Scrap searched for a just description. She was a spoilt, a sour, a suspicious, and a selfish spinster.

The glass doors of the dining-room opened, and the three men came out into the garden, Mr. Wilkins's voice flowing along in front of them. He appeared to be doing all the talking; the other two were saying nothing.

Perhaps she had better go back to Lotty and Rose; it would be tiresome to be discovered and hemmed into the cul-de-sac by Mr. Briggs.

She got up reluctantly, for she considered it unpardonable of Mr. Briggs to force her to move about like this, to force her out of any place she wished to sit in; and she emerged from the daphne bushes feeling like some gaunt, stern figure of just resentment and wishing that she looked as gaunt and stern as she felt; so would she have struck repugnance into the soul of Mr. Briggs, and been free of him. But she knew she didn't look like that, however hard she might try. At dinner his hand shook when he drank, and he couldn't speak to her without flushing scarlet and then going pale, and Mrs. Fisher's eyes had sought hers with the entreaty of one who asks that her only son may not be hurt.

How could a human being, thought Scrap, frowning as she issued forth from her corner, how could a man made in God's image behave so; and be fitted for better things she was sure, with his youth, his attractiveness, and his brains. He had brains. She had examined him cautiously whenever at dinner Mrs. Fisher forced him to turn away to answer her, and she was sure he had brains. Also he had character; there was something noble about his head, about the shape of his forehead—noble and kind. All the more deplorable that he should allow himself to be infatuated by a mere outside, and waste any of his strength, any of his peace of mind, hanging round just a woman-thing. If only he could see right through her, see through all her skin and stuff, he would be cured, and she might go on sitting undisturbed on this wonderful night by herself.

Just beyond the daphne bushes she met Fredrick, hurrying.

"I was determined to find you first," he said, "before I go to
Rose." And he added quickly, "I want to kiss your shoes."
"Do you?" said Scrap, smiling. "Then I must go and put on my new ones.
These aren't nearly good enough."

She felt immensely well-disposed towards Frederick. He, at least, would
grab no more. His grabbing days, so sudden and so brief, were done. Nice
man; agreeable man. She now definitely liked him. Clearly he had been
getting into some sort of a tangle, and she was grateful to Lotty for
stopping her in time at dinner from saying something hopelessly
complicating. But whatever he had been getting into he was out of it now;
his face and Rose's face had the same light in them.

"I shall adore you for ever now," said Frederick.

Scrap smiled. "Shall you?" she said.

"I adored you before because of your beauty. Now I adore you because
you're not only as beautiful as a dream but as decent as a man."

"When the impetuous young woman," Frederick went on, "the blessedly
impetuous young woman, blurted out in the nick of time that I am Rose's
husband, you behaved exactly as a man would have behaved to his friend."

"Did I?" said Scrap, her enchanting dimple very evident.

"It's the rarest, most precious of combinations," said Frederick, "to be a
woman and have the loyalty of a man."

"Is it?" smiled Scrap, a little wistfully. These were indeed handsome
compliments. If only she were really like that . . .

"And I want to kiss your shoes."

"Won't this save trouble?" she asked, holding out her hand.

He took it and swiftly kissed it, and was hurrying away again.
"Bless you," he said as he went.
"Where is your luggage?" Scrap called after him.

"Oh, Lord, yes—" said Frederick, pausing. "It's at the station."

"I'll send for it."

He disappeared through the bushes. She went indoors to give the order; and this is how it happened that Domenico, for the second time that evening, found himself journeying into Mezzago and wondering as he went.

Then, having made the necessary arrangements for the perfect happiness of these two people, she came slowly out into the garden again, very much absorbed in thought. Love seemed to bring happiness to everybody but herself. It had certainly got hold of everybody there, in its different varieties, except herself. Poor Mr. Briggs had been got hold of by its least dignified variety. Poor Mr. Briggs. He was a disturbing problem, and his going away next day wouldn't she was afraid solve him.

When she reached the others Mr. Arundel—she kept on forgetting that he wasn't Mr. Arundel—was already, his arm through Rose's, going off with her, probably to the greater seclusion of the lower garden. No doubt they had a great deal to say to each other; something had gone wrong between them, and had suddenly been put right. San Salvatore, Lotty would say, San Salvatore working its spell of happiness. She could quite believe in its spell. Even she was happier there than she had been for ages and ages. The only person who would go empty away would be Mr. Briggs.

Poor Mr. Briggs. When she came in sight of the group he looked much too nice and boyish not to be happy. It seemed out of the picture that the owner of the place, the person to whom they owed all this, should be the only one to go away from it unblessed.

Compunction seized Scrap. What very pleasant days she had spent in his house, lying in his garden, enjoying his flowers, loving his views, using his things, being comfortable, being rested—recovering, in fact. She had had the most leisured, peaceful, and thoughtful time of her life; and all really thanks to him. Oh, she knew she paid him some ridiculous small sum a week, out of all proportion to the benefits she got in exchange, but what was that in the balance? And wasn't it entirely thanks to him that she had come across Lotty? Never else would she and Lotty have met; never else would she have known her.

Compunction laid its quick, warm hand on Scrap. Impulsive gratitude flooded her. She went straight up to Briggs.

"I owe you so much," she said, overcome by the sudden realization of all she did owe him, and ashamed of her churlishness in the afternoon and at dinner. Of course he hadn't known she was being churlish. Of course her disagreeable inside was camouflaged as usual by the chance arrangement of her outside; but she knew it. She was churlish. She had been churlish to everybody for years. Any penetrating eye, thought Scrap, any really penetrating eye, would see her for what she was—a spoilt, a sour, a suspicious and a selfish spinster.

"I owe you so much," therefore said Scrap earnestly, walking straight up to Briggs, humbled by these thoughts.

He looked at her in wonder. "You owe me?" he said. "But it's I who—I who—" he stammered. To see her there in his garden . . . nothing in it, no white flower, was whiter, more exquisite.

"Please," said Scrap, still more earnestly, "won't you clear your mind of everything except just truth? You don't owe me anything. How should you?"

"I don't owe you anything?" echoed Briggs. "Why, I owe you my first sight of—of—"

"Oh, for goodness sake—for goodness sake," said Scrap entreatingly, "do, please, be ordinary. Don't be humble. Why should you be humble? It's ridiculous of you to be humble. You're worth fifty of me."

"Unwise," thought Mr. Wilkins, who was standing there too, while Lotty sat on the wall. He was surprised, he was concerned, he was shocked that Lady Caroline should thus encourage Briggs. "Unwise— very," thought Mr. Wilkins, shaking his head.

Briggs's condition was so bad already that the only course to take with him was to repel him utterly, Mr. Wilkins considered. No half measures were the least use with Briggs, and kindliness and familiar talk would only be misunderstood by the unhappy youth. The daughter of the Droitwiches could not really, it was impossible to suppose it, desire to encourage him. Briggs was all very well, but Briggs was Briggs; his name alone proved that. Probably Lady Caroline did not quite appreciate the effect of her voice and face, and how between them they made otherwise ordinary words seem—well, encouraging. But these words were not quite ordinary; she had not, he feared, sufficiently pondered them. Indeed and indeed she needed an adviser—some sagacious, objective counselor like himself.

There she was, standing before Briggs almost holding out her hand to him. Briggs of course ought to be thanked, for they were having a most delightful holiday in his house, but not thanked to excess and not by Lady Caroline alone. That very evening he had been considering the presentation to him next day of a round robin of collective gratitude on his departure; but he should not be thanked like this, in the moonlight, in the garden, by the lady he was so manifestly infatuated with.

Mr. Wilkins therefore, desiring to assist Lady Caroline out of this situation by swiftly applied tact, said with much heartiness: "It is most proper, Briggs, that you should be thanked. You will please allow me to add my expressions of indebtedness, and those of my wife, to Lady Caroline's. We ought to have proposed a vote of thanks to you at dinner. You should have been toasted. There certainly ought to have been some—"

But Briggs took no notice of him whatever; he simply continued to look at Lady Caroline as though she were the first woman he had ever seen. Neither, Mr. Wilkins observed, did Lady Caroline take any notice of him; she too continued to look at Briggs, and with that odd air of almost appeal. Most unwise. Most.

Lotty, on the other hand, took too much notice of him, choosing this moment when Lady Caroline needed special support and protection to get up off the wall and put her arm through his and draw him away.

"I want to tell you something, Mellersh," said Lotty at this juncture, getting up.

"Presently," said Mr. Wilkins, waving her aside.

"No—now," said Lotty; and she drew him away.

He went with extreme reluctance. Briggs should be given no rope at all— not an inch.

"Well—what is it?" he asked impatiently, as she led him towards the house. Lady Caroline ought not to be left like that, exposed to annoyance.

"Oh, but she isn't," Lotty assured him, just as if he had said this aloud, which he certainly had not. "Caroline is perfectly all right."

"Not at all all right. That young Briggs is—"

"Of course he is. What did you expect? Let's go indoors to the fire and Mrs. Fisher. She's all by herself."

"I cannot," said Mr. Wilkins, trying to draw back, "leave Lady Caroline alone in the garden."
"Don't be silly, Mellersh—she isn't alone. Besides, I want to tell you something."

"Well tell me, then."

"Indoors."

With reluctance that increased at every step Mr. Wilkins was taken farther and farther away from Lady Caroline. He believed in his wife now and trusted her, but on this occasion he thought she was making a terrible mistake. In the drawing-room sat Mrs. Fisher by the fire, and it certainly was to Mr. Wilkins, who preferred rooms and fires after dark to gardens and moonlight, more agreeable to be in there than out-of-doors if he could have brought Lady Caroline safely in with him. As it was, he went in with extreme reluctance.

Mrs. Fisher, her hands folded on her lap, was doing nothing, merely gazing fixedly into the fire. The lamp was arranged conveniently for reading, but she was not reading. Her great dead friends did not seem worth reading that night. They always said the same things now—over and over again they said the same things, and nothing new was to be got out of them any more for ever. No doubt they were greater than any one was now, but they had this immense disadvantage, that they were dead. Nothing further was to be expected of them; while of the living, what might one not still expect? She craved for the living, the developing—the crystallized and finished wearied her. She was thinking that if only she had had a son—a son like Mr. Briggs, a dear boy like that, going on, unfolding, alive, affectionate, taking care of her and loving her. . .

The look on her face gave Mrs. Wilkins's heart a little twist when she saw it. "Poor old dear," she thought, all the loneliness of age flashing upon her, the loneliness of having outstayed one's welcome in the world, of being in it only on sufferance, the complete loneliness of the old childless woman who has failed to make friends. It did seem that people could only be really happy in pairs—any sorts of pairs, not in the least necessarily lovers, but pairs of friends, pairs of mothers and children, of brothers and sisters—and where was the other half of Mrs. Fisher's pair going to be found?

Mrs. Wilkins thought she had perhaps better kiss her again. The kissing this afternoon had been a great success; she knew it, she had instantly felt Mrs. Fisher's reaction to it. So she crossed over and bent down and kissed her and said cheerfully, "We've come in—" which indeed was evident.

This time Mrs. Fisher actually put up her hand and held Mrs. Wilkins's cheek against her own—this living thing, full of affection, of warm, racing blood; and as she did this she felt safe with the strange creature, sure that she who herself did unusual things so naturally would take the action quite as a matter of course, and not embarrass her by being surprised.

Mrs. Wilkins was not at all surprised; she was delighted. "I believe I'm the other half of her pair," flashed into her mind. "I believe it's me, positively me, going to be fast friends with Mrs. Fisher!"

Her face when she lifted her head was full of laughter. Too extraordinary, the developments produced by San Salvatore. She and Mrs. Fisher . . . but she saw them being fast friends.

"Where are the others?" asked Mrs. Fisher. "Thank you—dear," she added, as Mrs. Wilkins put a footstool under her feet, a footstool obviously needed, Mrs. Fisher's legs being short.

"I see myself throughout the years," thought Mrs. Wilkins, her eyes dancing, "bringing footstools to Mrs. Fisher. . ."

"The Roses," she said, straightening herself, "have gone into the lower garden—I think love-making."

"The Roses?"

"The Fredericks, then, if you like. They're completely merged and indistinguishable."

"Why not say the Arbuthnots, my dear?" said Mr. Wilkins.

"Very well, Mellersh—the Arbuthnots. And the Carolines—"

Both Mr. Wilkins and Mrs. Fisher started. Mr. Wilkins, usually in such complete control of himself, started even more than Mrs. Fisher, and for the first time since his arrival felt angry with his wife.

"Really—" he began indignantly.

"Very well, Mellersh—the Briggses, then."

"The Briggses!" cried Mr. Wilkins, now very angry indeed; for the implication was to him a most outrageous insult to the entire race of Desters—dead Desters, living Desters, and Desters still harmless because they were yet unborn. "Really—"

"I'm sorry, Mellersh," said Mrs. Wilkins, pretending meekness, "if you don't like it."

"Like it! You've taken leave of your senses. Why they've never set eyes on each other before to-day."

"That's true. But that's why they're able now to go ahead."

"Go ahead!" Mr. Wilkins could only echo the outrageous words.

"I'm sorry, Mellersh," said Mrs. Wilkins again, "if you don't like it, but—"

Her grey eyes shone, and her face rippled with the light and conviction that had so much surprised Rose the first time they met.

"It's useless minding," she said. "I shouldn't struggle if I were you. Because—"

She stopped, and looked first at one alarmed solemn face and then at the other, and laughter as well as light flickered and danced over her.

"I see them being the Briggses," finished Mrs. Wilkins.

That last week the syringa came out at San Salvatore, and all the acacias flowered. No one had noticed how many acacias there were till one day the garden was full of a new scent, and there were the delicate trees, the lovely successors to the wistaria, hung all over among their trembling leaves with blossom. To lie under an acacia tree that last week and look up through the branches at its frail leaves and white flowers quivering against the blue of the sky, while the least movement of the air shook down their scent, was a great happiness. Indeed, the whole garden dressed itself gradually towards the end in white pinks and white banksai roses, and the syringe and the Jessamine, and at last the crowning fragrance of the acacias. When, on the first of May, everybody went away, even after they had got to the bottom of the hill and passed through the iron gates out into the village they still could smell the acacias.